T0278118

Praise for *The Grand Illusion*

'At last, something different, but also brilliant. A quirky, clever and compelling novel drawing on an extraordinary true story, and with a memorable heroine.'

Anna Mazzola, author of *The Clockwork Girl*

'A rattling good read. Historical crime at its quirkiest and best. Here be occultists, lads! Love it.'

Barbara Nadel, author of *Belshazzar's Daughter*

'A blend of glamour, stagecraft and espionage . . . had me gripped from the first page. I screamed aloud at one point! Impossible not to fall in love with the characters. Loved it.'

Rachael Blok, author of *Under the Ice*

'Gripping, strange, unusual. Beautiful writing and a brilliant heroine. I loved it.'

Sophia Bennett, author of *The Look*

'An intriguing novel, laced with insight and humour, and Daphne is a heroine who would shine in any age.'

Olivia Isaac-Henry, author of *The Verdict*

'A ripping wartime tale of plucky Brits fighting the Nazis with distraction, deception and darkness. Thrilling, inventive and fabulously entertaining. I loved it.'

Paddy Magrane, author of *Disorder*

Also by Syd Moore

The Drowning Pool
Witch Hunt
Strange Magic
Strange Sight
Strange Fascination
The Strange Casebook
Strange Tombs
Strange Tricks
The Twelve Strange Days of Christmas
The Twelve Even Stranger Days of Christmas

THE
GRAND
ILLUSION

SYD MOORE

MAGPIE
BOOKS

A Magpie Book

First published in Great Britain, the Republic of Ireland and Australia
by Magpie Books, an imprint of Oneworld Publications, 2024

ISBN 978-0-86154-160-7
eISBN 978-0-86154-161-4

Typeset in Dante by Hewer Text UK Ltd, Edinburgh
Printed and bound in Great Britain by Clays Ltd, Elcograf S.p.A.

This book is a work of fiction. Names, characters, businesses,
organisations, places and events are either the product of the author's
imagination or are used fictitiously. Any resemblance to actual
persons, living or dead, events or locales is entirely coincidental.

Oneworld Publications
10 Bloomsbury Street
London WC1B 3SR
England

Stay up to date with the latest books,
special offers, and exclusive content from
Oneworld with our newsletter

Sign up on our website
oneworld-publications.com

For Hugh Foster and Olivia Isaac-Henry

July 1940. Germany's rapid advance into Western Europe means the threat of attack is high on the British government's agenda. British citizens are nervous following the disastrous Norwegian campaign, which has resulted in Nazi occupation. The recent withdrawal from Dunkirk still stings and the Phoney War goes on.

All eyes are on the empty skies anticipating the bombs that will soon fall.

The country is in a perilous situation.

Morale is at a low ebb.

Paranoia rubs shoulders with fear, neighbour looks askance at neighbour, fifth columnists are invisible but everywhere. The military services are overwhelmed. Winston Churchill calls nineteen meetings during the first three weeks of his premiership to discuss the imminent invasion.

It is the eleventh hour, and the stage is set for nothing short of disaster.

Yet all is not lost.

Step forward, Daphne Devine.

You are about to change the course of the War.

Proposal of Prosecution for the Invasion of the United Kingdom

June 1940

Assessment

It is feasible to subjugate England.

Importance is attributed to gaining air superiority before commencing land invasion.

Geographically, Great Britain and Northern Ireland are made up of a smattering of islands which face the north of the Continent, largely France but also Belgium and the Netherlands.

A landing operation will eradicate the power of the mother country: England. Occupation of this, the largest country in the union, will mean there is no possibility for it to continue as a base in the war against Germany. Troops and supplies may then be convoyed across to the remaining countries and islands of Britannia.

Dover, an urban conglomeration with ports, is situated on the South Coast at the south-eastern point, across from the Pas-de-Calais in France. Here the English Channel is only thirty-two kilometres wide.

Within reach.

The Führer and Supreme Commander has decided ALL groundwork for carrying out this operation must commence with immediate effect.

2 JULY 1940

CHAPTER ONE

A spindly darkness advances over the skyline like a stalking horse, smothering monuments and rooftops, snuffing out light, dragging the curtain of night across the sulky sky.

Despite the dimness, the windows have been blacked out and the blinds drawn. The great room is illuminated only by a dull flickering in the hearth. Chiaroscuro shadows crawl flittingly, butterfly bruises, across the sombre faces of three silhouettes warming themselves there.

'How do we fit your plan, sir?'

The man addressed tenses his arms like a giant crow readying to take flight. Or gird itself for a squall. 'We need people who are not predictable in their thinking,' he says. His voice is a baritone, deep and richly textured. It echoes through the empty room and settles on the furniture.

Stirring across the fireside, the other man fills his lungs and exchanges a glance with the young woman sitting there. Although she is a good twenty years junior to both men, she carries a certain stillness which confers upon her a solid presence. The nature of her working relationship with the man she is watching often relies on communication not based on words, so she understands from the arch of his eyes, the position of his hand, that the statement just made has both flattered and perplexed him. She inclines her head a fraction to the left to let him know that she too is not yet sure what to make of it. It is different for women – predictability. The quality, she feels, is dull and uninteresting though regularly considered a dependable trait in her sex. Evidence of sound mental balance.

'Unlike our officers,' the man continues. He has lowered his voice to a volume just above a whisper. Perhaps he has noticed the echo too. 'Our British officers,' he repeats, 'who are gentlemen, and used to conducting war like a game of cricket. We believe the Germans are abandoning all rules. They are politically violent and murderous.' He lets that hang in the air between them, his eyes twin searchlights gauging his guests' response.

The young woman assumes a vacant gaze. She is able to apply it speedily, like cold cream from a pot, whenever she is scrutinised. Which is so often that she almost does it without thinking. In the opposite armchair her boss, Jonty, has done the same. Snap. She would laugh if it wasn't so, if the situation weren't so . . .

The man has raised his voice again, and she does not complete the thought. If she had, she might have used such a word as 'serious' or 'alarming'. Either would have increased her degree of tension and she might have giggled. Inappropriately. So it is just as well.

'The rejection of any collective notion of decency,' he is saying, 'at present gives the Third Reich an advantage.'

The German term makes her shudder. It is hard and aggressive. Fatal.

In his deeply upholstered chair Jonty lets out a low whistle and shakes his head.

The other man nods. 'It is vital that we are not hampered by our innate sense of fair play and justice. There are those who cling on to their idea of a "noble war". It no longer exists.'

'That it's come to this, Hugh,' replies Jonty and strokes his moustache.

'Agreed,' says the man. 'But there is no time for hand-wringing.'

The phrase makes the younger woman realise that although not quite wringing her hands, she has unconsciously let them stray to clench the hem of her skirt. She spreads her fingers and smooths out the creased fabric.

Hugh observes her, keen to dominate attention. 'We in the Security Service need young, quick, clever minds.'

The words 'Security Service' both surprise and appal her. This hadn't been mentioned before, not when they were invited to the meeting. Though *invited* was too generous a word for their delivery to the club. It had been more like an intervention. Or an order. Perhaps she should have worked it out, but my! the Security Service. Who would have thought? The thrill that goes through her is quickly followed by an internal voice that sounds like the disapproving instructress at the ladies' academy she attended: *You're neither agile, nor bright, nor connected enough to be an asset to such an organisation.* And then she is horrified that it's come to this: that the Secret Service has approached the pair of them. It smacks of desperation.

Detecting a change in her expression, Hugh leans his elbows on the chair arms so he is angled towards her. 'We need people who are not afraid to think differently.' He pauses, and though he does not move it seems to her that in a heartbeat he has grown darker, as if a cloud has passed over him. With emphasis, he says, 'Wickedly even. To come up with solutions, ideas, strategies, actions which our regular operatives cannot conceive of. Our remit is wide. Our position weak.' He fastens his gaze on Jonty for a good long minute without speaking, then on her and uses their names for the first time: 'Jonty. Miss Devine. We must recruit laterally. And now!'

The sense of his words sinks in. Her breath catches in the back of her throat, which has suddenly grown dry.

Jonty, whom she has momentarily forgotten, wags his glass so the ice in it clinks, and she remembers where they are: a gentlemen's club. Such an unlikely setting for so grave a conversation. And she is certainly no gentleman either. It is only possible for her to be admitted on nights like this, when the institution is closed, and so she takes a second to look at her surroundings. She won't come here again, she is sure. The dark wood panelling the walls is broken by several Corinthian columns, an architectural homage to the statues of Greek gods, who seem tonight to listen stoically from their positions around the room. She wonders how many battles and wars they have seen declared and ended – won or lost?

Jonty raises his glass to Hugh. 'That's all well and good with Daphne and the like. This little filly's as sharp as a box of tools. But I can't possibly see' – with his other hand, he thumbs his bony chest – 'what this old fool can bring to the war effort.'

In return Hugh jabs his own finger. 'Ah, well, there's the rub. It's not brawn we need, my friend, though God knows enlistment will have to be broadened. It's brains, imagination.'

Jonty does not reply. Daphne supposes he is turning this over in his mind, shaping how it is that the pair of them might fit in. Hugh Devereaux is sphinxlike in his riddles. It would be easier, she thinks, if he came out and told them what he wanted. But perhaps straight talking is no longer permissible. Perhaps it is another thing to be rationed.

Hugh regards them like a priest, putting his hands together as if in prayer. 'I am aware of your accomplishments,' he says like a man placating, as if they had objected.

Which leads Jonty to ask, 'Then what is it of which you speak?'

Hugh's cheeks reflect the flames, diabolically red, blue, yellow, a little glimpse of Hell in the hearth there. 'Illusions.'

'Ah,' says Jonty, and for the first time the corners of his mouth turn up. 'Magic?'

But Hugh is quick to dismiss. 'The Department prefers instead to use "deception, sleight of hand".' The delivery is sniffy and stiff.

His manner, however, intrigues Daphne; after all, he has commanded them here, so she asks, 'Why?'

Somewhere, in one of the club's labyrinthine corridors, a clock chimes the hour: ten. She wonders if it is significant, if she will remember this moment.

Around them the shadows darken. A stillness has crept into the air. The room itself is holding its breath, waiting for Hugh's answer.

But what he says next is a non sequitur. 'I'm sorry to tell you: Britain's fortunes are at their lowest ebb since declaring war.' The pain of conveying this news has him reaching for his cigarette case on the table beside him.

'Hang on, old chap,' Jonty counters, a touch of defiant patriotism in the lift of his chin. 'What about the triumph of Dunkirk?' He takes a cigarette from his friend's silvery case.

Striking a match, Hugh bends to light his friend's cigarette. Daphne has refused. Not knowing what the man thinks of girls who smoke, she errs on the side of caution.

'Mercifully,' Hugh says. 'We saved the British Expeditionary Force. Though not without the great sacrifice of good men. Our tanks, guns, transport and rifles, however – all of them were abandoned there.' The amber end of his cigarette bobs in the darkness, like a tiny detonating bomb. 'In France.' His forehead contracts so tightly that the furrows are visible in the gloom. 'We left the Germans at least seventy-five thousand tons of ammunition and one hundred and sixty thousand tons of fuel. As such, we are now completely unprepared for battle.'

'Well, I haven't heard that,' Jonty stutters and draws down deeply.

Daphne can smell the tobacco smoke and is glad of it. Now she wishes she had taken a cigarette.

'It's true, I'm afraid. Armaments from our factories are coming in at a trickle. Britain simply does not have the weapons to put up a prolonged resistance. And you are no doubt aware that German landings have been made in Guernsey and Jersey in the Channel Islands.'

'I saw something in the paper,' Daphne remarks. A bead of sweat has begun to form on her upper lip, though she is not over-warm. The thought of the enemy on British soil fills her with extreme anxiety.

'It seems obvious that Adolf Hitler's goal . . .' Hugh begins and then stops: in the corner of the room someone has appeared with a tray of drinks. Daphne watches the glimmer of starched collar, cuffs and frilly white apron approach.

They pause while the maid decants a bottle, deposits a carafe and glasses, and do not speak again till they hear the door close behind her.

How did she know their drinks had run low, Daphne wonders.

'Brandy?' asks their host. Without waiting for an answer he fills three glasses. 'It helps with the shock,' he adds and hands them over. 'If you *are* shocked. Can't for the life of me keep up with what's out there in the public realm and what is . . . suppressed. For morale, you understand. And none of this to go any further.' He passes over their drinks.

Jonty wolfs down half the contents of his tumbler in one gulp. Daphne, too, noticing a tremble as she takes the glass offered, swallows more than a mouthful. She waits for it to blunt her nerves and watches Hugh pour himself a large measure. Behind his spectacles the bold globes of his eyes glitter with flinty intelligence. The iris of one, she notices now, is slightly larger – no, not larger, darker – than the other. Or is it a trick of the light? She suddenly has the notion that beneath the bone of his skull there exists a huge whirring brain, the size of the universe, that is in perpetual motion, weighing, calculating, forecasting.

Without warning Hugh flicks these fascinating light and dark eyes at her, and she feels as if she has been caught out.

'As I was saying,' he says so softly she and Jonty lean in to hear him. His knees are close to her own. She is aware of the shortness of the gap between them. 'It is clear that Hitler's next move will be to mount an invasion upon these shores.'

'We have heard,' Jonty laments into his glass.

Daphne is not so easy with it. A shudder passes through her again.

In the grate, a log pops and splinters. Briefly the flames flare and rise higher, lighting the men's features, deepening the wrinkles in their faces, making them look like grim, exhausted versions of the statues around them.

Might the German fleet sail up the river and march into the Houses of Parliament? Could it really be true, Daphne thinks.

'So what is it you want from us, Hugh?' The liquor has done the job. Jonty's voice is steadier; now he is getting to the point.

Devereaux sinks back into his chair. 'You see,' he says, opening his hands. The action is sweeping and expansive, as if he is creating an invisible circle and drawing the two of them into it.

Daphne feels something imperceptible, tickly, shower down briefly from above. It is not unpleasant; it makes her feel strangely significant, something she is unused to.

Hugh is still speaking in his low, textured voice. 'I am one of those tasked with the job of thinking up measures to counter this ghastly eventuality. We are prepared to adopt every idea that offers any prospect of helping us meet the threat. In fact, the men of action in the government are cutting red tape as we speak, readying to hurl everything we've got at the Nazis. And to fortify Old Blighty to the death.' He pauses like a showman spooning out the suspense and eyes them both, his intense, mongrel pupils flicking from the man to his assistant. 'And this point is exactly where you two enter the frame. You are who we must turn to now – practitioners skilled in using imagination to conjure sleights of hand which the Germans will fall for. Who will trump them with trickery!

'There is something currently brewing which I have you in mind for. No details yet. But my feeling is you would be a good match, if it materialises. The Germans' designs on our fair isle must be thwarted, you agree. At any cost.' He pauses, then repeats for emphasis, 'At any cost.'

The effects of this passion on Jonty, however, produce a lethargy. He yawns, though Daphne knows it is not really an expression of ennui. 'Hugh,' he asks, 'don't you have trained staff for this kind of thing?' His posturing could be construed as nonchalance to outsiders, but both his companions know him well enough to understand it is fear well masked.

And Hugh responds without irritation. 'Unfortunately, although we are recruiting rapidly at present – when war was declared there were less than forty officers working for the Security Service – our serving agents are overwhelmed. Reports of German spies in the kingdom must all be investigated, and we are receiving many. Not to mention the interned enemy aliens who need to be processed.'

Daphne starts. Before she can prevent the words tumbling out, she hears herself saying, 'My mother is one of those.'

Hugh hesitates. Something changes in his face. Recognition maybe, or resolve. His jaw tenses before he says, 'On the Isle of Man, yes. And your uncle too, I understand, on a ship bound for Canada.' He looks at his watch. 'Set sail today.'

Daphne's mouth contracts into a small *o* of surprise. 'I didn't know that. Well, I mean, about Uncle Giuseppe. Mum was taken a few weeks ago . . . how did you . . .' She trails off without finishing the question.

Hugh is ahead of her. 'Of course, all those approached must be investigated. Circumstances and such,' he says. 'It would be foolish to not to check the background of a young, agile, healthy, unmarried woman of twenty-two years who was once a pupil with an exemplary academic record at the Girls' Grammar School in Southend, a record which was marred only by three disciplinary actions. The most splendid of which was the vandalism of a netball goal.'

Daphne frowns. 'Now listen . . .' She wants to tell him the infraction wasn't entirely hers. 'That was—'

Devereaux clears his throat and grows even larger in his chair. His shadow reaches across her. 'Though in truth, what the headmistress failed to uncover was that the damage was the result of no less than sixteen girls playing "war" in the court. A surge of attackers had resulted in congestion by the goal, which then toppled under their collective weight. The whole thing had been an accident. However, the punishment was stoically shouldered by the lone offender, "turned in" by a rival class, and who refused to surrender the names of her co-conspirators. A noble gesture, I might add, for one so young. Shows spark, however unladylike that may be.'

She opens her mouth. 'How the devil—'

He stills her with his hand. 'Loyal also to family. And, though there is little that can be done for your mother's brother, Giuseppe, it would be remiss not to communicate the fact that your cooperation will count for much when officials deliberate upon your mother's case for release.'

The brazenness of it all renders her speechless. Then her mind processes, weighs and calculates the impact of Devereaux's words.

So this is it, she thinks. The quid pro quo incentive. It changes things, of course, and she feels a surge of something close to anger.

'We are in the process of enlisting some of the finest minds in the country to consider options,' he says. 'I would like you to consider yours.'

The flames are subsiding, though the coals in the grate still glow.

Jonty steals a look at his assistant. He is not sure whether he should be troubled by the pursed lips he finds there. 'Daphne, I suggest we talk it over. Give us some time please, Hugh.'

Devereaux nods. 'Twenty-four hours. That's all I can offer.' Then he throws his hands up as if surrendering and says nothing more.

Daphne knows on the outside her composure is tight, but internally a sea is roiling which she is finding difficult to calm.

A click somewhere in the darkness of the room.

Though she has seen no signal nor heard any bell ring, the maid appears once more. This time she is carrying their coats.

Everything seems to slow down and stop in this tiny frozen moment. She thinks she hears another noise: a faint scrape of metal, springs, gears changing. In her mind's eye she sees above them, high up beyond the blacked-out glass ceiling, there in the aether amongst the cold constellations, the wheel of Fortune beginning to turn.

CHAPTER TWO

'Well, that wasn't how I saw our evening panning out,' says Jonty as they wait outside the club on the step.

'Nor I,' Daphne agrees.

The car that dropped them at the club has failed to materialise. They have been under the porch for ten minutes.

A creeping sense of vulnerability grows. Daphne squints down the alley into the dark city. The moon tonight is new and the fine crescent of silver lends but a futile light. The car had picked them up at twilight, but they hadn't reached the club until the day had entirely faded. She guesses that they may be in the West End. It is hard to sustain a sense of direction these days: cars dim their headlights or don't use them at all. Street lamps, facades, the few pedestrians that dare to brave the blackout all look as if they have been showered in soot.

'If he doesn't show soon, I think we should get the Underground,' says Jonty. He stamps his feet, though the night is not cold.

'Come on then,' says Daphne. 'There's a main street up there. We'll be able to ask where we are. Must be a Tube nearby.'

Jonty grunts and they begin to make off up the side street. It is narrow. The buildings are tall and lean into each other.

As they pass under an arch, there is a high squeal of tyres. A car is starting up ahead of them. Going at some speed by the sounds of it. Jonty appears not to have heard and is saying, 'A bit much to take in, isn't it?'

But Daphne has her eye on the black mass of metal coming down the alley. For a minute she thinks it will clear them, but astonishingly it swerves. A second more and it has mounted the pavement. Jonty is in its direct line.

Even before she processes what she is doing, her hand has shot out and grabbed his jacket. With a mighty yank she jerks him back, out of its way, and then turns and throws herself against him.

There is an enormous bang as the car hits the wall. The screech of steel on brick, a shower of sparks, bits of metal flying off in all directions. One piece shoots past her ear. She feels the heat it leaves behind pass over her skin like a comet's tail. Instinctively, she braces. But the driver has regained control and steered back onto the cobbles. Instead of braking, she hears him hit the accelerator. The engine roars and she looks up just in time to see the car hurtle ahead.

'What in damnation?' Jonty is not happy to find himself in such an undignified mess. Though he is luckier than he realises.

Daphne gets to her feet. She has skinned her knee and the stocking on that leg has ripped open. She curses inwardly; nylons don't come cheap these days.

'Didn't even stop to check us!' says Jonty with justified outrage.

The car has reached the end of the street and turns right into darkness. Unseen, another car horn goes off. Jonty straightens himself. 'Bloody blackout drivers.'

Daphne says nothing. She is not sure she agrees. It feels too much of a coincidence after the conversation they have had with Hugh Devereaux. Though who would want to injure Jonty and herself?

They haven't even agreed to anything Hugh suggested. Indeed, they are still civilians right now. Though, she muses, the driver did not know that.

Should she report it to Mr Devereaux? Internally she makes a note while she is extending her hand to Jonty. He takes it and uses it to stabilise his centre of gravity, then he dusts himself down. He has come off unscathed.

'Thank you, dearie,' he says. 'I hadn't seen that coming.' She thinks his mouth curves a wry line, but she can't be sure. 'Another thing,' he says. 'I will have to brush up on my divination techniques.'

She knows, by the way his words sound, that he is smiling.

'You are good to me. So quick,' he says. 'I am lucky to . . .' He peters out, then she discerns a faint 'thank you' as he swallows. 'I'm quite all right,' he says. 'Are you?'

'Yes. Grazed my knee.' Then she sighs. 'And ruined a stocking.'

'Oh, Daphne,' he says to the latter. 'I'll buy you another pair.'

'People will talk,' she says, and sends a wink which he cannot see.

'If indeed I can find any,' he adds.

As they are smoothing down their clothes another car approaches at a far more acceptable speed. It decelerates as it reaches them. The door opens and the driver within asks, 'Mr Trevelyan? Miss Devine?'

They stare at him. Daphne is besieged with anxiety. Is it the same car that tried to run them down? They all look the same in the blackout.

But Jonty replies cheerfully, 'Yes. That's right.'

'Orders to take you to your billets,' says the driver.

They don't have billets. They have homes. But the word makes them both feel as if the world is changing beneath their feet.

Jonty gets in. He seems unmoved by their close shave. Daphne however is possessed by the notion that something has ended. As she enters the car she feels as if she is crossing an invisible threshold. I'm going through the looking glass, she thinks. Just like Alice.

She is not wrong.

Out on the main street there are more cars and more people. The driver swerves to avoid a rotund man in a dark suit, worse for wear, who has tottered off the pavement. He has his shirt tails out so as to be noticed, thank goodness, otherwise the outcome might have been worse than that they have just experienced. Which makes her question again whether their near miss was purely accidental. The larger part of her gives it the benefit of the doubt, but there still lingers a disquiet she cannot extinguish.

The motion of the vehicle has caused Jonty to roll slightly into her. They pick themselves apart, without the delicacy and embarrassment that others demonstrate in similar positions. They are familiar with each other's bodies in a way that inclines others to salacious gossip. Helping each other in and out of small, confined spaces, holding hands, reading signals from barely visible gestures – flexed muscles, eyebrow movements, fingers. All of this requires the suspension of conventional manners. While acceptable in their circles, the greater social sphere often titters over them. Daphne is viewed by several grand dames as tainted, improper, lacking decorum, while adjectives thrown around to describe her boss include 'debonair', 'roguish' and 'dastardly'. Though the latter two, when spoken by men of his age, are laced with an awed respect. It bothers the pair not at all or very much depending on their circumstances. Tonight they do not think about it. The driver has his eyes sharpened into two black darts set firmly on the obstacle course ahead of him.

'A bumpy ride,' says Jonty.

His assistant is unsure if he is talking of this journey, the future or their route from stage door to Mr Devereaux's club. She turns to Jonty and says, 'Yes,' and her mind goes back to before any of this happened, to the afternoon matinee, which had not been smooth either. Perhaps it was an omen? The show had been running behind. Some hold-up in the ticket booth meant they were late starting. It happened sometimes. With everybody rushing around, rearranging the timings with Smoking Chieftain and the Basset Girls, no one remembered the dove concealed for longer than intended in the lid of the pan, quietly running out of air. Poor Coco.

When Jonty – or, as he is known onstage, The Grand Mystique – tapped the empty hat with his wand, a limp Coco dropped out of the hidden compartment into the bottom of the pot with an audible clang. Not having the wherewithal to flap her wings, the bird was stunned upon impact.

Daphne did not notice this when the magician passed it over, so presented the theatre with what appeared to be a dead bird.

A small girl in the stalls began to wail.

It was awful and yet Daphne felt an uncomfortable giggle rising in her throat. She stifled it and brought down her vacant expression while The Grand Mystique, with a flash of his cloak, drew off the attention, picked up his linking rings and began his next trick.

Daphne danced to the waiting stagehand in the wings and swapped the stunned dove for her more alert twin, Bobo. As she twirled herself back to centre stage and took a bow, she released Bobo, who obediently flew up to the rafters.

The little girl in the stalls, however, was still not buying it. 'He killed the bird!' She pointed at The Grand Mystique. 'The other one is dead, it is.'

A ripple of disapproval ran through the house. Several members of the audience tittered.

Fortunately, the disapproval was directed at the child, who was now being disciplined in an amplified show of parental chiding by their mother. It was one of society's more senseless norms, Daphne thought, that a child speaking out of turn could never be right. Their behaviour was to be censured no matter if they had glimpsed the truth. A characteristic they shared with young ladies.

The Grand Mystique exhaled loudly, fluttering the ends of his moustache, and signalled they should move next to the cutting cabinet. Slicing up women pleased people.

'With the scimitar plucked from the arms of a dying whirling dervish, I will slice my beautiful assistant in two!'

The scimitar was a saw adapted by a welder from Sheffield. But in the eighteen months Daphne had been performing, no member of the audience had yet questioned its veracity. Showgoers, like the public at large, generally saw what they were set up to see.

'Audiences,' Jonty had once told her, 'are on your side, whether they know it or not. They want to be thrilled, to transcend normality, they want to be fooled, to believe. The job of the stage magician and his assistant is merely to help them on their way. All illusion is in the mind.'

The gold and red of the walls with their elaborate baroque decorations brightened hopefully.

Daphne sent her smile to a prune-lipped woman in the dress circle, then retrieved the lacquered cutting case from the wings. It smelled of enigma and polish and held a special place in her heart. The width and length of a small coffin, covered with exotic oriental motifs, this heirloom had once belonged to Jonty's father, and before that to his father too. The art of illusion was a Trevelyan family secret: mysteries passed down from generation to generation. And performing was in their blood. It was easy to see how it became so: the glamour and greasepaint, the buzz of anticipation as the curtain went up, all of this had imprinted itself on Daphne.

She wheeled the case into the circle picked out by the spotlight.

Jonty had already selected a volunteer from the raised hands in the auditorium and invited him to the stage. The man began to make his way down the aisle.

'Come, sir, come to me. That's right.' The Grand Mystique beckoned and spread his arms wide in welcome. It gave him the opportunity to expand his shiny emerald robe and reveal the full length of a ferocious scarlet dragon embroidered across the front. Everything had a purpose here. 'Come test the strength of the Turk's scimitar.'

With one hand on hip, one in the air, Daphne stepped up to the blade, feigning horror at its sharpness, then threw a red silk kerchief in the air.

With a skilled and well-practised demonstration of dexterity, The Grand Mystique whirled the heavy curved sword above his head and with a shout of triumph sliced the silk clean in two.

By this time the volunteer had arrived onstage. Daphne skipped over and extended her hand. He took it with a leer, winked at his friends in the cheap seats, and allowed himself to be led over to the illusionist.

In his late twenties, the chap was casually dressed for the theatre. He had shed his jacket and rolled up his sleeves. She wondered as she walked if Jonty had picked the right one; it was hard to see into the womblike darkness of the far stalls with the lights training down.

The Grand Mystique handed over the scimitar to the volunteer, who inspected the knife. Daphne again urged him to inspect the inside of the cabinet, which he did, employing many knocks. Level with Daphne's chest, he winked at the audience. 'This one's certainly well made.' She closed her ears and fixed on her beatific smile. Holding out her hand, she asked him to assist her into the cabinet.

With a kiss on her ring finger, the volunteer clicked his heels and, as if playing the part of a Russian courtier, performed a low, exaggerated bow. It wasn't what they needed. If he didn't start behaving, the audience would think he was a stooge. She felt his eyes upon her as she climbed the wooden steps, watching her intently as she lay down.

Concern wrinkled his forehead. She clasped her hands together. 'Don't you worry about a thing,' she said and let her fingernail slide gently over the skin on his exposed fore-arm. 'Please communicate the authenticity of the Turkish scimitar.'

With a conspiratorial grin he turned, blinking into the spot-lights. 'Oh, the sword's real enough all right,' he announced. Having fulfilled his obligations, the illusionist dismissed the volunteer, and he shuffled back to his seat.

The pianist in the pit moved his fingers to the lower keys. Immediately the atmosphere changed: the act had darkened.

The Grand Mystique assembled his features into a grimace.

Appreciative of the spectacle, the audience sat up straight in their seats: with a bit of luck, something horrible was about to happen.

A couple of well-dressed young ladies in the balcony covered their eyes.

With another sweep of his hands The Grand Mystique produced a box from the air. It was black and satanic, decorated with ominous occult symbols. The audience oohed and aahed. He opened it and slid his long fingers in, removing two thick and shiny chains which he wrapped around his shoulders like a snake charmer handling cobras.

When he tied her hands together Daphne winced, then the lid of the case came down with a loud bang.

Only her head from the neck upwards was visible. She poked her feet out of the other end, where they wriggled and squirmed. She did not smile.

Inside the coffin-shaped box, Daphne felt her way. She had been here before many times and was as comfortable with claustrophobia as she was with the spotlight on her shapely legs.

She made herself small.

Her calf rubbed against a lever and flicked a switch which swapped real feet for two mechanised likenesses. This added a macabre realism absent in other illusionists' interpretations. All she had to do now was . . . she grimaced . . . hang on . . . the metal . . . the catch . . . it wasn't there . . .

Realising the error, the assistant's whisper rang out, louder than anticipated: 'Just a minute now. Wait.'

The Grand Mystique, however, had not heard it, and brandished the fearsome blade over the centre of the box.

The audience began to shift in earnest. Many had come with the sole purpose of witnessing this. And yet, now that their appetites were about to be sated, the courage of some fell away.

'Stop!' Daphne shouted. Her head lifted up to the magician.

A woman in the front row clasped her hand to her mouth.

In the coffin box Daphne cried out, 'Wait! I say wait—'

Unheeding, he brought the scimitar up and back behind his shoulders to lever more swing.

Daphne turned away and appealed to the audience. 'Help!' she screamed.

Frenzied mutterings in the dress circle. Two men in the stalls stood up in alarm.

'No, no, no.' Daphne's head shook from side to side. Her hair swished back and forth.

But it was too late. The knife caught the spotlight and flashed as the magician brought it down and, with a thrust, jammed it hard into the lacquer cabinet.

Daphne let go a heart-clotting scream. A viscous scarlet liquid began to seep from the cabinet.

'Oh God . . .' Daphne's voice became audibly weaker.

But her exclamation was pointless. The magician continued to force the blade through to the other side, his movements jagged, arduous, thick. With a final thrust, it burst out of the bottom of the cabinet, sending red droplets to the boards.

Daphne at once went limp.

Standing back and panting, The Grand Mystique scratched his turban and took stock. Thick, reddish-purple globules were oozing out of the cabinet, dripping down the black lacquered legs.

Now screams filled the air.

The magician seemed to falter, then mania regained him and he threw himself at the ornate cabinet and pulled the now-separated sections apart.

From the balcony a man bellowed, 'Murderer!'

'Where am I? Help . . . I can't feel my legs . . .' moaned the assistant.

Mr Peterson, the stage manager, rushed into the spotlight. Looking to the side, he gestured wildly to the wings. 'Curtain! Quickly.'

The velvet curtain fell, blocking the sight of grotesque dismemberment from the baying crowd and marooning The Grand Mystique front of house.

Most of the men in the audience were on their feet, blown full of outrage and passionate venom. Some were already half-way down, threatening to storm the stage.

Ushers appeared in the aisles.

'Do something!' shouted a woman in the dress circle.

Responding, The Grand Mystique nodded and held his hands high. 'Stop!' he commanded. Perhaps grateful for leadership and order in the escalating chaos, those about to engage in violent protest faltered.

A quiet hush engulfed the theatre.

'Oh mighty Isis,' the magician began. 'If I ever needed real power, I beg of you, grant it me now.'

A crash of drums.

A mighty flash.

The place was filled with a bright, blinding light.

Smoke appeared and encompassed the stage.

As the clouds began to recede The Grand Mystique could be perceived, head hanging low, shoulders shaking with grief, arms outstretched, his huge emerald kimono fully extended now. The striking dragon embroidered across it shimmered.

'Please accept my apologies . . .' he began, his voice tremulous.

A movement, down by his knees.

'This,' he continued, 'has never . . .'

A chink in the satin. A slim white hand.

Some of the audience spotted it, gasped, pointed to their neighbours.

An arm, then a torso, then a real-life and whole magician's assistant opened the silk. Daphne stepped out and twirled her hands up high.

'We're sorry,' she joined with Jonty to announce, 'but that's it, ladies and gentlemen – the end of the show.'

For a moment silence pooled.

Then a roar of appreciation filled the theatre to the roof.

Those already standing no longer bridled with rage. Relief gave way to delight then flipped to relief once more. A startling realisation that they'd been had transformed their passion into amused admiration. Who'd have thought the magician and his assistant might do something so unexpected and queer? Now they understood why London was atwitter with their act. What a clever, elaborate but quite vulgar joke. How had they done it?

The clapping began.

There were whistles, there were shouts and a dozen flowers thrown into a heap at the feet of the pair onstage.

Then, in the blink of an eye, the two performers nimbly disappeared.

In the dressing room afterwards, they had discussed the faulty lever and giving up the butcher's blood. It was expensive now. Might they continue to have the same effect on their audience without it? They decided to leave it off for the evening performance. As it turned out, the trick had gone down just as well.

It is only now, as they roll through the dark night, that Daphne remembers she had meant to talk about Coco. They should set an alarm clock or something similar when they put the dove in the lid. But she had not got the chance, as Hugh Devereaux had turned up with a driver outside and given them no choice but to accompany him. Still, as she thinks of the poor creature, something stirs in her memory.

'Don't they represent something?' she says absently to Jonty, who is biting a fingernail on his right hand.

'What's that?' His eyes are baggy and lined around the edges.

'Doves,' she says. 'They're a symbol of something else. Not just magic.' Then she remembers Noah and the ark and the bird that came back with the twig in its beak. It told Noah there was land somewhere ahead. So the bird must represent hope, she thinks.

Jonty does not ask where the non sequitur has come from. Perhaps he has been reviewing the performance himself. 'You're quite right there,' he says, 'They stand for peace.'

Daphne winces. Suddenly a suffocating dove seems not funny at all. She lapses into uncomfortable silence.

Soon they are at Jonty's house.

'I am full of fatigue,' he says before he gets out of the car. 'Can we talk about all this tomorrow?'

'Of course,' she says and waves goodbye.

But the conversation does not happen.

Events overtake it.

Though they do not yet know it, their decision has already been made.

GERMANS TORPEDO SS *ARANDORA STAR*

Without warning, in the early hours of yesterday a Nazi U-boat opened fire on British liner
SS *Arandora Star*. The 15,500-ton vessel was
just off the west coast of Ireland at the time
of the attack and was struck on its starboard
side. The former cruise ship was carrying
hostile Germans and Italians on their way from
Britain to holding camps in Canada.

  The *Arandora Star*'s lighting system was
destroyed and its engine room staff had to
scramble through fire, darkness and water to
get to the decks. Early reports suggest that
900 enemy aliens and as many as 100 Britons –
soldiers, guards and members of the crew of
300 – are missing.

4 JULY 1940

CHAPTER THREE

Daphne's relaxed posture belies the pulse of her veins. She does not know how she feels. She does not know how she wants to feel or how she should feel. A turbulence of thoughts – the war, the meeting and now the news – blows through her head in a disordered and unpleasant stream. Up, down, up, down. Around. Her breathing comes and goes in fits and starts. She is perspiring, although it is only dawn.

Her hair is brushed to a shine and pinned up at the sides. It glides down from the crown and, at her neck, swishes about like the line of black tassels sewn into the hip of her costume. While she has inherited the colour from her mother, her father's curls are visible in the drop of hair as it touches her back. She cannot see it but when she moves her head, reddish threads catch the light. Her lips are bare and her skin powdered sparingly. She looks the very model of a good girl. Thoroughly finished.

In truth, she never rises at this hour. And so when she appears in the kitchen Mrs Thomas, her landlady, is flustered. The older woman rarely grabs ten minutes to read the morning paper, though today she sits on a hard stool by the fire. Despite offers from her husband it has never been upholstered. Mrs Thomas prefers it that way. She does not want to be more comfortable. It is, she says, perfect for a housewife mindful of her duties.

Mr Thomas had been fed and watered and dispatched to the paper shop to open up and sort the news before the sun peeped over the chimneys of terraced houses across the road.

Mrs Thomas flushes, feeling she has let herself down. 'Oh, it was just a breather,' she says, and folds the paper away.

Daphne makes a movement with her hand as if she is patting the side of an invisible horse. 'Stay.' She is pleased to see her at ease. Mrs Thomas is always in a state of perpetual motion: washing the stove, scrubbing steps, cleaning the house from the top rafters to the cellar, stirring pots, clipping recipes from the National Food Campaign. She follows their advice and is thrifty, keeping all food scraps. Over the way, past Borough Market, her cousin belongs to a Pig Club. Sometimes Daphne helps her take the pails of waste to the corner on a Friday morning, where they are picked up by the pigswill man from the allotments. If they are lucky some bacon may come of it.

Mrs Thomas transfers her weight to her knees and pushes up awkwardly. She rubs her back as she rises and winces. 'Rheumatism.'

'Oh, please don't,' Daphne protests. 'I can fix myself something.'

The landlady is having none of it. 'You sit yourself down.'

Normally, Daphne would insist on helping, but this morning her mind is not level. She pulls out a chair at the table by the window. It overlooks a small yard and outhouse. Alfie, the ginger tom, is stretching out on the roof of the coal bunker, enjoying the early sun. He stares at her, twitches his whiskers and blinks. Unimpressed, he looks away.

Her fingers smooth down the chequered tablecloth and tidy the crumbs left by Mr Thomas, straighten the knife by the butter dish. Mrs Thomas bustles in and sets down a pot of stewed tea and a plate of bread and butter. Tension hunches her shoulders, accentuating the dowager's hump that has been emerging since November. 'Any news, dear?'

Daphne does not want to answer, to use words, maybe the wrong ones. She knows that everything which originates as thought can be born into actuality once articulated. The Aramaeans understood this with their 'Abracadabra' – which, Jonty taught, translated to 'I create as I speak'. Language, she understands, has a magic of its own. Sometimes it is how real fear begins. She shakes her head.

Biting her lip, Mrs Thomas retreats into the kitchen.

Sleep was woven with the most unusual images: sailors, regarding her through drowning eyes, pushed Uncle Giuseppe, with his jug ears and hair still black, down beneath the cold green waves. While in the sky above them chattering witches, straight out of Grimm's fairy tales, bending spiky noses to spindly fingers, flew on broomsticks. Werewolves. There had been werewolves too, slowly metamorphosing, fangs dripping gore as they howled.

Mrs Thomas coughs beside her and holds out the last of the jam to sweeten what she thinks will inevitably be a bitter pill for her lodger.

Information has been hard to come by. Daphne's father has called the port authorities in Liverpool. The switchboards are constantly jammed. With nothing useful to occupy his mind, he has boarded a train heading north, intending to reach the Isle of Man and locate her mother, Carabella, at the internment camp. She, Daphne thinks, will be beside herself with worry about Uncle Giuseppe.

Her father has promised to alert her as soon as he hears anything. It is a strange limbo to live in.

She had been relieved to the point of collapse when Jonty arrived at the house last night. On hearing the radio reports of the *Arandora* he had hailed a cab and made his way to Southwark where, he told his assistant, there was now no choice.

'My dear. Although I was reluctant,' he said, 'to give up our liberties – we still have a good run left at the Oriental Theatre – Hugh assures me an arrangement can be made. I am aware of your mother's situation. Every ambition we once harboured must now be turned towards getting her out of that camp. You heard what Hugh said. Your, our, cooperation may vouch for the good character of your family.' He affected a yawn. 'The seas are perilous. The Germans had their own on that ship, you know. Their own people! Just as Hugh said, no scruples. I would never forgive myself if . . .' He abandoned his affected lethargy and drummed his fingers on the table. His back hunched, eyes reaching over her shoulder into the past. She knew he was thinking of his wife, buried less than two years since. A warm woman with turquoise eyes, Mrs Trevelyan caused Jonty to both glow and visibly relax whenever he was in her presence. Though he remained haunted by his last image of her, at their cosy fireside, gripped by a severe headache but insisting he should not cancel the matinee to stay with her. 'The show must go on, Dear One. Of course it must.' He found her there, cold, on his return. She had suffered a brain aneurism. The doctors insisted that there was nothing he could have done. Guilt refused to hear it and hung like a dead albatross across his shoulders. She could almost see its weight across his posture. It flapped as he said, 'We cannot permit your mother to be sent off like your poor uncle. We simply can't. There is too much death and disaster around us already. Further calamities must be stopped at any cost.'

She recognised those last three words. Mr Devereaux had also used them. Jonty had repeated them on purpose and she understood his choice. There were so many things to consider before they agreed. It was not just a matter of liberties, there were financial impediments to consider too. And yet he was here. She took his hand and brought it to her lips and kissed it. 'Are you sure, Jonty?'

'It's not like I've got anything to lose,' he said and gripped her tight.

It wasn't true, but she appreciated the solidarity.

And the sacrifice.

Breakfast helps rouse Daphne somewhat.

The tart sweetness of the greengage jam on her tongue sparks a recollection: summer at home in Essex, feeding jam sandwiches to the horses at the bottom of the garden. Before the new houses were built. Before the world changed. Before the light dimmed across Europe.

She experiences an impulse to walk out of the house and catch a train and go back there. Then she remembers – her childhood home will be empty.

Nothing will ever be the same.

Prompt, excited, anxious and nervy all at once, she is ready with her bag, waiting outside the house when the car arrives. She is surprised it isn't a military vehicle but a Hillman Minx just like her father's. He loves his motor car. Sometimes, when she was home for the holidays, she used to help in the garage. She recalls how, as he bent over the engine, her father's oiled hair would unstick and stand up off his head, like a cockscomb. It would make her giggle as she passed over the required spanners and tools. 'Wrench, Daphne! Oh come on, it's not that funny.' The consequences of these occasions have had an impact on her grasp of rudimentary mechanics. She's more finely tuned to dynamics than any other stage assistant Jonty has employed. She has a vague idea of this but does not think on it. Just now she is summoning the smell of cleaning rags and petroleum, and finds herself comforted fractionally.

When no one gets out to open the door for her, she lets herself in and slips along the back seat, putting her bag between her feet.

The car moves off more bumpily than her father's ever did. It is probably the chassis loosening. Again she thinks of him and wonders if he has made it to the Isle of Man yet. She is glad he is trying. Her parents need to be together.

'So do you do tricks then?'

Daphne assumed the driver would be the same sullen man who bore them over to the gentlemen's club. However, a pair of light blue eyes, bright and open, stare from the rear-view mirror. A woman, age indeterminate.

'Don't you?' asks the driver again.

Daphne meets the woman's persistence with frank ambiguity, if that was a thing (and she thought it might be now), mindful of Hugh's sniffy dismissal of Jonty at the club. 'Depends what kind you're referring to.'

'Aha!' says the driver with a grin. At least, Daphne supposes it is a grin. She can't see the shape of her mouth, only the frizzy blonde hair pulled back and held in place by clips. The outline of her left cheek, though, bulges outwards. 'Good answer. Devereaux has clearly been at you.'

Been at me? Daphne turns it over and considers what 'being at her' might feel like. Her eyebrows lift. She inspects her fingernails to make sure they are clean.

The driver prattles on, filling the air. 'I hear you're quite the performer. You and The Grand Mystique.'

'Yes,' Daphne answers, truthfully. Why not admit it? She is good at what she does. Though etiquette dictates she should decline flattery, compliments on her skill are better received than those on her appearance. The way one looks is just a happy accident, or an unhappy one. How one performs – well, that is a different matter. Hard work and attention to detail are required to become a stage assistant. Great dexterity and intuition are necessary to become a better one. 'I am,' she says. 'And so is The Grand Mystique. We work very well together.'

'Orders to pick him up next,' the driver says. 'Do you have a stage name too then?' She is very upbeat, quite enthusiastic.

Daphne doesn't have such a name. Most assistants are referred to as 'box jumpers'. But she doesn't want to admit this so says, 'La Petite Charisma, or Cha-Cha for short.' A little lie.

The driver claps, which Daphne thinks unnecessary and dangerous. 'Bravo!' she says. 'How marvellous.'

Daphne wants to tell her to keep her hands on the wheel but finds herself doing the opposite and poking her arm between the front seats. She offers her hand and says, 'I prefer Daphne. Daphne Devine.'

'Well, that sounds quite a name in itself.'

Yes, she supposes. It probably does, though she has never really thought about it.

Her chauffeur snorts. Daphne still can't tell if she is smiling, but there is a little crease to her visible cheek.

'And I'm Barbara,' the driver offers. 'But you can call me Bunty. Everyone does.'

Daphne lurches in the back as Bunty puts down her foot on the accelerator. Clearly she does not favour slow, cautious driving.

They gun down Pall Mall. Daphne presses a hand against the window. Everything moves much faster in daylight. Outside, above the pavements, the air is shimmering. The Quadriga at Hyde Park Corner has its own guardian angel floating near – a barrage balloon dangling almost invisible chains, protecting from the clouds. They are all over London and have created a spider's web of metal to tangle would-be bombers.

Daphne is pleased that she has chosen a light cotton dress. It is one of her favourites, duck-egg blue with daisies woven into the pattern. The fabric is fine, airy and cool. Pedestrians on their way to work have shed their outerwear already and carry jackets over their arms, dabbing their necks with handkerchiefs.

Despite the sunshine, the air is full of pressure. Thoughts frown across perspiring foreheads.

Soon they come to a halt. Daphne winds down the window on the kerb side.

Jonty is leaning against the railings, dressed in his civvies and smoking a cigarette. With the sunshine on him today and without his thick pancake of make-up you can see his skin. He looks older, more lined and craggier, late forties rather than earlier in the decade.

Bunty honks the horn. Jonty jumps, frowns. He takes a final drag on his cigarette and coughs, tosses the butt of his cigarette into the gutter.

'Your chariot awaits,' Daphne says as he opens the door. He smiles. Good. His mood is even.

She slides over to the other side to make room. Her boss gets one leg in the car, though before he can sit down and close the door Bunty has pushed off from the kerb. He lands with a thud beside Daphne. 'I say,' he splutters.

'Can't wait, sorry,' Bunty declares from the front. 'If I put my foot down, I can get you a bit of a tour in before the briefing starts, all right?' She revs the engine and goes at it full pelt, enjoying the speed and emitting a little squeal, like a young piglet.

'I still can't quite believe this, can you?' Jonty says once he has managed to sit upright. His movements are groggy, eyes red.

Daphne guesses he left the Thomases' last night and then adjourned to Soho. A man's downfall, she thinks, does not come from battles or circumstances out of his control but often, merely, one more drink. When in his cups Jonty's mood can go up and down. She sweeps her hand around the interior of the car and twirls it, as if pointing to one of their great reveals. 'Seeing is believing,' she says.

'No, it isn't. As well you know.'

Daphne laughs. It is good to keep him on this level. She prefers Jonty buoyant, not needing support. Though she is there, should a helping hand be required. She owes him, and will always be grateful. It was he, after all, who introduced her to London, leading her through an assortment of illusions during the day and the streets of the city with all its questionable delights after the sun had set. At the beginning he had invited her to dine in the family home. And it had become a regular thing until Mrs Trevelyan had passed. After that, home-cooked suppers were exchanged for restaurants and dive bars. Daphne did not always accompany him to these establishments.

Lips curved with a smile, her employer asks after her sleep. 'No, me neither,' he replies once she has confessed her night full of bleak visions. 'I woke at four o'clock with a sense of foreboding and, try as I might, just could not get back to the Land of Nod.' Then he remembers her position and says, 'But then again, I stopped off for a quick one on Greek Street. The wine must have been corked. It was probably that.'

She does not press him and says, thinking of one of the places they have both visited, 'L'Escargot?'

'Dear Lord, no,' he says. 'Still can't get to grips with how they eat the slimy buggers. Would have quite turned me. Mr Gaudin has a snail farm in the basement, did you know?'

'I hadn't heard.'

'Funny things, foreigners, aren't they?' She does not reply and he quickly catches her silent rebuke. 'Oh, I didn't . . . you're . . . you . . . your mother, or uncle . . . Not them. They're practically British. I meant . . .' Despite his dexterous contortions onstage, when off it he has a habit of putting his foot in his mouth.

'I know what you mean,' she replies but keeps her eyes fixed on the windscreen. She is aware of the ears of the Secret Services, or at least the Bunty Division. Best not to leak information about sympathies for those with ancestors not born on these shores. Or her own Continental parentage. An Italian mother and quarter-German father are not the finest credentials for governmental work. Though Hugh Devereaux has more than the measure of her. Evidently it is no bar. It provides leverage. For them.

'Quite,' says Jonty and, knowing he has blundered, tries for diversion. 'Has our lady driver told you where we're going?'

As if on cue Bunty takes a sharp right, sending Jonty over to Daphne. He manages to grab a strap hanging from the roof and corrects himself crossly. As he settles back into the seat, his gaze snaps to something through the windscreen. A loud gasp, eyes widen in genuine dismay.

Daphne notes the change and turns to see what has provoked it. Usually Jonty is able to conceal such a reaction.

'Stop the car.' Jonty uses his loud stage voice: 'At once!'

'I intend to.' Bunty pulls up the handbrake. The tyres slide on the road. 'We're here.'

'But this is preposterous.' Jonty grips hold of the headrest, his already florid cheeks flushing a deeper shade of lobster. 'There must be some kind of mistake!'

The iconic towers are distinctive in their patterned brickwork, bone white against brown. Daphne has seen them before. Though not in person. Perhaps in a newspaper photograph. Something to do with a murder. Or a murderer, was it?

And then she places the high wired walls, grey-dark against the summer sky. A crushing feeling comes over her.

They have arrived.

Before them looms Wormwood Scrubs.

CHAPTER FOUR

'I shall be speaking to your superiors,' says Jonty. Beyond the haughty imperiousness lies a tone of dark fright.

'Oh, did they not tell you?' Bunty tries to suppress a grin.

'Did they not tell *you*?' Jonty's finger trembles as he waves it at her. 'We cooperated: we did. We've volunteered to work. We agreed.'

Getting out, Daphne catches up with the driver, who is striding to the entrance.

'He's right,' she says, modulating her tone so that her words sound conciliatory. 'Mr Devereaux can vouch for us. We haven't done anything wrong.'

'HQ has relocated here. Nothing more secure than a prison,' Bunty explains.

Daphne feels they might have been told, but then she realises thoughts like this, manners, etiquette, they are all from the old world, back before the war. They have indeed gone through the looking glass.

Once inside, they are directed to a tatty wooden bench by the front desk and told to sit. Three guards and two plainclothes staff are on duty in the lobby.

A woman in a hairnet with a bored toddler, another visitor, is working through a pile of forms. The child wanders to

Daphne and stares at her with a grubby face and a quizzical look, holding his hands out either side for balance. His gas mask does not help matters and swings out as he wobbles. Gently, Daphne turns him around and sends him tottering back in the direction of the woman.

Jonty looks at the child sternly. The Trevelyans had a daughter once. Jonty has never explained what became of her, and Daphne has not wanted to pry. But she notices, without ever commenting, that sometimes when she is bold he smiles proudly, the way a parent might.

Bunty is speaking quietly to a desk officer, and then the guard calls them. They are each asked their name and address, whom they are visiting. At this the new recruits swivel their eyes to Bunty, who announces 'Colin Scott.' The name is followed by Bunty's low whisper: 'Always Colin Scott, you see.'

They don't, but Daphne files it in her mind for later use.

Once the relevant documentation has been filled, or waived, they are allowed admittance.

Wormwood Scrubs, Daphne thinks. What would her parents say? An image of her mother enters her head, fingers crooked and gnarled, her hair once luscious, thick and black but now shot with grey, frazzled and dry. Probably even white now with Giuseppe lost somewhere. She reminds herself this is why she is here. Her muscles tense: she must impress.

They descend a flight of concrete stairs into a corridor with low ceilings and exposed pipework, graceless and severe. No doubt its intended effect.

Daphne senses desperation. She does not like it.

Doors are unlocked and then locked behind them. They go down two more staircases until they reach the bowels of the prison, which are almost certainly subterranean.

At the entrance of a wider and slightly loftier corridor Bunty stops and checks her watch. 'Mmm, the briefing might have started but I can give you a bit of a heads-up. Just so you've got the gist of it. I'm not sure how much Mr Devereaux has explained.'

'Nothing at all,' Jonty says.

The driver turns to the first door, which is made of thick metal with a grille at eye level. She knocks: two light bumps and then a heavier one using the palm of her hand.

A voice inside: 'Enter.'

Bunty guides them through.

The little cell contains two men. The younger has on a turban not dissimilar to The Grand Mystique's stage costume. His skin is dark against a light linen suit. He scribbles on a wall. It is daubed with calculations in black chalk paint. The other man is older, rotund in military khaki, and is puffing on a cigar. He holds a paper chart. Daphne glances at it and immediately their Metamorphosis box is summoned to mind. It has zodiacal symbols, she can see, and chirology diagrams.

'What's this?' the older man says.

Unless Daphne's ears are deceiving her, this man is German. Unexpectedly she experiences relief, for if he is permitted here then her background must definitely be acceptable. But still – a German. Here, of all places, at the Secret Service headquarters.

'Captain,' says Bunty, 'this is The Grand Mystique, and his assistant Cha-Cha.'

Daphne has forgotten her white lie, and quickly she glances at Jonty. He's not looking at her, but doesn't seem perturbed by the name.

The captain bows. He gestures to the young man in the turban. 'My assistant Rashnid. And I am Captain de Kohl.' He looks intently at Daphne, his expression ostensibly open and mild, but she is well primed in the art of concealment and knows there is something going on beyond the upturned mouth.

'Are you coming to the briefing, Captain?' Bunty asks.

'We were updated earlier,' he says, as if this means something else. 'Work to do here.'

The captain and Rashnid bow, synchronised like dancers, and turn their backs.

Outside the captain's room, a couple of men in suits enter the corridor.

Bunty points to a wooden door at the opposite end of the corridor. 'Section W.'

Their footsteps as they walk are faint, almost unnoticeable. The floor is covered by a strange lino – parts of it sparkle. They pass other cells, emitting strange sounds which make Daphne wonder what on earth is going on inside.

And then they are there.

The door to Section W opens.

CHAPTER FIVE

The interior is the length of five or six cells and three times as wide. On the ceiling Daphne can see rough patches where pieces of masonry stick out, suggesting walls have been hastily knocked down to create this underground meeting room.

On the far end charts and maps are tacked to a pinboard that extends from floor to ceiling. It is difficult to see any great detail through the cigarette and cigar smoke which hangs in loose strips in the air, though the outlines of the British Isles and the north edge of the Continent are visible on the widest map. In the English Channel there are red dots.

A wide table runs down the middle of the room. Around it, under harsh suspended lights, sit a dozen or so personnel. Again Daphne is surprised to see everyone is in plain clothes. While several appear somewhat ordinary, perhaps civil servants, others are less so. She is drawn to a skinny man in a bottle-green suit, with keen eyes, who is also watching her, and she senses his curiosity. Next to him is someone who regularly features in the gossip columns. A poet with a reputation for rowdy behaviour. It is all very curious.

There are no seats left at the table and despite several men noting her entrance, none have risen or offered their chair.

Bunty nods at Daphne, indicating she should move closer to the front. It is like a bunker, with not one single window. She slinks along its wall.

At the head of the table a portly man with a military bearing stands erect. Positioned in front of the maps and charts, he has the best view of those gathered. He is dressed in a double-breasted suit, an uninteresting grey the colour of pigeons' necks and not a good fit, being tight around the waist. Despite his inexpedient sartorial style it is clear the man is in charge.

Daphne, self-conscious, finds herself straightening her spine as if standing to attention.

'The commander,' Bunty hisses to Jonty and Daphne.

The man tilts back on his heels. 'Right,' he says, with a touch of irritation. 'Now, as I was saying. Supernatural thinking is at the very core of Nazi strategy. Since the thirties our sources in Germany have reported on Himmler, Reichsführer of the SS.' He squints at a girl with reddish-brown hair standing at the side of the room and then explains in a softer tone, as if she might be ever so slightly dense, 'The commander-in-chief. Almost an equivalent rank to me.' Then authority reasserts itself into his voice and he addresses the room again. 'He has created a department called the Ahnenerbe. Some are calling it the SS Occult Bureau. It seeks evidence to confirm Himmler's belief the Germans are descended from an ancient Indo-European race, the Aryans.'

A smaller man, balding around the crown, seated near the speaker, pushes his spectacles up his nose.

'It's worth saying,' the commander adds, 'that scholars, archaeologists and historians, both here and in Germany, do not accept this claim.'

'Sir William.' Bunty identifies the fellow with the thinning hair and specs.

'And yet it gains ground there,' the commander snaps. 'The National Socialist German Workers' Party have long been engaged in political manipulation. Techniques of mass suggestion have lodged this belief in the minds of their people.

Even the pauper begging on the *strasse* believes he has biological superiority over other races.'

Around the table someone snorts.

The commander acknowledges the sentiment: 'Indeed, some have suggested they are the descendants of the lost civilisation of Atlantis.'

Sir William clears his throat and adds, 'Another myth they have adopted, also lacking empirical evidence. It is false information.'

'Propaganda,' the commander agrees. 'Cyril over there,' he says, addressing a young man who is dressed more flamboyantly than the others, his flashy hairstyle brushed back messily. 'You have confirmed this, from your work in the field?'

Daphne can't help but notice that Cyril is dashing. His style is raffish. He would not look amiss at the Leigh Yacht Club regatta.

However, when Cyril opens his mouth, his delivery is grave: 'They will use anything to reinforce the idea that they are chosen, different, exceptional. For many ordinary Germans their Führer's ascent to power has encouraged the perception that he is a messiah with otherworldly powers. A view he is in no hurry to dispel.'

His words send a shock wave through her: she has never heard of any of this.

'Added to that,' says the commander, 'the German people are now abandoning their Christian ways and turning to superstitious magical beliefs: sun worship, the old gods. There is an appetite to believe. We have photographic evidence of pagan torchlit ceremonies.'

Daphne's throat tightens.

Cyril does not respond but his neighbour, the man in the bottle-green suit, coughs gently as if in warning.

'Other agents,' the commander adds, 'have described Himmler as half-cocked.'

Other agents? Daphne muses. So the Cyril fellow is one? He does not look like her idea of a spy. Not with the hair and the loose tie. Though perhaps that is the point.

She watches Cyril's chest rise as he speaks again. 'The occult holds a dark fascination for Himmler, we are certain.' His voice lowers. 'He also runs the Witch Bureau. A pamphlet published five years ago claims the Germanic witch hunts were an attempt to annihilate "Aryan womanhood". We must remember: this is a pursuit of power designed to control. To achieve global domination.'

To what point? Daphne wonders. The rewards are illusory . . . After all, the top of the tree is the most precarious position. There will always be others on the branches beneath who covet it and wish to topple those there. It is a place that exists without rest or tranquillity. Or peace. And what for? What *is* it ultimately for? What happens when the greediest man in the world has eaten everything? What happens to him?

The commander has shifted to one side. His buttons glint under the light. 'What we do know is that Himmler is a proponent of Luciferianism – of the view that Lucifer was unfairly expelled from Heaven. Thus the Devil is a force that can guide and endow with diabolical powers: a bringer of enlightenment who opposes the Jewish God. The Reichsführer has created a new mystic order with this SS of his.'

And it is at this point the lights above them blink.

Everyone's attention snaps to the ceiling.

Only the commander stays focused. His lips form a thin line. 'They are committed to the belief that this dark magic can be put to use in the conquest of Europe.'

Something above their heads sizzles. There is a flash, and they are plunged into deep subterranean darkness. Daphne wonders if this is a show, well organised and well timed. Or an elaborate joke? Jonty reaches for her hand.

Chairs scrape against the floor. Some shuffling by the table. A glass smashes. And a man says, 'Do not concern yourselves. It's the generator.'

There is a sudden fizzing as matches are lit. Someone transfers a flame to two candles, which flicker then illuminate a small patch of table. It is the girl who had been at the side of the room only seconds before.

Atop the candles naked flames, the colour of ghosts, tremble. The girl withdraws into the blackness and returns with an oil lamp. Setting it on the table, she lights the wick. It is quick thinking for someone the commander addresses like a simpleton.

The candles splutter. Above them black air ripples and warps, as if a sentient creature.

They can hear us, Daphne thinks, then administers a mental reprimand to bring her imagination under control. It is always such a problem with her.

In the room the mood has altered and feels charged with electricity.

The hairs on Daphne's neck prickle as the pooling shadows collect behind her back.

The commander, who has not moved throughout this episode, draws everyone's attention with a loud summoning statement. 'It's all claptrap, of course.'

His words may have been designed to soothe the collective disquiet but a couple, an older man with a shock of white hair and a middle-aged woman in a felt hat, share a glance. Daphne sees they are not happy. Who are they? Why would they be offended by his assertion?

'We know Hitler ordered the Imperial Regalia to be removed from the Kunsthistorisches Museum when he invaded Austria two years back. That collection contains the Spear of Destiny.' The commander points at an old lady with thin silver hair gathered into a bun. 'Margaret?'

She looks like somebody's grandmother. But when she moves forward into the globe of light cast by the oil lamp, Daphne notices her dark sparkly eyes. 'The Reichskleinodien, regalia of the Holy Roman Emperor with many symbolical pieces. The Spear of Destiny is also known as the Holy Lance, and reputedly belonged to the centurion who pierced Christ's side at the Crucifixion. It is said to be infused with his blood as he transmuted from mortal man to godhead.' She lets a murmur run through those gathered at the table and proceeds. 'The "God particles" on this lance thus wield unfathomable super-natural power. A belief exists that whosoever holds it will be given powers to bend the destiny of the world to their will.'

These words trigger a reaction in the young man in the green suit. He jerks himself upright and asks, 'And we can confirm it is in Hitler's possession?' He has a soothing voice despite his rigidity.

Margaret nods grimly. 'I'm afraid so, Septimus. It was displayed at Nuremberg during the September 1938 Party Congress. Though I doubt it has magical powers.'

'Even so,' the young man, Septimus, says. 'It is illogical. Nonetheless, the psychological effect – the Spear of Destiny in the hands of their leaders – will flame a belief in the populace that they are unstoppable.'

The commander interjects. 'That is not our concern, remem-ber. Others are already occupied in a strategy to counter it. There are four Spears of Destiny currently in existence, all claiming to have breached the Lord's side. And the Nazis have just one of them.'

'Then we should let them know about this,' says Septimus. 'We could drop from aeroplanes information detailing the other spears.'

Daphne thinks it is a good idea, but no one makes notes or takes it up. Instead it seems the commander is readying for his final point. 'Now, I know that in this prestigious grouping we have experienced academics and writers who may not believe in this sort of thing, but the point is – the Third Reich does.' He crispens his diction for emphasis. 'While they may well imagine that untapped supernatural forces are contained within these ritual objects and suchlike, we understand that this – their preoccupation, this *credence* – gives *us* power.' A pause. He crunches his brow. 'It presents opportunities. It is, in fact, a weakness which we can exploit.'

Sharp nods round the table.

'Militarily,' he says, using the word to anchor his words in a more earthbound subject, 'we need time to regroup and restock. In order to produce this space, we must utilise these ideological beliefs to create cracks.' Sweeping the room with his eyes, it feels like he is making eye contact with every individual present. 'We need to be creative. You here today represent some of the wiliest and most brilliant brains in the kingdom, and you have been selected for your strengths and expertise in areas that may not, at first, seem relevant. But your sagacity, wisdom, ideas, your cleverness – these are our weapons against the enemy. We charge you now to join us in putting them to use in the defence of the realm.'

The map behind him flutters, alerting the commander to the door in the corner opening, and a very tall man enters the room. He stands for a second. The candlelit gathering looks like a seance. It is evidently not what he expected.

Who would?

Above the table the light flickers and buzzes. This time, however, it turns back on, flooding the room once more with light. A collective sigh of relief goes up.

Hugh Devereaux squints into the room.

The light makes him look different. She has only seen him in the low-lit lounge of the gentlemen's club. Now his broad forehead and features are noticeable. For his age, even with white hair, he is handsome: neat side parting, perfectly combed; dark eyelashes; strong jaw; good shoulders.

'Ah, pardon me just a moment, Brigadier.' Spotting Daphne and Jonty lurking at the back, he slips round the table, light on his feet for a man of such stature. 'Come on.' He beckons, indicating she and Jonty should step into the spotlight near the commander. 'I need to introduce you.'

Suddenly Daphne's cotton dress is too girlish. She touches the hair at the back of her neck. This too should have been piled up neatly. She feels out of her depth.

Hugh Devereaux's eyes flash.

Jonty follows her to the pinboard.

'This,' says Mr Devereaux, 'is The Grand Mystique, aka Jonty Trevelyan, a master of illusion.'

Jonty readies for a speech but is swiftly nudged aside by Hugh, who thrusts Daphne so far forward that she almost bumps the brigadier. She is left with little room to manoeuvre and stands awkwardly closer to him than is decent.

'And this is Daphne, his assistant.'

At last, Daphne thinks. Now they might learn what she and Jonty will be doing. But the brigadier thrusts a handful of paper at her with the instruction, 'Go Roneo these notes.'

'No,' says Jonty. 'She's *my* assistant. A stage perf—'

The brigadier cuts him off. 'Here you share resources.' Then he takes Daphne's elbow and spins her around. 'Now hurry along. Fifteen copies. Bunty will show the way.'

And Daphne is outside the room before she knows it.

CHAPTER SIX

An austere woman in the secretarial quarters occupies a large desk positioned at the front, like a teacher watching over her classroom. Although above ground this room has just one window, high up and barred. It's not a classroom.

The office is artificially lit, like the briefing room, by several unshaded bulbs. Rows and rows of women sit behind desks, hammering away on typewriters. The air is filled with a continuous buzz – the click clack click of fingers on keys, like hundreds of metallic butterflies opening and shutting their wings.

Ordinary workaday cabinets, at the far end of the room, are piled high with the day's filing. Behind them, screens section another space. A gap has been left as a makeshift door to an area beyond, too far away to see into.

Bunty announces them to the head clerk. 'She needs access to the Roneo please, Miss Prendergast.' Her voice is raised to be heard over the clatter.

The woman at the desk stops arranging papers and peers over pince-nez to inspect the interruption. There are lots of tiny wrinkles on her top lip that face powder has failed to reach. She has the look of someone who does not need to shout to get what she wants. Like the teachers at the Institute where Daphne was sent by her parents to be 'ironed out'.

'And what department is this for?' Miss Prendergast's voice is calm though taut, as if braced for whatever may come but at the same time wearied by the effort.

Daphne wonders if this is what is meant by 'going on a war footing'? Must she also expect to exist in a perpetual state of readiness?

'Section W,' says Bunty.

'Oh,' Prendergast replies.

What is that in her voice? Disapproval? Disappointment? Awe? The head clerk does not look like someone who is overawed very often. Everything about her is brisk, efficient and polished, but dour.

'Jolly good. I'll leave you to it.' Bunty's breeziness is getting on Daphne's nerves now, and she's happy to see her go.

'Wonderful,' says Miss Prendergast in a manner that suggests the opposite.

'Splendid.' Bunty lets her hands drop to her sides, nods once more at Daphne, then bounces off down the corridor.

The head clerk's gaze falls on to the new recruit, who changes her mind about Bunty's absence. Safety in numbers.

'So, Section W?' Miss Prendergast proffers. 'What does the W stand for, do you know?'

'I thought you might be able to enlighten me.'

Miss Prendergast does not smile. The unpowdered wrinkles deepen as she holds out a pink hand. 'Notes please.'

Daphne passes them over and shrugs. 'Is it, perhaps, W for War?'

'Popular hypotheses,' says Miss Prendergast, inspecting the pages, 'include "witchcraft".'

'Oh,' says Daphne.

'Indeed.' Prendergast's mouth twists into a fleeting but unpleasant smile. 'Have you Roneoed before?'

Daphne has no idea what a Roneo is. 'Not exactly.'

'Wax paper,' the head clerk says. Daphne thinks she is talking about the W again and does not know how to react. Then Miss Prendergast points to a box of the stuff on her desk. 'Please.'

The head clerk inserts it into her typewriter. 'There have been other suggestions. Woeful. Witless. Wicked.' Miss Prendergast removes her hands from the typewriter and counts out the names on her left hand. 'Widdershins. Weird. Worrisome.' Her fingers dance onto her other hand. 'Water and . . . Wrong. So you're their new secretary?'

'I don't think so.'

Prendergast gives Daphne another once-over. 'Well, what are you then?'

'A stage magician's assistant.'

The older woman winces and mutters under her breath. 'We're going to lose this war.' She turns her head to the screens. Her hair is wound into a French plait. It is pulled so tight that the skin at the roots is red. 'Next, once you have the wax in place, simply copy. Over there.' She returns to Daphne. 'If there are diagrams involved, you'll have to get someone else from the secretariat. Miss Wilberforce is efficient. Line 3, desk E.'

Daphne scours the rows of desks. There is nothing to identify each one. When she returns her gaze to the head clerk she sees that Prendergast's wrinkles have disappeared, just briefly. Her lips match the thinness of her contracted eyelids: something in the notes has given reason for alarm. Conscious of her failure to hide her reaction, Miss Prendergast darts a glance at Daphne. Seeing nothing but a pretty yet empty face, Prendergast masters herself, swallows and then revisits the text, keeping her eyes on the letters being thumped out of the red and black ribbon.

Daphne, however, has made a decision: she is going to read the pages once left alone with the Roneo device.

The head clerk stands up and barks, 'Follow me.'

It is an order, so Daphne does as she is told and scampers after her.

Over her shoulder, Prendergast calls, 'I'll show you the Roneo. You'll have to sort yourself out in future.'

They go through the gap between the screens into an area where several young women hunch over different pieces of equipment.

'Watch carefully,' says Prendergast. 'I daresay you'll become well acquainted soon enough.' There is a glint in her eye, like a warning.

As it turns out, a Roneo is a duplicating machine. Prendergast wraps the wax paper around a cylinder. 'You have to turn this handle.' She demonstrates. 'Copies come out the other end. How many do you need?'

'Fifteen.'

'Good. I'll leave it to you. Let the ink dry for a bit before you give them out or they'll smudge.'

Daphne is not fazed. It can't be more complicated than a Chinese sword cabinet. Soon leaves of paper are churning out of the machine. She gathers them up and places them at the end of the table to dry as the other women are doing.

It is impossible *not* to notice the words typed there beside a series of initials:

```
JG - Nostradamus, astrology, metapsychol-
     ogy, occultism.
HG - World Ice Theory, cosmology.
RH - Astrology, cosmobiology, Nostradamus,
     parapsychology, clairvoyance, psycho-
     kinesis, magnetism, fortune-telling,
     astral travel, occultism.
HH - Luciferianism, World Ice Theory,
     reincarnation (King Henry), occult
     magic, Ariosophy, Nostradamus.
AH - Ariosophy, astrology, DEATH
     RAYS.
```

'You're meant to copy them, not read them.'

'Just checking there are no smudges.' Daphne looks up. 'Oh, hello.' It is the girl who lit the lamp earlier. She is older than Daphne had earlier assumed. Not a girl but a woman. A few years her senior, maybe two or three. Perhaps mid-twenties. Lipsticked mouth as vivid as a pillar box. Her eyes are bright, cornflower blue, and sharp. Very sharp. She holds her body alert.

'We're returning the notes, then you're to follow me,' she says briskly.

More orders, thinks Daphne. She is only halfway through the duplicating so goes back to the handle and cranks it again. 'Where to?'

'You'll find out soon enough,' says the woman.

It is all getting a bit irritating, this cloak and dagger. Daphne can't quite stop herself from saying, 'Of course, I suppose I should just resign myself to the fact I'm here to be rounded up like a sheep and nosed in any direction.'

The woman chuckles. It is a full-throated sound. 'That would imply that I'm a dog. A bitch to be precise. I'm not so keen on that.'

Her tone reminds Daphne of someone. A friend. This person standing upright in roomy slacks and a gauzy blouse is as bold as her old pal Enid, who taught Daphne to exhale smoke rings leaning out of the window at the Institute. The thought evokes an immediate warmth for this woman.

The newcomer finishes with the Roneo, gathers up the papers, looks Daphne square in the face and smiles. 'Brigit Harkness.' She thrusts out a hand. 'And yes, before you ask – I am a relation. The brigadier's niece, for my sins.'

Daphne experiences a moment of confusion. Who is she referring to? Then she remembers – yes, the commander in the briefing room, he is the brigadier.

'There's not much of a family resemblance,' says Daphne. And there isn't. Where the brigadier is barrel-chested and squat, Brigit is tall and slender. Their genetic bond is expressed through a similar red in their hair. But even so, Brigit's tresses are more caramel. She is glossy and groomed and supple-skinned.

'Glad you said that.' Brigit Harkness tosses back her head, reminding Daphne fleetingly of a thoroughbred.

'Oh no. Now I see you're not like him at all. You're . . .' Daphne flounders. 'Brighter . . .'

Brigit snorts through her nose. Daphne feels she is laughing at her.

'I take it you observed the manner with which dear Uncle addresses me?' Brigit's tone is wily. 'Oh no, I prefer to play it that way. Saves a lot of bother. You know how men are with intelligent women. Unnerves them. When Jesus preached that one shouldn't hide one's light under a bushel, he was talking to his disciples. And they were all chaps.'

It is consoling to hear these profanities drop from a pretty mouth. Daphne is cautious, though, and simply blows on the papers she is holding.

'All right then.' Brigit takes a portion of the notes and they exit past the screens, through the desks full of typists, past Miss Prendergast busy with another set of papers, and back to the corridor.

'I'm not well versed in clerical duties,' Daphne says.

'Yes, I thought as much.' Brigit nods. 'Stagehand, aren't you?'

'Magician's assistant.'

'Quite. The brigadier means well but he's not entirely up on personnel. I dare say he knows only a quarter of those at the briefing today.'

'Mmm,' says Daphne. 'I heard him call a lady by name – Margaret?'

'I can't really answer that, I'm afraid. We're not officially here, like I said. Hence the civvies. If people saw uniforms coming in and out, they'd soon cotton on that the prison wasn't being used for the sole purpose of locking up crooks.'

This at least explains the dress code. 'Makes it difficult to know who's who.'

'That's the point,' says Brigit.

'There was a man in the briefing room,' Daphne ventures, 'who I do know – the poet. I have heard rumours that he takes drugs.'

The last part of the sentence doesn't faze Brigit. 'Oh yes. Aubrey Sharpling. He has a highly individual way of thinking. It's best that you forget everything you've read in the papers and just take people for what they are.'

'Well, what's that?' asks Daphne. They have reached the briefing room. Brigit does not answer. Daphne senses she has rinsed out all the information that Brigit is willing to give. So she thanks her and says, 'I expect I shall get to know them over the coming months.'

Brigit raises a finger to the air. 'Sooner than that. Once we've delivered these, I'm to take you to your boarding house. You must pack a bag. Only essentials. As quick as you can. I think they have a job. They're sending you off to training tonight.'

This is not what Daphne anticipated. It unlooses her somewhat. 'Tonight!' Brigit has got it wrong. 'No. I'm sorry, we have a show.'

Now Brigit's demeanour changes, as if the patience she had been extending has instantly dried up. She catches Daphne by the arm. 'Look, tonight's performance has been cancelled. And those thereafter.' She does not keep her eyes on her for long but switches to the door and points to those on the other side. 'We are at war. There cannot be half-hearted commitments. This work is something you do not pick and choose. Your man Jonty knows about the shows already.' Brigit's words fall upon her like little hammers.

'We've still got weeks left of the run . . .' says Daphne. 'There are costs involved, Brigit.'

Brigit releases her and steps back, then a different light comes into her eyes. 'Beg pardon,' she says in a voice Daphne has not heard before, as if she has forgotten something. 'There's been a development.' Her eyes narrow, the porcelain skin on her forehead cracks slightly. 'We have scuttled the French fleet.'

Daphne cannot immediately make sense of this. She thinks 'we' refers to the people in the briefing room. Then she realises Brigit means the British military, and the horror of the statement hits her. But the French, she thinks, they are our friends. 'How could we? They have suffered already.'

'Italy has entered the war. It is true that France has been wounded, but now the country has fallen,' Brigit says with steely conviction. 'Their ships cannot find their way into German or Italian hands. The Axis's naval strength is greater. What folly it would be to let them grow stronger still. The French fleet in Algeria has been neutralised: battleships, mine-layers, torpedo boats, minesweepers, submarines, tugs, trawlers, sloops – they have all been destroyed.'

Daphne pictures the men in the vessels, the panic and fear as explosions fill their ships with sound, fire and ocean. She thinks of Uncle Giuseppe with bubbles trailing up from his mouth.

'There was some negotiation, but it was futile. In the end overwhelming force *had* to be used. Hitler assumes the war is already won.' Brigit's face hardens in a way that Daphne finds absolutely frightening. 'It is only us, Britain alone, who stands against the Axis States.' The muscles in her cheeks contract. 'A message has been sent to the Führer and, indeed, to the rest of the world. We will not surrender. We will fight.'

Daphne pulls her mind from the oceans and its fresh harvest of souls and lets Brigit's words in. She hears herself ask, 'Casualties?'

'Haven't heard, but it will be inevitable.'

Inevitable. What a way to describe those lives cut short and the pain that will now consume all those wives, mothers, fathers, sons, daughters. Hundreds of lives changed forever in a strategic instant. And what for? To stop a lunatic from enacting some potty delusion. She knows her eyes carry anger in them.

Uncomfortable under Daphne's gaze, Brigit bristles and thickens her voice. 'So you see – you must pack your bag and we must gird ourselves for retaliation.'

The door of the briefing room swings open. All Daphne can see is darkness and smoke.

An omen.

Germany calling, Germany calling.

The Reichssender Hamburg broadcasting from Station Bremen.

You are about to hear our glorious German news in English.

It is the most feeble of understatements to say that today the British Empire is in great, great danger. Never before, in fact, has it been in such peril.

So we are not the least bit surprised to learn that panic and confusion are gaining ground in Britain day by day, hour by hour, minute by precarious minute. Food shortages are so severe in England that looting has broken out in most of your major cities. Of which there is no reporting in your news.

The only wonder is that the people of this small, doomed island took so long to realise the dire position into which their leaders and politicians have led them. But now realisation seems to have come with a vengeance in the country lanes and city streets, the villages, towns and cities. The wealthy, the upper classes are all seeking safety in flight. They have plenty of resources available to them to which the larger population lacks access. These affluent refugees have thoroughly used England for their own purposes, and now, when the worst is about to arrive on the country, they quietly vanish from the scene.

It won't be long before we are over in England and then through to the furthermost reaches of Britannia.

I say to you, People of Britain, the time has come to meet the bill, the extortionate bill that the flagrant Mr Churchill and his foolish accomplices ran up for you and which everyone of you, who remains, will be called upon to pay. Unless you force your government to meet it.

As to the immediate future, what do the stars foretell?

Why it is success.

German victory.

'So he is prepared to sacrifice,' says the man with the moustache. He dismisses the raised arms with a tight, distracted salute.

In the room the air is still and thick, heavy with cigar smoke. Fastened into the atmosphere is a peculiarly sour stench of sweat. It has something keen to it, acute, tinged with a feral mustiness and the faint taint of panic, as if somewhere in the room, unseen, there trembles a cornered animal, reeking.

The gathered try hard not to breathe.

'I will not tolerate it. Never.' He pounds the desk once with his red fist, solid, powerful.

One of the men starts at the sound but quickly masters himself, containing the discharge of energy within his body and puffing out his chest in an amplified display of fortitude and solidarity so none might witness his weakness and report it. Two more standing feel their hearts beat faster – oh, the strength, the fervour, the passion.

'Never. Never.' Slam. Thump.

Beside him the simmering man in spectacles smiles. Violence is power. He approves and lifts his chin to their leader, opens his mouth and breathes in his essence. Only a minute movement of the lips, but in his head he sees himself sipping greedily, gulping, from this spectral radiance as if it were a stream. No, a fountain. His soul billows out.

A heartbeat later the man with the moustache changes. He is as mutable as quicksilver. A new thought extinguishes the fire and yields instead vexation. His shoulders drop. He puts one hand on his hip and with the other strokes his naked chin. 'General. What say you of their situation?'

The summoned man displays flashes of red and gold at the collar of his crisp grey-green uniform. He has been biding his time. He appreciates the profits of patience, but once summoned cannot linger, and steps into the light provided by the single bulb that hangs over the map. 'It is desperate. Full of bravado. An attempt to throw us off. But we know they are exposed.' He wills his words to satisfy. 'They shall come to see it soon.'

It is a small measure of appeasement: one can never know how long the leader's shape will last.

To enforce his meaning, he adds boldly, 'Otherwise we can smash them.'

All eyes switch to the leader. They wait with pains in their chests.

Conscious of their gaze but unconcerned by such trifles, the man with the moustache clasps his hands behind his back and bends to the map. 'They are vulnerable.'

Is it a question or a statement? The general, like everyone now, errs on the side of caution. 'They can be made weaker,' he says with a firmness he does not really feel.

But there is no response. Tension creeps back into the room. The air crackles with impossible angst. Beads of sweat collecting on the lips of the clean-shaven threaten to slide down into the corners of mouths. They resist the urge to lick them.

Where will the wheel of Fortune land – cruelty, steel, zeal?

The man's eyes trace the frayed band of blue on the map and frown.

Pressure builds.

Capillaries expand.

Blood reaches the furthermost parts of the anatomy.

It is as if thought-tentacles stretch out from the man in every direction. They all feel them.

He continues to lean at this strange and hard angle over the desk. Hanging. Motionless, frozen in a moment, as still as a statue and just as grey.

Someone breathes out stutteringly, trying not to make a noise, attract attention.

In this hollow pool the spectacled man manoeuvres forward. 'There are forces that may be rallied to empower us yet still.'

General Halder shudders.

Far above, in the complex, a door slams.

Reading the signs, the spectacled man persists. 'I have volunteers,' he says.

It is untrue. There is no one who would willingly submit to such ritual. But the man with the moustache understands his meaning.

'Every channel, every possible means to reduce them should be used now.' The Führer straightens, and with a curt nod he agrees. 'Do what you will.'

The man in spectacles grows a little taller. He sees the intangible shadow-thing which lurks on the edges of this present liminality reach and spread its wings.

10 JULY 1940

CHAPTER SEVEN

She shudders, jolts, flinches.

Her feet kick out at the sheet.

She has cried out, though her words have been strangled before they are born. The sounds dying in her throat are incomprehensible once consciousness dawns.

Something viscous, slimy, still clings to her. Not able to tell whether this is real or imagined, she puts her hand beneath the blanket. Sweat has soaked through the sheets. She leaps onto the rug, perceiving the wetness as blood. Holding her hands to her mouth, she lets out a wail.

She tries to stifle the noise, her fleshy palms instinctively smothering the shrill notes of her scream. But not all of it.

'Come on now. Pull yourself together.' A distinct voice.

Brigit, living and breathing. Real, not a phantom in the night.

Brigit, solid and flesh-made, fragrant of Sunlight soap. In her nightdress, two feet firmly planted on the ground, she stands behind her. One hand is on her shoulder; the other gently unpeels the fingernails digging into the flesh of Daphne's jaw.

Closer now, Brigit is saying, 'It's another one of your nightmares, Dee.'

The words serve to pierce the strange otherness Daphne has woken into. Like a radio station cutting through ghost static.

Normality. Reality.

Yes.

This is it.

In time – she knows not how long – her breathing composes itself into a more disciplined rhythm. A breath march. One, two, one, two, attention.

At ease.

She lets her hands drop and, at last, her head stops its spinning. The darkness recedes and the grey walls of the cramped room she and Brigit share sail into clear view.

A thin, watery light flows between a gap in the curtains. Morning.

Daphne catches her breath at last. 'I think you're right. A night terror.' Though she regrets the words as soon as they are spoken. An admission of weakness, born into the world. Night terrors sound childish and flighty, when in fact she has always considered herself to be robust and sturdy.

She exhales, blows the images out of her mind, then sinks down onto her bed. It bounces under her weight and squeaks with reassuring mundanity.

It has only been five days since she arrived in Farnham. However, they have been so full and intense that in some ways it is like a lifetime has passed. Or perhaps more that she has passed into a different life. The stage has been swapped for the theatre of war.

Here, jeopardy sits on the edges of consciousness like a vulture waiting to swoop and feed. Anyone who evidences fear becomes vulnerable, becomes prey. Which is why they keep themselves buttoned up.

Wit finds its way in, though, and laughter erupts at the absurdities of war. Much is ridiculous.

Of course, there is serious work to be done. Murmurs of missions, vague and unsettling, circle the ranks. Some talk of France, others of conveying messages behind enemy lines. But nothing is confirmed. Secrecy is the word. They have been told, firmly, that if they speak of what happens here dire consequences will follow. Someone has said they will be shot. Daphne is not sure whether that was a joke.

In any case, routine helps keep the mind occupied and disciplined. Each morning is full of drills, instructions and exercises. Some of these are carried out on Farnham Castle's high keep, a large walled circular ground at the rear of the castle where the lawn is mowed every day at six o'clock.

The afternoons are spent with other new recruits, a few of whom had been at the briefing. Aubrey Sharpling is here. His friend, Vivian Steiner, the couturier, has been *in situ* for longer. He is as full of mischief as the poet. John and Frank are painters, Roger is a sculptor, Percival a university don, Harry a zoologist. Marc is an art collector, Bernie does something in electrics, Ross creates ventriloquists' dummies, Christopher designs magazines, Donald the sets of films, while Kingsley has previously managed a roaming circus. And then there is Jonty. He has struck up a friendship with the zoologist, which pleases Daphne. Harry, with his fastidious parting, three-piece suit, shrewd eyes and dark-rimmed spectacles, looks more like a bank manager than a man who has spent a great deal of time studying crocodiles in Africa. And although disparate in terms of occupation, Daphne discerns a mutual respect between the two men.

Their brief is to start thinking about camouflage, distraction and dazzle, and how they might use their skills to confuse the enemy.

As the days draw on new ideas begin to hatch, many inspired by these daily rounds of lectures at which attendance is compulsory. A certain camaraderie establishes itself. They are all in it together. Apart from a singular group of men who do not mix and eat separately at dinner. Rumours persist that they are developing a new technology of some importance which is top secret.

Daphne's bed bounces. Brigit has come to sit beside her. They share the small room, located at the top of the castle, with the female servants.

'You've had bad dreams since Mr W showed us that film,' Brigit says.

It is true. She has underestimated its impact.

Cyril, who had been at the London briefing, turned up at the castle a few days ago. He had once been a film-maker and worked in the expanding industry over in Germany. Though it had been cover, his remit being to find out exactly what kind of philosophies were influencing those in government.

The screening had formed part of that afternoon's lectures. The team were ushered into a shaded room and told to take their seats. There were no comfortable chairs, only hard wooden benches, most likely to keep them awake.

Cyril contextualised the briefing – this was a flavour of Nazi propaganda produced several years prior to the outbreak of war. The Third Reich had shown it everywhere they could, in Germany and overseas.

Translating the titles, he explained that it was 'framed as a documentary about the National Socialist Worker's Party conference. Produced by order of the Führer. But,' he said, stepping away from the screen and addressing them, 'it is so much more than that. It couches the "suffering of the German people" in their defeat at the end of the last war. Their rebirth and new-found strength is portrayed here' – he tapped the screen – 'as the result of Hitler's pure will.'

'How narcissistic,' Jonty whispered in her ear.

'This,' said Cyril, 'has been taken to heart by the nation. You'll note the euphoria of the crowds when they glimpse him.'

And then the film rolled. Cyril continued to stand at the front while it played.

Black and white and full of thousands upon thousands of joyful subjects executing those strange Nazi salutes, the German people seemed united in fervour, in love with their leader.

Reading the expressions on the audience's faces, Cyril interrupted to narrate. 'It must be remembered that the film has been choreographed. It was propaganda designed to impress, and to that end some of the sound has been added later.' He drew attention to Hitler's second in command as a figure of interest. A peculiar man; as Daphne inspected him delivering a rousing speech to the masses, she thought there was something ape-like about the pronounced brow and the deeply recessed eyes that hid in constant shadow. 'Hess,' Cyril noted, 'as some of you may be aware from the briefing at HQ, has a bent for all sorts – astrology, Nostradamus, fortune-telling, astral travel, occultism. There's got to be something there for us. Set your minds as to how his obsessions might be exploited and put to good use.'

The film continued through toady speeches in which various members of German High Command salivated and dribbled praise upon the manly might of their leader, which Daphne thought surprising given she had seen juggling clowns with a better physique. Then came the displays of tremendous military force.

'Some of these scenes' – Cyril pointed to the screen – 'were rehearsed and then filmed again and again until they were just right.'

His insights were effective in dismantling the cinematic veil of perfect synchronicity and precision. As he talked she began to see the film through Cyril's eyes as a celluloid product, like an animated advertisement for 'Destination: Fascism'. It took Daphne back to Mr Thomas, her landlord, who had once attended a meeting of the British Union of Fascists with one of the shop regulars, Mr Neward. He was terrified of communism and believed only the fascists were taking the threat seriously.

The two men, however, had come away disappointed, declaring the people at the rally to be the most unsavoury types, full of bitterness and spite, with a leader who was vain. No good could come of them, they felt. And as she watched, Daphne remembered their words and thought the same.

The film culminated in shots of Hitler addressing the thousands there assembled. The camera roamed over rows of standard-bearers assembled like a Roman army. Cries of 'Heil Hitler' or 'Sieg Heil' rang out as he finished his speech. The Neanderthal man with the recessed eyes, Hess, came back and raved again about his boss, then the film ended.

Yet there were images that had plastered themselves on the walls of her mind. Indelibly so. Symbols with power – those sinister black wreaths that looked like satanic nests for their hook-beaked eagles, and that four-pointed cross, the swastika. The film projected a unity around these that bordered on frothing delirium. Even if it had been stage-managed, parts of it showed authentic adoration. The audience members, she felt, were fuelled by passion. And were strikingly militarised. It was a stark contrast to the stolid everyday folk Daphne knew at home. The possibility of becoming overwhelmed by this efficient war machine seemed not vague at all and no longer a distant menace.

And that, she supposes, is what has mobilised her fears so that they creep into sleep. At least that is what she *thinks* is happening.

But it isn't. It will take ten more months for her to see what these dreams really mean.

Until then, she will interpret with a degree of latitude that will ultimately guarantee her sanity.

Some futures we should not know.

* * *

'It's nearly six o'clock,' Brigit's voice is a shepherdess's crook hauling Daphne's thoughts back into the present. Her friend has left the bed to rummage through an open drawer in the chest they share. 'I say, you haven't borrowed my stockings have you, old girl? I have a single good pair of silks. Well, when I say "good", they've only one ladder at the back of the knee.'

Daphne shakes her head. 'I wouldn't borrow anything without asking first, Brigit. You know that.'

Her roommate kneels back on her heels and bites her lip. 'I'm sure they were here. Oh well, have you got a spare pair?'

She has only one set, but she cannot refuse Brigit after her care this morning. 'Yes,' Daphne says, and finds the bag she keeps them in. Brigit catches it with a nod. 'All right, duckie, with thanks.' She sits back on her narrow bed and pulls her skirt up, exposing slender legs. Carefully she gathers the fragile material and slides it over her toes. 'We might as well get brekkie. We'll be out on lawn for drill in no time at all.'

Daphne sighs. She would prefer to go back to sleep and find a peaceful vision to latch on to. Something that might take her away from the uneasiness lingering in the shadows of her mind.

But she knows that Brigit, ever the pragmatist, is right. An army marches on its stomach. She needs to fill hers.

Grabbing her washbag, Daphne pads across the oilcloth and heads down the corridor to the bathroom. She scrubs the night out of her.

It is, apparently, of great necessity that the girls understand how to march. Nobody knows why this is the case, but it is best not to ask. At least this is the advice of the sergeant major who has been saddled with the task. A kindly man with a short temper, he attempts to obfuscate his indignant bewilderment with breathy mutterings about the expansion of the military and importance of discipline, but really he takes this new responsibility as an affront to his rank and speedily delegates the role to his sergeant, Dobson, who also views training girls as a slur on his masculinity.

The other men are going through similar instructions, but mixing the sexes in this exercise is felt to be improper. Thus, after reporting on the keep, she and Brigit are each morning dispatched to a different part of the castle, whatever is not being usefully used, to irritate Sergeant Dobson.

Daphne finds the art of synchronised walking boring and often lets her attention drift. Her resulting errors incur many furious reprimands. She is grateful to Brigit, who tries to practise with her in the evenings. The latter's orders are to remain at Farnham until Daphne's basic training has been accomplished, or at least until any sexual threat from the group of homosexual, married and uninterested male artists and entertainers has been thoroughly eliminated. In contrast to Daphne, Brigit is like a duck to water. Clearly she has been marching for most of her life. Her performance soothes Dobson, though only marginally.

While Daphne manages 'at ease', 'left face', 'right face' and 'face to flank', the 'attention' position often catches her unawares. 'Quick time' uses up all her powers of concentration, despite the fact that she is very accomplished with the foxtrot. Years onstage spent distracting the audience from Jonty's sleight of hand cannot be erased overnight, however, and the odd wiggle or sashay often sneaks into her routine. These do not amuse Sergeant Dobson.

Daphne reminds herself that it is not a routine but a drill. Much time is spent executing the proper hand salute.

Yesterday, when Daphne bobbed a curtsey before raising her hand, she realised that she had also forgotten to tuck in her thumb. Dobson's right eye had contracted into very visible twitches. Today, when they arrive at the keep, she notices that it continues to spasm.

It is the men who are dispatched elsewhere this morning, and Daphne and Brigit see there are other women present. Dobson has seconded the cook's assistant, a mousey girl called Mable, as well as the head gardener's daughter, who wears large spectacles and answers to the name of Sarah. None of the female retinue exhibit much gumption. This is what makes them an acceptable presence at the castle, which has for many centuries been the chief residence of the Bishops of Winchester. The current incumbent has, upon occupation by the military, withdrawn to a section aptly called The Retreat. He is rarely seen except for Sundays, which is felt by both sides to be a good thing.

Sergeant Dobson spends an hour trying to inject some coordination into the delegation, marching them round the perimeter of the grassy yard. Daphne's mind wanders. She does not hear the order to halt and bumps into Sarah, the gardener's daughter, sending her glasses flying into the stone wall. One of the lenses shatters into lots and lots of sharp little pieces. As she and Sarah clear up the mess, Daphne notices at the knee of Sarah's stockings there is a ladder. It is wider than Daphne's, but then so are Sarah's legs. While Brigit tries to distract the sergeant from entering into a state of apoplexy Daphne hisses at Sarah, 'Ask before you borrow.'

'What?' The gardener's daughter's voice is low and mournful. Behind her singular lens her right eye is large.

Daphne digs her finger into the small of Sarah's knee. 'Brigit has a pair like this. She can't find them.'

'They're mine,' Sarah bleats. Her protestation is half-hearted, almost as good as a confession.

'Would you like me to point the ladder out to her? Then she can decide what to do.'

'No!' Sarah is quick to answer.

'Put them back and I'll say no more. But you owe me,' says Daphne. 'Sorry about the specs.' She drops the shattered glass into the hand of Sarah, who darts her one last reproachful glance then scuttles off to the relative safety of Sergeant Dobson, whose right eye is closing twice every second.

Brigit steps back and they form a line to recommence the exercise but then, thankfully, Aubrey Sharpling, the poet, trots onto the keep. His appearance does not usually appease the sergeant, as he is not the most athletic of the new recruits, being quite pudding-faced, with a similarly doughy body which, prior to army uniform, was often clad in golfing knickerbockers. His hair is pale and curly and piled up on top of his head like a pyramid. But today he brings with him the message that Daphne and Brigit are required to take lunch at once, then report to the Tudor wing for 1300 hours. Sergeant Dobson listens. His eye stills briefly as he dismisses the women.

'I wish they didn't make us do that,' Daphne moans as they descend the steps to the courtyard and make their way to the Great Hall, where lunch is served. She has decided not to disclose where her friend's silk stockings have gone – knowledge is useful. These days she is learning that it is also power. 'Seems a pointless exercise,' she continues, feeling bolstered by her little victory. 'How is marching going to help us defeat the enemy?'

'It's not,' says Brigit. 'But it's preventing you making matters worse over here.'

Daphne allows herself a private smile: Brigit doesn't know everything. But she plays along with her. 'I'm not sure Sergeant Dobson would agree.'

* * *

Having filled their stomachs with a thin soup and bread roll, the two make their way to the Tudor wing, where Vivian Steiner, the couturier, has a small workshop. His task has been to fashion the prototype of a wool serge uniform for women. They are all aware of this. Now, he tells them that he is almost there but would like the girls to try on the new suits and test their durability. The men at the castle have already exchanged their civilian garb for starched Austin Reed uniforms with polished brass buttons. Brigit and Daphne think they are quite natty.

'I need to know if it has enough stretch,' Vivian says, throwing back his curly black hair. There is always a haughtiness to everything he says and does, as if he has a hundred and one better things to do. Daphne thinks no one can be that confident and entitled so assumes he is uncomfortable here.

She and Brigit gather up the khaki pieces. As they take them off to get changed, Vivian throws over two coloured bundles. 'Good-quality silk stockings,' he says. 'The fibres in the skirts are harsh. Put these on and they'll chafe less.'

Daphne laughs as she catches them. 'Yellow and peacock blue! I'm sure they're not regulation.'

'It's the best we can do,' Vivian takes his glasses off to clean.

Daphne catches an odd grin that touches his lips before his curls flop down and obscure his face. Some of the men here are difficult to fathom.

Brigit snatches the blue, leaving Daphne with the pair that are buttercup bright. 'Needs must, I suppose,' she says. 'I shall look like Malvolio.'

'What?' says Brigit with irritation.

Honestly, thinks Daphne, for a privately educated woman sometimes Brigit is very ignorant. '*Twelfth Night*, silly. They made him wear yellow stockings so he looked a fool.'

Brigit snorts. 'Well, I wouldn't worry. No one's going to see them. Let's get this over and done with. Percival told me there's to be an important briefing in an hour.'

The fit is baggy. She and Brigit discuss how they might give some shape with belts fastened around the waist and tailored darts under the bust.

When they return, Aubrey has appeared again. Now he is in conversation with Vivian. The two men are well acquainted. They talk together in low voices. Aubrey chuckles. He always chuckles. Daphne regards him with suspicion. She cannot erase the memory of him labelled a hellraiser in the gossip columns. Something he delights in. He has never been particularly civil to her. Never paid her much attention before.

At Victor's insistence, she and Brigit walk the length of the room. But the couturier, who is eyeing the hems of the khaki skirts, says, 'Mmm, not sure. It would help awfully if I could see you in action. Do you think you could march in them? There's no point producing something that isn't fit for purpose.'

Daphne sighs but assents.

The couturier opens the lid of a nearby chest, rifles within it and produces two pairs of court shoes. 'Now, the uniforms will be worn by all sorts,' he says, holding them up to his chest. 'Come on. These are roughly your sizes. Let's get you out in the courtyard and see what you can do.'

The girls slip their feet into the shoes and follow the men out into the large courtyard where the others take their drill practice.

'Right,' says Aubrey, positioning himself at the front just as Sergeant Dobson does. 'On the left, quick MARCH!'

And off they go. Up, down, up, down until Vivian announces he needs to see how much the fabric will give. 'When you reach the end of the yard, do a turn and then leap. Really stretch your legs. Our girls might need to run in them.'

Given their current situation it is a fair comment. Who knows how quickly they might be forced to flee when the Germans arrive.

'Oh right,' says Daphne. 'A leap? Like an assemblé?'

Vivian grins, then coughs. 'Yes, that's it. An assemblé. If you please.'

She notices the scowl on Brigit's face but accepts the task and sets off quickly. Her friend is slower to comply.

'Left, right, left, right,' Vivian calls after them. 'And now as you reach us, yes, assemblé!'

Desiring to demonstrate her superiority in this exercise, Daphne decides to assemblé and then move into a jump. As she lifts up into the air, however, she hears the distinctive sound of cotton splitting. Her skirt, now loose at the seam, begins to slide down her hips.

As her feet touch the ground, a chorus of catcalls fills the courtyard. She spins round to see that on the top floors of the buildings which line the courtyard the men are leaning out of their windows guffawing. Someone whistles. A few are slapping their foreheads.

'Oh damn,' says Brigit. 'I think we've been had.'

Aubrey is now beside himself, doubled over as he watches Daphne's attempts to halt the progression of the fabric to the floor. 'What a caper!' he says in a high, stifled voice through tears of laughter. 'What a pantomime!'

She has worn less onstage. Aubrey's words have already summoned one of her favourite film stars to mind. She digs deeper and fetches one of Mae West's great comebacks.

'Darn it,' she says, and would put a finger to her cheek if she had not needed both hands to hold the scraps of fabric to her thighs. 'I used to be Snow White,' she quotes, 'but then I drifted.'

The applause is thunderous.

She thinks about throwing in a little curtsey, but the state of her dress is too precarious.

It is only moments later, when the clapping starts to ebb, that she detects another voice booming over the cobbles: 'What in God's name is the meaning of this!'

Instantly everyone in the courtyard stands to attention.

The men at the windows vanish and she sees, coming out of the door in the corner of the courtyard, the formidable figure of Lieutenant Colonel Franklin.

'Just a little spot of dancing to raise morale, sir,' Aubrey ventures.

The man is completely shameless.

The lieutenant colonel splutters as he approaches. 'Marching! Marching in heels. You could break your damn necks. What in heaven's name possessed you?' Then, to Daphne, 'Where's your salute, girl?'

Everyone else, she realises, has raised their hands promptly. It is she alone who appears to be wilfully disrespecting his rank.

'I'm afraid I can't—' she begins.

'When in the presence of your superiors you damn well salute,' the lieutenant colonel thunders.

Left without any option, Daphne executes the perfect salute, of which even Sergeant Dobson would be proud.

Under the lieutenant colonel's cold, cold stare her skirt quietly slips to the ground.

CHAPTER EIGHT

It is in some ways fortunate that the lieutenant colonel is on a mission, so to speak: that of assembling troops into the Great Hall in precisely one hour. An urgent communication is to be relayed. So the disciplining of the instigators and participants of the prank is to be put on hold and dealt with later.

They are ordered to their lectures for the interim and assemble in the room used for such activities. It is located in the tower.

The men had got fed up with the layout, declaring that the rows of chairs made them feel as if they were back in a classroom. Much to the annoyance of the unit instructors they broke up the formation and arranged the chairs around tables, a design the thespians amongst them referred to as 'cabaret style'. As one of the military instructors commented, 'One can evidently take the men out of the theatre. Taking the theatre out of the men, however, may require surgical intervention.'

A couple of them look sheepish; most, however, are in a state of excitement.

Daphne sits in a pair of borrowed trousers and laced-up boots and smoulders.

Harry the zoologist, who has given several lectures, attempts to bring some order to the group and takes the fore, positioning himself in front of the blackboard that has been fixed to the southerly wall. When he speaks it is with authority and people usually listen. Though now he has to clear his voice, tap the lectern and call the recruits to attention.

'We have an announcement in a little under thirty minutes, and I am not privy to what it is.' He has to say this twice. After the second repetition the men settle. He waits for silence then continues. 'I suggest we refresh our memories regarding the principles of camouflage that I have gone over during the last few weeks.'

A couple of the men groan. Someone, possibly the ventriloquist, says, 'Boo,' but no one can tell which side of the room the sound has come from. Harry ignores it. 'Remember, Nature is the greatest teacher. From She we learn.'

'Well, there's Art too,' interrupts James, the artist. 'There's a lot that can be done with paint. Different greens and browns and the like.'

'Yes.' The zoologist is unfazed by the derailment. He has taught in universities and is familiar with students showing off. 'And if you paint the underside of certain things a pure white, just like the tummy of the gazelle, we now know the contrast flattens things out and obfuscates the real form. We can apply this technique to tanks and shelters. It works. Now what about the other techniques I've outlined: merging? Who remembers that?'

Aubrey, the terrible poet, puts up his hand. 'Matching the colour to the background.'

'Correct,' says Harry. 'Example, please?'

'Oh, oh, I know, I know!' says Kingsley, the middle-aged circus manager, sticking his entire arm as high into the air as his seated body will allow. Despite their protestations that the new seating arrangements do not make them feel like schoolboys, when Harry asserts himself as teacher many regress to 'the taught', resurrecting all the juvenile behaviour that they associate with that part of their lives.

'Yes, Kingsley?' Harry gives him permission to speak.

Smiling with pride, the ringmaster answers. 'The polar bear in the Arctic. Their white coats so strongly resemble the tundra that they can be mistaken for snowdrifts.' He pauses and turns into the room to face the others seated there. 'But did you know that under that fur they have black skins?'

There is a mumble of appreciation at that little nugget.

'Oh yes.' Kingsley gives them a long, knowing nod. 'Now, I was told that by a strongman from Siberia. He was married to a bearded lady. Her legs were so hairy, he once mistook her for their dog.'

Hoots. The mood of hilarity that has been bubbling away under the surface since the courtyard brims again.

'Sounds like she could give Daphne a run for her money,' shouts Vivian.

The class erupts into laughter.

Jonty, at least, scowls.

Daphne, however, is not going to let that go. Her visits with Jonty to the dive bars of Soho have equipped her with enough confidence to engage in repartee. 'I'll have you know, fellas, I shave mine each day with a cut-throat razor. I was trained to use it by Jack Dagger, the Impaler.' It's all rubbish, of course, but she has to say something.

A chorus of *ooh*s and an *oh la la* circle the room.

'I'd be careful.' Jonty pipes up. 'There's a fair few who have crossed Daphne and come away a little less of one.'

'Less of a what?' Vivian asks with a derisory snort.

'Why, a little less of a man, if you know what I mean.' Jonty's eyes twinkle.

'Oh,' says Aubrey. Vivian crosses his legs.

This time Harry clears his throat very loudly. 'Now, what about "disruption", eh? Of the animal kind. We've had quite enough of yours. We're in a war, may I remind you. Who can tell me how disruptive camouflage works?'

Chastened by this reminder, his audience recompose themselves.

'Disrupted . . .' Bernie the electrician puts up his hand. 'Jarring coloration? That which breaks up the outline, the structure. You showed us skunks with their white streaks.'

'That's absolutely right,' Harry confirms. 'Well done, Bernie. The form is confused. Sends misleading signals to the eye. Then we have "disguise".' Harry's expertise is evident. 'Dazzle also works like this. But not to conceal. To confuse the predator, so they cannot efficiently estimate range and speed.' He can tell his audience is getting restless, so hurries on. 'Then there are smokescreens, false displays of strength, dummies, decoys and misdirection.'

'Also the element of surprise,' says Aubrey. He is keen to wrestle back the spotlight. 'Seeing things in places that you don't expect to can disorientate.' He sends a devilish smile to the zoologist then adds, 'Like yellow stockings.'

Heading off the chuckles, Harry quickly interjects, 'Well, I think we're all up to speed now.' He looks at his watch and decides the best thing is to get them into the Grand Hall early. 'Assemble at the door.'

Daphne thinks it will take a good deal more to dampen the men's spirits. They have been desperate for some lightness in the dark.

Under the arches of the great vaulted hall the summoned men and women wait. A buzz of jolliness continues to hum over them. As Lieutenant Colonel Franklin takes to the podium, the noise ceases. They know their mood is about to be crushed. The expression on his face is bleak. He wastes no time communicating the announcement.

'Unfortunate news,' he says at once.

It is effective. Those in attendance stop fidgeting and concentrate.

'There has been increased activity along the south coast by enemy aircraft whose primary objective, we believe, has been to disorder convoys and also to test the resolve of our island population.'

Murmurs ripple through the hall but die off quickly.

'Enemy bombers, from the occupied Pas-de-Calais, this afternoon have come in and attacked a merchant navy convoy on the coast north of Ramsgate. Over one hundred aircraft of ours and those of the Luftwaffe have been engaged in a dogfight. Reports are as yet unclear: some have said that over a hundred and fifty bombs were dropped on our fleet.'

Some near the front sit up straight in their chairs.

'Reports suggest that one of our ships may have been sunk.'

Frowns break out.

The lieutenant colonel continues his grim delivery. 'We have lost men. Good men. At present we are unsure of the navy casualties.'

Daphne feels the familiar return of dread and knows she is not alone. This is what it is like now: the tone of her life, of all of their lives, can tighten up in an instant, move to lightness or pitch without warning. There is no certainty. She sends her gaze through the open windows in the direction of the Channel. Clouds are gathering. Dark ones, with ominous underbellies.

'We know the 111 Squadron fought back heartily. Two Hurricanes have been shot down with their pilots and the enemy have moved inland.'

Large drops of rain begin to fall against the open windows. Leisurely at first.

'We must brace ourselves,' he says. 'This is the beginning of an invasion.'

It starts to rain.

'So you can see why I have summoned you.'

He lets them have a minute for the implication to move into their brains and begin to fuel.

'Some of you have been here a short while, others have already found their way. War moves quickly, and we have now come to the point where we must turn, with speed and urgency, to the fortification of the south-east of our island. This being the most likely point of entry for the Germans.'

Daphne cannot pull her eyes from the rain.

'It is not enough in warfare to be courageous,' says the lieutenant colonel, 'if this means giving yourself up as an easy target. Intelligence, cunning and concealment must be used.'

The *pit pat pit pat* of rain becomes a squall, a *rat-a-tat* like machine-gun fire against the castle walls.

'The Home Guard have been consigned the task of confronting enemy strikes at crucial tactical points. They are ill-equipped and need as much help as possible. Our enemies are ruthless and already are exploiting every means of deception. We have people developing instructions on how the Home Guard may train their men in warfare. To that purpose you, here, must develop tools and techniques that will encourage them in their efforts to disguise themselves and deceive hostile aliens on our terrain. You have been engaged in the art of camouflage. Now you must be ready to move from the theoretical into the immediate development of your designs. To this end, I am announcing an inspection next week. Commander Lieutenant General Lord Bailey-Rae will oversee this. Expectations are high. You will put your ideas into practice, to impress. I have no doubt that you will all do us proud.'

He pauses and eyes the men, some of whom have shrunk since the mention of Lord Bailey-Rae, a known stickler for detail and commitment.

The lieutenant colonel finishes with a salute. 'Dismissed.'
With a great thunderclap the storm clouds break.

Jonty, Brigit and Daphne regroup in the courtyard, the scene of
her humiliation, which has already left her mind. The words of
the lieutenant colonel have affected a change in the entire
group, most of whom have used the break to smoke, despite
the rain. The atmosphere is charged, not only with the electric
storm but the prickly feeling of anticipated action. The enemy
is near.

'Dazzle,' Jonty says at length. 'I've been thinking about it
since Harry mentioned the technique this afternoon. Come.'
Obediently the girls clip-clop down the stone steps and around
the side to the front of the castle.

The rain is easing. A small consolation. The storm clouds
have moved further inland, though they can still see some forks
of lightning pitching to the ground.

The trio sit on the castle's low garden wall, which is still
wet. Brigit offers round her pack of Chesterfields again.
They each take one: their nerves are jangling. Brigit swings
her legs like a child, bumping the wall with her heels. She is
usually so composed; Daphne realises her anxiety is finding
its way out.

Daphne herself sucks in a lungful of smoke and views the
town below. Many of the shops are boarded up, bracing
themselves for the German invaders. There is the pub down in
the main street, the Bush. Brigit has suggested they should
patronise it when they have time to spare. Canadian soldiers are
billeted in the town and known to frequent the hostelry. Daphne
likes the idea of Canadians, though she has never met one.
From the off, they too have perceived the threat to Western

civilisation posed by the Germans and have wasted no time in lining up beside Britain.

Behind her the castle looms. Built on the crest of a hill, surrounded by trees, it has grown up over the medieval and Tudor periods. Castellated turrets and three-storey quarters give way to a complex of rooms and buildings connected by passageways which will undoubtedly be draughty in winter. The rooms are furnished with rugs, tapestries and fine art, and most of the furniture is antique. But the grounds are the real treat. Some flower beds have not yet been given over to the kitchen. Roses in full bloom scent the air. If circumstances were different she might enjoy staying in such palatial surroundings. Sometimes it is too beautiful and makes her feel guilty. It doesn't seem right when men are fighting. When men are dying.

It is still hot. The storm has increased the humidity.

'I'm sorry, gals,' says Jonty, breaking the silence. 'I didn't know they were going to do that. With the skirts.'

Daphne did not think he would comment on it.

Brigit crushes her cigarette on the wall and throws the dead end into the long grass on the slope that leads into the moat. 'I've had worse,' she says. 'Lots of brothers. We grew up in an army house. You sink or swim.'

Daphne suddenly understands Brigit a bit more. She wonders if she should say something, but having delivered condolences Jonty is keen to move on.

'Now listen,' he says. 'I've a plan to make them all stop *and* take us seriously. *And* pass the inspection with flying colours. *And* show them what can be done with a bit of imagination. The colonel is right. We have to put our minds to this – for the country. We can all feel it, can't we? The enemy at the door.'

They nod gloomily.

'Is there space for me in your plans?' Brigit hedges.

'Of course,' says Jonty. 'We'll need help.'

'With what?'

'Yes, quite. But I'm getting ahead of myself.' Jonty twists round and instructs them to do the same. He points to the front of the castle. 'Regard this flat wall. It is smoothish and light. A perfect screen, in fact. And on top of a hill. We can use our skills to create lines of distraction, lights, sound, projections.'

Brigit shrugs.

Jonty sees how Daphne is taking it. 'You've got it, haven't you, Daphers?'

She has got the gist but not the detail.

Brigit swings her legs off the wall and stands. 'I've heard a couple of the chaps talking about covering machine-gun posts and concealing tanks. Vivian was discussing weaving coir netting and scrim. Hessian "leaves" were suggested.'

'Mmm,' says Jonty. 'It's to the brief but I think it a little conventional. I've got something more ambitious in mind.'

'Smoke and mirrors?' asks Brigit.

'That's the ticket,' he says. 'They can certainly be of use. But if we pull off what I think we can, then we'll really give Lord Bailey-Rae something to think about. And show the rest of them that we're to be reckoned with. Not *trifled* with.'

Daphne agrees. She knows what Jonty is capable of. Despite a sometimes shambling impression, his mind is acute: he has developed the most ingenious illusions. As did his father, and his father's father before him. Show business might be the end product, but deception is at the heart of his calling. She is emboldened and adds, 'Aubrey and Vivian are so competitive. The best revenge would be to outshine them spectacularly. Beaten by girls and a magician, in an inspection too. They'd never live it down. I have an idea.'

'Right then,' says Jonty. He has come to life now and, despite the mood, strives to lift them. 'Let's get this show on the road.'

Brigit looks askance so Daphne remarks to her boss, 'You're cornier than that field.'

But Jonty is unstoppable, full of his own visions. 'I think, my dear,' he declares with a wink, 'you'll find that that there is sage.'

Lessons in Fieldcraft
CAMOUFLAGE

This is a particularly ambitious subject on which to instruct. It presents challenges to members of the Home Guard who have lived in cities and towns for all their lives. However, there are opportunities which may be put to good use for the defence of the realm. Particularly with respect to the ground and darkness, amongst other terrain.

We must assume open country is the setting.

It is intended that landscape targets that you have already manufactured for Fire Direction Orders will be used here.

Initiative, cunning, craft and intelligence must be brought into play while camouflaging posts, especially from air observation. Here are a few points with which to start:

1. Trenches: when digging, it is essential to avoid straight lines.

2. Spoil from digging must be distributed evenly. Dark bumps and small hillocks may be seen as signs of industry or work by an astute aerial observer.

3. We have opportunities to alter the landscape so that it does not look as it should on a map. This may disorientate our enemies. Though they may take time to manufacture, craters are very useful in this regard.

4. Instruct men to gather local vegetation: grass, crops, leaves, branches. These can be applied over fish netting or wire netting to cover an object or position. It is vital to remember to refresh supplies often. Once they have died and turned brown they can give you away.

5. Conceal carefully all tracks left by any type of vehicles. Brushes and brooms can sweep away footprints and tyre marks. Even the humble bicycle may reveal your location.

6. When required to move from place to place, ensure that movement is kept to the shadows of walls and hedges. Stay within the shadows of tree lines.

7. Texture is significant. It must be matched to the background. At times a difference in surface textures may attract the eye. There are locations where this is more important than colour.

8. All helmets must be darkened. This can be done with mud or boot polish and other stuffs. Never allow your protective head coverings to shine. Anything that reflects light will be seen. Break up the hard lines of your helmet with hessian and foliage held in place by clips provided. Unless under cover, do not look up.

9. Draped netting over a gun and limber will reduce the lustre of the metal. Brushwood will add texture and interrupt the outline.

18 JULY 1940

CHAPTER NINE

Commander Lieutenant General Lord Bailey-Rae is a man of bold constitution and poor patience. Of these qualities his driver, Douglas Fairbanks (no relation), is acutely aware. Which is why, despite the cloudy day and temperate conditions, his upper lip is already beaded with sweat. The needle on the petrol gauge had forced an unscheduled stop on the way into Surrey, which was not the young corporal's fault. He had been promised a full tank by the officer who handed him the keys to the truck. Some of the petrol, however, had been siphoned overnight. Everyone is at it these days. Even in the army.

The refuel at a small town south of London displeased Bailey-Rae, who was not succinct in his expressions of displeasure at the resulting delay.

It amused Frederick Mathers, their assisting navigator, who privately calls Fairbanks a 'right goody two shoes', or, when ladies are not in company, which usually they are not, 'an arse'. Unable to conceal his glee, he stroked his moustache and made a show of taking out his map sheet and guiding them with clipped, precise and clear instructions down to the base at Aldershot for the commander's appointment. For which he was late.

As they left, an hour later, he needled Fairbanks. 'Got enough juice to get us all the way to Farnham?'

The driver returned him a curt nod, whitened his knuckles on the wheel and set his eyes on the road ahead, stoic and silent.

Mathers continued to call out directions. He was loving it.

Fairbanks fumed but kept his lip stiff.

Fifteen minutes later, however, he turns to Mathers and asks in a very loud voice, 'Now listen here, are you sure we should be taking this road?'

Mathers does not even look up from his map. 'Absolutely. Straight on, then the next right.' He is doing his best to shine in front of the commander, as any young soldier with ambition might.

'Only,' Fairbanks goes on, 'it looks like we've hit a dead end.'

'What?' Mathers snaps and flicks his eyes to the windscreen. No, that can't be.

But, sure enough, instead of continuing through open fields, the road has petered out into a dirt track and brambles. Wild and tangled woods lie beyond them. 'I don't understand. This isn't on the grid.'

In the back seat the commander grunts. 'Have you got the right bloody map?'

'Yes sir. Absolutely sir.' Mathers, quick to respond, cannot hide the strain on his vocal cords.

'Something's gone awry.' Fairbanks eyes the trees. 'I'll take this left and see if we can sort ourselves out.'

'Thank you, corporal.' Bailey-Rae sends a withering glance at Mathers's back. Though he cannot see it, Mathers feels the commander's eyes burn the skin on his neck. He wants to touch it but restrains himself. He must make up for his mistake.

The new route takes them out of the wood and back into the countryside.

Mathers does not recognise it. His throat is dry. Perhaps his map is old. Then again, his compass seems to be working just fine and should be able to compensate. Why can't he orientate them?

The country lane snakes another mile up a hill. Either side the hedgerows lower, giving Mathers a chance to view the pastures full of sheep lightly grazing. As they crest the top, he searches for landmarks. But there is a hillock ahead, where according to his map there is a pond. Beyond it stands a wood where there should be pasture. Mathers silently curses and turns the map the other way. Has he got the approach all wrong?

They pass a sign to Aldershot which has not been taken down. Though they have just departed from there and it is pointing in the direction that they are heading.

'Dear God!' The commander sights it. 'We're going the blasted wrong way.'

Out of nowhere Fairbanks hits the brakes. Mathers lurches forward in his seat, surprised but pleased nonetheless that the driver has stuffed up. They jerk to a halt.

'Now what . . .' Bailey-Rae begins. Then, 'What in Hell's name is this?' For there, about a dozen yards ahead, in the middle of the road, a cowgirl sits astride a zebra.

There is a brief pause as the men, unable to absorb the shock, try to square the image within the limits of geographic plausibility. They fail.

Mathers's eye is caught by something to their left – a ragged figure in blue, zigzagging in a twitchy, juddering manner across the nearby field. Still unable to think before he speaks, he yells, 'Watch out! Is that a Jerry? Is he—'

His words, however, are obliterated by a sudden crack. There is a flash and then smoke fills the air, followed by wisps of wool.

Fairbanks and the commander duck. But Mathers, who is in some state of befuddlement, says, 'One of those sheep just blew up and killed the German.'

While the other occupants of the truck check that their bodies have come out from the explosion intact, Mathers scans the horizon for planes. Seeing none, he gets out and staggers to the mounted woman. Her blackish hair is neatly tied back and held under a flat military cap, which he could swear was a

Stetson just a moment ago. She pulls on the reins– no, not a zebra but a horse – and noses it towards the place where the detonation has occurred. The manoeuvre gives him the briefest opportunity to marvel at her unruffled comportment. Despite the loud detonation her pace is leisurely, the horse calm as if exploding sheep are a regular part of both of their lives.

'Yes,' says the woman, matter-of-factly. 'They're just sheepskins wrapped round explosives. But they don't arf look like the real thing from a distance, no?'

Lord Bailey-Rae, who has crawled out of the back seat and is now gawking at the woman's black mare, says, 'I'd swear you were riding a zebra back there.'

'Seconded,' says Fairbanks.

'You're half right,' Daphne says, and turns the beast to reveal one side painted with white stripes. 'Now, I'm assuming you're lost. Please follow me. I'm here to guide you to Farnham Castle.'

Fairbanks glances at the commander, expecting him to go the same way as the unfortunate sheep, but he simply nods, open-mouthed, and watches the horse and rider canter away. 'Well, I'm damned,' he says. 'Farnham Castle. Should have known it. That lot are all about deception.'

'Well, they're doing a bleedin' good job of it, I'd say, sir,' says Mathers.

He is not reprimanded.

CHAPTER TEN

They follow the rider through various lanes and turnings to a narrow village street. Not a trace of the cowgirl that all of them had seen is evident in the crisp khaki suit she is now wearing, leaving each one of them to wonder about their eyesight.

Pointing to a small tavern with a thatched roof, the Red Dragon, Daphne alights. 'Refreshments,' she mouths at them, and ties her mount to a lamppost.

Above the sun, which has appeared between the clouds and has not diminished in warmth, is sailing close to the rooftops.

'Hmm,' mutters the commander. 'Surely we're moving on to dinner at this hour?'

Fairbanks parks and the men get out.

Again Daphne beckons them and, although it is not the custom for women to do so, she pulls on the brass handle of the pub's old wooden door and holds it open while they enter.

The creak of the hinges reminds Lord Bailey-Rae of the tavern near his country estate. He is filled with nostalgia, and the idea of a decent ale passes over his mind. He can almost taste the hops. It is a pleasant sensation, and he finds his mood ascend.

Daphne tracks in behind them and squeezes past. 'Right, sir, if you'll follow me.' She leads them down the tight passageway, which has watercolour paintings of the pub in various centuries and decades affixed to the wall. It is clearly a very old building. The ceiling is low and bisected by dark, weathered beams.

There is another door at the end of the hall. Daphne stands to attention before it. She does not open this one. 'Sir,' she says and points to the handle, then takes a step back – an invitation for him to enter first.

The commander takes out a silk handkerchief, removes his hat and dabs the perspiration on his forehead. He must make himself presentable before the lower-ranking officers behind the door. He replaces his kerchief, rolls his shoulders and extends himself, then nods to the navigator.

Mathers is glad to have been selected and opens the door into – into . . . 'Well, I'm blowed,' he says.

Not a parlour.

Or a quiet back room.

Not a kitchen.

Or a yard.

But a field.

'Heavens.'

The commander, navigator and driver stride out onto bushy grass, blinking.

'It's quite the thing, isn't it?' says Daphne.

The commander turns to the sound of her voice and sees that the sweet country pub, which was so welcome a minute before, is an illusion. The walls, the interior and exteriors – the entire high street down which they have just driven – are nothing more than facades put together, painted onto canvas and erected onto chipboard, supported by long wooden beams. 'Good grief,' he says, speaking for all of them. He has once visited a film set and has viewed scenery which looked like this. What a clever trompe-l'œil. It *is* quite the thing.

Without waiting for an answer (her question is hypothetical anyway), Daphne marches past them. 'The men await your inspection, sir.'

And yet the field is fallow. Only trees in full leaf cluster along the drainage ditches. To the far end stands a solitary barn and a lonely haystack. There are no men to be seen.

Baffled by the field of endless green, the commander starts, 'This is preposterous. Where are the troops? Now look, if this is some kind of joke—'

From behind him a voice announces, 'There are thirteen men in this field, Lord Bailey-Rae, a tank, two vehicles and one pillbox.' Lieutenant Colonel Franklin salutes. 'Once you find them, tea will be served.'

The commander visibly softens at the sight of the lieutenant colonel. 'Ah, Freddie, there you are. You mean it then?' They evidently know each other well, as men of rank often do.

'Indeed,' says the lieutenant colonel, pleased with himself for once. 'Deception is what you ordered, sir.'

'Hmm, right. Well, perhaps you could give me a clue.'

Lieutenant Colonel Freddie Franklin calls out, 'Herzog! Reveal!' and it seems to the commander that at that moment several shadows unpin themselves from a cluster of trees less than ten yards away. Taking a few steps forwards into the sunshine, they materialise into hairy green creatures who with remarkable synchronicity stand to attention and salute.

When the commander looks more carefully he sees that their helmets have been dotted with leafy twigs, so they resemble the shrubs and bushes lower to the ground.

The creature on the end is wearing khaki painted with dark stripes which zigzag across his tunic and trousers. It stands out now the chap has moved into the field, though it must be an excellent match with the trunks and foliage of the copse. On top of their uniforms they have heaped on leaves. He isn't sure how they got them to stick, but the look is striking. And what is more, it works. In fact, he would undoubtedly lose sight of them if they took a few steps back and crouched down. 'Excellent,' he says. 'I didn't see that coming.'

'And that is exactly what we hope the enemy will say. Please lead on.'

Trailing Mathers and Fairbanks, the Lord Bailey-Rae marches into the field. Feeling like it is himself who is being inspected rather than the men, he decides to reassert his authority by way of criticism. 'Though this is all very good in summer, but what about winter, eh?' He is uninterested in any answers and is purely buying time to sharpen his eyes. 'I've found four men in the woods. That leaves nine out here. Am I right?'

'Yes sir.'

'Well then,' says Bailey-Rae. 'Mathers, Fairbanks, let's see what you can do.'

Noting the commander has falsely declared the detection of the tree soldiers as his own, Mathers steps forward immediately. He knows what Bailey-Rae is like – if there is some success out here he'll claim it. Any failures, then the driver and navigator will be blamed. Mathers, for one, is not prepared to be thrown under the bus for his superior's failings. Quite the opposite. This presents an opportunity. A time to catch up. To impress.

Both soldiers move out across the grass, Mathers in an easterly direction, Fairbanks towards the haystack. While Mathers surveys the ground with caution, Fairbanks breaks into a trot.

'Halt there, Fairbanks.'

Fairbanks obeys and waits while Lord Bailey-Rae catches up. Panting, he asks, 'You spotted something?'

The driver points to the north. 'That's an odd sort of location for a haystack, sir. It's only July, Commander.'

'And?'

'June was wet, sir. The air needs to dry the hay before it can be stacked. Most folk back home are still growing their crops.

Won't harvest them yet. I don't see why Farnham should be any different.'

'Farm lad, were you?' Bailey-Rae falls into step with the young driver.

'That's right, sir.'

'Perhaps the weather here has been better, Fairbanks. Doesn't make the erection of a hayrick a crime.'

'Seems to me that' – Fairbanks's speech slows as he realises, with some surprise, that his point has been missed – 'this regiment are using decoys like the Gerry soldier Mathers saw, and distractions such as exploding sheep. Nothing is what it appears, including those soldiers cleverly hidden in the trees. The haystack may well conceal more.'

Worried it might be another detonating device, Bailey-Rae orders, 'You walk on then, Fairbanks, see if your notion is right.'

At which point Mathers, who has been crossing the field behind them, gives up a yell. When the commander and driver turn round he has completely disappeared. It is only the muffled cussing that gives his position away.

On first sight it appears that the navigator has fallen into a dip. But then the ground on which he is sitting, shirred grass on grey earth, moves.

Moves and roils.

Moves, roils and is then pushed back to reveal two more men in a crater that has been dug out, and who are evidently none too happy about thirteen stones' worth of navigator landing on their backs.

'Not bad,' says the commander as the two soldiers squirm out. They help a grumbling Mathers to his feet and salute their senior officer.

The commander returns it. 'Well done. I cannot believe that one can hide so many men in what is apparently an open field.'

Lieutenant Colonel Franklin watches, unable to let a smile bend his lips. 'The methodology has been to identify threats and future worries, to bring them in, if you will, into the comfortable and safe setting of the classroom so that we can deconstruct, understand and then undermine them, sir. Once we have been through this process we then turn over the possibilities generated by lateral thought. In this way the men, who come from a range of unconventional backgrounds, are able to invent new tactics to weaken those threats. Thus we shift the balance of power. Praemonitus, praemunitus.'

'That it is indeed, Freddie. Forewarned is certainly forearmed.' The commander's tone conveys great satisfaction. He had thought the setting up of such a regiment, a crackpot idea when he first heard of it, rather too left-wing and frivolous. Yet it is becoming evident that they are on to something. It is crafty, certainly, but this could very well aid warfare. Franklin's technique, albeit peculiar, seems to have distinct benefits.

There is no time to reflect further, for Fairbanks shouts, 'Over here, sir.' The driver is pulling hay out of the lower part of the stack. Instead of diminishing or collapsing, the structure stays firm – a dark hollow which has been concealed by the straw is becoming visible.

He watches as Fairbanks kneels and sticks his head into the tatty opening.

'Ah, there you are,' Fairbanks says. As he pulls out his head and stands up, two more soldiers come crouch-walking out of the hollow. Fairbanks's eyebrows hoist themselves up over his forehead. He can't help but laugh. 'They've only got a pillbox under there sir.' He shakes his head in disbelief and reviews the stack. 'Not bad at all.'

Ingenious, thinks the commander.

A cracking sound ricochets across the field and draws Bailey-Rae's eyes to the barn. It ripples and warps, and he realises what had seemed like a solid farm storehouse a few moments ago is yet *another* deception – a flimsy painting. It takes a great deal of restraint to remain silent as it falls gracefully to the ground, revealing behind it (of course, there has to be something behind it) a splendid green infantry tank. More startling, next to it is a table covered with a brilliant white cloth, some buns and biscuits and a tea service set for afternoon tea. A waitress stands there in a starched apron.

Brigit steps forward. 'Refreshments, sir?'

The commander does not censure his smile this time but lets the colonel see his appreciation. He turns to the woman. 'I really don't mind if I do.'

Once they have been refreshed by perfectly brewed Earl Grey served in china teacups, the lieutenant colonel accompanies Lord Bailey-Rae back to his car and they set off for HQ.

Lieutenant Colonel Franklin is hoping for some words of praise from his commander-in-chief, but Bailey-Rae has other things on his mind. The temperature still hovers in the high sixties despite the dusky sun. He orders the windows to be rolled down. 'I heard that there is a marvellous keep at the castle with excellent views,' he muses, checking the outskirts of the historic town as they make their way through. 'I'd hoped that we might have pre-dinner drinks there. It's almost sunset now.'

'You'll want a drink all right,' says his old friend Franklin.

'What's that, Freddie?'

'I said, "I'll get you a drink, quite right." The castle is not far.'

'Good, good. And we can discuss some of these techniques you are developing.'

They pass an old coaching inn. This, he sees, is not a deception. Inside, the landlord is closing the curtains against the light.

'Blackout,' says Franklin, watching the middle-aged publican run his fingers over the diamonds of tape, 'is not the only form of camouflage we must deploy to deceive the Axis. As it is not just the human eye we should seek to delude. We don't know how many enemy planes might already be coming over, taking photographs. My men tell me the terrain can give us away. Under moonlight, when the Luftwaffe come, roads shine. Any metal shines. Regular patterns are likely to be man-made, they must be hidden, and everyone must play their part.'

'Quite,' remarks Bailey-Rae, feeling rather tired and hoping the lieutenant colonel might shut up. But Franklin does not stop.

'On your way here you have experienced acoustics, lights, loudspeakers, dummy devices, decoys. Your knowledge of the terrain has been confused. I am certain your navigator doubted his abilities.'

'I did, sir,' pipes up Mathers in the front, though he has not been asked to comment.

Franklin's voice becomes ardent. 'And that is what we need to pursue: that moment of hesitation, of confusion, disorientation. In combat, in war, this saves lives. It is the difference between a bomb dropped on target or slightly askew. Camouflage works this way too. A man who is not seen, not spied, not observed can bide his time, lie there forever watching for the enemy to reveal himself and then hold his fire until his target is close enough for him to hit with one hundred percent accuracy. He can take out the occupiers as they move across the land. The advantage given to us is that we are on home territory and can deploy our native skills.'

They are driving up the hill now, past the little Victorian cottages, larger Regency homes, a great Tudor residence. All the eras of architecture are presented here like a history lesson, Lord Bailey-Rae thinks, and wishes to linger on them, but Lieutenant Colonel Franklin is making his point.

'There are scientific methods behind camouflage and deception, sir,' Franklin says. 'The art should be treated seriously. It is not inconsequential or trivial, as some of your colleagues would suggest.'

Lord Bailey-Rae does not disagree. The ardency of Franklin's speech requires some validation, however. He looks at the lieutenant colonel and nods.

The incline of the road steepens as they ascend to the castle approach. Only a lightness of stone can be glimpsed through its border of cedar trees.

A soldier halts them at the gate to the castle and checks their identities. Bailey-Rae is surprised to see the other sentry abandon his post and run up the slope to the castle's entrance which, he presumes, is hidden by a bend in the drive.

Franklin coughs very loudly. 'Sir.' The commander understands that he must transfer his attention to him. 'Yes, Freddie?'

The lieutenant colonel's eye contact is curiously intense and demanding. Bailey-Rae gives into it. Anything else would be rude. Freddie is clearly impassioned by his commission here. 'All of this . . . It can be transformed into weaponry,' he says.

The soldier at the window accepts their identities and waves the vehicle through.

They climb the drive and take the bend but have to stop for a girl in spectacles to cross their path. She takes her time and waves as she reaches the other side.

'At times the practice' – Freddie's voice rises – 'can be only described as an act of warfare in itself. Visual warfare, sir.' And as the words leave his mouth an ear-splitting blast erupts from the castle front. The noise booms over the walls of the outhouses and shakes the car. Inside, everything vibrates.

There is smoke in the air again. Thick, dark smoke.

A blaze of light blinds everyone.

The car halts.

Earth, grass and pebbles rain down from above.

'Good God,' says Fairbanks. He can smell sulphur.

'What the—' Mathers begins, for as the air clears he sees a fireball engulf the castle.

Orange, yellow, green flames licking up its front, leaping from the ivy to the roof, catching at the curtains. Bubbling, sizzling, spitting, the dry timbers blaze.

A terrifying whistling sound, mechanical, metallic. Then *thud, bang, snap.*

'My God, we're being attacked,' he hollers and flings himself on the ground to crawl under the car.

The whining becomes louder, transforming into a hiss . . .

Lord Bailey-Rae opens the door and, dazzled by the sight, overwhelmed by noise, smells, smoke, staggers out. By sheer force of will he keeps his eyes open and compels himself forward.

Someone cries out, 'It's a Messerschmitt.'

Bailey-Rae's gaze shoots to the angry smoking clouds and sights a black-winged shadow crossing them.

A thundering sonic boom, like a cannon, except with such volume that it makes him duck and cup his ears and blink again.

An intense flash, magnesium-white.

The commander shuts his eyes tight, braces and waits for impact . . .

But none comes.

Abruptly the cacophony of fire ceases, to give way to . . .

Silence.

Nothing.

In the long quietness of those perplexing seconds, he opens one eye . . . then another.

The hellish inferno has vanished.

No longer gripped by the colours of danger, the ancient fortification has returned to its state of dignity. It is restored, in a restive state of calm, untainted stone.

The windows are not sooted, tattered or scorched, the ivy no more a network of acidic flames. Surrounding shrubs, which had just been the most diabolic cradle of destruction, are simply, visibly, pretty, well-trimmed bushes, criss-crossed with shadows.

And it is out of this very ordinary foliage Lord Bailey-Rae perceives two figures emerging: the young woman who had ridden the zebra and an older, lean fellow.

Without pause or a second glance, unperturbed by the pyro-technics, sonic fireworks and spectacular dazzle they have discharged, the pair march up to Lord Bailey-Rae.

Lieutenant Colonel Franklin smiles and takes his chance, buying into the drama of the moment. 'The latest of our recruits, Edward. May I present Mr Jonty Trevelyan and Miss Daphne Devine, who are responsible for this "attack".'

'And who in Hell's name are these people?' splutters Bailey-Rae. His heart has not yet returned to its regular pace. 'Sorcerers? Witches? Devils?'

'Almost,' says Franklin. 'They're magicians.'

This time, instead of bowing, the two deftly salute, perfect manoeuvres without a curtsey in sight.

Lord Bailey-Rae puffs out his cheeks. 'Well, I'm darned. You've certainly played your ace, Freddie. Really had me going there. Couldn't work out what was fake or real. What a performance! It really was.'

Unable to resist, Jonty smiles and hedges his bets. 'Indeed, sir, all the world's a stage, don't you know.'

The Führer and
Supreme Commander,
Armed Forces

Führer
Headquarters,
7 copies

Concerning the invasion of England

The country confounds me. It is an utterly
hopeless situation militarily. However,
despite our military superiority, it is
evident that Churchill is not readying himself
to meet our terms. His misplaced stubbornness
gives me no choice but to initiate plans for
invasion.

Each of our armed forces will be issued with a
directive that will outline their objectives
and responsibilities. It is vital that all
preparations for the entire operation must be
concluded no later than the middle of August.

The invasion will bear the cover name Sea
Lion.

[. . .]

Signed: ADOLF HITLER

CHAPTER ELEVEN

Jonty and Daphne are toasted as the stars of the show. Despite some initial reservations from certain members of the team, they did indeed lead to victory, in the inspection, at least – an achievement that even Aubrey and Vivian have to concede, albeit grudgingly, is well deserved. The coordinated display, created with the use of stage props, sound effects, projections, amplification and gunpowder, has also benefited from the cooperation of four cleverly concealed volunteers, dressed in black. Brigit, Mable the kitchen maid and Bernie the electrician had thrown themselves into the organisation of what Daphne keeps calling 'the show' with an enthusiasm and zeal that none of them had expected. Variously they assisted with rehearsals, erection of the set, fireworks and the throwing of earth, stones and soil upon the commander's car. Bernie had borrowed drums from the local Salvation Army band and discovered a new calling. The short-sighted Sarah had been uncharacteristically enthusiastic in volunteering, which had surprised Brigit and Jonty but not Daphne, who understood she was repaying a debt of sorts.

'It was one of the single most inventive experiences I have yet encountered,' Lord Bailey-Rae comments later. 'Though I still don't know how they got the Messerschmitt to fly over like that.'

They hadn't. The effect had been produced by a plywood plane no more than a foot long, painted black with a metallic veneer. As Lieutenant Colonel Franklin tells him, 'The idea was only suggested. As I have learned here, our eyes see what we expect them to.'

So this evening the camoufleurs are given time off. And rightly so. A lot of effort and sleepless nights have gone into the inspection. Their ambitions have been realised. As such, their reward presents the opportunity for a little dose of cheer in their landscape of worry and they descend upon the old coaching inn for a congratulatory ale or three.

Daphne is not used to ordering drinks, so Brigit puts in a request for two port and lemons.

Some of the men have gone into the public bar. The floor there is sawdusted and makeshift barrel-tables dot the room. Daphne chooses the last free table in the saloon, between the window and the huge inglenook fireplace, which is not lit tonight. The interior is nicer – proper chairs and wooden tables to sit at, and a piano currently used as a repository for empty glasses.

All the windows are open, allowing air to circulate, though the number of bodies crammed into the space is elevating the temperature. There are indeed Canadian soldiers here, as Brigit had told her there might be, in their uniforms and dapper caps. Only their patches differentiate them, although they seem smarter than the British – their uniforms are certainly a better quality. But it is their voices, like liquid honey, that draw her to them. When Brigit brings the drinks to the table, the Canadians' eyes follow her like signets after a swan.

Brigit hands over the port. It is sweet and sickly. Daphne notices that the Canadians are nudging each other, looking in their direction. She straightens her skirt. A powder-blue ribbon sewn down the seam matches exactly the shade of her blouse. She knows it is flattering.

The front door swings back powerfully and hits the wall. A young man strides in and crosses the floor to the Canadians. He is not wearing uniform but shares their accent. Full of confidence, he says something to the soldiers and grins. One pats his back. Another thumbs in her direction. The newcomer turns round to view them, mouth open and laughing, and she is instantly shocked by his features. Never has she seen such perfect symmetry in a masculine face. His nose is slightly too long but balances the rest of his face miraculously. It is a tiny flaw that highlights the perfection of his other features: the fine eyebrows, darker than his hair, lashy eyes, lips full and fleshy, cheeks like mountain ledges, high and planing smoothly to the jaw. The effect is stunning. She casts a glance at Brigit to see if she has noticed, but her friend is occupied by a British officer at the door who is giving her the eye.

'Brigit,' she says in a shrill whisper. 'Look, look.'

Brigit reluctantly pulls away her gaze and straightens her shoulders in a manner that is coquettish – almost a twitch but somehow sensual. She tosses her hair so that it falls off her shoulders and down her back. It is very good hair and appreciated by the officer, who puts a finger to his moustache and neatens it.

Brigit leans over the table and displays the full length of her back, from her long neck to the supple buttocks shaped and rounded by the tailoring of her pencil skirt. The officer's tongue nips out and moistens his lips. He is good-looking, with dark hair and eyes, but nowhere near as handsome as the Canadian.

Brigit stretches out her legs, glossy in stockings that reappeared mysteriously after the inspection was announced. Knowing she is being watched, she reaches down and slides her manicured fingers over her calf. She half expects Daphne to chide her for her shameless exhibition, but her friend is staring over her head.

'What?' says Brigit. Her face is open, the smile intended for the officer loitering on her lips.

'That man over there, behind me.'

'Which one?'

'What do you mean "which one"? The fair chap in the blue shirt. Tall. Just joined that group of Canadians.'

'The fellow with the shoulders?' asks Brigit and appraises the collection of men. Daphne cringes. Brigit is so obvious – he will see that she has spoken about him.

'Shoulders?'

'Broad shoulders.' Brigit's eyebrows rise in appreciation.

That hadn't been the first thing Daphne had noticed. 'Really?'

'I'll say. No Charles Atlas, though most definitely well built.'

'But look at his face. Look at it.'

This time Brigit lights a Chesterfield and lengthens her neck as she exhales the smoke. Using it as cover, she peers through the cloud. 'Pleasant enough, I suppose.' Her hand flops out and flicks ash onto the floor. 'Not my bag. The lieutenant is more my style. You watch, he'll buy our next drink.' She twists and moves her legs to the side, then crosses one and swings it, letting her shoe slide off her heel. This, she has told Daphne, accentuates the shape of her calf.

'But he's, he's an Adonis,' says Daphne. She can't understand why Brigit is not overcome. The man's looks put her in mind of a Greek god – his hair is a burnished gold and wavy, pushed back to reveal a wrinkle-free and squarish forehead. She can't resist looking back again.

This time his gaze hits her and she experiences an electrical shock through her body. It paralyses her for a good while. His eyes, light blue like marbles, have speared her. How can they be that colour? How can they be so luminous? It doesn't seem real. She is utterly astonished again by his beauty. But he will think she is being inappropriate if she continues to gape like this. So she forces out a breath, and it breaks the spell.

His lips have formed a curve. There is something cocky in it, which she immediately likes. He is smiling. He is smiling at her.

Unable to take any more, she looks away.

'What are you doing?' hisses Brigit, observing Daphne's disengagement. 'You've got him there.'

Daphne shakes her head fractionally. 'I can't. It's too much.'

Brigit rolls her eyes and finishes her drink. As soon as she replaces the empty glass on the table, the lieutenant is at her elbow. 'Can I get you another?' His voice is crisp and accented, full of wealth.

'Why, thank you. That's very kind.' She puts out her cigarette and sends him a wide-lipped grin.

'And one for your friend?'

'I'm fine, thank you.' Daphne has barely touched her port, although as soon as the officer goes to the bar she takes a large gulp.

'He's got a friend over there too,' says Brigit, as if encouraging her to the officer's companion. He is stout and stiff with lecherous lips and is perspiring heavily.

Daphne is going to tell Brigit that she is fine by herself but stops, hearing musical notes begin behind her. One of the Canadians has got on to the piano.

He taps out a few more and everyone in the pub smiles. Even without the trumpets it is instantly recognisable: Glenn Miller – he is popular with all the troops. This tune has a jaunty rhythm and infects those listening.

A soldier starts to whistle. A few in the corner applaud. Then the group in the middle of the pub get to their feet and drag their table over to the window. Daphne and Brigit stand up, and another chap moves their table to the wall.

The floor is being cleared. A couple who have been at the bar swing onto it and start to dance.

Daphne feels a tap on her shoulder and turns to find the lieutenant's stout friend. He glances meaningfully at Brigit, who now is somehow at the bar with her admirer. How did Brigit get there so quickly? Then he nods at the dance floor, which already has four couples swirling across it. 'Are you "In the Mood"?' He takes her hand and before she knows it she too is being swung by the gleeful fat man.

His hands are hot on her. She can feel his heat dampen her skirt. He hums as he throws her around, but he is out of tune and has not yet found the beat. She feels slightly sickened by the smell of his sweat, which has a strong scent, like pork crackling.

Brigit sends her an arch look. Approval is in there. But it makes Daphne feel even queasier, so she is pleased when the song ends and she is able to excuse herself to visit the powder room.

Another woman is in there, splashing her face. 'So hot,' she says.

Daphne recognises her and nods.

She is half of a couple who has been dancing. 'Got to make the most of it,' the woman says. 'Not long now.'

Unsure of what she means, Daphne murmurs 'yes' and fishes out a lipstick. The red looks good against her green eyes and blue blouse. She powders her nose and forehead, then goes out. But the woman's words linger. They refuse to be directed to the back of her mind and sit instead like a crow on a gravestone, waiting to swoop.

Benny Goodman is starting up on the piano. Another upbeat joyful tune that has seduced more dancers. It lifts her spirits. The crow retreats. Though it doesn't leave.

Outside, night has come down. The windows have been shuttered and curtained, the door closed. Inside, it is clammy and muggy. No one seems to mind. Everyone shines.

Halfway across the floor, she feels another tap and sighs. She does not want to dance with the fat man again and pinches her lips in. 'Look, I'm sorry . . .' she turns to reply, beginning a polite refusal.

But it is not the fat man. It is the Adonis. His head is tilted to the side, a rueful smile blooming. Or perhaps not blooming, but frozen halfway to fully coming into being.

'Are you?' he says. His voice is not all Canadian honey; but half infused with an English accent too. Still, it is just as delicious.

She is momentarily blinded by his eyes again. She blinks.

'Why are you sorry?' he repeats.

It is as if she is dazzled by his brightness. In her self-conscious confusion she cannot remember what she has said and stutters, 'Yes. No. Pardon?'

His lips recommence their bloom. 'Fancy a spin?'

She swallows, unable to speak, and nods.

He takes her hand and leads her into the room.

Look at me, she thinks. All the girls must be so jealous. I am the one who has been chosen.

The way he handles her is slick. And he has got the beat.

'You local?' he whispers. She can feel his breath on her ear, tickling it like a butterfly wing.

'No,' she says, then, 'Yes.'

He laughs. 'And do you always give two answers to any question?'

This time she looks into his face and says, 'Yes, I mean – no.' Then she laughs with him.

He moves his face closer to her and says, 'I like that.' And then he twirls her. She moves away a foot. He pulls her back firmly into his arms and they turn together, round and round the floor.

She catches sight of Jonty peering in from the public bar as she whirls, laughter spilling out of her though she knows it is unbecoming. Her friend's eyes are not smiling; they are loaded with caution. Why a warning? she wonders. It is not like him to be conventional in his outlook. Sometimes he can be overbearing. Though it is born out of love. But this is war. No one knows what tomorrow will bring. Young people must make hay while the sun still shines, as they do not know how long it will last. She realises this is what the woman meant, yet does not feel the presence of the crow. Instead, there is a strange release and she lightens and slinks closer to her partner, feeling his body touch her in unfamiliar places. A longing begins deep inside. The tempo jumps and she grips him more tightly. It is wonderful.

She does not notice the commotion at the door until she looks up at his face and sees distraction there.

Raised voices are coming from the entrance. They halt abruptly, and he releases her. She stands with her hand in the dance position as if still holding his.

A couple of the Canadians at the door are engaged in dispute with a warden. Brigit's officer is there too. The fat man isn't.

As people notice, the room quietens and the piano peters out. The pianist turns on his stool and regards the commotion.

Someone throws a punch. The officer staggers back. Daphne can't tell who has hit him. There is a brief pause, then the room goes up.

A surge of bodies.

Someone screams.

Her arm is tugged. Jonty. 'Quick, Daphers, here.' He whisks her off to a back room and out over a yard. Several of the castle team are already ahead of them, making their way up the hill. Brigit is with them. 'Can't get caught up in that,' Jonty tells her. 'Can you imagine what Bailey-Rae would make of it?'

She agrees, but is beyond disheartened so does not answer. Perhaps she will find her man another evening.

Just before they take the curve, under the branches of the castle's boundary trees, she looks back. She can see men outside the pub but doesn't know if he is amongst them.

'Come on!' Jonty almost shouts at her, so she gives up and scampers after him. 'I'm sure you'll see him again,' he says.

She realises she does not even know his name.

19 JULY 1940

CHAPTER TWELVE

The inspection is not as extensively celebrated as might have been. In war there is no pause. No stillness, no time for rest. Always there is something dark occurring in corners unseen, machinations murmuring, whisperings of desperate ideas, difficult decisions made.

The next day, when they are nursing sore heads, news reaches the castle that Yeovil has been bombed. Ross, the ventriloquist, has a sister who works in a factory there. Though he does not say it, they can see he fears the worst. They all do. Information and news of casualties, about relatives, are hen's teeth.

Daphne feels a ballooning of fear in her stomach. It is getting closer. However, her mind is full of the man from the Bush. Thinking about him makes her feel lighter. Over breakfast she is preoccupied. She recalls the way his hands felt on her body. It makes her flush.

'Are you all right?' Brigit says. Daphne inspects her face, anticipating a mischievous inquisition, but Brigit is pale. 'We're all worried about our families,' she says.

Her friend's words provoke an overwhelming sense of shame. Daphne's father has not yet managed to find Carabella in the camp, though he knows she is registered there. At least the government has declared no future plans to relocate internees. The tragedy of the *Arandora Star* swims through the collective consciousness of the nation. The watery dead lurk in the corners of the War Cabinet. Though there has been an effort to deal out blame, like a pack of cards, to several different parties, guilt clings damply over many of those in command. Not all the alien enemies consigned to the mass grave at the bottom of the Atlantic could have been innocent. But it is fair to believe a lot of them were.

More victims of other people's war.

And yet still nothing is known of Uncle Giuseppe.

A quietness comes over Daphne, as it does over every single one of them stationed at the castle. It starts on the inside and gradually works its way out through the pores of the skin.

The domestic staff can sense it.

The eccentric, curious castle camoufleurs radiate silent concern. It wraps around each individual like an invisible cloak.

In the days that follow, their movements become muted, restricted. They hold things closer to their bodies, thin their lips, narrow their eyes and hunch their shoulders.

They work faster, longer, harder.

Above them the air squalls with Hurricanes and Spitfires and enemy Messerschmitts.

Daily dogfights, fatalities, the steady advance of the Germans.

Stomachs tighten. Meals become rushed, subdued affairs. Pit stops for refuelling.

On the fourth day it is announced they are to go to the nearby airbase for advanced training.

No one complains.

And this is how Daphne comes to be bent over an aerial photograph of the South Downs, shoulder to shoulder with the dreaded Aubrey Sharpling. Against all odds the lieutenant colonel has accepted Vivian's elaborate and long-winded explanation of the marching/stockings incident as a valid justification for an exercise designed to test the elasticity and therefore flexibility of the women's uniform prototype. Largely this was due to the lieutenant colonel's dislike of the terms the couturier used: 'bias cut', 'baste', 'selvedge' and 'warp'. It was far too peripheral and trifling; he wished not to spend one moment longer occupied with unmasculine concerns and discharged the group without discipline as long as they promised to engage in activities 'somewhere else', and, after a pause for good measure, 'with chaperones'. Both Brigit and Daphne thought it highly unlikely they would be in need of such safeguards in the company of the couturier and poet, but they all recognised the opportunity to de-escalate and agreed to the terms with good grace. A grudging truce has formed between the four.

To his credit, Aubrey has a good eye for detail and can point out landmarks like factories and runways on the paper. When first presented, Daphne thought it a diagram. It transpires, however, that this is an aerial photograph taken from a plane. The technology these days is marvellous.

'The geometry comes from square farm buildings, ploughed fields and roads,' Aubrey tells her.

Under his tutelage she soon begins to see how shapes, seen from above, can indicate potential targets for the enemy.

'The importance of air power to the outcome of the war is highly significant,' the poet explains. 'In the last one we were dominated by the air and were not air-minded.'

This chimes with what their instructor has told them of the Germans' intentions to destroy aircraft production and the infrastructure on the ground. The question he poses to the camoufleurs is, 'So how can *you* disguise them from the bombers?'

This occupies much of the discussion. The artists think that paint can be used on the floor to disrupt the lines. The sculptors argue that texture is harder to replicate.

They mull over various ideas until their instructor announces that they have turned down a cul-de-sac and so perhaps it is time for lunch.

While they gather their notebooks and return the photographs to him, he adds that after dining there are flights arranged. Photography is no substitute for the real thing. Practice in flying will train them to understand the aerial view when creating their schemes.

Daphne has never been in a plane before. She and Aubrey exchange a look of mutual delight, a feeling that most of the team share, judging by the level of enthusiastic babbling that accompanies them into the canteen, a breezy, high-ceilinged room with a lino-covered floor. The acoustics amplify the volume of voices, the clatter of their feet and murmurs of excitement, which means that their loud and garrulous entrance draws the gaze of every occupant at lunch.

Fastened into uniforms with polished shoes and well-groomed hair, the team look less ridiculous than they had done on arrival at Farnham. However, there persists an air of intense difference about them that is clankingly obvious to military eyes. Too old, too fat, too flabby, too thin, too noisy, too showy, too expressive – anyone can see they aren't soldiers, as hard as they might have been pressed into the mould.

While the airmen seated at the tables raise eyebrows and incline their heads, a group of women smile over. One of them, in flying gear (flying gear!) waves at Daphne. She looks around to see who is behind her – Jonty, Harry, Bernie and the rest of the boys are there in animated enthusiasm, intensely discussing which planes they might fly in.

Her gaze returns to the female pilot. The woman nods and mouths, 'Yes, you. Come over.'

She could do with a bit of female company, quite frankly: none of the men are particularly interested in talking to her and Brigit has stayed back at the base with a headache and cold. There is nothing to prevent her peeling off from the herd.

The small group of five have picked the table in the corner

with a double aspect which gives the best view in the canteen. It looks onto the runway and hangars where mechanics are busy with the planes.

They are chatting over cups of tea and the crumbs of lunch. Two of them wear overalls, their elegant fingernails stained dark with grease and oil. Women engineers, Daphne thinks. What progress we are making. The thought has crossed her mind that she and Brigit were desperate aberrations, pulled into the field to satisfy some commander's whims. Seeing other women here is reassuring.

Another pair are in navy uniforms: smart tunics, skirts and black stockings. She is interested to hear what they are doing too. Might ask if she gets a chance.

As she draws closer she realises the pilot is familiar. Her bobbed hair shimmers and waves like the waters of the estuary at home. It is the same muddy brown too. Though the cut is dated – an It-Girl, twenties style – it is also iconic.

At two feet away recognition finally flares. Who could fail to recognise those finely painted eyebrows, the delicate cheekbones and lips –a perfect Cupid's bow?

'It's you,' says Daphne. Of course it is. The woman is a hero. 'I didn't know you were working—'

'Joined up,' the pilot cuts in.

The rest of the women glance at Daphne's face, which has taken on the wide-eyed arrangement of the pleasantly starstruck. They are used to it and chuckle. Johnson regularly has this effect. People still remember her flight from London to Australia. It was all across the papers. The whole journey on her own and she but a woman. Amy is teased about it by the men, some of whom call her Gypsy Moth after her beloved plane.

'Well, my friend,' says the pilot, pronouncing it *frynd*, 'we've all got to do our part. I'm flying planes from base to base.'

Her voice is high and soft. Surprising. Daphne imagined it would be deeper, have more bassy resonance, though she doesn't know why. Perhaps because the woman has, well . . . she has done something that only men are able to. But then why should that make her less female?

'I'm Daphne—' she begins.

A woman in a boiler suit examining her keenly asks, 'Not Pearson?' as if it is a trick.

'No,' says Daphne. 'Devine.'

'That's a shame,' says the engineer. Letting her face drop, she shrugs and returns to her tea.

'Sorry to disappoint.' Daphne adds.

'Oh no.' The pilot speaks up. 'Don't worry. We were just talking about her. One of the WAAFs in Kent. Did a tremendous job recently. Rescued a pilot from a crash.' She bends closer and lowers her voice theatrically. 'World's turned upside down – women rescuing men, whatever next?' Daphne laughs and sees Amy is pleased by this. 'You know,' the pilot continues, 'when we started there was an awful lot of cynicism. But us gals are getting there. Pearson has helped enormously.' She slaps a free chair at the end of the table. 'Come, take a seat. Tell us what you've been doing with that bunch.' She inclines her unruffled hair to the rest of the camoufleurs still traipsing in in twos and threes. 'We've been wondering who they are since brekkie. Are you the Entertainments Troop?'

Daphne stifles a giggle. 'No, not quite. Though I can see why you might think that. They're a different sort of sign-up. Non-typical, if you like—' But at that moment one of the engineers gasps and takes everyone's attention. Her face is aghast at some activity taking place below, outside the large arch of the aircraft hangar.

'Amy,' says one of the girls in a boiler suit. She has used her name like a warning yet does not turn her head to the pilot.

Daphne follows her stare and sees there is a man in flying gear on the tarmac. He is involved in a dispute with another person hidden by the fuselage of the plane. 'What's Brewers doing at the Spitfire?' says the girl. 'It's only been fuelled. Not done the checks yet.'

Amy has risen. 'Haven't the foggiest. But that's got the new wing configuration. They've only just added armoured steel plating to it. Not been out yet.'

The other boiler-suited girl gets to her feet. Daphne senses alarm.

'Is he checking it?' the other engineer asks. 'He's not got authorisation.'

Oblivious to the concern he is causing in the canteen above him, the fellow clambers up to the cockpit.

The men on the table next to them have become interested. Daphne hears one. 'He's not going to . . . is he?'

Back on the tarmac two mechanics stroll out of the hangar, one still rubbing down his hands with a rag. Their lips are moving as they approach the male pilot belting in. One of them puts his hands on his hips and shakes his head. The other breaks into a jog towards the Spitfire. In response the pilot pulls his visor down. The plane's engine chugs into life.

On another table a young RAF chap clamps his hand over his mouth. His neighbour starts, 'Good God, no. Someone has to stop him. Open the window. Call out!'

Both girls in blue have already pressed up against the window and started banging on the glass, trying to draw the attention of the workers down below. All personnel in the canteen have stopped what they are doing and come to gawp helplessly.

The aeroplane is taxiing to the runway, gaining speed as it approaches. One of the mechanics sprints after it as it readies into position.

'What is Brewers playing at?' asks Amy. Urgency steeps her words.

Another man curses. 'A note was sneaked under our door that there was a price of £50,000 for anyone willing to fly one of our latest aircraft to Germany.'

At which the canteen breaks into a clamour of furious, outraged voices:

'The traitorous fool. They'll kill him as soon as he touches down.'

'Why in Hell's name didn't you tell me?'

'I assumed we'd all had them and that you did too. I ignored it.'

'Who else got one?'

The plane squares itself at the runway, the mechanic still attempting his fruitless pursuit, clearly outpaced.

Now there is a second Spitfire emerging from the hangar.

'Who's that there? Is he going after him?' someone asks.

An angrier voice spits, 'Brewers will be shot down.'

The aircraft's flaps go up, its engines roar as the pilot applies maximum forward pressure and increases the power so that it rushes down the runway.

'No, no, no,' says Amy, but the traitor's craft lifts off from the ground and climbs, wobbling, into the air.

Realising the futility of its position, or perhaps instructed to return, the second Spitfire begins to slow.

'He won't catch him now. He's gone,' says another airman, watching the rogue plane sail into the heavens.

Then the canteen door bursts open. An officer in a state of agitation marches into the group. 'Who is it?' he barks. 'No one is permitted on that one yet.'

Someone says, 'Brewers, sir.'

The aircraft is growing smaller and smaller, a painful black blot in the sky.

But no one is able to speak. They are calculating the implication of such a betrayal.

'There's a fox in the henhouse,' murmurs Amy.

At which point the officer growls, 'Trevelyan! Devine! Report to Office 105 at once.'

All eyes turn on Daphne.

Their hostility is barely concealed.

Surely they can't think she had anything to do with this.

Little pulses flame in her cheeks.

CHAPTER THIRTEEN

'We didn't do it! We weren't even here when the note was slipped to Brewers!'

'They must know that.'

'Then why the Hell have they dispatched us to this room?'

'Language, Daphne!' Jonty moves on quickly. 'I don't know. It was so quick, wasn't it? I'm not sure how they might have come to that conclusion . . . Unless . . .' He darts a sideways glance at his assistant. 'Well . . .' He winces now, regretting his folly.

His assistant has seized on his mistake. 'Unless what?'

He should not have spoken nor jumped to such conclusions and wishes not to finish the sentence he has started – there will be no let-up until she has prised it out of him. With these hesitations she can be like a hound after the fox. She knows him too well, understands his speech, the intonation and lingerings, his microscopic facial tics, far too well for him to easily obfuscate and retreat. 'Unless,' he says, already fatigued by the reaction that will come, 'they have found out about your parentage.'

Daphne halts and slaps her hands hard on her hips.

Jonty does not want to look – her cheeks will be hotter than ever. Her eyes will open and burn like green flames in faulty gaslights. Copper streaks in her hair will remind him of fiery Welsh dragons, and the two little darts that appear on her top lip when it is puckered will be there like arrows pointing to her mouth. From which, no doubt, something scalding will blow forth, like steam from a geyser. She does not know that her words often scorch him. His assistant exhibits the same pluck and energy as his daughter, Olivia, when she was alive. It was a quality that had endeared Daphne to him when she had first strutted out onto the stage two and a half years ago with no experience and no training. Only a diploma from an Institute, a ladies' finishing school which he had never heard of. When she had replied 'no' to his enquiries regarding dance certificates, stagecraft and other dramatic arts, some of the other girls auditioning started to giggle. Daphne had jutted out her chin, picked up her skirts and bobbed a curtsey to them. It had made him laugh. And, though it was unwise really, he had given her the job.

Nobody in the Oriental Theatre thought she'd last three months.

She was a quick learner, though, and soon began to display some calling for the art. A little over five feet tall, she was not as diminutive as some of his assistants, but rapidly became proficient in the contraction of certain muscles and was nimble enough to squeeze inside the smallest of boxes and cabinets. Her timing was good and, as she had become more confident in the role, her personality began to shine. Playful and saucy (when allowed), the audience warmed to her. But mastery of her emotions has been harder to come by. God knows he has tried, with little success. She is still so forthright. Candid also. Far too independent of mind. Women with such troublesome tendencies, he thinks, rarely make good wives.

Jonty had hoped military training might smooth out the rough edges. Daphne is, however, showing no signs of malleability. Much as he sympathises, the episode in the courtyard should have taken her down a peg or two. Instead the lieutenant colonel has let her off and she has continued on her downward spiral. The dancing in the public house was worrisome, the reckless abandonment in her face evidence of her lack of restraint. And with a Canadian too. She usually had her head screwed on when it came to matters like this. Everyone knew what these foreign soldiers got up to with local girls. And they'd be gone soon, when the war ended, leaving all those silly misses in the lurch and some, no doubt, with child too.

He is determined to have her matched someday, and soon too: a pairing with a decent chap, able to provide. And British. He is aware of his persistent cough, the bloodshot phlegm: he is getting older and knows that in the none-too-distant future he will vanish from this worldly stage one last time. With things being the way they are, it will more than likely be in a puff of smoke. Or an explosion. At least there will be some poetry in that.

Jonty continues walking, outpacing her. His legs are longer. He savours the brief separation.

'What do you mean, my parentage?'

He knows she knows exactly what he means. She is being wilful again.

'You know . . .' He swallows hard.

'I don't.'

'You do, Daphers.' The use of her pet name is calculated. On occasion it softens.

'Jonty, there are others working for the government with worse heritage than mine. We met a German at Wormwood Scrubs.' She continues to pout, a pace behind him. He knows from her tone what her expression is: her lips are pursed, creating a curved shadow under her bottom lip and above the fleshy part of her chin; between her eyebrows there will be evidence of a dark but small crinkle. It all reminds him of a pug the stage manager used to keep who was sweet-natured but ferocious when vexed.

He is unsure of what to say and keeps his eyes on the end of the corridor, a wall with paint peeling, dull brown. 'De Wohl must have defected,' he counters eventually.

'And I'm English. Born here. And so was Father.'

'But perhaps it has given them cause for concern?'

'Then why let me in in the first place?'

They have reached 105.

'Well, that Spitfire theft was certainly nothing to do with me,' Daphne says emphatically.

Childish, he thinks.

'And,' she continues, 'I'm pretty damn sure it wasn't you.'

Her loyalty pleases him. But she still needs to be shaped. 'Language, girl!'

His reprimand has no effect. Instead she puts her finger to her lips and points at the door. Voices within the room are engaged in discussion. He hears the word 'priorities'. Then four that make him shiver – the end of a question: '. . . they are not indispensable?'

Surely no reference to them, he assures himself. He hopes not. He thinks probably not. Although . . . no. He brings the lid down on the thought. Clearly they are discussing the pilot who has flown off with the plane.

Daphne has missed it, for which he is grateful. He knows she would have reacted with strength. Though she believes herself to be an outstanding camoufleur of expression (long before he had ever heard the term), to him she is an open book. He watches with misgiving as she bends to the door and puts her ear to the keyhole.

Fretting, he cautions, 'One day this impulsivity will get you into real trouble.' He means it.

'Shh,' Daphne says. She is too loud, though, and the door of Office 105 springs open.

A stern voice within commands them to enter.

CHAPTER FOURTEEN

Lieutenant Colonel Franklin sits behind a desk. After her most recent brush with authority Daphne is not overjoyed to see him.

The feeling is mutual. Lieutenant Colonel Franklin glowers.

She and Jonty raise their hands to their foreheads and execute a synchronised salute, then smile at each other in appreciation of their successful coordination. It does nothing to ease the prickly tension in the office.

The lieutenant colonel rolls his eyes. His face resumes its stiffness. When they have managed to stand still a little longer, he says, 'You're to be reassigned.'

It is a curt dismissal. Even Jonty is surprised that it has come so soon.

Daphne's mouth drops open. Before she can check herself, it all comes out. 'But we had nothing to do with the theft.'

Franklin's eyebrows rise. 'What theft?' he asks.

She feels Jonty brace himself but finds it not within her reach to stop. 'I thought that . . . there was a pilot, sir . . . unauthorised. He has flown a spitfire out. To the Germans.'

Jonty has had more experience with the treatment of messengers. 'I don't think it is right for us to comment yet, sir. We are not aware of the full facts. My assistant speaks out of turn.'

The lieutenant colonel tenses and sits up rigidly. He shifts his eyes to the corner of the room. 'Then it's true,' he says. 'There are traitors amongst us. Enemy agents.'

Out of the shadows steps Hugh Devereaux.

Initially, Daphne does not recognise their recruiter. Her first impressions are of a man in a dark grey suit with a distinct masculinity and authority that make her shiver slightly. Not as the lieutenant colonel does with his frosty demeanour. No, this is like eating something spicy – one of her mother's exotic pasta recipes that used to get her school chums fanning their mouths and chugging on glasses of milk.

'Hello,' says Hugh. 'I'm afraid it's back to London for you.'

Now she sees it is definitely him – her enthusiasm does not fade.

Jonty nods with apparent relief but Daphne immediately asks, 'Why?'

'We have been alerted to your inspection success,' Hugh tells them and settles himself by the window next to an iron coal burner. 'You have excelled yourselves.' He pauses. 'There is no time to correct and continue further training. That will have to be done on the job. We have a mission for you. There's a car waiting outside, and you'll be briefed in London.'

'London?' says Daphne. The hot flush of feeling has reminded her of the man from the Bush. If she leaves Farnham she may never see him again. And she dearly wishes to. 'But our things—'

'Already in hand,' Hugh says. 'Being packed as we speak.'

The disappointment is crushing.

Jonty is thinking of Harry and how he still has so much to talk about with him. So much which will not be turned over and spoken of. He has become a good friend, a confidant.

Their lack of urgency irritates Hugh so he says, 'That means now. Downstairs. Ask for Mathers.'

The King has graciously approved the following award:

The medal of the military division of the Most Excellent Order of the British Empire, for Gallantry.

At approximately 0100 hours on 31 May an Avro Anson of No. 500 Squadron crashed near the Women's Auxiliary Air Force quarters at RAF Detling, Kent. On impact one of the bombs it was carrying exploded, killing the wireless operator outright. The pilot and two crew were injured. Hearing the crash, Corporal Pearson (880538 – now Assistant Section Officer), who had been in her bunk, dashed out to the site and, on meeting it, saw that the aircraft was on fire. Despite knowing that there were bombs aboard, Pearson fearlessly climbed into the wreckage and grabbed the stunned pilot. She then freed him from his parachute harness and dragged him clear of the burning plane. When they were only 30 yards away, a 120 lb bomb went off. With no thought for her own safety Corporal Pearson at once flung herself on top of the pilot, covering his face with her own tin helmet and shielding him from the blast and flying splinters and shrapnel. Without a doubt her swift and courageous actions saved the pilot's life.

She is the first woman to be decorated for bravery in this war.

CHAPTER FIFTEEN

There is some comfort to be found in the return to Wormwood Scrubs. It surprises Daphne. In fact, she very much doubts that many, if any, of those who cross the threshold find much solace in the place. Prisons are not designed with that purpose in mind. As they sign in their visitation to 'Colin Scott' and trundle down the corridors into the basement maze of the lower headquarters, she notices that the murky, fetid smell does not repulse her so much.

In truth, she has experienced conflicting emotions since the lieutenant colonel's announcement. The unknown does that. There is part of Daphne that swells: the idea of deployment in a proper military operation is exciting. She feels special, like being picked first out of the whole class for the hockey team. A *secret* mission too. What can it be? She cannot wait to find out.

They expect to return to the castle after they have completed it. Whatever it is. So her hopes of meeting The Man have restored themselves to that hidden nook at the back of her head where she keeps furtive memories, unruly desires and delicious dreams. She ruminates on them quietly when alone in bed at night. They are delectable.

Before Jonty knocks on the briefing room, she stops to ask, 'How do I look? Competent? Tidy? Polished?' and smooths down her hair. Polished shoes, neat skirt, no make-up.

Her hair has come loose from the band fastening it at the back but generally he approves. 'You're all right.'

Not an overwhelming compliment, but she takes it anyway and signals that Jonty may knock.

Hugh Devereaux opens the door and summons them in. She isn't sure how he has managed to get there before them. He had left after they had departed the airbase, or she thought he had, though their driver insisted that they stop at a facility outside Twickenham to refresh themselves and change into civilian clothes. However, this diversion only lasted forty-five minutes or so. And yet here he is, perfectly groomed and impeccable as ever.

Their contact acknowledges them with a nod of the head and gestures to two spare seats at the long table.

The light is different. It has been replaced by two smaller ones which do not flicker.

There are fewer people here than on their first visit, and Daphne and Jonty take the number to eight.

A man with a handkerchief poking from the breast pocket of his dark green suit goes to the back wall, which is covered with new photographs and what Daphne thinks might be a large map. He pulls down a blind across it.

She recalls that he had been present at their initial briefing. Someone had called him Severus, or some posh old-fashioned name that was clearly code. He had worn the green suit then too.

As he comes closer to seat himself at the table she sees that he is only a few years older than her. Somehow she had thought him far more senior. A high forehead gives him an air of nobility. His grey eyes are strong, his hands large and capable. Possibly it is rank that confers authority, though she does not know what his is.

Another man, sitting at the head of the table, is not the brigadier this time but definitely older, with a lined face. Although his moustache is black and bushy he has a bald pate and thinning grey hair, a pointy hawklike nose, and a pale complexion which suggests days spent inside offices or underground. Wearing a pinstripe suit, he has the mannerisms of an office worker. A senior civil servant? Without revealing his own name or station, Pinstripe introduces them to the circle.

Daphne is right about the man at the board, who they are told is indeed Septimus. He remains standing. She remembers his concern over the Spear of Destiny in German hands. The thought of this unnerves her too. Just the name of the thing is full of power. Especially when 'destiny' is at the forefront of all their minds. Not long now, she thinks, recalling the words of the woman at the Bush.

A chap in the chair next to her volunteers his hand and announces, 'Wheaters, dear. You probably recognise me. Yes, you do, don't you?' He winks and lets out an aromatic chuckle. Clearly he thinks himself both famous and irresistible. His air of confidence, she suspects, has something to do with the potent reek of port coming off him whenever he opens his mouth.

She draws away and sits on the edge of her chair, though the canvas makes it impossible to lean. The fabric is worn in the middle.

The man in pinstripes calls back her attention: 'Thank you, Mr Wheatley.' He dismisses the other chap. The chief's eyes glitter like the onyx necklace her father gave her when she was sixteen. The beads were cut so that the light caught them on their hard edges. The chief's shine because they are animated – full to the lens of a distinctive energy that might burst from their watery confines. What is it? Urgency? He continues to extend his palm across the table in the direction of the man with the shock of white hair. Daphne also recognises him from their last visit. Tall and lanky, he is the oldest in the room. His long, white, straggly beard lends the impression of wildness. 'This is Mr Potter.'

Who in response says, 'Gerard.'

It is unusual to encounter this level of informality; in fact it is bordering on uncomfortable. But this last year has changed everything, turned all conventions on their heads.

'Miss Sabine,' the chief continues, indicating the woman beside Gerard Potter, perhaps a friend. A plaid two-piece and a lemon blouse are the very essence of respectability. Because of the heat she has unbuttoned the top two buttons, probably the most risqué she ever gets. Although she has a large, mannish face, there is something compelling about her. Attractive.

'Cyril, whom you know. And Hugh, your recruiter.' His forehead contracts into several deep furrows.

They all nod, and Pinstripe gets down to business. He has not introduced himself. 'The facts of the matter are . . .' he begins.

At last! thinks Daphne.

'We would like to involve you in an operation that may seem rather off-piste.' He leans towards them and clasps his hands together loosely. 'But as you are aware, the imminent invasion means that nothing is off the table.' He turns his eyes to Gerard. 'Perhaps you would care to explain?'

'Everything?' Gerard asks. His raised eyebrows are bushy, the ends whipped up into points. With his narrow chin the effect is goatlike. Devilish even.

'Just enough.' Pinstripe pats the table with his knuckles. 'Perhaps the context.'

Gerard fixes intense eyes upon them. 'As the chief has mentioned, we are in the greatest crisis in our country's history since the Spanish Armada.' He side-eyes his female companion, a look that is an invitation.

Miss Sabine picks up the torch of his words and continues. 'An invasion which failed,' she says simply. 'Now that our very civilisation is threatened and dark armies approach our shores again, we must tap into the forgotten sources, unleash all Hell.'

Wheaters chortles in his chair. 'Yes, let the Devil ride out,' he says, enjoying the drama, then adds, as an afterthought to himself, 'I say, that one's not bad,' and writes on his notepad.

Pinstripe shoots him a warning glance before addressing Daphne and Jonty. 'And this is where you come in.'

Daphne has no idea what they are talking about. She is not sure anybody does.

'How so?' asks Jonty. She is pleased he also requires more explanation.

From the corner of the table, Hugh speaks up. Good, thinks Daphne, he will be coherent. 'Your demonstration at the Farnham inspection has shown you are capable of complex . . .' He pauses and changes tack. 'We are in need of your expertise in this area.'

'You can count on it,' says Jonty.

Hugh Devereaux's voice becomes brisk and purposeful. 'Now listen here: this undertaking does not come without peril. There are those amongst us, invisible enemies, fifth columnists, who are ready to rise up and enable the enemy to take over the country when they arrive. And others too. Those sympathetic to the Germans, and some who are already working actively on their behalf. Be alert as you go about your tasks. Should anybody seem suspicious, report it right away. Be on your guard.'

Daphne isn't sure how to react other than to nod. 'All right,' she says cautiously.

'If you agree, then you will be briefed on arrival,' says Pinstripe.

'On arrival?' she asks.

'I am afraid we are unable to divulge locations at this point.'

So they must agree to a mission which is dangerous, without knowing why or what it entails. This is madness, Daphne thinks. Can operations really be run in this way?

Pinstripe pushes them. 'What say you? There is no room for hesitation.'

She doesn't answer. Jonty, though, is already nodding, shaking his fist lightly. 'No one has ever doubted the Trevelyans' commitment to their country. I will lay down my life for my England, have no fear.' He adds, 'Although I'd prefer to avoid that.'

'Then it is agreed,' says Hugh, taking Daphne's silence for consent. 'You will be assigned immediately to Operation Reynard.'

Daphne blinks as he says the name. Reynard. She wonders if it is named after the fox in the fable, who was sly and amoral. Will they have to embrace those qualities too?'

Pinstripe takes over as Hugh leaves through the door in the corner of the room. 'Your sacrifice will be remembered,' he says dispassionately. 'Be ready to leave at 0800 hours.'

The meeting is over. Everyone else gets to their feet.

Except for Pinstripe, who gestures for the blind to go up again. He and Septimus have more work to do.

But she has been dismissed. That is it. Briefing executed.

She finds she is sweating.

What has just happened? What are they doing? Why are their lives in danger? What will be sacrificed? Things are whirling away from her. She feels adrift, as if she is being sucked into a large air tunnel.

Miss Sabine catches Daphne's eye across the table. 'I will see you soon,' she says. 'Your future will be . . .' she begins to say, then changes her mind and rephrases. 'The next phase of your life will take up every resource your body is capable of. Get as much rest as you can.'

And then, conversely, a stark coldness comes over Daphne, like the touch of a barn wall on a winter's night. It makes her think of owls and damp graveyards in autumn mist. A vague depression rises.

The words written on the pages she had to Roneo return to her again: *Luciferianism, occult magic, Ariosophy, Nostradamus.* She is seized by a terrible sense of foreboding. She cannot help herself – mental panic forces itself through her limbs, and she shudders.

The woman turns away.

But as they leave Jonty frowns. 'Someone walk over your grave?'

'No,' she says, as a peculiar clarity washes over her. 'But someone is planning to.'

And suddenly she knows this is true.

CHAPTER SIXTEEN

Mrs Thomas is pleased to see her. 'I'm so relieved,' she says and enfolds Daphne in an unexpected embrace. For once Daphne enjoys the smell of her damp apron – mothballs and flour. Her breath is sweet like hay.

Neither are particularly accustomed to physical affection, so they sit down quickly by the hearth, where they proceed to drink two watered-down glasses of homemade lemonade.

'So tell me,' says Mrs Thomas. 'How is the telephony course going?'

'The what?' Has she heard rightly?

'The telephony course,' says the landlady. 'A woman dropped by and told me they'd recruited you. Telephony. Yes, that's what she said, I'm sure. A very respectable profession, I might add. You might get the chance to meet a nice engineer.'

'Theatre work' was how Daphne had vaguely described her previous occupation. Telephony appears to be a promotion in Mrs Thomas's eyes. She tries to look keen. 'Very true.'

Her landlady bends closer, almost half off the seat of her chair now, 'They told me not to rent your room.' She taps the side of her nose. Twice. 'Gave us what they called "a small stipend". I'd never heard of it before, thought they meant a stick at first.' She flutters her hand forward playfully and with the other covers her mouth. 'Turns out it's money. And none too shabby is it neither. Mr Thomas and I are both extremely grateful. Times are hard. We've all had to draw in our belts. Lots of customers going on the never-never. Of course, we're happy to help, but we can't carry on like that forever.'

She talks greedily, as if she hasn't conversed with a human being for quite a while. Daphne finds herself content to sit and listen. After the dour mood of the castle, and the afternoon in Wormwood Scrubs, Mrs Thomas's chatter about the habits of the neighbours and fortunes of the customers is a welcome relief. Daphne hopes that an immersion in the trivia of Mrs Thomas's blather will vanish the heavy anxiety she has carried out of the briefing room.

Jonty asked if someone had walked over her grave. It is worse. As if a boa constrictor like the one in Harry's photographs is tightening its grip around her heart. Indeed, it is so unpleasant that her mind has started configuring possible means of escape – can she return to the castle instead of involving herself in something that has great risk attached? Not that it is perfect back there, not at all. But the chief and Miss Sabine have unsettled her. Hugh too. Danger that way lies. Daphne can sense it, and this knowledge is gnawing at a primal survival instinct, which in turn is raising her hackles. The hairs on the back of her neck stand up when she thinks about the mission. Warning signs – they are everywhere.

Mrs Thomas had once told her the story of a suffragette who had dreamed that she died in a fire. She was on holiday in Atlantic City. When the woman woke up she knew instantly that she must return home. Later that day, the hotel burned down.

It is foolish not to heed such omens.

Perhaps tomorrow she will return to the prison and find Hugh and explain her feelings. He will be annoyed, but there must be others who can step into her shoes. Perhaps she could help Vivian with the women's uniforms. Or Aubrey could give her some lessons in aerial recognition. Anything really. Just not the mission.

Something very bad is going to happen. She knows it.

'Oh,' says Mrs Thomas suddenly, as if she is interrupting another person. 'Sorry, I forgot. You had a letter come.' She reaches to the mantelpiece and fetches it. As she hands it over she adds, 'Postmark's Isle of Man.' Then she bites her lip.

'Oh right,' says Daphne, heartbeat accelerating.

'You'll want to read it in private, I'm sure.' Mrs Thomas is gentle. 'I'll start sorting out the linen. Your bed's not made up.' She clears the empty glasses. 'Will give you a shout in an hour for tea. Better not leave it any later if you've got an early start.'

'Thank you. You're very kind, Mrs Thomas,' she says, and glances at the letter.

In her tiny room Daphne kicks her shoes onto the rag rug and sits on the edge of the bed. Even without sheets it is so much softer than those in Farnham, though smaller, all that can fit into an attic room under the eaves.

The air at the top of the house is stale, so she unhooks the latched window. Outside, the street is quiet as twilight takes hold, smog above the rooftops a pale green mist just visible under the last of the sun's rays. Across the road the Petersons' boy, Laurie, is off for a night shift. He has an impediment which has prevented him enlisting. The family are quiet on what that is and loud about his volunteering as an auxiliary fireman. Laurie Peterson must be proud of his uniform: though the July warmth still thickens the evening, he wears his steel helmet and rubber boots. The young man whistles very loudly as he rounds the corner and disappears. He needs people to see he is doing his part.

Daphne inhales the air. It is nothing like as fresh as the castle's: soot, the muddy stink of the Thames at low tide, diesel fumes. And dust, she thinks as she returns to her bed.

She places the letter on her lap and turns it over. Usually she would tear the envelope open immediately.

Not today.

Here is the stamp, red, with the King's and Queen's faces staring stonily at her address, which is written in her father's immaculate hand.

She does not know what she wants to hear. She hopes the news is good, but she has this feeling in her stomach which is like a curdling. Is it all bound up with this letter? Or is that simply fantasy? Is she piling things up, unnecessarily dramatising the significance of the missive?

She'll never find out if she does not open it. So, with fingers that tremble slightly, she removes the sheet of paper from the envelope and unfolds it.

Dear Daphne,

I hope this letter finds you well as can be expected in these difficult times. They say the theatres in London are still open so I expect you will be working hard to keep everyone's spirits up. Please give my regards to Mr Trevelyan.

I am, myself, writing this in my room at the Hotel Lanson and am glad to inform you that I may soon be joined by your mother. The internment camp is made up of several hotels with barbed wire all around. There are locals in there too who come and go freely. I am just outside of the camp and must report that my surroundings are very pleasant indeed.

Your mother has, as usual, charmed the local officers in charge of the camp for, as I said, they are allowing her to come and stay with me next week. In fact, although I err on the side of caution, a couple have dropped hints that she may not be inside the camp for much longer at all. Everybody seems keen to do the best by each other. That's what we've all got to do in these times. I am optimistic for a good outcome.

Unfortunately, the same can't be said for Uncle Giuseppe. I have not yet been able to find any more news of him. Your cousin Luciana went to live with Aunt Bertha a few years ago, after Gladys passed away. I don't think Giuseppe ever got over her loss, so in some ways, if we have the worst news then we can take some comfort in the thought that they will be reunited in Heaven. Bertha and Uncle Wentworth have written letters to the Ministry. Luciana is continuing at school and doing well from what I hear. Your mother is of course out of her mind with all of this worry, but it seems there is little we can do but wait. My liaison officer tells me that if we, her family, can prove that we are good, faithful and patriotic citizens who work hard for the country, then a case may well be made to release her from the camp. I am doing everything I can to follow the rules, and we think that Bertha and Lucy are too. Your mother has been told that there is a lot resting on the next month. I have no doubt that you are doing the best you possibly can, dear Daphne. You have always had a courageous heart, of which no one can doubt.

Let us hope everything turns out so we can get Mum back home as quickly as possible.

Fingers crossed.

Must be quick to catch the post. Try not to worry.

Love, Father

24 JULY 1940

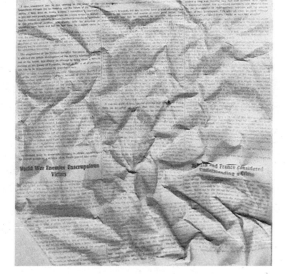

CHAPTER SEVENTEEN

'What does he say then?' Fairbanks addresses his question to Jonty, who is smoothing out the crumpled paper on his trouser leg.

The leaflet had been plucked from a hedge when they stopped to stretch their legs halfway into the journey. It was the suggestion of their driver, Fairbanks. He recognised the pair of them from the Farnham inspection and had much to say about the delight it had caused in the barracks afterwards. Daphne guessed that he had become a bit of a celebrity in the meantime, as he regaled them with comments the soldiers had made, mostly in response to the shock and confusion that the lieutenant general, Lord Bailey-Rae, had experienced throughout that day. Though some of the scenarios, she thought, might have been enlarged by an active imagination. She had, for instance, ridden a black horse which on one side had been covered in stripes, and had worn a Stetson. However, Fairbanks described a cowgirl in chaps toting a pistol and cracking a whip as she rode a zebra. It bore small resemblance to her own account. Though did it matter in the grand scheme of things? Probably not.

Their driver has developed a great deal more confidence since she last noticed him. She thinks, on balance, this is a good thing. War shreds the nerves and dampens the spirits. It is important to laugh when you can, and Fairbanks has had them chuckling a few times on this westward journey.

'My eyes are no good,' Jonty complains. He sighs, gives up and passes the leaflet over to Daphne in the back of the truck. Room is tight: the seat next to her is loaded with wooden crates. 'You have a go, dear,' Jonty instructs.

They are driving at over fifty miles per hour. Everything is rattling and shaking. It makes it hard to stay still and focus on the words. But she is best positioned to try. She reads the heading.

'Nazi propaganda,' she says, skimming it. 'A speech Hitler made to the Reichstag last week, allegedly.'

'Go on,' says Fairbanks, changing into a higher gear. The metallic pattering of the engine escalates. 'What are they trying to scare us with now?'

'Mmm. It's more about justifying their actions.'

'Pah!' Jonty exclaims. 'How?'

'Because of the Treaty of Versailles.'

Jonty makes a sucking noise with his teeth. 'That entitles them to invade France, does it?'

It is a rhetorical statement. She ploughs on. 'He says Mr Chamberlain obviously wanted a long war because we invested in weaponry shares and bought equipment for armament.'

'Rubbish!' This comes from the driving seat and is followed by a great snort.

Daphne concentrates – the translation is not good and the print difficult to read where Jonty screwed the leaflet up in contempt. 'Mr Chamberlain also spat at him, or something along those lines—'

'A likely story.' Jonty picks up the fabric of his trousers, shakes it free of creases and crosses his legs with disdain.

'Churchill, Eden and Cooper are warmongers, etcetera. We did something bad to the German fleet.' She squints her eyes again. It is so awfully composed, managing to be rambling, turgid and bilious at the same time. Quite a feat. 'Paragraphs on Norway. Finland. He blathers on about the Nazi German Reich being an incredible thing and then says everyone is going to be extremely grateful to them in the future.'

More scoffing back and forth. Fairbanks adds a laugh into the mix.

'Bluster, swagger, swagger, threat, threat, lies,' she goes on, bolder as appreciation wafts from the front seats. 'Good Lord – if this is a speech, he must have gone on for hours. Pity the poor audience.'

'Serves them right. Elected him, didn't they?' Fairbanks is correct, but she supposes not all Germans could have voted for the National Socialists. Though how many of those dissidents had survived the purges, nobody knows. Terrible rumours are coming out of Germany. Things that make a good woman with principles despair. If they are true, then what has become of humanity?

She breathes in and wriggles her shoulders to stop her thoughts derailing into a mental swamp. 'Anyway, he says that these months of war have strengthened their zeal.'

'Yet *another* likely story,' Jonty interjects.

Fairbanks slows as they turn into a road recently widened but not yet surfaced. 'You all right in the back? May be a bit of a bounce coming up.'

'It's fine,' says Daphne. The vehicle is equipped with an ill-sprung rear seat incapable of absorbing shocks from bumps on the road. It has been quite undignified at points.

'Cut to the chase then,' says Fairbanks, gripping the steering wheel. 'Where's the appeal to our sanity?'

'To "reason",' Jonty corrects in a mocking tone. It is aimed at the writer of the leaflet, not the driver accompanying them, so to differentiate he hastily adds, 'Reason – of which we have much, and of which that Charlie Chaplin impersonator has little. I mean, who was ever going to take him seriously when he's modelled himself on a clown? I really don't know.' He flops his hand across the open window then nods to his assistant. 'Please continue.'

'All right.' Daphne runs her finger across the page. There is so much bravado here. It doesn't even make sense. 'He says Churchill wants all-out war.'

Fairbanks yells over his shoulder, 'If that means not surrendering then fair enough, I'm with him. "We will fight them on the beaches." '

Daphne lifts her head to the driver and paraphrases. 'Hitler says he believes the prime minister has deserted the country. That he is probably in Canada with some children.'

'The dog's barking up the wrong tree there, ain't he?' Fairbanks titters.

'Quite.' She thinks it is highly unlikely Churchill will leave the country, as suggested. He is made of sterner metal. 'Ah, here we go: large amounts of suffering will begin. The Empire will be destroyed. But he says it is Britain that will be entirely annihilated. Mr Hitler can't in all conscience continue without warning our people of this.'

'Very good of him, I must say,' Fairbanks grunts.

'Any more?' asks Jonty.

'No,' says Daphne and begins to rip the paper into little pieces. She wants it out of the car.

'Weakened your resolve, has it, Mr Trevelyan?' Fairbanks asks with a snigger.

Jonty affects disinterest. 'Hardly. It's strengthened my resolve never to get stuck at a party with the buffoon.'

'You want to be careful about saying things like that,' cautions the driver. 'People might misconstrue you've been at such an occasion, in company like.'

'Good job it's only me, you and Daphers then.'

'Walls have ears, Mr Trevelyan. Mark my words.'

They turn into a smaller lane cut from forest. There is not a single human habitation in sight.

'Anyway, if that's the best they can do, then they must be desperate.' Fairbanks sounds quite cheerful about the impending invasion.

But Daphne is relieved. When Jonty spotted the leaflet dropped by German planes, she had felt her stomach fall once more. Her mood had been dire all night after she had read her father's letter and understood the message conveyed – unwittingly, she suspected – by the statements made to her mother and passed on: if she does not accept this mission, and all the sacrifices required, then it will not bode well for her mother's release. Those in command would absolutely know that this information would filter through via her father to her. It was something of a low blow, but then again, she is dealing with people responsible for devious espionage. And there is more at stake than the feelings of one woman. So when the car had arrived at her door this morning and she had been waved off by a beaming Mrs Thomas, she departed full of determination. She may have been left with little choice on the matter, but she could exercise free will over her attitude. Where some might feel manipulated into defeat, she would bring fortitude and effort to the mission. Her father thought she had a 'courageous heart'. She hoped it was true.

When the city sprawl had given way to fields that would be harvested soon, her spirits had lifted. Just a nip. It was good to be out of London again. They had not driven south to Farnham but instead taken a route to the West Country. Fairbanks informed them they were to be transferred to a headquarters in the New Forest. Other than that, there were no more details forthcoming.

For most of the way the sky had been cornflower blue above them, specked with white clouds, a light breeze taking the heat out of the morning. She had momentarily felt like she was going on holiday, the dampening fear of last night forgotten. But then they had stopped by the wayside and seen the leaflet. Though she finds now that she has been partly reassured by the contemptuous remarks of her companions. Britain will not be defeated. Germany will be. And she is to play her part in that. One day she might even tell her grandchildren about it. If she ever has any.

'*And do you always give two answers to any question?*'

She thinks of the man again. His hands on her waist.

Unable to repress a quickening that shoots through her stomach, she shivers. Perhaps this has something to do with the survival instinct that Harry has spoken of in several of his lectures. The flash of an image: two frogs engaged in an act of fornication. No, not fornication, reproduction. It is different if you are an animal. Or a reptile. If you are an animal or a reptile then it is necessary for the propagation of the species. If you are a *homo sapiens* and unmarried then it is a wicked fornication – and the shame of it, the shame of it, can stain you forever. This has been drummed into her by every grown-up who has ever been charged with the instruction of Daphne Devine and her peers.

Which makes her suspicious. Though she does not think herself the kind to get into that sort of trouble. Some of the girls, in the Soho dive bars, have already told her about equipment that can be used to prevent such a thing. They all sound grotesque. Not to mention what happens if you get pregnant and can't marry. She remembers one young woman who got herself in the family way and visited a lady reputedly skilled in magicking away unwanted babies. But the girl never came back. Some said she had gone away. Others that she had died in the operation and her body been disposed of.

It is a dangerous act.

Still, she imagines what it would be like to try it.

Imagination is the safest way.

Harry the zoologist had forgotten that ladies were present in that particular lecture and quickly sped the frog slide on – to the wolf whistles and wisecracks of the rest of the men. Neither she nor Brigit had blushed.

She wonders if Brigit has ever fornicated.

'Not long,' Fairbanks calls from the front and snaps her away from such thoughts. 'There's a good pub in that direction,' he says, and points to a lane coming off the main road. 'The Trusty Servant. Landlord does excellent ploughman's, all local, and sometimes he gives the Services a discount on the beer.'

'Oh really?' Jonty's languor transforms into enquiry. 'How much? Do you know, old fellow?'

'Not been. I've got a cousin down this way – Home Guard. He told me. I wouldn't mind going for a refresher now, if I'm honest. My mouth is as parched as a . . .' – his eyes swivel to Daphne in the rear mirror – 'desert.'

'Well, that is very parched indeed.' Jonty's voice is laced with great optimism.

'Gawd, I'd love to.' Fairbanks gets the drift. 'But the sergeant would have my guts for garters. Hopefully they'll have a brew going at the HQ.'

Planes have flown overhead constantly on their journey down. She has spotted a Halifax. Now she knows what Spitfires look like she keeps her eyes out for one. She has not seen any yet.

Through the window a picturesque little town has opened up, all shops and inns fronting a high street.

'Oh, this is nice,' remarks Daphne, though she thinks it old-fashioned. 'Are we staying here?'

'Not far,' says Fairbanks. 'A few of the officers are billeted at the Crown. We're just a bit further south. Burleigh Hall is your

HQ. And quite nice it is too. I'm sure you'll feel at home, Mr Trevelyan.'

Daphne rues the fact that they aren't staying in Lynthurst. The Crown is an old three-storey building with gables. Red brick gives it a solid and elegant look. It is directly opposite the church. The clock face tells her it is four, but there are no bells calling the time.

She must have murmured out loud because Fairbanks says, 'They're all quiet now. Will only be rung as a "Call to Arms" when, you know . . . the balloon goes up.'

She falls quiet. There it is again, that black shadow watching from the edges of everyone's consciousness, keeping them alert, second-guessing, vigilant.

No one speaks again until they see a group of ponies on the outskirts of the town.

'Look,' she says. 'Wild horses!'

A silly, girlish observation, but Jonty chuckles.

Fairbanks sniffs and with gallows humour observes, 'Won't be around much longer if rationing continues.'

Daphne decides she has gone off him.

A few miles on, the track cuts a sharp right. They motor up a small country lane, passing through a smaller village, nothing more than a hamlet, then take a path through a cluster of trees. Not forest but a wood, though it is thick enough to prevent the eye penetrating its dark shadows.

When they emerge the other side of it, the view that opens up is spectacular.

Burleigh Hall is bordering on palatial. A large Georgian building with wings on either side. It would be splendid, like something out of a Jane Austen novel, if not for the fact that the grand drive is a parking lot for various utility trucks, military cars and army vehicles. Nissen huts flank the building on all sides.

They pull up beside them and unload their bags – one each, packed with 'just the essentials'.

Part of the lawn has been turned over to a drill and exercise ground. There are soldiers marching in formation.

'Here you go,' says Fairbanks, slamming the truck door. 'Not bad, is it? For the foreseeable, this is what you'll be calling home.'

CHAPTER EIGHTEEN

The place is a hive of activity. People everywhere – fetching equipment across the hall, poring over papers in the corner. Unlike in Wormwood Scrubs, many wear uniforms.

She had supposed their headquarters would be devoted to their secret operation, but this is evidently a large base attending to other functions as well.

An officer has set himself up in the corner of the entrance hall, with a makeshift reception desk that once served as a kitchen table. A small flock of staff hover around him, like birds waiting to land.

Their driver strides up to the desk. 'Corporal Fairbanks, sir. Delivering Mr Trevelyan and Miss Devine. Operation Reynard, sir.'

The officer does not remove his eyes from the form, even as Fairbanks speaks. It is only at the mention of Reynard that he refocuses his gaze on the trio standing before him. Looking them up and down, a sudden smirk comes over his face. 'I see,' he says. 'Civvies.' It is a remark that Daphne thinks belongs nowhere. A pointless observation that he feels the need to articulate to himself. 'Please park your broomsticks outside and fly along to Room 11. Down the corridor, beyond the kitchen. The rest of the coven awaits you.'

For a moment none of them say anything. Daphne has frozen with horror. Not just at the content of his remarks but at his tone. So disrespectful and dismissive. And what is he talking about? Who is he?

Jonty has taken exception. 'I beg your pardon!' He is unused to being spoken to like this. Fairbanks and Daphne, both being of inferior rank, hasten to him.

'Thank you, sir,' says Fairbanks and salutes.

'Report back to me for assignation of quarters,' says the officer to the other two. 'Once you're fixed there.'

Daphne does not know how to address these men of military rank. It is all confusing. She turns, and with Fairbanks they usher Jonty's attention to the corridor.

Once they are out of range, Fairbanks makes his farewells. He hands them their bags and they struggle down the corridor.

'The cheek of the man,' says Jonty.

But Daphne is more concerned with his words. 'What does he mean, broomsticks and coven?'

'A coven is a group of witches! It was insolence. He is clearly sending up my profession as a magician.'

This pacifies Daphne a little. 'I didn't like it,' she says. 'You remember what they were saying in the initial briefing. All those dark arts that the Germans are intrigued by. What if we have to . . . I don't know . . . get involved?'

Jonty is elsewhere, though. 'He's clearly unaware of my pedigree. It does annoy me, the way these men of military rank think that the world revolves around them.'

'But we have been entertainers,' Daphne says. She wants to shake him and tell him that he's missing the point.

'Even so,' says Jonty.

The words the officer has used do not alarm Jonty. In fact, his reaction is starting to make her pause. Perhaps she is being oversensitive.

He is easily distracted. 'This place must have been

requisitioned in haste,' he says as they pass open double doors that lead into a fine room.

Some of the original fittings and paintings remain, but they have seen better days. No doubt anything of value would have been removed with the former occupants. Utilitarian tables and metal chairs take up space on the carpets over dark patches where large pieces of furniture must have lived for decades.

Here,' says Jonty. 'Room 11.' He knocks. A voice from the interior tells them to enter.

Furniture is scarce, but somehow the room looks like a Victorian painting. Dark, still and enclosed. High decorative ceilings and plaster corbels, original features probably, which have been kept intact. A beam of light creeps through curtains the colour of faded roses and illuminates dust motes spinning in the air. The picture would be completed by the insertion of a lady in a long silk gown, embroidering by the French windows.

But she is not there in the picture, frozen in time. Instead, in the corner two men and a woman are gathered about a table. It is very high, and it is only as they approach that Daphne sees that it is constructed from a door nailed onto two ironing boards. This operation has been set up quickly with whatever they could lay their hands on. And here is Septimus, if that is his real name, Cyril the agent, and another woman, whom she had seen at the first briefing in Wormwood Scrubs. Bunty had informed her that she was a priestess of a group called the Golden Age – Dodo Blaze.

She doesn't look like a priestess now. More like a teacher or something plain – the lady of a country house who enjoys keeping horses or grouse shooting. Her hair is rolled up, her green blouse un-frilled, skirt long, brown and unflattering. Her one concession to frivolity is a jade necklace.

Blaze is speaking firmly as they approach. She continues to hold the men's attention, even as Daphne and Jonty stand waiting for acknowledgement.

'. . . and was caught in a shower,' Blaze is saying. A larger lady, she has great presence, though her voice is light and soft. 'At the time I was seeking divine guidance and asked for a sign. It was then that I saw, in the east, a rainbow. And that's it, you see. That's what we must do. Now it seems obvious, but it hadn't occurred before. We must attune all efforts to turn Gerry's thoughts to that point – the east. Let them doubt the wisdom of coming west and turn instead to the east. The Order must be inducted into the ritual. This I feel with a great certainty. I will work on language to include.' She turns at last to the newcomers. 'Please come and be seated.' Blaze indicates a couple of stools.

Septimus stands up to greet them. His eyes are hooded, shadows beneath them. 'Ah, yes, do come and sit. I hope your journey wasn't too exhausting.'

Tea is on the table, a solid symbol of all that is good and civilised and British. Though next to the cups and saucers and teapot a buff-coloured folder is open. Its contents are spread across the tabletop. A chart has spilled out. She remembers the symbols from that visit to HQ. The zodiac is represented on it.

Without waiting, Septimus reaches for two cups and saucers.

Cyril's hand supports his chin. His pose is self-contained. His eyes flit across the paperwork. 'Dodo, here,' he says at last, 'has brought us Captain de Kohl's astrological chart. She has been talking to us about the importance of rituals and different seeds we can plant in the Germans' heads.'

She and Jonty look at Dodo. Dodo nods.

Septimus passes over the tea and says, 'Which is a good place to start with you. How much do you know about Reynard?'

Jonty takes his tea and shrugs. He is easing back into his deflective nonchalance now, which means he is concerned.

'He was a cunning fox who exploited greed and lust for power to his own ends,' Daphne offers.

Septimus appears amused. 'Apologies.' He dips his head. 'I was referring to your briefing. Operation Reynard.'

Propping an elbow on the table, Jonty leans back and stifles a yawn. He is very worried now. 'But, old chap, we haven't been told anything yet.'

Cyril clenches his fist and presses it against the fleshy parts of his lips.

Dodo blinks and shakes her head.

Septimus says, 'No instructions? No letter?'

They shake their heads and wait for him to proceed.

'Right,' he says. 'We'd better get on with it then.'

Daphne straightens, all ears, slightly afraid.

'Yesterday,' Septimus says, 'we spoke of the grave threat that we face, a threat that has been countered by our island before.'

'That's right,' says Jonty. 'The Armada.'

Cyril takes up the conversation. 'A victory, in that particular war,' he says.

Jonty, who is still trying to give off an air of indifference, says, 'Won because of Drake's immeasurable nautical skill.'

A glance is shared by the other three.

'That is what history tells us, yes,' says Cyril. 'But have you ever wondered about the story of the admiral playing bowls?' His pronunciation is distinct and tightly clipped, slowing for emphasis. 'Legend has it that when he was given news of the sighting of the Spanish Armada he announced he would finish his game before setting off. He was on the Plymouth Hoe at the time. The Spaniards were very close. Why such a leisurely approach?'

Jonty makes a scoffing sound with his lips. 'Pfft. Probably he'd worked out that the tides and winds weren't favourable to the enemy advance. Anyway, that's just a story invented by teachers to stop the schoolboys dozing off in History.'

'Is it?' Cyril asks. 'What is history if not stories?' He spears Jonty with a look, eyes murky. 'Have you ever stopped to consider who writes them? Why and who for?'

The question also gives Daphne pause. She has never considered such things before. But of course, yes, the history books are only one side of the story. Historians can't know *everything*.

'And who decides what is left out?' Dodo speaks now. She taps her finger on the table and moves her ample bosom forwards. The top of her blouse opens and Daphne sees a glint there. Previously concealed by the collar is a complex silver star with many points, shiny under the dull light, like a moving puzzle of lines contained within a circle. 'Especially when secrecy, the defence of the realm,' Dodo is saying, 'is what is at stake.' Her nostrils flare. She closes her mouth into a straight line and sits back. The shiny pendant withdraws behind the lapels of her blouse. When nobody, not even Jonty, speaks, her posture relaxes. Pleased to have elicited a silent, thoughtful response from her audience, she leans back and surveys them. 'There have always been rumours or stories, as we shall call them now, that Drake was a magician.'

Beside her, Daphne feels Jonty tense. He thinks the integrity of his profession is about to be debated.

If she has detected a change in Jonty, Dodo does not show it. 'He was friends with Thomas Doughty, who you would not have heard of. The mariner was executed for treason and . . . witchcraft. Drake too was alleged to have practised the dark arts. In fact, some put down his decision to finish his game of bowls to another tale. One which states that he, and a coven of witches, had carried out a powerful ritual the night before to raise a storm in the Channel and repel the invaders. To ensure an English victory.'

Cyril takes over the narrative. It is as if they have done this before. 'And this is what we intend to do. To gather a coven, some of the most powerful magical practitioners in the land, to recreate this dangerous ritual – the Cone of Power.'

Daphne is confused. When he says 'magical practitioners', does he mean illusionists? Though the word 'coven', Jonty explained, involves witches. But Miss Blaze is not being rude or humorous here. She has used the word as a descriptor.

'It is tricky and potent and dangerous,' Cyril is saying. He leans his knuckles on the table. 'It will exhaust us almost completely. And some of us will die.'

Now Daphne is alarmed. Why will there be deaths? Surely not human sacrifice?

'Which is why it has been undertaken only in times of great crisis – the threat of the Spanish invasion, once during Napoleon's reign. And now.' Cyril's voice is resonant. She can feel the boom of it in her blood. It is reacting there, speeding her heartbeat.

It is as if she is missing a large part of information and cannot understand his words. 'Stop,' she wants to say. 'Go back and start at the beginning.' But she restrains herself again. If nothing else at least she is learning that.

'Well, I don't believe in it,' says Jonty. 'It's nonsense.'

Such a quick and impulsive dismissal is impolite. Cyril makes a half-surrendering gesture, palms up, a shrug, so Septimus steps in. 'You'd think that, wouldn't you?' he says. 'We're learning a lot about the mind at the moment. There are specialists, not occultists, but those who study it and who believe that is where ritual resonates.' He taps his head. 'Here. In the inner landscape. And this, too, is where our power resides.'

Jonty agrees. 'I am aware that the power of suggestion lies in our brain, yes.'

'You use the word "power", for it *is* such,' says Septimus.

Cyril moves on. 'It is all the more easily accessed if we can utilise prompts – external signifiers, symbols – which amplify the human response.' He is coming to the point. 'And this in turn elevates consciousness to a certain level. Once harnessed—'

Septimus raises his hand and halts Cyril. He can see Jonty is not convinced. 'We have more faculties within than we yet realise. Ancient man, who had to fight each day for survival, knew this instinctively. He used such props.'

Daphne can see, in her mind's eye, cavemen donning horns to hunt. She is remembering headlines in the papers last year about extraordinary treasures unearthed at Sutton Hoo. It makes her think of Vikings and the old gods, the German Woden. Then her mind comes full circle back to the Nazis and the sinister fascinations which have brought her here. A different sense of foreboding visits her – not fear for herself, or for Jonty or her parents. But anxiety for the whole of the human species. How will it end?

'And used ritual to help them harness the forces within,' Cyril is saying. He understands the tack Septimus has taken with the magician. He follows it. Jonty needs to have his intellect fully engaged. 'And these forces are still there,' Cyril continues. 'We have not left them behind in prehistory. Though somehow we have let them fall into disrepair.' He pauses and watches Jonty keenly to gauge his level of belief. And commitment.

In the large room all is quiet. Daphne hears noise outside. It draws her eyes to the window. There, the gentle thud of a ball as it hits willow. A young man cries 'Out'.

It is incongruous that there should be men playing cricket in the middle of all this. But she is aware that this is life now – absurd and chaotic. Full of contrasts. Light and dark.

Darkness.

Of many shades.

It has settled over them.

She feels it near. An evil.

Though he does not translate it into words, Jonty is aware of a disturbance in the occupants of the room. Daphne's teeth have crept over her bottom lip. Gloom-laden thoughts, he muses. They will trouble us into paralysis. And that is no good for anyone.

Although he is uncertain and sceptical, he *is* interested in the proposition. As, of course, he was always going to be. He has no doubt that, since Hugh Devereaux knocked on his dressing room door, his old friend already had his strategy in place. Hugh was brighter at school, distinct, tactical, head of house and chair of the chess club. Himself and Daphne might have believed they had come here of their own free will, but all this time they have been herded. And here they are now, watching Hugh's endgame.

'So what is it you want from us?' Jonty asks. He has broken the spell that has held them.

Cyril looks up and places his arms on the table, palms flat. 'The ritual is called the Cone of Power. So that is what we need you to create.'

The agent has lost the magician and his assistant, though. Septimus sees this and adds, 'To *build* a Cone of Power.'

Jonty brings back his head and inclines it to show his confusion. 'But isn't that, as you said, all in the mind?'

'Yes,' says Septimus. 'But we need the participants to *feel* it is happening too.'

'Don't they all believe that anyway?'

Septimus shakes his head. 'We haven't enough real esotericists to perform the ritual so are recruiting local Canadian airmen. Jonty, you must use all your skills to create and exaggerate the visual representation of enormous power: the aethereal cone.'

At last Jonty understands. It is all tricks, smoke and mirrors. The muscles in his shoulders relax and he breathes out slowly. Well, he thinks, I can certainly do that.

'You, Daphne' – Septimus transfers his gaze. The girl is more important than the briefings state, though Hugh hasn't explained why or how – 'are to learn the ritual then aid the teaching of it. To train our personnel to perform it. The more realistic, the better.'

'But it is real,' says Dodo.

No one remarks upon this.

Jonty holds up a finger. 'Wait a minute – you want this "cone" to be seen?' There is a touch of something that is mistaken for disdain running through his words. 'Isn't that rather the opposite of all this cloak and dagger? If it has any real power, and I'm not saying it does, won't you want it kept secret?'

'We're working on that,' Septimus says. He has had the same thoughts but awaits further clarifications. 'You leave it to us. For now we must pledge you to silence. The "cloak and dagger" to which you refer is a necessary precaution. You will not breathe a word to anyone outside of this room unless you are given authorisation to do so. This will come from Mr Devereaux, and only from him.'

'Now,' Septimus says, bending over the chart on the make-shift table and pointing towards a circle with an arrow bisecting it, 'if the auspices are to be read correctly, the stars favour us at some point in September.'

'September!' spits Jonty. 'It takes at least six months of planning, engineering and testing to develop a new illusion. It's July, for goodness' sake. Totally unacceptable to timetable anything so soon.' He has one hand up and is shaking his head.

Daphne knows this is true. She has watched Jonty work with draftsmen for months, sometimes years, developing plans, producing prototypes and assessing different aspects before scheduling as much as a practice run.

'We're not calling the shots here,' Septimus says with quiet restraint. 'Adolf Hitler is, and he doesn't care about your standards of professionalism.'

The truth of this is dawning on Jonty, though his mouth seems to be operating independently of his will. 'You're suggesting we aim for a performance—'

'A working,' Cyril interrupts. 'That's what we'll be calling it: a working.'

'All right,' says Jonty with fading irritation. 'Scheduling "a working" with my illusion in barely two months based on a horoscope? It's a nonsense.'

Wondering if she should step in to calm him, Daphne leans forward and opens her mouth.

But it is Septimus who speaks next. 'We know there exists a high degree of belief in astrology in the enemy's High Command. If they think we are favoured on the fifteenth of September, it will undo them. That is what we focus on. It is the date you must work to. Think of illusions you have created before which may be adapted. And remember that there is method in what may appear madness. You are a small part of a larger picture.'

Daphne can see this has got through to Jonty, because he doesn't react any further.

'Now *again*, I must ask you to keep to yourselves the details of the mission. We have made available some of the finest men in the country to help you. But they need not be party to the overview of the operation. In fact, we advise against you disclosing details to anyone without clearance.'

'And how do we know who has got clearance?' Jonty asks. It is a sensible question.

Cyril smiles. 'Why, you have already met them.' He sweeps his hand over the table, indicating all present.

The gesture has an air of finality, as if he is concluding the meeting, which Septimus picks up on. 'Quite,' he says then taps his fingers on the table, twice, and speaks to Jonty. 'Given the timescale and your concerns, I suggest you start thinking about

what this cone might look like. At once. Go and familiarise
yourself with the workshop we have allotted. You will find it in
the last pasture before the lake.'

So that's it then, Jonty thinks. He had expected to be treated
with more reverence, such as that with which he was served at
the Oriental Theatre. Though this is the army, he acknowledges. Different priorities, no time for niceties or manners. If
this really *is* the army? Or is it the Secret Service? Or something
else? No one has actually told him. He thinks about grumbling
out loud, though his mind is already turning over ideas: power
equals electricity equals light. What does a cone created from
thought-matter look like? What about pure will? Does that have
a colour?

Daphne, however, is bewildered by the abrupt dismissal. She
does not know where she is to learn this 'ritual', from whom or
when. 'Don't we need badges or something to get through the
grounds?' she asks.

'Oh yes, that's right,' says Septimus and leaves the table for a
sideboard on the far side of the room. It is the only other piece
of furniture here. He selects two forms from a small pile and
waves them. 'Sign these, please, and then you must report to
the desk in the entrance. The officer will direct you to your
assigned accommodation. Drop your bags, check the workshop
and then we'll meet back here after dinner. There is much work
ahead of us.'

'I don't know,' says Daphne when they are out of earshot. 'It
all feels very strange.'

'It is what they want from us.' Jonty sounds assured, she
thinks. But then he knows what his role is – to come up with a
design for an illusion of sorts. He has done this many times
before and will be confident of his remit. It makes sense now
that they have selected him for this operation, however wild
and crazed it seems.

She, however, must learn a rite, work with occultists. Occultists, for heaven's sake! Who were they? What did it mean to be an occultist? She has no idea. Her landlady, Mrs Thomas, attended a weekly table-turning meeting, attempting to reach out to her brother long since passed. She had gone along once but never really taken it seriously. The notion that she might be working with lots of old women dressed up like Gypsies and speaking in tongues is foolish and ridiculous.

But then Daphne remembers a film she saw at the Palais about a golem brought to life by dark magic. Another flashes across her internal screen: a zombie resurrected by Voodoo. And a man bitten by a werewolf, enchantments from Tibet, demonic invocations. No, no, no. They are fantastic creations. But based on what? 'There's no smoke without fire' is her mother's favourite saying.

It is her imagination again – her deep fault. She is letting fancy fray her.

Stop. *Pull yourself together, girl.* She takes a deep breath. Nevertheless, the memories of the films have left a residue in her mind. Daphne does not want to acknowledge it, to say it out loud, to make it real, yet there *is* a thought looming in the recesses of her brain. A thought that is not easy to accept: what if it works? What if this ritual opens up, brings something new into the world? Into her?

No! As her lips move she realises she has said it aloud.

Jonty stops. His face changes. 'Daphne, I know I may have appeared reluctant. But it is our duty. We must cooperate.'

'Of course,' she says. His words have been spoken with a conviction that she now realises she must share. She recalls a tip from one of the showgirls in her early stage career: 'You can get away with anything onstage – if you do it with conviction.' And it is true. And this is a performance, after all. The decision is made. She feels it alter a part of her psyche and her pulse rate lowers. It is extraordinary, she thinks, how her mind changes from one minute to the next, and she understands that, at some point in the future, it will probably change back again and waver.

There is a new man on the desk when they hand in their forms. He has a sallow complexion, oiled black hair and a look about him that suggests he is going to shout at them. Daphne remembers his face – he was at the initial briefing. A cool cucumber who had said very little even when the lights failed and plunged them into darkness.

As they hand over their registrations, his eyebrows stretch. Underneath them his eyes are flush against his skin like a hare's and just as bright. His lips twist. 'Ah, Trevelyan, Devine. Yes, I've heard about you.' His voice is sharp, aristocratic, with a public-school confidence embedded there. He sniffs, holding his head at an angle so he is literally looking down his nose at them. 'Captain Tuckett.' He introduces himself with unnecessary reluctance. 'I shall be overseeing the operation here at Burleigh Hall. So you're to report to me.'

Is this true? Report to him? Surely Hugh is the one, or failing that, Septimus? She opens her mouth to question the instruction and then shuts it. She will only make matters worse. Instead she looks at her shoes. What is it that has made this man, and the one before him, so very cold-mannered? Is it her age? Her rank? Her class? Or is it her sex?

'I wouldn't let chorus girls anywhere near this base if it was up to me,' he snaps as his eyes run down her body. 'But it isn't, so behave yourself, keep quiet and run along. Chop chop. You,' he says to Jonty, 'are to be accommodated on the third floor. Your assistant is in the girls' quarters. Huts on the former croquet pitch.' And then he waves them off with his hands as if he is shooing away a cat.

Daphne's cheeks burn. Jonty whispers in her ear, 'I'll meet you at this workshop in half an hour. Is that enough time for you to unpack?'

She tells him it is, and picks up her bag. It is not heavy, but she thinks about when they travel for work. Ordinarily there are porters to help her out.

Now, though, her life is very different.

CHAPTER NINETEEN

Daphne discovers the workshop before Jonty. It is a good half mile from the main residence, surrounded by a thick circumference of trees. Mostly dark-leaved conifers, but there are some silvery birches in amidst them. It is secluded, so she has to circle twice before she finds the path that takes her into the enclosure.

The puzzle has the benefit of calming her nerves. She is slightly worried by what she may find there.

She need not have been concerned.

'The finest men', as Septimus had called them, turn out to be Ernest, a carpenter from the village in his sixties, and an engineer called Jack, who has apparently gone to fetch some water.

Ernest perches atop an upturned wheelbarrow on the lawn. The grass needs a bit of a trim, full as it is of dandelions and daisies. There is an old outbuilding made of wood, not much larger than a shed, laid into concrete foundations. The sun is dipping behind the tops of the ash grove that borders the plot on the west. Though it is still light, the tree-shadows crawl to their feet. Soon, twilight will yawn across them. The birds know it and are starting their nocturnal call to the nest.

'That's your workshop,' says Ernest between puffing on his cigarette and eating one of the several sandwiches on his lap – thick-sliced ham with pickles. His speech is accented with the local burr. Slow and casual.

The workshop doors are open: there is a small oil stove inside. The wooden sides are rickety, with cracks between the boards. 'It looks like it might blow down at any minute. Are you sure it's safe?'

'Been standing for a good hundred years, I reckons,' says Ernest. 'My father used to work here. Been like that since I was a child and no structural problems. Not yet.'

What Jonty will make of it, she doesn't know. She notices flowers planted in buckets and tubs around the side. They strike her as peculiarly beautiful.

'I brought cuttings from home,' says Ernest, watching. 'So much of the land has gone over to veg. I know we have to do this, keep the country fed, but seeing a splash of colour counts for a lot these days, don't it? Raises my morale, I'll tell you. And I know some of the boys stationed here.' He nods in the direction of the manor. 'They ain't got much and they're worried about where they'll be sent and what's going to happen next. Plants, flowers' – he pronounces it 'fleurers' – 'when they look lovely like these do, they make you think of better things. A living reminder, ain't they, that everything has its time.'

She agrees. 'We had some geraniums at home. They're cheerful. Not as healthy as these though. London smoke.' She shrugs.

'You one of those girls co-opted in?' Ernest asks, not in an unfriendly way. She thinks he is assessing her frame. Although she is slight, she can be sturdy.

'I'm not, no. I'm The Grand Mystique's assistant.'

This affects a change in Ernest. 'The heck? I thought you was from the Royal Engineers?'

Oh, she thinks. So she *is* missing a large chunk of information. Best play along with it. 'That's right,' she says, backtracking, and is about to go into some fabricated details enlarged from her training but Ernest's eyes move off her face to a point behind her and he breaks into a smile.

She turns round, and there HE is.

She cannot believe it.

The shock of his face hits her like a lightning bolt.

The Man from the pub.

He puts down a pail of water by his feet. Brigit is right – he *has* got well-muscled shoulders. As he straightens up and strides towards her with his hand outstretched, she becomes slightly breathless at the sight of him in breeches and braces, white shirt open at the neck.

'Here's Jack,' says Ernest, oblivious to the change of energy in the air. But Daphne can feel it quickening around her.

Jack – so that is his name! – takes her hand and shakes it. The excitement of the palm of his skin touching hers infects her with a prickliness which is not unpleasant but makes her super-alert. Is she holding it for too long? Is he? She begins to pull her fingers free but he twists her hand and raises it to his lips and plants a little kiss there. She is at once appalled by his audacity and in love with it. He laughs, reading her expression.

'This is Daphne,' says Ernest. 'Come to work from the Royal Engineers. With the Grand Mystique.'

'Is that right?' he says with a puckish grin. She smiles back and feels something go off in her stomach – like she has dropped an Alka-Seltzer in there which is starting to fizz.

She is starting to fizz.

'Yes,' she says. 'Well, no . . .' Then she laughs, remembering that night.

'Do you always answer like that, Daphne?' Jack asks playfully.

This time she says, 'It appears so,' and rolls her eyes and makes a face, as if she has been caught out. I'm like a silent screen actress, she thinks, all exaggeration and hyperbole. It is not how she imagined. In the well-rehearsed fantasy which had carved itself into her brain, she was in control, gliding into the Bush, tapping him lightly on the shoulder, ready to eat up his joy as he recognised her. He should have been the one taken off guard.

Ernest has at last tuned into the familiarity that exists between them. 'Do you two know each other?'

This time Daphne is on it. 'No, I mean yes.' She side-eyes Jack, who is appreciating her little quip. He pulls up another bucket, an empty one, and turns it over.

'Our initial meeting was unexpectedly cut short by a fight,' he says. 'Not between us.' He gives Ernest a wink and heads towards the open doors of the workshop. 'I'll fetch a stool. Can't have Daphne sitting on a pail.'

Her eyes follow Jack into the darkness of the hut and she realises that she has clasped her hands together tightly in front, has pulled in her head with delight and is practically squirming with pleasure. Like a blushing schoolgirl. She wriggles her shoulders out and makes them lower and unlocks her fingers. Takes a deep breath in.

Atop the wheelbarrow Ernest lets out a stream of smoke and narrows his eyes. 'You don't sound Canadian,' he says with suspicion. 'Not like 'im.'

'Oh no,' says Daphne. 'I'm not. Jack and I met in a pub.' His name is like liquorice on her tongue. She wants to say it again.

'Can't be too long ago. He only just got here last week.'

And he is back, with a robust three-legged stool that looks like something a milkmaid would use. She catches his scent as he passes. He plants it on the grass as though it weighs the same as a feather. His hair flops forwards. The sun lightens the golden threads in it. Then he stands and pushes back the wavy fringe to reveal clear sky-blue eyes and beckons her to sit.

She has him pegged at just a few years older than her. He has the confidence to show for it too. There is more than a touch of Errol Flynn in the way he holds himself, his purpose-ful carriage – long strides without self-consciousness, like he owns the place. Definitely one of the finer specimens of manhood that she has come across. Magnificent, she thinks. Really special.

'Reassigned,' he says, and offers his hand to help her sit down. She declines and tries to sit down elegantly. It is hard on a stool, though. 'What do you do?'

'Jack of all trades,' he says, taking out a packet of smokes from his shirt pocket. 'Engineer and explosives mainly.'

'Ah,' she says. 'That explains it.'

'Well, I'm glad you've said so,' he says. 'I was hoping someone might. Any clue as what we're to do? I've set up worktables and some easels for design. Not sure why though.'

'Oh well. It's probably best to wait for Jonty . . .' she begins and hears his voice coming from the bushes. 'Talk of the Devil and he is sure to appear. That's him,' she says and cocks her head towards the path where Jonty is sauntering in, hands in his pockets, looking like he hasn't got a care in the world.

As he emerges into the last of the sunshine and sees the grouping, his face clouds. He takes his eyes off them and glares at the shed. 'This is it then, is it?' he says, drawing up beside Daphne. Curtly, she thinks. He barely registers the two men, occupied in his appraisal of the hut. His mouth purses with obvious disapproval. Then he sighs and turns to them.

Ernest has hauled himself up. Unsure of how to address the newcomer, he salutes. Dressed in overalls with a rolled cigarette in one hand, it is quite a look.

Jonty at last smiles. 'At ease with you, dear chap.'

'This is Ernest,' says Daphne, and they shake hands.

Jack has also got to his feet. He introduces himself. Jonty exchanges greetings without enthusiasm.

She realises that they have used first names and wonders if

she has made an error in disclosing her own. Though she is sure she will be corrected if in breach of some rule. She motions to the workshop. 'I haven't been in so far.'

Jonty makes no move to enter it. Just stands there, his hands back in his pockets, turning something over in his mind.

'Allow me,' says Jack. He disappears and returns with a dilapidated canvas picnic chair. Daphne is pleased to see that Jonty thanks him for the courtesy.

Lowering himself into it, the magician sits down and fingers his collar. 'I'm parched. You haven't got a drink, have you? It's a hike from the main house. I had no idea.'

'They have a stove,' says Daphne. 'Tea?'

But Ernest points to his barrow and says, 'It's late now, sir. I've got a few flagons of home-brewed cider, if you don't mind taking the rough with the smooth?'

The effect on the magician is like oil over water. His eyes light up. 'That will do very nicely,' he says.

Jack is off again, as quick as you like, to retrieve some clean mugs and a flagon.

And so they sit in the half-light, on this most agreeable evening, and as Jack pours the drinks, Jonty details the practical basics of their brief.

'It should,' he says, 'resemble something that visually represents tremendous thought energy.'

'Why?' asks Jack.

'Because that is the requirement,' says Jonty firmly, giving nothing else away.

Ernest stifles something in his throat. 'What does thought energy look like then? Don't reckon I've never seen it.'

'It's a fair point,' says Daphne. 'I think, in my head, that energy is orange, maybe yellow or gold. Like a flame.' She sees Jack looking at her. A buzz of energy courses through her veins and heightens her wit.

'Good,' says Jonty, who has begun taking notes, a sheaf of papers balanced on his lap. 'I'm thinking of something like a giant lantern.'

'But without the casing?' Daphne asks.

'Possibly,' says Jonty. 'It'll need to be dug into a pit, for it will be used outside.'

'Where?' says Jack.

'Somewhere here, of course. In the New Forest,' says Daphne. 'I presume.'

Jonty necks the remains of his cider. 'So what have you got? Equipment-wise?'

Ernest leans onto his knees and pushes himself up in three jerky movements, then rubs his back. 'Old lawnmower, some wheels, iron scraps, and a fair bit of wood I've managed to snaffle.'

Daphne watches Jonty's face to see what expression will cross it now. He turns to the barn. 'I see,' he says, squinting through the open door. 'This may well take some time.'

'Till the fifteenth of September,' Daphne reminds him. She is suddenly sad that it is less than two months, but brightens at the thought that she will spend all of that time with Jack.

'All right, clever clogs,' says Jonty. 'I know.'

'She is though, isn't she?' says Jack, looking at her again.

His eyes burn. She can feel them strobe her cheeks.

'What?' This from Jonty.

'Clever.'

Daphne starts to glow.

'Oh, she is that,' says the magician, though he does not smile. 'As I'm sure you'll find out.'

The deputy treads lightly down the stone stairs. The two men descending after him synchronise their footsteps. Theirs is a heavier tread. Both officers are bigger, and he knows that if he were to halt, they would have to use every ounce of concentrated effort, every muscle in their legs to still themselves and avoid a humiliating tumble. On other days he might have stopped to see what would happen – turning around, striking a pose, one finger perhaps lifted into the air as if he had remembered leaving something of importance in his office. But today there is no need. The prospect of other activities appeases.

Ahead, behind the curve of the stair where the steps meet the dungeon's floor, he hears scuffling. A sentry is rousing himself, scrambling up, urgently checking his uniform. There is a cough. A whispered word, 'Quick.'

They will be standing to attention, readying themselves to greet him.

He enjoys the feeling he inspires in others.

Fear has its own consolations.

All those years spent overlooked, underestimated, unheard. If only he had known what was to come. No one dares ignore him now. Far too aware of what might happen if they incur his wrath, it has bred a certain type of loneliness, but he thinks, all in all, that it is a fair exchange.

The soldiers' acrid sweat is tinged by a surge of adrenaline, the odour of panic. He smells them before they come into view. It would *make him smile, but that is the entirely wrong signal to give. He lets his shoulders broaden as he marches into the subterranean stone lobby.*

The stench down here is not pleasant. Damp and mould mix with another feral scent. No wonder the guards have chosen to close the doors. He doesn't blame them. It is disgusting, the odour of weakness.

Here they are then, the two sentries. Despite the temperature, sweat coalesces on their lips. They stand stiffened, their faces immobile, eyes focused straight ahead on the other wall.

He nods to the door.

The guard on the right, closest to the lock, about-turns and bends to fiddle with it.

The deputy hears the click and the door is pulled open. But the officer does not go straight in. Instead, hesitation blends with repulsion as the concentrated odour wafts through and engulfs them all.

He clears his throat. There is no choice now but for the officer to open it fully and enter. 'In,' he commands.

The guard obeys.

The corridor within is lit by flaming torches. Burning oil adds another tone to the meaty, sulphuric smell that he associates with this place and a couple of others he has visited recently. One of the officers behind him gags. He chooses to overlook it.

The lights are an unnecessary flourish, he thinks; they seem overly dramatic, almost feminine. 'The torches,' he tells the soldier who is pacing down to the next door. 'You do not need them.'

'Oh,' says the guard. 'Yes sir.' And he reaches up to take one. Dark patches in the armpits stain the guard's uniform. 'There is a water butt. I will extinguish them.'

'No,' he says impatiently. 'Not now. Afterwards. Light is not necessary down here.'

The guard is momentarily confused and turns his body from the waist up towards him, his arm still in the air, half extended.

'I shall need a torch.' He tuts and rolls his eyes as the guard, flustered, returns his arm and takes down the torch, offers it over and salutes.

Needless, he thinks, but takes the torch, which is warm in his hand.

'The larder.' He nods to the door. Really he should stop using that term. It is what the guards have named it. This grim humour helps them suppress their own horror, he supposes. Which is weakness. But still. 'Open it,' he barks angrily, though the anger is only with himself.

'Yes sir.' The guard springs into action, hops round and unfastens a key from his belt.

Now he cannot stop himself holding his other sleeve to his nose as the door swings out and the stench intensifies. It is utterly repellent, even to him, but he cannot show this. He takes a deep breath and enters the darkness.

It is funny how they always look like meat to him. Sides of pork or hanging cow carcasses stacked up against the sides. You can only fathom their humanity in the threads of cloth still attached to them. Some hardly move.

The torch illuminates their faces. Though he thrusts it close to them, most no longer register nor recoil from the flame. Their senses surely fled some time ago. But one, young, raggedly bearded, turns his face to the light.

It is a slow movement, but something flashes in those dark eyes.

Though it is gone in a blink, he imagines it is the lingering residue of defiance.

'This one.' He licks his lips and points to the bearded face. 'Bring this tonight.'

25 JULY 1940

CHAPTER TWENTY

'You must empty your mind of all other thoughts.' Miss Sabine's voice rings out like a brass bell.

Right now, Daphne is still alive.

The future is in the present.

Her heart beats a little faster, invigorated by the prospect of romance, of sex and of purpose. She replies to this woman, who Septimus described as an occultist, 'Easier said than done.'

She is not being flippant. Last night she was unable to sleep, kept awake by the snoring of one of the girls, Esther, a seamstress from London who had come down to help Vivian Steiner manufacture the 'ritual' robes for the working.

She had bumped into the couturier at supper in the mess. Or rather, outside it. The girls had to wait until all the officers had been fed before they were seated. It hadn't been like that at the castle, and she was very put out. The other girls looked at her with disapproval. One muttered about ideas 'above our station'.

Steiner had a large antiquarian book stashed tightly under his arm. Evidently he had been promoted. Or had wormed his way up the ranks. Knowing Vivian, she suspected the latter. The couturier greeted her like a lost friend. 'Miss Devine,' he said. 'I say, you know they've attached me to the Royal Engineers now. That's what we were apparently. At the castle. Nobody tells me anything, what.'

She understood the feeling well.

'Been dispatched here to run up some magical-looking robes. Objectives: to shock and inspire awe.' He was enthused and spoke in a rush as if to get all his thoughts out before they ran away from him. 'Wouldn't mind you running your eye over them, as you've been in the same kind of business, haven't you? And no, don't worry, it won't be like Farnham, I promise. Aubrey Sharpling's still there, you know. Aeronautics. There's some sort of performance going on. No, not there. Here. You in on it? It's all very hush-hush as far as I can gather.'

'Yes,' said Daphne when she was able to find a gap in his monologue. 'I know.'

He poked wire-framed glasses back up his nose and grinned. 'Fascinating stuff,' he said. 'This mystic whatnot. I've been looking at symbols in the Key of Solomon. Chap called Gerard Potter sent it through.'

'Oh yes.' She remembered him from the briefing in the Scrubs. A tall, wiry fellow with bushy white eyebrows. Another occult practitioner.

'That's right, give it some authenticity, or, you know.' He swung his hips a little to the side and hugged the book to his chest. 'Pentagrams.' Then before she could work out what he meant, or what it related to, he was off again. 'I've recruited some of the local girls and requisitioned sewing machines. I'm thinking black silk, if I can get hold of it. If not, something with a sinister sheen. Would you care for a look at the studio? I won't make you model the prototype, promise,' he added with a grin.

She declined, reluctant to lose her place in the dinner queue, but agreed to visit another time.

The couturier leaned his dark curly hair to her and lowered his lips to her ear. 'Bad news about Ross's sister, I'm afraid,' he whispered.

Ah, the ventriloquist from Farnham. She remembered his unfortunate relatives in Yeovil. 'Oh no,' she said. 'What? Did they find her?'

'Survived the bomb blast, but won't walk again. In hospital for the foreseeable.'

'That's terrible,' said Daphne. 'I will write to him.'

And so later, when she had retired to her quarters, she penned a note of condolence. It was thoughtful and long and sincerely written. She was pleased with it but knew there was another letter she too must send. Resting a book on her knees to lean on, she penned an epistle to her father. It was harder going than her note to Ross – this communication was likely to be intercepted. No doubt the contents would reach the ears of her commanding officers, and certainly Hugh Devereaux, whose right side she needed to stay on.

After sucking on her pen for a good twenty minutes, she succinctly expressed passionate delight at the opportunity presented: to play a part in the war effort. Telephony, she added, was not for everyone, but she was learning a great deal every day. Hopefully it would be enough to encourage her mother's release. Though she suspected it would not happen quickly; her mother's fate was a carrot dangling before her. The authorities would be reluctant to relinquish such leverage.

And yet, though her dedication had been committed to paper for all to see, the words remained insincere: not all of her submitted so easily. There still lurked a dark worry at the back of her brain. Something that seemed small, like a crow, but which could rear up and spread its wings, like those of the three-jointed albatross, and become huge. It took effort to will it away. Fighting against such instinct was counter-intuitive. Like so much she was becoming involved with.

When she had finally fallen asleep sometime between 2 a.m. and 4 a.m. she had dreamed of dark things, castles and Uncle Giuseppe, trapped at the bottom of the ocean, breathing bubbles that were pearls, speared by the beaks of kingfishers. Crabs crawled across his eyes. On his head he wore a crown of thorns.

She awoke with a moan, thankful not to have disturbed her roommates in the surrounding bunks. But her mind, coupled with Esther's snores, would not let her return to sleep.

So when she arrived in Highcliffe, eight miles south of Burleigh HQ, a few hours later, she felt fatigued. She did not like this separation from Jack either. It made her feel slightly fearful, though she wasn't sure why. Was she jealous? Worried someone else might nab him? Or was it another feeling she couldn't put a name to? She had decided to concentrate on the positive aspect – that they had met again. How fortuitous, how lucky. What destiny.

This focus worked.

In the bathroom she began to hum the Benny Goodman tune they had danced to. Jack's eyes as he spun her, the pleasure of seeing him again. It was all so . . .

Her host, Miss Sabine, allowed her a half hour to refresh herself but primly told her not to dawdle and that there was much to be done if she was going to learn how to approach the 'working'.

Daphne washed in a small pink-tiled bathroom, then was given a shapeless robe to wear. As she slipped it over her head, she saw in the mirror that it resembled something a monk might wear, a habit of sorts. Though it was lighter. Like herself. The effects of both rationing and drilling, she supposed.

She folded her day clothes and left them on a wooden chair, then was directed into a room which Miss Sabine called her 'temple'.

It was hard to believe anything of a spiritual nature might occur in this twenty-year-old bungalow. Externally it looked the very picture of suburban respectability. On the outskirts of Christchurch, not far from the sea, the streets around Miss Sabine's home were neat and tidy, formed of rows of squat bungalows with unadventurous front gardens, some turned over to vegetables now. It spoke of quietness, conservative tastes and conformity. So at odds with her tutor's particular esoteric practice.

Daphne's imagination had already created the notion that a temple would be full of gold leaf, intricate carvings, jewelled ritual tools and unknown deities, but she was disappointed to discover that Miss Sabine's was a second bedroom off the narrow hallway that ran widthways across the house from the entrance. It had no bedroom furniture and was sparsely decorated with rugs over the boards and a number of scatter cushions. There was a large bookcase with lots and lots of hardbacks. Some looked very old. And spooky. Across the mantelpiece over the hearth, stood a pile of candles in different colours: red, purple, black, yellow. Above were pinned images of occult symbols.

Her instructress bade her sit, and lit a candle. Then she too sat on a cushion cross-legged, with her hands on her knees, like some Eastern pagan deity, and told her to empty her mind.

'Focus on the flame.' Miss Sabine's accent is almost queenlike. Yet she is most certainly not aristocratic. Not living here.

'Yes, I will,' says Daphne. Then, 'Why are all the candles different colours?'

'Shh, later. Look at the flame,' she commands in her perfect English.

Daphne's eyes travel back to her strong-jawed, handsome face.

'Look at the flame. See the colours within.'

Daphne obeys.

A translucent globe, edged with purplish, blueish shades. Above it the round-tipped gaseous ball bobbing, reaching higher. All that exists is not always visible, she thinks as she watches.

After a few seconds: 'Close your eyes.'

Behind Daphne's lids the flame tip is there, a light brown halo.

'Breathe in deeply.'

She does.

'Relax.'

She awakes to find Miss Sabine standing over her. Somehow she has fallen asleep and has no memory of anything after the candle.

Her instructress has Daphne's clothes in her arms. She holds them out. 'I intuit that you need some fresh air and a change of scenery. It seems I may have underestimated the toil your duties have taken thus far. Please dress and meet me outside.'

It is gusty this afternoon and they set out. Miss Sabine wears a hat and holds it to her head. They walk past an open stretch of land that is being fenced off by soldiers. 'Aviation,' she explains.

Daphne nods. She doesn't say anything. She is just glad for this small freedom to walk outside and remove herself from all the imperatives that persist in the narrative of her present life. It is a welcome break.

In a few minutes they have reached what looks like a natural harbour at the beachside. They stroll along the seafront. Fishing boats are returning from the trawl, trailed by looping seagulls who know there will be fish guts to feed on soon.

'There,' says Miss Sabine and points to a bench. They both sit down and face the sea.

The older women emanates a certain mental stillness which draws Daphne. After a while in Miss Sabine's presence, people calm.

A strange, almost liquid tranquillity pools around them now as they gaze out at the Channel. An island in the distance rises out of the gauzy heat shimmer. The Isle of Wight? She isn't sure. Her geography has never been that good. The sight of it prompts the memory of another very much in her thoughts. How is her mother? she wonders. Will her letter ease the anxiety she must be feeling as a prisoner in the camp? Might her father show it to the authorities? Will he even have to? She thinks it is likely it will have been read and reported as soon as she handed it to the post boy in the manor.

'Breathe it in,' says her instructress and takes down a whole lungful of sea air. 'Marvellous, isn't it?'

Once again Daphne obeys.

'You've lost someone already,' says Miss Sabine suddenly.

She looks at her, shocked, unsure if this is a question or an observation. She treats it as the former. 'My uncle was on the *Arandora Star*. We have not received any news of him.'

'Very worrying,' agrees her tutor. 'War disrupts everything, but it is here. And we are here, in these incarnations, and can do little to avoid it.'

'Incarnations?' Daphne thinks of choirs singing and people chanting around fires.

'Not incantations,' says the esotericist, as if hearing her thoughts. 'An incarnation is a lifetime, spent in this particular vessel.' She taps her pale wrist and the watch strapped there. 'The body you inhabit. Some believe that when you die, your spirit is reborn into another vessel, another body.'

'Oh?' says Daphne. 'So you never really die?'

'The belief is that you work through different problems in each lifetime.'

'Is that so?'

'Some believe our souls are on a journey. Towards enlightenment. The Hindus call it the atman, an immortal self.'

Daphne thinks the process sounds exhausting.

Sun is coming through the clouds to the west and is dazzling upon the water.

'There are two approaches we can take to the obstacles that we face now. We can wring our hands and be frightened, or we can accept what it is we face and be grateful that we can act, confront it.'

'I worry about things,' Daphne says. 'About what might happen.'

Miss Sabine lays a hand on her arm. It is the first time any physical contact has passed between them. 'We all have concerns about the future,' the older woman says. 'So many are depressed. And with good reason. There are things one can do, however. You asked about the candles.'

It is not the turn of conversation she is expecting. She is thrown a little.

'You have a powerful aura. I can see it, Daphne.'

Instinctively she puts her hand to where the older woman is looking, somewhere over her hair.

It makes her tutor smile. 'Don't worry – it is a psychic phenomenon which only the initiated can "see".'

Initiated into what? Daphne wonders.

'There are practices,' Miss Sabine goes on, 'that you can use to channel your energy into defending your loved ones.'

'But how?'

A light goes on in her tutor's face. 'Oh, I see what you mean. Yes, we believe that we can only sense a fraction of what is going on around us. That there are dimensions we cannot perceive but which exist. Like dogs – they can hear a dog whistle which is so high a frequency human ears don't register it. We are deaf to it. Similarly, in the Order we think that there is more to the universe than that which we experience and currently comprehend. We use magic to channel and tap into these unseen elements. For we believe they have force, power that we can put to use.'

Daphne has heard her reference this 'Order' before, but that is not what has pricked her attention. 'How do I protect those I love?'

'Yes, the ones you love.' Miss Sabine's eyes contract and narrow, as if Daphne has trod on something inside her. 'I trust, as you are unmarried, the love you mention is pure?'

Daphne feels the older woman's eyes roam over her figure, searching for clues.

Miss Sabine's lips wrinkle. 'Please tell me you have controlled your appetites? Not yet experienced fleshly sin?'

'Oh.' Daphne now understands. Part of her is outraged, part of her is nonplussed. It is a strange dichotomy. 'I'm a virgin, if that's what you mean?' She thinks she might be pouting and looks out to sea. The waves are foam-topped: white horses storming angrily. Her stomach grumbles too.

'It's important we know.' Her tutor's voice has a plaintive quality. 'The ritual, your part, it's reliant—' She stops suddenly, as if she has let down her guard, said too much. 'No matter.' She adjusts her tone and returns to Daphne's initial question. 'To shield your loved ones you must use the spectrum of blue. The brighter the better. It is the colour of protection. When we go back, you can visualise a sphere which surrounds them. And that sphere should be filled with an electric blue. Think of the bars on a heater, the blue you see sometimes in a flame. Catch it, fill it with your energy, then imagine it surrounding the ones you love. And while you're at it, you can put one over my house.'

With fresh intention Daphne nods and says, 'I think I'm ready to give it a go.'

'Excellent. Purpose distils resolve and concentration. I should have thought of it myself before we embarked on our first exercise.' Miss Sabine holds her hand to the path down which they have come. 'It will be a good test before we conduct the ritual tomorrow.'

Daphne has been told that the real instruction will take place then. 'I will, but I'm rather famished. Haven't eaten since breakfast.' She sends her tutor a hopeful gaze.

'Well, that is splendid,' said her tutor. 'Hunger always sharpens the mind.'

And strangely, it does.

In the temple, cross-legged and sitting opposite her tutor, she lights a blue candle and imagines a large globe which she takes time to fill with brilliant azure. She enlarges it over the seas, over the land and settles it over the Isle of Man. Then she puts a smaller one over Jonty, Ernest and Jack. 'Protect the ones I love, protect them all.' Only later, as she fades from the room and the darkness clouds around her, the thought passes: 'To whom am I praying? Whom do I ask for help?'

Miss Sabine and these people are not Christians.

So if not God, then who?

She silently curses.

The British government wouldn't rally the forces of darkness. Would they?

26 JULY 1940

CHAPTER TWENTY-ONE

When Daphne emerged from the temple, the bungalow was empty. In the kitchen she saw on the clock that that she had slept for fourteen hours. Fourteen hours! She couldn't remember the last time she had slept that long.

Her dreams had been vivid, full of colour and energy.

Dreams had always been of interest to her, but for entertainment purposes, not by way of finding meaning in the mundane. She preferred not to think of her recent nightmares.

A note from Miss Sabine, on the kitchen table, instructed her to make an omelette: fresh milk was in the pantry. The eggs were laid out beside it. The lines of vegetables stored in the dark cupboard were indeed a sign that she was out of London and somewhere near farms. They had nothing like that back in Southwark.

After breakfast she dressed and went into the back garden. She sat, then lay down on the neat lawn with her arms behind her head. Someone had mowed it a few weeks ago. But now daisies and clover were pushing up through the grass. It had been a good while since she had had some time to herself.

Clouds were blowing leisurely across the sky to the north-east, allowing intermittent shadows to float over her. Sweetened honeysuckle scent wafted in from an adjoining garden.

A black cat poked its head through a rosebush and stared at her. Miss Sabine had mentioned that she had one but it had so far stayed away. No one was around. Maybe she might take the opportunity to roll down her stockings and let the sun get to her legs. They were very pale.

Soon the clang of metal upon metal gives way to a rusty squeak. Someone is coming through the gates at the front. She sits up and pulls her stockings into place. Minutes later Miss Sabine pads out of the house with a bunch of roses in one hand and a half-filled bucket in the other.

'Good afternoon,' says her tutor and carefully places the roses head first into the pail. 'Glorious sunshine today. The auspices are good.'

Daphne doesn't know what to say and so nods.

Her tutor fetches an old wooden deckchair and sets it up next to her on the lawn. 'Do you need one for yourself?'

'Why not?' says Daphne.

'There's another in the shed, and a small table.' Miss Sabine points to a small structure at the back of the garden. 'Tea?' she asks. Daphne thinks she looks much prettier when her features lift.

'Lovely, yes please.' She pushes herself up onto her knees, brushes her hands of dead grass and walks down the garden path to the shed.

It is dim inside. The wood retains the heat of the day. Sweat wicks into her clothes. There is the deckchair and a small table the size of a piano stool. As she picks them up, a sheet which has been lightly covering another piece of furniture comes too, revealing a board with the alphabet printed in a semicircle at the top. On one side, there is a circle which reads 'YES'. On the other, 'NO'. A Ouija board. She has seen them in films. Generally with poor outcomes for the users.

It dawns on her that she does not know enough about the people she will meet. It has been assumed that because she and Jonty had their backgrounds investigated by the Security Service before Hugh's approach that everyone else has too. But this is built on logic, not evidence. They are separate things.

Even if Miss Sabine is channelling entities or engaged in dark practices, it wouldn't prevent her working with the government. The brigadier and Hugh Devereaux have made it clear that the country is in such a dire state, invasion so close, that anything is possible. If that means invoking demons and devils, then so be it. But she does not like the idea.

She hears the instructress returning to the garden with a tray – pieces of crockery are knocking each other lightly. 'All right there?' Her voice carries concern. Or is it disapproval? So hard to tell without seeing the expression framing the words.

'Yes, yes,' she says and covers the board again quickly.

They put up the second deckchair opposite the first. Miss Sabine sets the tray on the little table. There are scones on a plate with jam and a pot of tea and cups. She offers a pot of cream. No butter. 'Please help yourself.'

'I'm not particularly hungry now,' says Daphne. She hasn't long eaten, and now there is a knot in her stomach that extinguishes any appetite.

Her instructress checks her wristwatch. 'You must. But then nothing else until we've done the working. We'll eat afterwards.' It is a statement of fact.

From under her fringe she watches Miss Sabine spread jam on both scones. Clear grey eyes and a very pale face framed by gingery hair. She could easily pass for a member of the Women's Institute or the Women's Voluntary Service.

'Before we commence the ritual tonight,' she says, adding cream to the scones, 'we will cast a protective circle.' She pours the tea and adds milk. 'We must only work within its perimeter. Do not step outside it.'

Daphne takes the offered cup of tea. It is hot and scalds her throat. 'Why?' she asks, doing her best to hide her feelings of disquiet.

Miss Sabine bites her scone. Next she takes a tiny sip of her tea, then licks her lips. 'We aren't the only creatures on earth drawn to others' energy,' she says, as though speaking of such commonplace irritants as the wasps that have begun to hover round the jam. 'Occasionally otherworldly beings come out to see what's going on. Several are curious. A few might be drawn by the fancy of a little nip. Others won't have the best intentions.'

Daphne tries to wrap her mind around this and turns over what other beings there might be. Miss Sabine, she guesses, does not refer to mice or foxes.

'They may be vampiric in nature,' her tutor continues.

It startles Daphne. Her teacup wobbles and splashes liquid over the side onto her skirt. 'What?'

A flash of displeasure wrinkles Miss Sabine's nose. 'Oh, nothing like that. It's a metaphor,' she says matter-of-factly. 'Vampires take. They do not give.' Her composure and attitude speak of complete acceptance of their existence. She might be explaining a card game. 'I'm sure you know many people like that. Half an hour in their company and one finds oneself exhausted. Thus it is wise to repel those with such capacities. Some elementals.' She takes in Daphne's widening eyes. 'Paracelsus's sylphs, for instance.' When her mentee's expression does not change she adds, 'Air spirits,' and then, 'Oh, never mind. Forget about that. We haven't got time to go into it now. Leave the protection to me. Just ensure you remain in the circle.'

Her pupil nods. The instructress is either as crazy as they come or the wisest woman she has ever met. A shudder takes hold and finds its expression in a jerking of her shoulders.

Miss Sabine notices. She is not pleased. Her voice hardens. 'If there is anything us Britons are good at it is sangfroid. You need to use it now,' she says. 'Button up.' Her eyes bore into Daphne.

It is uncomfortable to be inspected with such intensity. To misdirect the woman's attention she drops the half-eaten scone and catches it with her plate. The scone crumbles into pieces. It is classic sleight of hand.

'Oops, no harm done.'

Daphne makes the decision to press on with another question that has been on her mind: 'So does this, I mean, the magic, the ritual, does it have anything to do with the Devil?'

Miss Sabine's eyes flash. Daphne wonders if she has gone too far. But then the staid older woman throws back her head and hoots. Her shoulders go up and down, up and down. The laugh that comes out of her is not ladylike at all but full-throated and genuine. She throws her hands up in the air and then brings them down with a light clap as her body rocks forwards and backwards, to and fro. After a good two minutes she is able to regulate her breathing enough to manage speech.

'Oh,' she says at last. Her hand flies up to her mouth and covers it in a late show of modesty. 'Goodness me, I must apologise.'

Miss Sabine takes a breath and plucks a handkerchief from her sleeve. 'In our circles,' she begins and wipes her eyes, 'we are not limited to one god.' She wheezes, and folds the handkerchief and drops it into the hammock of her lap. A bird flies across the garden and casts a brief shadow over her face. She rearranges herself in her chair and takes another sip of tea.

'Hitler,' Daphne adds, 'is a Luciferian.' She remembers the paper she had to Roneo. 'At least, I know some of the High Command are followers.' And another thought comes upon her as she speaks: that she will find this out first-hand.

'I am not surprised,' the older woman says.

Daphne is struggling to dismiss her foolish and unprovoked notion. How absurd she is. The idea is a product of her uncontrolled imagination. And bad dreams.

'Lucifer,' says Miss Sabine, 'is an agent of chaos and destruction. The pictures of Wieluń.'

Daphne immediately understands her meaning. It has been all over the papers, photographs capturing the destruction of the town, rubble, dust, crumbling buildings. The place was pummelled into the ground, as if the aggressors' intentions had been not to conquer or dominate but to annihilate simply because they could.

'Sickening,' her host continues. 'All those innocent civilians. It was nothing short of terrorism. Which makes our work even more important.' Her jaw tenses with resolution.

'I suppose they think they're right in some way? To do that.' Daphne cannot imagine why else one might commit such atrocities.

Miss Sabine's voice drops. 'Power has its own darkness. Like a drug, an opiate. It is an intoxicant which inspires avarice and greed for more. For some it is a god. Certainly we can see from history that once it is worshipped, it takes over the soul of its devotee. Nothing else matters to them. Not their conscience, which is excused, swept aside in the pursuit. And not their people, who may be seen as purely an organism, a faceless mass that must be bent to the user's will. Like the railway train, they are fuelled by its energy: power. All they wish is for more and more: absolute power. And, as a wise man once pronounced, *that* corrupts absolutely. Ultimate power cannot sustain itself and so sickens, poisons its vessel, like a virus or a disease. Likely it's some type of inbuilt safety catch, as it were?' she asks herself.

'And thus it ensures that the man who seeks it will fall and fail. Perhaps it is the greatest illusion of all.' She drifts off into her own ruminations.

Despite her misgivings, Daphne has not yet heard such a lucid analysis of the present war in Europe. All of it is the collateral damage of one man's thirst for expansion.

In the near distance the whine of a plane brings Sabine back. 'But that process of decline can take time,' she says, 'and that is exactly what we haven't got.'

Their moods have changed. Daphne forces herself to sit erect in the chair.

Mustering momentum, the instructress slaps her lap, looks at her charge and says, 'An important element of the ritual you will see tonight is the chalice that will be passed around. You must drink from it. Such sharing occurs in many rituals – think of the Mass. All elements are present: earth, air, fire and this water. It is holy, from a local well that is sacred, full of healing properties. Miracles have taken place there.'

Daphne is starting to feel excited. How will it feel, she wonders, if magic happens?

'When you are asked to pour in your will, you must do it as you have with the candles. Imagine it travelling out of your physical being to the point indicated. And that, my dear, is all you need to know.' She lets her hands drop to her sides and her voice becomes teacherly again, assuming a higher status to her mentee. 'We should prepare.' She starts tidying up the empty cups and saucers. 'Wear your summer coat over the tunic. Bring a cardigan in case it gets cold later.'

'Bring it? Aren't we doing the working here?'

'Hardly.' Miss Sabine wipes a crumb from her mouth with the handkerchief. 'We're to go over to the Masons' temple. Don't fret. It's not far. They have a section of wood in their grounds which is quite private, no one will be heard or seen.

The trees are thick. There's a clearing. Mr Eldridge will be along in a little while to pick us up. So do hurry along.'

'Hurry along to where?'

She narrows her eyes. They ignite with impatience. 'Did I not say? I am certain I did. You must undertake a ritual cleanse. Get those roses out of the bucket and shred the petals into the bath. There's a dish full of salt on the wicker table beside it. Take two handfuls and mix it in. It'll purify your aura and prepare you, should you be chosen as the vessel.'

This brings Daphne up short. She does not like the sound of that. 'Chosen as the vessel? What does that mean?'

Usually Daphne is good at keeping her features in check, but Miss Sabine reads her. 'Oh, don't give me that look, Daphne. Keep focused and watch what goes on. I suppose, after your time on the stage, you may find it dry, perhaps, possibly even dull.'

It will be the very opposite.

CHAPTER TWENTY-TWO

On the surface, Arthur Eldridge looks about as esoteric as Postman Joe doing his rounds back home on Sutherland Street. He has an identical moustache to the mailman, long and neat, similar horn-rimmed glasses, and is approximately the same age. Just like Joe's, his hair is giving up the battle with grey. He has decided to inject some colour by way of bright handkerchiefs, which the postman also does when visiting the social club on a weekend. But Arthur Eldridge does not talk of football coupons or the price of stout like Joe. No, this gentleman's conversation takes an entirely different trajectory.

'But today is Friday,' he argues. They are overtaking a tractor and Daphne hopes he will return his eyes to the road ahead. 'Freya's day. I would have thought we should have a priestess in the saddle, so to speak.'

The farmer on the tractor doffs his cap as they pass.

Daphne has completed her ablutions and changed into a fresh tunic cut from a silky material. It is peacock blue with a tasselled cord that fastens at the waist. It feels pleasant on her skin. She wears her summer coat over the top, as Miss Sabine has instructed.

'I understand that.' Her tutor is testy, replying to Arthur's observation. She is seated in the passenger seat next to him. 'The eleventh hour on a Friday, however, is ruled by Saturn. Dominant. Then the god of gods himself, Jupiter. We need a man to hold that strength.'

The car is not as noisy as the army truck that brought her to Highcliffe, but Daphne has to lean forward between their heads to hear the conversation,

Arthur is not cowed. 'Hmm. I'd say you were just as capable as Alex in that regard. Don't be so down on your sex.'

'There is such that a priest can do and there is such that a priestess is good for. That has been the way for aeons, and it will be for aeons more.'

'I wouldn't be so sure,' says Arthur. 'Look at this lot here.'

Up ahead a group of women tramp along the side of the road in a loose formation. Some bear agricultural tools – spades, rakes, trowels – while others wear gloves, overalls and jackets. Their clothes are dirty with mud and stains. The roof of Arthur's car is down so they can hear the women's chatter as they approach.

'Land Army,' says Arthur, and to drive his point home, 'Look at them. Fine women doing jobs that men once did.'

Miss Sabine's eyes roll skywards and she literally turns up her nose. 'And regard their loss of femininity.'

'How do you mean?' asks Arthur.

Daphne assumed that Miss Sabine's views would be largely nonconformist, due to her membership of the Order. However, the instructress does not budge. 'They're dressed as men,' she says.

'I think trousers are a darn sight more practical than skirts when you're farming. And getting dirty,' Mr Eldridge replies.

Miss Sabine knuckles down. 'They say that women who wear trousers have loose morals.'

Daphne thinks this conflicting. From the back seat she calls out, 'Well, make your mind up. They can't be masculine like men and loose women at the same time, can they? Or does wearing men's clothes make you loose like a man? Is that what you mean?'

To which Arthur lets a laugh burst out and hoots on the horn, calling to the group, 'Well done, girls, keep at it!'

A couple wave, but now they are closer, she sees that most are exhausted. The sun is sinking behind the land girls, catching their hair, so they look like a gang of tramping angels. The phrase 'an honest day's work' comes to her.

'What do you think of it, Daphne?' asks Arthur. 'Women at work.'

'I think . . .' she says, gazing at their shrinking form, which is collective and herd-like. 'Most of us' – she shifts round and settles back into the seat – 'have known for a long time that women can do just as much as men. It's just the men who like to think we can't. But then I've been a working girl for a long time.'

'I wouldn't call yourself that, dear,' says Miss Sabine with an aggrieved wobble of her head.

'Well, I've worked for a living without the support of a man. Unless you count Jonty.'

Arthur is looking at her through the rear mirror. 'Who?'

'My employer. The magician – The Grand Mystique. But I earn my living. It's not like he just gives me money.'

'I should hope not!' her tutor tuts.

'What I mean is . . .' She pauses to find the word. 'It is quite possible for women and girls to meet the challenges accepted by men and boys. Sometimes they can even be better.'

In the front seat Miss Sabine's lips smack. 'Even without the necessary physicality?'

'Onstage I can move hulking chests, huge and heavy cabinets . . .'

'But that's a trick, I presume.'

'Is it? I cannot mobilise them on my own, so I have machinery to enable me. That's what I'm talking about. You find out how to do it and then you do it, using what you have to accomplish your objective. Machinery sometimes. Strength isn't everything.'

Arthur nods in the driving seat. 'Radical, radical.'

Her tutor does not reply. She sits upright and still with her hands neatly laid one on top of the other, in her lap, her lips unmoving.

A frosty sort of silence rolls out into the car.

'Things are changing,' says Daphne to break it.

'I know,' say Miss Sabine and Arthur at the same time.

Only one of them seems happy about it.

When they reach their destination an old housekeeper ushers them through the premises. 'The Masons' is not anything to do with a Masonic lodge, as Daphne had presumed, but is the residence of one Mr and Mrs Mason.

Their home is an early Victorian manor, full of dust and heavy furniture, damp and sprawling. Daphne is unsure if this is better than a Masonic lodge or worse. While it lacks the rigid rules and formality of a recognised group, it does not have the safety of such: should anything go wrong, it will be far easier to keep things quiet here in the sprawling grounds than in a lodge.

They are sent down a corridor through uninhabited servants' quarters then out into a beautifully landscaped garden. A shingle path on one side winds through ever-thickening foliage, where a couple of insomniac crickets are enjoying the warmth of the summer evening. Above the trees she can see a crescent moon slowly rising.

Gigantic cedars spread huge branches over their heads. Some are so big they look prehistoric, survivors from the last ice age, when mammoths and megafauna roamed the earth. Through their leaves dusk is already painting the sky with purple ripples.

A single owl hoots. From higher up comes the faint cry of a seagull.

Arthur points to a pinprick of light ahead between the tree trunks. 'There,' he says.

'Ah yes,' agrees Miss Sabine and softly adds, 'Home.'

There is a metaphorical meaning to that declaration.

Soon they come upon what Arthur described as the 'magic cottage'. It is little more than a single-storey hut, better made though not much bigger than the Nissen huts at Burleigh Hall.

'Take off your shoes.' Miss Sabine is back in instructress role. 'Wait here.' Then the two of them make off round the corner of the cottage, out of view.

Daphne bends down and removes her outer shoes, putting them underneath a holly bush. Hopefully she will remember they are there when she leaves.

A slice of orange light falls against the foliage as the door of the cottage opens. The faint aroma of incense is released, something spicy and sweet. She catches a snatch of whispered murmurs and then the door closes.

There is no light now, only the celestial constellations shining through the navy fabric of night. To the south-east she identifies Jupiter. Or perhaps it is Mars; she has never been much of a stargazer. Is Saturn there too? That is a thought – what had Miss Sabine said about someone needing to hold Saturn's strength? Was she referring to the planet, astrology? Or did she mean the god himself?

In the contemplation of these questions, a change comes over her. She has well and truly left the ordinary behind. The garden chat and the car journey over, now feel like a lifetime ago.

Standing in the quiet light, on this warm summer night, surrounded by things in the trees, wildlife hushing their breaths, occasionally moving, agitating the leaves so they quiver visibly, she feels a distinct energy unfurling and infecting the air around her. As though everything nearby that is living or breathing understands – or not even that, perhaps is simply just aware, has a notion – that something is about to happen.

The muted sounds of voices rise in a chant: 'Demera . . . Hachety . . .' or words like that.

Ancient names, she thinks. But surely the old gods are gone, defunct? Or is it wrong to assume that because they are no longer worshipped, they are dead? Maybe they are dormant. Have *been* dormant. For there are evidently people who pray to them. Perhaps these old gods will wake up again? And what will that mean?

A loud creak.

The door of the hut must have opened, because a stream of people emerge down the side and begin to process out in front of Daphne, onwards, curving away, through the shadowy trunks.

In the dimness she can make out men and women, ordinary but for the clothes they wear: marvellous tunics, all colours of the rainbow, long gowns, togas that sweep the floor. A few of the older women have wrapped themselves in long black cloaks. Their hair is undone so they look like witches. All are barefoot.

As they pass, they acknowledge her with a silent nod. She spots Miss Sabine at the back, who motions to her protégé: come hither.

She goes over quickly, quietly.

Side by side now, Daphne notices the instructress is shorter than her. 'To the glen, now. Just follow me and copy what we do,' she whispers.

The path snakes downwards on a shallow incline through a cluster of trees and out into a leafy glade. In the middle stands a large cauldron piled with tinder and twigs. The adepts form a circle around it.

Daphne follows and takes her place.

Something else is positioned near the cauldron: a stone altar covered in a black shiny cloth. Upon it various tools have been placed, and a vessel like a silvery grail.

It is a difficult sight to rationalise. She is very aware of herself, an outsider, in this occult working. A flush of nerves courses through her.

Keep your head, Daphne. It's a performance, she thinks as a man with long grey hair curling over his shoulders detaches himself from the others. He wears a loose kaftan, whitely luminous, covered in embroidered patterns and fastened at the waist by a wide gold belt. When he reaches the altar he bows low with great solemnity and picks up the metal cup with both hands. This must be Alex, the leader. Or is he a priest?

The man raises the chalice to an invisible host, over the heads of those facing him. In a deep, sonorous voice, he intones, 'I offer thee to the spirits of the air.'

His words chill her. She thinks of spirits, forms, entities in the space around them and remembers Miss Sabine's caution about breaking the circle. Her heart beats a little faster.

Next he passes the chalice to a woman in the circle who repeats the actions, drinks from the vessel and hands it on. The grail moves round the circle from acolyte to acolyte, each taking down the liquid with practised reverence.

'Tonight,' the priest says, raising his arms and his voice, 'the veil between the worlds draws thin. We come together to raise power. To empower our island and to weaken our enemies. Never have the stakes been higher.' He holds an unlit torch made of brushlike twigs to a point six feet above the cauldron.

A sense of disquiet begins to grow.

The priest's hand goes to his belt. With a start Daphne notices a knife which has been concealed between the folds of white silk. He does not touch it, though. His fingers pass to the pouch fastened there and produce a handful of fine white crystals. With these glistening in his open palm he walks a circle and traces a line of salt onto the grass. They are now a circle of people within a circle of salt.

Her hands are moist with sweat. She flicks them as if she is drying them in the air.

A nudge on her arm and Miss Sabine passes over the chalice. 'Have a good drink,' she hisses. 'Two sips at least for you.'

Daphne raises it. As she feels the cool silver on her lips she hesitates. Does she really wish to do this? Though it does not form into a statement or warning in her head, she understands that once she has drunk of the cup, she will not be able to turn back. She will have passed an invisible line. She will no longer be an observer. She will be a participant.

Miss Sabine has noticed the pause. 'You must be open to miracles, remember – the miraculous.'

She takes down a deep draught.

Sour and musty, there is an earthy cuddiness, the taint of an organic component like fungi, sweet mushrooms, and a rusty note too. She hopes the well is not stagnant. Perhaps the water gains its metallic taste from a stream nearby. Minerals are often deposited into springs. She takes another, longer gulp and hands it over to the man on her right, who she now realises is Gerard. He smiles a silent greeting, raising the vessel to her in salutation, drinks deeply, closes his eyes and turns his face to the night sky. His lips move, though she does not hear what he is saying.

The priest is behind her now. Anxiety begins to crawl up her back, over her shoulders.

She fidgets. Underneath the soles of her feet she feels dried grass, slightly damp, covered with leaves and twigs.

The priest has paused between the two circles – human and salt – with the circulating water. She is aware of the elements. They lack only fire now.

Behind her, he inhales. All of a sudden, and so loudly he makes her jump, the priest bellows out to the air, 'Raphael, bestow your protection upon us now.'

It is an order, a command, a decree.

And it changes everything.

It is as if lightning has struck at the centre of the circle. As if they are in a magnetic field.

The archangel's name continues to resonate through her ears. The vibrations move into her brain and drum into her skull. A fleeting image of herself, an infant, in church, kneeling by a nativity scene, hushed, waiting for the godhead to manifest into flesh.

Then – a new reaction within – energy ignites. Animation. She starts to feel very much alive.

'I call upon thee, Gabriel, to bestow your protection upon us.'

The air is charged. Her hands are becoming hot.

'I call upon thee, Michael, bestow your protection now.'

The priest slips between two people and creeps to the cauldron with practised ceremonial gait.

Daphne glances down and sees Miss Sabine take her hand. Gerard takes her right with a firm grip. When she looks up again, the priest has lit the torch.

Fire. The four elements are all in place.

'Demeter, Hecate, Diana, Selene, Ishtar.' He puts the flame to the stack of wood and dried branches in the cauldron. 'Jupiter, Isis, Amunet.'

The conflagration catches instantly. Flames huge and powerful release strange aromas into the night: spices, petrol, woody bark smells and something golden. Daphne breathes it all in. Her senses are becoming overwhelmed by the intense stimulation.

Night has darkened the glade. With the fire casting shadows

against the trees, she appreciates at last that they are onstage, their audience formed of eyes hidden in the darkness, watching them, waiting.

The show is beginning. The curtain not going up but drawing thin, like the priest declared.

'Demeter, Hecate, Diana . . .' All have joined in voice.

Gerard pulls her anticlockwise.

'Jupiter, Isis, Amunet.'

As she circles the strange heat, energy, rising from the ground like an invisible mist, courses upwards, from her thighs and into her stomach, filling her, making her feel like she is sparkling within.

The circle spins round and around. In the firelight, all glows.

'We take this power and we turn it against you.' The priest's words echo. 'Turn east, turn east.'

'Ishtar, Jupiter.' A Greek chorus of chanting.

Circle, dancers, acolytes blur together, trees lean like giant ogres. Their footsteps beat a maniacal rhythm like the whole thing is a carnival hurdy-gurdy speeding out of control . . .

Something like a bee is buzzing in the background. No, too noisy for that. It can't be a bee, she thinks, then laughs out loud at her words.

Be a bee. Bee bee. Bibi. They make no sense.

How has it come to this?

She doesn't care.

Round and round, with the sounds and the smells and the stiff heat rising, out through her eyes, which are rolling. With the buzzing bee louder, louder, and the voices growing stronger, stronger . . .

And then the very ground is vibrating.

Incredible!

Miraculous, yes!

All the energy in the world rising, pushing up through them, out of them. Tremendous force into the air, making it yellow or . . .

'Go east, go east,' intones the priest.

'Yes,' she says, 'east!' and throws back her head laughing at the stars pulsing, planetary flares . . .

Somewhere in the cacophony, the bleat of a goat.

Eerie whines . . .

A dark shadow flies at them . . .

'No!' someone cries.

A shattering crash.

The earth shakes.

Everything—

Everything explodes into fire.

27 JULY 1940

CHAPTER TWENTY-THREE

'There can be no visual clue,' Daphne says. 'I must tell Jonty. We were so preoccupied with the working that we were careless.'

Captain Tuckett does not regard her with contempt this time. Instead he is all ears, like the hare he reminded her of. They all are. Him, the Wren assisting and a small man in an army uniform whom she does not know but who switches his eyes to the bruise on her jaw. It is purple now, and no amount of powder is able to cover it up entirely. When she arrived, he had muttered something under his breath. But Daphne had caught it: 'Beauty is your duty.'

It is a phrase that is catching on. Troops need girls who keep themselves pretty and well turned out. Ladies' appearances must be kept up or morale might plummet.

They are sitting in a small office off the main entrance to Burleigh Hall. A couple of typists are pretending not to listen in to the conversation. Another woman is moving tiny vans and tanks across a map ironed onto the surface of a large table.

The girl taking notes on a stool smiles at her apologetically, and something passes between them which encourages Daphne.

Clearing her voice, Daphne tilts her chin upwards. She needs to be heard. 'The bonfire must have attracted the attention of the Luftwaffe . . . We simply cannot have light on the night,' she says.

Whatever had fallen had just missed them, though the carnage she had glimpsed on their way home was terrifying. Ashen and black, the crater was the size of a house. Sooted shrubs and vegetables, smouldering greenhouses, flaming trees splintered, bent and crooked like paralysed people with their hair on fire. The air full of smoke and cinders. Such chronic destruction was a shock.

It had been so frightening. Nothing like the bomb they had simulated at Farnham, which now seemed laughable by comparison. They could never have replicated such noises, the deafening explosion, the earth-splitting tremors, the shock wave and terror unleashed, the disorientation, the fear.

Never.

In the chaos afterwards, Daphne had come round with her face pushed into a hollow between the roots of a tall oak tree. She didn't know how long she had been like that. It could have been seconds, minutes or hours.

At first she struggled to move – something was pinning her down. She wriggled her fingers and discovered that one hand was beneath her chest, another behind her back. Her legs were stuck under something heavy. She tried to move. The weight of it held her fast.

Yet this would not defeat her. Contortions in various magical cabinets meant she knew that she would find a space, no matter how tiny, and use it to bend her body. She had been in tighter squeezes before. Though perhaps not so disorientated.

A dip in the ground by a large root allowed her to insert a knee and push up the upper part of her body. Something hard and rectangular began to slide off her back and released her other hand. She twisted round, stretching her muscles painfully.

The altar had been blown over and come to rest on her legs. Though it was heavy it had not broken her bones. She could feel her extremities and move her toes. With her free hands she grabbed the chipped surface of the altar and shoved it hard. It scraped some of the skin from her calves – a small price to pay to free her legs fully.

She laid against the tree's trunk and caught her breath. And beheld the awful scene before her.

It looked like, it looked like . . . Hell.

Blackened roots, smoke, fire.

Against a blazing backdrop, people were running around with pails of water, lifting the wounded, disappearing into the inferno.

The landscape was strangely muted.

Her head was aching. And ringing.

Then, a hand in front of her eyes.

Gerard. Hair dishevelled. Bits of earth in his beard moving up and down as he spoke.

She could not hear what he was saying.

He extended his arms and lifted her up.

Again his lips moved and she heard nothing. This time, though, she understood the soundless words: 'Are you wounded?'

Good question, she thought, and checked herself. Apart from a few scrapes and a bloody knee she seemed unhurt. She ran her hand over her left jaw, which had been on the bark of the tree when she regained consciousness, and stretched her mouth. The skin there was swollen and stung, but no permanent damage. Nothing broken. She shook her head and stuck up her thumb. Then said the words, 'I can't hear you.'

'It'll come back in a bit,' he mouthed.

She nodded back.

He said something else but she couldn't understand. Daphne shrugged and shook her head. Gerard gave up trying to communicate and offered his arm. She took it and was led back through the woods, up the path, past the hut to the back of the house. The door was open. He pointed, then turned around and went back to the glade.

Inside there was light. She followed it and found the large drawing room.

Members of the Order were in various states of shock. Some were sitting, others talking, severe, taut, pinched. One man was asleep or unconscious on the floor. Two women were crying soundlessly. Others were nursing injuries. A young female servant was applying a bandage to an older man's head.

She drifted, still dazed, into the centre of the room. Someone touched her arm. It was Arthur Eldridge.

Gesturing at her ears, she tried to say, 'I can't hear,' though didn't know if she said it loudly enough.

More words she couldn't make out, then he pointed to a chair where Miss Sabine was sitting, covered in a blanket, drinking tea. Her cup was trembling. Daphne tottered over to the footstool by her feet.

Miss Sabine put her hand on Daphne's shoulder and stroked it. 'Are you all right?'

The words registered faintly, as if they were spoken underwater. Again she nodded and watched the older woman say something to Arthur, who went away and came back pushing another well-upholstered armchair. He lifted her and guided her into it. Miss Sabine covered Daphne with her blanket. She tried to give it back, but the older woman put a finger to her lips, which pursed.

So she relaxed.

Someone gave her a sweet drink: tea.

She took a sip, then put it down.

Exhaustion overwhelmed her.

* * *

So now is the time. 'Captain Tuckett,' she says emphatically. 'The ritual must be scheduled for a full moon. Hopefully it'll mean a clear night and we'll be able to see without assistance.'

'Ah, yes.' He strokes his moustache. Underneath, his mouth is shaped again like an upside-down *u*. 'Things have changed somewhat.'

'How's that?'

'We have just received intelligence that Hitler has brought the proposed assault forward.'

'Right,' says Daphne. 'So we'll have to speed things up.'

'There is absolutely no question of that. According to our sources, the date mooted for invasion is the tenth of August.'

'Hang on.' She is calculating in her head. Days, weeks, months. What date is it? Thursday, Friday, Saturday. 'That's, that's only two weeks away!'

'Indeed,' says the captain. So terse.

'I'm not sure Jonty will be able to pull everything together in that time.'

'What time?'

'A fortnight.'

'No, he won't. The idea is to repel the Nazis, not welcome them with a little dance. As such, Operation Reynard takes place on the night of the fourth.'

'The fourth of what?'

Tuckett pauses to take a deep breath, suggesting that he is trying to control himself. 'The fourth of August.'

Her mind takes a second to work out the timeline. 'But that's just over a week away. An illusion cannot be worked up in mere—'

The captain holds up his hand to silence her. 'This isn't negotiable. It's doubtful that you are used to them, Miss Devine, but this is an order. You don't get to challenge such things.'

'Surely that's not enough—'

His eyelids flutter as he rolls his pupils. 'Well you'd better stop wasting what little you've got and go and give your magician the news.'

'Do you mean he doesn't yet know?'

The captain has turned back to his notes.

Daphne is appalled. There will be so much to do. The illusion may well have to be scrapped and reinterpreted. They need to think about how to portray power without using brilliant light. How can that be achieved? And so quickly?

Noticing she has remained, he pipes up. 'No, you can have the honour of breaking the news. Now trot along like a good little girl.'

CHAPTER TWENTY-FOUR

Jonty will be devastated. Already she can picture his face. He will try hard to conceal it but she will know by the cracks around his eyes, his over-amplified languor.

She does not realise it but walks the entire length of the grounds with her head down, eyes on the grass.

When she reaches the hut Jonty is there outside with Jack, Ernest and Septimus. The latter, despite the heat of the afternoon, is still wearing a dark green suit and tie. Ernest has gardening trousers on and Jonty sports a boiler suit smudged with oil. Jack, who she had been looking forward to seeing again before her encounter with Captain Tuckett, wears knee-length shorts. He has well-shaped calves which look solid and tanned. She feels guilty for noticing.

As a group their pose is tense – lots of folded arms and jittery movements. Judging from the looks on their faces, she thinks, they must have already got the memo. Or something else has gone badly wrong.

The sun is dappling the ground through the trees, casting lacy shadows on the grass, and she thinks instantly of the burned black leaves in Christchurch. She shudders. It could have been so much worse.

'Good God!' Jonty exclaims as he sees her. 'What's happened to you? They didn't try to sacrifice you, did they?'

Daphne's hand flies to her jaw. 'No. But, but . . .' She stammers and is embarrassed, tries to correct her demeanour, straightens her jangling nerves. 'But it wasn't good,' she says firmly.

Jonty puts his arm over her shoulders like a protective parent and brings her into their circle. 'You're back now. I'm here.'

His words quell her.

Ernest inspects her jaw and says, 'I've got a poultice for that. Give me a couple of hours and I'll make it up for you.'

She can feel Jack's eyes on her but is hesitant to meet them.

'Sorry to hear that,' Septimus says with sincerity. 'Is it painful?' He tries and fails to conceal a wince of sympathy.

'Not really.' Daphne squirms under the scrutiny of four pairs of eyes, having skimped on the make-up and not pin-curled her hair. She realises she is desperate to see what Jack makes of her appearance and, with a jolt of adrenalin, sees a look of extreme outrage.

Jonty rubs her shoulder, which is still a bit tender. 'Can you talk? Tell us.'

'Yes, I must.' She starts to say, 'There isn't much time . . .' but then she wonders if the news of the new date might derail all other conversation. Probably.

So: first things first. She sketches out what took place during the ritual, the props that were used and the motions. Everything they must know.

Jonty surmises, 'the principal players – Alex, the leader of the Order. He acts as a sort of priest. Right, I think I've got it. I can work with this.'

'I know you can,' she says. 'But I'm afraid there is some new information. About the ritual.'

'Oh yes,' says Septimus. 'They've brought it forwards. I was just explaining.'

Her shoulders drop and she relaxes briefly. Thank goodness for that. Jonty appears not to have been floored by the reduced schedule. In fact he nudges her. 'We're making good progress.'

She is pleased to hear this and allows him to nudge her again, this time onto the stretch of lawn with him. The daisies and dandelions have gone. Someone has clipped the grass back almost to bald.

He comes to a stop by a hole that has been excavated in the centre of the enclosure. From it protrudes a device, a giant hexagonal crate like a lantern. It puts her in mind of their Metamorphosis illusion, allegedly a Trevelyan family tradition. Although a plate-spinner from Manhattan had once informed her that Houdini had demonstrated it many times over. She has a great admiration for the escapologist's work and uses one of his techniques herself when bound for a trick. Recently she has noticed how her body reacts automatically to the touch of a rope or chains, tensing muscles and filling out the space around her. It is amazing how her limbs can remember what to do. The slack that is created when the body relaxes allowed Houdini to work his 'magic'.

Their own Metamorphosis box has butterflies painted across its sides, ostensibly to represent change. This is far less alluring and is only decorated with chalked-on geometric patterns.

'No butterflies?' she murmurs out loud, momentarily transfixed by the sight.

'Ah,' says Jonty. 'No, Vivian – have you seen him? – there's a book in his studio we're using for decorations, etcetera, etcetera. It's all part of the brief – the Key of Solomon or some such. Interesting symbols though. Might make copies for when we get back on the boards. There's a few bits and pieces need refreshing. Anyway, this lantern will be painted up properly after the mechanics are finalised. Once we've finished with it the whole set will look quite esoteric.'

And yet it was no Metamorphosis box. Much of the internal machinery is visible via hinges which allow the side of the hexagonal box to slide open at the top. A magician never reveals what goes on inside his magic cabinets, never lays open his secrets for all to view. Secrets which can be copied. 'Our own Cone of Power,' he says with a flourish.

'But you can see inside.' Daphne is puzzled.

'Ah,' says Jonty in understanding. 'It's not that kind of trick. As it starts to spin, the centrifugal force will allow the sides to fall open a few inches.'

This confuses her.

Jonty reads her face. 'Wait for it,' he cautions. 'We have dug a trench, which will be covered so that no one can see the cabling that enables the rotation. Jack will be operating the lantern over there.' Another piece of machinery twenty yards away pokes out of a mound of earth. It is fashioned from the end of a pipe. A steering wheel with a handle attached is fixed at the top. 'This will give the impression that the cone is turning of its own accord.'

'Or by other forces,' Septimus comments. He has followed them into the centre of a roughly chalked-out circle where the lantern stands.

'It will perform well, I think,' Jonty goes on. 'There will be tinder and gunpowder in the bottom of the box. We plan to have it lined with non-flammable material, possibly clay, whatever we can get our hands on, so that when lit the flames will create a whooshing effect, as if tremendous energy were spouting up into the sky.' He smiles at his cleverness. 'Our hypothesis is that the motion of rotation will cause the flames to weave and plait, as it were, to become a spiral or indeed a cone.' Jonty is animated. He gets like this whenever he is engaged in new inventions and illusions. 'However, we haven't worked out how to do that just yet. Our best guess is someone should remain close to it, and as the ritual climaxes they'll have to light the tinder. Unseen, of course. There's only one person I know who's more than capable of that.' He winks at her but then sees something in her face. 'Don't worry, it will be quite safe. Sleight of hand and speed is required and I know this is your forte, my dear.'

'Yes.' She must tell him now before he gets more carried away. 'About the fire . . .'

Jonty's eyebrows stiffen.

'We can't have any light,' she says with firmness.

'What?'

'It's simply too dangerous in the blackout. We nearly had a terrible mishap – it could have been disastrous.'

Despite her worst fears, Jonty does not get cross. Instead, he taps his forehead hard. 'Oh Lord,' he exclaims. 'We haven't factored that in. At least, not enough.'

Ernest, for once, frowns. She has not seen him do that before. Septimus tuts. Jack drops his head to the floor. His hair, long and luscious, flops forward so she cannot see his face.

In the silence they hear the rumble of plane engines crossing some other part of the forest. All of them look up.

Then Daphne says, 'No, we didn't either. I mean they didn't.' She qualifies her plural. 'The Order. None of them. And it wasn't a big bonfire.'

'Who? What is the Order?' asks Jack. He is up again, alert and now by her side. 'Sounds intriguing.'

He is so near to her that she feels his energy. Her cheeks heat. She senses him moving a fraction closer. 'I can't say.'

Ernest opens his tobacco tin and offers ready-mades to everyone. Jonty takes one and inhales deeply.

'So we are to give the impression of a fire giving the impression of energy without using light.'

Jonty's irritation is clear.

'In fact,' says Septimus, 'your brief is to give the *illusion* of power, which is something different. And to this end, Daphne, you will visit the Canadian camp tomorrow, in the forest. Teach them the basics. Jack, can you drive her? How long do you think it will take?'

The warmth in her cheeks becomes a full flush at the prospect of Jack's company. 'A couple of hours?' Daphne kicks the grass with her shoe.

'Good. Now do you have secretarial skills?' Septimus asks Daphne.

'Me? Oh no.'

'Can you write?' he asks. Then a thought occurs to him which makes him smile. 'You've been a showgirl, haven't you?'

Jonty sniffs with disdain and calls over, 'An illusionist's assistant is the correct term, Septimus.'

Without waiting for an answer, Septimus replies, 'Even better. Follow me. I have a job for a couple of hours and need an assistant. You can spare her, can't you, Jonty?'

The magician has one hand held to his forehead. With his other he makes a circular motion. His meaning is clear: *Yes, yes, go away.*

'You won't have to do much,' Septimus tells Daphne. 'I'm interviewing a few of the locals for some positions. It's quite simple. I'm sure you can manage it.'

Back at the manor, Septimus leads her down a long service corridor, then up through a waiting room, where several local men who are not wearing uniform sit and chat and smoke. He smiles at them as they march through to the double doors at the far end. 'Thank you for coming,' He is most polite. 'We'll not keep you waiting much longer.' Promptly, the men say thank yous.

Pushing open the doors, they enter a room of very large dimensions, with a parquet floor. Daphne thinks it must have at one time been a ballroom. She is coping with her new task well, starting to understand the haphazard nature of the work. You do one thing, you return, you get pulled into another task. There are no limits to what one is expected to do. You must simply put your all into everything that is required, as and when. She realises, as she as she follows Septimus, that to live usefully in war one must abandon the expectations of pre-war life, when working and leisure time were delineated. This is what war means. A taking over of a person. A requisition. Countries are invaded and people are too. She will rise to the new challenge.

The ballroom is mostly empty but for a desk stacked with paper at the end closest to them. At the other end, French windows open onto what was once a lovely garden. Perhaps the rockery. Another requisition. Now it is full of tents and huts, and the notion of a garden established for pure delight suddenly feels like an absurd indulgence.

She alters her gaze to the centre of the room, where a couple of dozen skittles, the type one might find in a bowling lane, are laid out in a triangular shape on the floor. What is this? she thinks. Surely not a recreation? She would not have been pulled out of the planning with Jonty, Jack and Ernest for something so hedonistic.

Septimus's voice cuts through. 'The men outside are potential fire wardens, We need to start assembling shifts so we may work out who is on duty the night of the operation.'

'I see,' says Daphne, eyeing the skittles. They start to make sense. 'So you're looking for skills of dexterity and accuracy?'

'Not exactly.' He hands her a stack of index cards. 'Can you write on each "How many skittles here?" And then "What do you see?"'

'Two questions?' she asks. There is a greater function here. These are not just skittles. This is not just leisure.

'Yes, that's all. Now, have you got any lipstick? Would you have a quick tidy-up, put on a pretty frock?'

'I suppose so,' says Daphne. Now she is thrown again. But she trusts this man, Septimus. He is not frivolous. She can tell that he is intolerant of time-wasting.

'Can you do it in five minutes?'

Of course she can.

When Daphne reappears she has put on one of the two frocks forwarded from Farnham. Her hair is brushed and done up. Scarlet lipstick stains her lips (Hitler allegedly does not like women with red lips so she feels it is both acceptable and defiant, at least until the lipstick runs out). On her feet she wears a pair of flats borrowed from Miss Sabine. Her own shoes had been lost in the chaos of the air raid.

The men whom she passes in the waiting room have formed themselves into an orderly queue.

'Much better!' says Septimus as she hurries to his side. 'So.' He passes over a large placard on which someone else has written the same questions in a very orderly hand. 'If you please, I would like you, once the men have assembled, to wait at the side of the room. When you see my cue,' he says, sending her a floppy salute, 'please walk into the centre of the room, hold up your card, then return to the side.'

'And that's it?'

'You can give it some of your show business spin, if you like? The men will answer the questions and wait outside for our decisions.'

'Yes sir,' she says, though she is still at a loss as to why Septimus, he who is so much more interested in history and matters of perception, is delivering an observation test.

The agent half opens the door and calls in the men, directing them into a straight line with their backs against the display of skittles so they cannot see them and have an unfair advantage.

When they have settled he gives each one a card that Daphne has written on and a pen, then asks them to write their name at the top.

'When I say "Start!"' he announces, 'you must turn around and follow instructions. You will have sixty seconds to complete the exercise. Does everyone understand?'

Nods and affirmations.

'Add your names to the postcards if you can, please.'

They lean their cards on each others' backs so they can scrawl their details on one side.

Then, when they are all ready and waiting, Septimus yells 'Start' and gives the signal to Daphne.

She bows at the side of the hall. With all eyes upon her, she slips into her role and skips to the centre, curtseys at the assembled audience, then holds up the placard proudly with a big grin.

The men's eyes quickly scan the question written there. Septimus gives her another nod. She bows and sashays back to her place.

The men have galvanised into action. Some of them are counting on their fingers, others are sweeping their eyes across the room from left to right. She decides to count the skittles herself and, as she surveys them, she almost lets out a laugh.

For there, at the back, is a short fellow got up in a Charlie Chaplin outfit. He dashes to the furthest cone, twiddles his cane, jiggles his eyebrows and then waddles across the back of the room, through a door there and out onto the rockery.

Septimus holds his watch up and yells, 'Stop! Time's up. About-turn.'

The men obey instantly. They are well trained to respect authority.

'Next to me please, Daphne,' Septimus orders. She goes to him and sits on the chair behind the desk.

The agent calls the first man over. The others have started to talk to each other and compare notes. Septimus does not object.

'Twenty-five, I believe,' says the first man, who has a limp. 'Is that correct?' he asks.

'Spot on,' says Septimus. 'So you're Alfie.'

'That's right.'

'Well, Alfie, can you please go and wait in the waiting room?'

'Absolutely.' Alfie is pleased with himself and hobbles off.

'But,' whispers Daphne, with surprise, 'he didn't see Charlie Chaplin.'

'Shh.' Septimus calls over the next, whose answers are the same.

'Splendid,' says Septimus. 'Waiting room, please. And not a word to the others.' He gives him a conspiratorial wink.

'I'm not sure about that one,' says Daphne. 'I've a feeling he might tell.'

'All the better.'

It is truly perplexing.

The next candidate arrives.

'Twenty-five.' His voice is low.

The number is repeated by all of the men, until, that is, they come to the last one standing, who does not need to be asked to come to the table.

'I counted twenty-five skittles, sir, like the rest,' he says. 'Though I think Mr Chaplin presented something of a skit. Does that count?'

Daphne claps her hands together and laughs. At last!

'Ah, very good,' says Septimus. 'What's your name?'

'James,' says the fellow.

'Well James, you will be in Fire Warden Section A. Please go home. We'll be in touch.'

The man is taken aback. 'You don't want me to wait?'

'No, you've earned your place in the team. Thank you for your time.'

And, although he was not expecting that answer, James simply shrugs and then leaves.

'Right,' says Septimus and collects up the papers. 'Time to brief our fire-watchers for the night of the operation. Will you accompany me to the waiting room?'

'Of course,' says Daphne. 'But I don't understand. Why would you choose these men who did not notice the clown, the man dressed as Chaplin? None of them saw him, but he was so obvious. Don't know how they could have missed him.'

'Astounded you need to ask, Daphne,' he says. 'The men were told to count the skittles, and count the skittles they certainly did. Concentrating so much on them that they failed to see the bigger picture, the hall or Private Paskins executing what I think you'd agree is a strikingly good impersonation.'

'Ah,' she's got it now. 'Is it misdirection?'

'In a manner of speaking,' he says, striding to the door.

'But why would you select the least observant? A fire warden's job requires a keen eye.'

'Don't you worry – James will head up a team and hopefully transmit his skills as he does so. But for the night of our operation, it is of the utmost importance that people see what we want them to see. The power of suggestion is a very useful thing. You know that,' he says as he opens the door.

He turns brightly to those in the anteroom. 'Hello gentlemen. Thank you for waiting. Many congratulations on passing.'

28 JULY 1940

Lumberjills

Hear them marching through the glades,
Those fine young girls in green,
With crossed axes and a saw,
Whatever can they mean?
It's the Women's Timber Corps of course,
Here to lend a hand
Felling trees from dawn till dusk
All across the land.
We'll do the job and earn your trust
Till bells of peace ring out once more
Until then it's up to us
To help win this blimmin' war.

CHAPTER TWENTY-FIVE

The morning dawns with a bristly friction.

There is a pressure and tint in the air which makes Burleigh Hall's limewashed posterior pulsate with light. The grass in its lawns snaps to attention and, like tiny bayonets, whips ankles and fires loaded dewdrops across bare skin.

The birds can sense the difference, though their reaction manifests in an enervated shrill to their song which few human ears detect.

Full, florid and ferny, the tree trunks send over their branches to the leaves, an order to scratch and brush against each other, so the sound might rustle out like a crackling SOS.

Sitting side by side in an open-top truck with Jack, Daphne does perceive a difference. However, because her attention is occupied by more immediate concerns, her lazy hind-mind interprets it as a detection of sensual potential. This in turn gives rise to a half-cocked question which forms silently in her head: is her luck on the up?

Perhaps so.

For here she is on a beautiful day, out in the fresh air, in the countryside, with company that is not much of a chore to keep. She has thrown caution to the wind and, aware that Jack is to be her driver, has selected a skirt from her civilian wardrobe. It is olive green, and though the cut is more daring than standard issue, the garment hangs off her hips in what she has been told is a complementary manner. It is one of the few clothes she has packed from her pre-rationing spree, which is evident in its opulent satin lining. The fabric is so light it is like wearing clouds which swirl as she walks. If anybody challenges her as to why she is not dressed in uniform, she can say she needs freedom of movement to demonstrate a particular drill for the operation.

She has brought a coarser army-grade jumper to set it off, just in case, though she has not put it on. The temperature is still too mild. She sits back and enjoys the satin on the bare skin above her stockings and the sun's rays strafing her hair.

By turns hilly then flat, purple, yellow, green, brackish brown, the land flashes past. She has heard people who had been to the New Forest announcing that it was beautiful, but she is not prepared for the broad flat moors and shady, verdant woods, teeming with life and wildness. So different from Essex, which seems domestic by contrast. And London, well it is a world away. She finds the pronounced contours of the hillocks and slopes sensuous, female – the land is a jade goddess sleeping on her side.

It is not blackout London, but the roads here are still narrow and twisty. Jack drives quickly. She is not sure whether to be exhilarated or terrified. And when they take a corner she clamps hold of the door handle.

'Oh behave,' he says, smiling widely. That jaw is so firm. Perfect teeth. He is too good to be true. 'You're in the forest now. No rules here. Well, not that many. Just . . .'

Daphne can't hear the rest. Air shrieks through the radiator grille and bumper. And the engine is not quiet. She contents herself with smiling back, and that seems to go down well enough with Jack.

They come out under a canopy of branches and turn left onto a road. It is nothing more than a cut through the woods. But there is an obstacle yards ahead. A low truck. It is full of young women, sitting on logs.

'Ah,' says Jack, with his foot on the brake. 'The lumberjills are up and about already.'

'Lumberjills?' Daphne lurches as their speed comes down and puts her hands out onto the metal frame to steady herself.

'It's what everyone calls them. Jills as opposed to Jacks – women who do the forestry. Frees up the men to go to the front. A pretty vital part of the war effort. People don't realise how essential their work is. You, I mean, the United Kingdom, Britain, have a timber shortage.'

Daphne is getting used to his accent. It is only when he mentions her country that she remembers he is a foreigner.

She wonders what Canada is like. She thinks it is probably green and has buffaloes. It most certainly has lumberjacks. Which might be how he knows so much about lumberjills.

'Are they part of the Land Army?' Daphne asks. 'I saw some of them when I was in . . .' She trails off, remembering the importance of secrecy.

But Jack hasn't heard. He grins and blows the horn. 'What's that? Land Army? No, Timber Corps. Completely distinct. Different caps and badges. And their work is more physical than the land girls'. Dangerous, to be fair.'

She wonders what it is like to work like a man. Probably the same as working as a woman, only without disapproval and control. Women are stronger than men realise.

The lumberjills' truck pulls to the side to let them pass, and they move on. The woods thicken, filtering more light out of the arbour. Their road slants, twists, steepens.

Jack takes his foot off the pedal, changes gear and decelerates into a pace that borders on meandering. 'Not far now,' he says as they motor past a small black and white cottage nestling in a clearing. It is one of the first human dwellings she has seen for miles. The forest is very depopulated. Essex has few patches left of uncolonised land.

'Where are we?' she asks.

'Between Lynthurst and – oh damn!'

She laughs at the exclamation. 'Fine name for a wood!'

'Damn.' Jack says it again and hits the steering wheel. 'I was meant to bring a technical drawing, a pattern . . . for a part. A cog. Never mind. I'll have to go back and get it.'

'All right,' said Daphne, not sure why this matters.

They are cresting the top of the hill. The trees have thinned out. Some show evidence of forestry: trunks have been felled and rolled to one side. Presumably the work of the lumberjills. Round a corner, then they emerge out of the treeline. Jack pulls onto a flat piece of scrubland and cuts the engine. His lips fall into a straight line.

This is not the camp. Why has he stopped here?

'It's stunning, eh?'

She follows his eyes to the horizon and sees they are on a ledge. Beyond, the land dips into a valley and then rises up the other side in a thick wedge of green forest. She agrees. It is.

They sit enjoying the stillness. It is not silent, but there are few sounds. A buzzard soars effortlessly on a thermal. Then Jack asks, 'How long do you think it will take you to do what you've got to do at the camp?'

'Hmm,' she says. 'An hour? Two?'

'Only I thought I might take you for a quick drink at a pub not far from here.'

Doubtless to say, Daphne is delighted by the proposition, although simultaneously uncertainty clouds her. 'We're on a very tight schedule. I don't know if Jonty will want me back at—'

'It's also Sunday,' he tells her. 'We've been told we can have the afternoon to ourselves. If we get all our work done. And I sure could do with some rest and recuperation.'

This is news to her. No one has bothered informing the 'chorus girl' about this. They probably think she had her time off in Christchurch, which was exceedingly unrestful and for which she feels she needs a decent stretch of recuperation. 'Well,' she says, recalibrating her schedule, 'it depends how many people I have to instruct and how well they take to it. But I'm sure I can speed it up.'

He presses her: 'A couple of hours? Three? Four?'

'Oh, I shouldn't think more than two.' It won't be any longer. She has decided it won't be.

'Good. I can drop you off, go and get the plans. I'll pick you up at three and we can have a nice drink. Then I'll pop you back and go and see this man about a dog. I mean cog.' He winks at her. It unleashes another fizz in her stomach. 'That will do, won't it?'

She nods. 'But the pub – it's Sunday. It will be shut by then.'

'There's a particular one I'm thinking of that caters to the Sundays of servicemen. The landlord is happy to flex his opening times and the local bobby turns a blind eye.'

'Splendid.' Daphne had no idea such things happened.

She waits for Jack to restart the engine, but he doesn't. He is still gazing out over the valley. She watches him close his eyes and draw the air into his lungs. 'I'd like to get away after the war,' he says. 'Perhaps buy a piece of land, have a smallholding. Somewhere far from everyone with all their warring ideologies and orders. Start afresh, you know. Clean. New name and everything.'

He'll be able to get away, she thinks, go back to his country. But she says, 'Everybody believes things will be different once we get out of this and peace prevails once more. It's a noble aim.'

To her surprise, he leans over and taps her knee. 'You are quite remarkable, you know that?'

The skin underneath where he's touched her skirt sparks with electricity. At least it feels that way. 'Sometimes,' she says, refusing to blush.

He starts the truck. Before steering back onto the road he throws a sideways glance at her. He is smiling.

They register at the camp. Jack drops her off by the entrance and she waves him goodbye, sorry to see him go but full of anticipation for the promised delights.

An officer collects her and escorts her deeper into the base. 'Won't take long, will it?' he asks as they pass a construction site. Hangars are being put up like those back in Surrey. The base isn't yet finished; soldiers and construction workers are erecting a vast many buildings.

'Not if they pick it up quickly,' she replies, starting to wonder about the reception she might get from these men, clearly in the middle of a huge building operation themselves. 'I'd like to be away by three.'

The officer continues to march at a pace. 'We're not entirely sure what your operation is about. Any chance you might enlighten me?'

She has to half walk, half jog to keep up with him. However, she remembers her briefing: only those who knew need to know. 'If you haven't been briefed already, I don't have the authority to go through it.'

'Very well,' he says, by which time they have reached a parade ground carved out of a cleared forest area. A group of men are sitting or standing by a row of three tents, all with their flaps rolled up. The soldiers immediately stand to attention on sight of the officer. He introduces Daphne and orders them to take her instructions. Then, to her dismay, he withdraws, leaving her alone. She feels exposed and silly in her flouncy skirt.

'Right,' she says, and raises her voice to sound authoritative. 'If we work together we can make this quick. There are some words you need to learn first of all.'

She pulls her notebook out of her bag. There is a rough sketch of the set-up as she had seen it in Christchurch: X marks the position of the altar, Y the cauldron, encompassed by two circles, one of which has arrows on it demonstrating the direction they need to move.

'Here we go.' However, when she looks up from the page most of the men have resumed their previous positions and are chatting and smoking. 'Hello?' she says, trying to get their attention. 'If you could repeat after me.' She clears her throat and raises her voice. 'Demeter, Hecate—'

A thin man with beady eyes throws his cigarette to the ground and starts walking towards her with a look on his face she hasn't seen since the dark alleys of Soho.

'Listen,' he says. 'We're not 'ere to muck around. We've got work to do.'

The lack of respect is infuriating.

'No, YOU listen.' She is surprised to hear her voice so full of command. 'You may think this is "mucking around", but your commanders don't. The German government has a weakness that not many are aware of. And this is what we are going to counter.'

The other men have turned their faces now, drawn by the possibility of entertainment.

But the lanky soldier will lose face if he backs down. He keeps it coming. 'What kind of mumbo jumbo is this? Nonsense.'

Daphne puts up her hand, palm out and flat, to halt him and sees hesitation flick over his eyes. A couple of those sitting are getting to their feet, readying for action.

Good, she thinks. At least it's getting through to a few of them.

'It doesn't matter what you think. Especially if it is saving your life and those of your hosting countrymen.'

Some of the men begin to stand still and erect.

Their compliance emboldens her. 'And that's what is most important here,' she says firmly. 'Do as I say and you will be actively fighting Hitler.'

'Yes, quite right. Thank you, Daphne.' A voice from behind.

She spins round to see Septimus, Gerard and Miss Sabine. Oh. So this is why the men have stood to attention. Internally she breathes a sigh of relief. Whatever one thinks about the eccentric trio and their civilian garb, there is something in their stature, their confident but urgent gait, which is arresting. The men have seen it and understand at once that playtime is over.

'Now,' says Gerard, 'I suggest you do what the lady said and start learning your lines.' He eyes them with disdain. 'Unless of course some of you want to die?'

It all goes more smoothly after that. Although anyone can see their hearts are not in it, the soldiers submit to instruction.

Septimus, she notes, is watching and busily scribbling on a ledger. It looks like he is assessing them. This helps as the men learn to re-enact what Daphne had witnessed that night.

After they are sure that the soldiers understand what is required, Septimus dismisses them and tells them to take the afternoon off as a reward. A cheer goes up for that.

'I don't know,' says Gerard when they are alone on the parade ground. His beard and his eyebrows, Daphne realises now, have been trimmed, effecting a look which is less eccentric and more formidable. 'If they don't believe it, it might not work. There has to be commitment.'

Miss Sabine nods. 'Yes, we need to throw everything at it if it's to work to disrupt the German plans.'

Septimus tuts. 'It's going to be a tall order.'

There seems little more to say. They walk back to a vehicle bay near the entrance. Arthur Eldridge is in a car waiting for Miss Sabine and Gerard. He waves at Daphne and points at his ears and mouth. 'All back now?'

She smiles and says, 'Yes. I'm fine, thank you.'

He mouths, 'Good. No doubt I will see you soon,' adding hand gestures and pointing to his eye to reinforce his meaning. Then he cranks the engine on.

Septimus offers Daphne a lift back to the manor, but she declines and tells him a walk will do her good.

Then, as quickly as she can, she hurries to the sentry point.

Jack is already waiting.

CHAPTER TWENTY-SIX

Late afternoon. Sun gauzy in the west, hidden behind a mackerel cloud bank.

At the top of the trees, leaves ripple like fingers on a piano, playing a sibilant *shh*.

The heat lulls.

Breathing out a sigh of gratitude to the clouds, the bumpy limewashed walls of the former coaching house relax and contract minutely. Above them, in the rafters, beams creak. Dormice settle into their nests.

An amber wash bathes the pub's beer garden.

Dotted about on tables and benches, workers sit and chew the fat. The occasional laugh punctuates the soft hum of chitter-chatter. Off-duty soldiers, some with Canadian accents fresh to the Kingdom, mix with local girls who have told their parents they are somewhere else.

Shirtsleeves are rolled up, newspapers folded into makeshift fans.

Glasses clink.

The mood is cheerful, flirtatious, fun, a welcome respite from the commotion and chaos that whirls throughout the week, tightening souls and foreheads both.

Snippets of conversation:

'Ain't Arthur? Behind the barn. I saw 'im there, I swear.'

'And then she said, "Not in *my* bloomers, you don't!" '

'Half a pound I reckon. Poachers' Moon coming fast.'

Daphne does not know what most of them are talking about. The soft snatches need context. Yet there is comfort to be had in knowing there is life outside, that people can find time to be ordinary.

No one has given them a second look since they have arrived. It is almost as if she belongs. Or perhaps no, not belongs – *deserves* to be here. A sudden sense of joy fills her. There hasn't been much of that lately in her life, Daphne realises, what with the close shave at the ritual and the rescheduling of the operation. And there, always there, bubbling away at the back of her brain, Uncle Giuseppe, head down, arms out, floating, spiralling, in the dark depths of unknown fate. Her mother will be going out of her mind.

But there is not much to be done about that, so she pushes away the thoughts. Or else they might grab hold of her and pull her under too.

Stop.

Pause.

Yes, pause. This what is going on here, she thinks. Everyone has paused. She should too. There is no one here to watch her with a critical eye, assess, judge, categorise.

She is off duty.

She breathes deeply and, at last, tension begins to drift from her, out of her. In her mind she pictures it as a balloon, purple like a bruise, on a string floating off a few feet over to the right, up to the sky. Much as she would like to kiss it goodbye, she understands that it will be needed again soon to sharpen her wits, so she cannot relinquish it completely. But for now she can park it over there, be free of it. Of all of it. For a little while.

Jack has settled them at a table with a view of the road and gone to fetch the drinks. Daphne, erring on the side of polite convention, has requested a cup of tea.

Beneath her feet the earth continues to bake. She undoes a

shoe and lets her stockinged toes touch the grass. Warmth. A dragonfly, luminescent, feathery, flies over her shoulder and hovers above the wooden trestle table.

The creature fires a memory: the woods back home, a few years since, with her parents' friends, the Daltons. They had gone for a picnic. A walk was suggested by young Roy Dalton, the eldest son, and he and Daphne ended up sitting near the slow-moving brook. Dragonflies darted over the surface. They tried to keep their eyes on them, describing the most dominant colour on each. It had been an entertaining diversion on a lazy and dull Sunday. Then Roy took her hand: his feelings were deeper than she had assumed. The word 'engagement' was used. She was so horrified she scrambled to her feet, without another word to the would-be suitor, and bolted for home.

Her mother was mortified to hear what had occurred on the young people's walk. Daphne, she yelled in her incandescence, had shown them up. Roy was of good stock, his family of some standing. A match would have been fortuitous. Her father was less upset, though he instructed her to be more gentle with men. They had not seen the Daltons again.

She wonders, as the dragonfly spins off upwards, what Roy is doing now. All the young men have been conscripted. Carabella, she thinks, may have mentioned the RAF. Without realising, she lifts her eyes to the still, blue sky that is streaked with feathery clouds.

There are places in Soho where you can catch a drink out of hours, but they are not above ground like this, in full view of any passing magistrate. Nobody here seems at all worried.

By the hedge that outlines the garden's perimeter she spies a gang of lumberjills. A couple of them must have lodgings in one of the local villages or towns as there are two bicycles leaning against a nearby oak tree. Most are still in their uniforms, although a handful wear civvies.

On one of their bench tables a plate is piled with iced buns. Her mouth waters. It has been a long time since she's seen them. Not since the rations came in. How decadent it would be to have one with a cup of tea. A real Sunday treat. She thinks, given the dearth of such unmitigated luxury, it is surprising that they haven't all been wolfed down. However, the main attraction is on the other trestle table, where some of the girls are drinking half pints of what looks like apple juice but is likely to be cider. The lumberjills are in fine spirits, chirpy and talkative. Their camaraderie is evident.

A pang of envy goes off in Daphne's stomach. She is the only woman on her team, and she feels it.

One of the girls has noticed she is watching them. Daphne turns her head away, worried she appears nosy. After a moment, when she looks back, the same woman is smiling at her. She returns the gesture.

'Fancy a bun?' the lumberjill calls. 'There's some going spare.' She holds up the plate and tilts it towards Daphne: an offering.

Half-inclined to say no for modesty's sake, she begins to shake her head but then a thought intrudes, a memory of doughy softness and sweetness on the tongue, the gentle mastication that is perfectly complimented by a cup of China tea. Before she even registers herself saying it she feels her mouth twitch and the word 'Absolutely!' is out. The lumberjill grins.

Pleased with the response, Daphne disentangles herself from the bench in as ladylike a manner as possible. It is difficult in a skirt, as she must raise one leg and then the other. The flesh between her legs is exposed to the light for a fraction. Shorts, she thinks, observing several of the lumberjills, are so much more practical. Though ironically probably viewed as daring down here. Daring! she tuts – only three months ago she had been tottering around in high heels, fishnets and far tighter shorts. You can get away with almost anything onstage. But this is not the West End.

At close range the buns are even more enticing. 'Gosh,' she says. 'How did you come by these?'

'Ladan,' says the lumberjill and points to one of the dark-haired women on the other table pouring herself a glass of amber liquid. 'Boards with a landlady in Lynthurst. The old girl's a dab hand at baking. Sent them over for our Bible class.' She winks, raises her cup and says loudly, 'Amen.' Upon hearing her exclamation, the nearby girls raise their cups or glasses and repeat, 'Amen,' as if it were a reflex.

'Would you like to sit down?' the lumberjill asks. Daphne shakes her hand and takes a proffered bun. 'I'm Penelope, by the way,' she says. 'Call me Penny.'

'I can't,' says Daphne. 'I mean, I can't sit down. I *am* able to call you Penny.'

Daphne rolls her eyes with disdain at her poor communication. 'I meant . . .' She points to the back of the pub. A wooden barn door is wedged open by the careful placement of a large red brick. 'I'm waiting for someone.'

Penny winks again. 'Lucky you.'

'Oh, it's just a friend,' Daphne hastens to add.

But Penny does not appear to hear her and says with a sigh, 'Most of the chaps here just rag on us.'

'Really? Why?' That is surprising.

'They say they're only joshing, but you can tell a lot of them are of the view that it is unbecoming for women to do men's work. My own mother told me it was "common". Not impressed when I joined up,' she says in her loud, emphatic voice.

Daphne makes sympathetic noises and thinks again of Carabella. It is likely she would be of a similar opinion to Penny's mother. It has been her ardent desire to marry Daphne

into English respectability and thus justify all the money they
spent on schooling and the Ladies' Institute. She supposes that,
although she will be unlikely to tell her parents about the type
of work she is doing now, they would think it more acceptable
than the Timber Corps. The thought makes the option attractive again. 'How did you come to choose the Timber Corps?'
she asks Penny.

'I didn't want to work in a bomb factory really. I like the
outdoors, you know.' Her face, pretty in a girlish way, opens up
as she speaks. She is freckled with light skin and blonde hair
which is bobbed at the shoulders, very curly and a bit too frizzy.
There is something about the wideness of her mouth and her
snub nose that suggests a mischievous nature. 'Father wasn't
very keen on me doing farm work,' she says. 'So that was that
– forestry it was.' Penny brings up her legs to hug her knees,
which Daphne notices are slightly scabbed and scratched. A bit
like her own. 'What about you?'

'Oh,' she says. Should she tell? 'I don't think I'm allowed
to . . . you know . . . disclose.'

Penny's eyebrows rise. 'I say . . . doing what?'

Daphne hesitates. She remembers that Vivian told her the
Farnham team were in the Royal Engineers. She gives it as cover.

'How interesting,' says Penny. 'Do tell me more.'

Daphne has not anticipated further questions and is on the
verge of inventing some bridge-building project – though the
only famous engineer she knows is Isambard Kingdom Brunel,
having once visited the Clifton Suspension Bridge. However,
she is saved by a prod in the back. It is lucky, as there are no
wide rivers in the New Forest. Penny's eyes greedily draw in the
sight of the newcomer.

'I'm putting these on our table,' says Jack. He is holding a
pint glass and a cup of tea, the latter of which looks rather
gauche now. 'Just need to get one more. Oh, is that a bun?'

Daphne realises she is still holding one. 'Oh yes, from Penny. This is Jack, by the way. We're working together,' she adds, feeling the need to justify their appearance here. 'We've just stopped by before we have to get a part, for our, er, engineering enterprise.' The lie trips out before she can stop it. She glances at Jack, whose right eyebrow rises ever so slightly.

A couple of the other girls have stopped talking and paused to study Jack. Penny is staring. So it is not just her, thinks Daphne. Jack *does* have broad appeal.

He returns to the pub, whistling and jingling the change in his trouser pockets as he goes. Both she and Penny watch him. He has changed his shirt since this morning. This one is a royal blue which, even from behind, is exceptionally fetching, defining his shoulders and setting off his thick blonde locks to perfection.

'A very pleasant workmate indeed,' says Penny in a brazenly wistful voice.

I *am* lucky, Daphne thinks. She takes her leave, thanking the lumberjill.

The iced bun is balanced across the top of the cup of tea. In her other hand she has Jack's pint. She tiptoes across the garden like a tightrope walker, depositing the provisions precisely.

The bun now lies on the table before her, glistening. Unable to wait any longer, she breaks it in two and places one half next to Jack's pint. Then she gobbles up her portion. It is lovely, barely touches the sides, probably because she hasn't had anything to eat since breakfast.

Perhaps she should eat. Jack would know if they served food here – she supposes a ploughman's might be on offer. But when he returns he has a drink in his hand, which he waggles in front of her. 'Port and lemon,' he explains. 'I thought you might fancy something stronger. If you don't want it, I'll have it.'

She does want it. This particular drink was one of Mrs Trevelyan's favourites. And Brigit's too. She associates the thick sweet taste with comfort and congeniality and has to exercise great restraint to prevent herself from guzzling it down at the same speed she demolished the bun. After the first gulp she forgets she is hungry and quickly becomes garrulous.

Jack asks her what she did before the war, and she finds herself trilling out a stream of humorous anecdotes about the stage. She recounts the time a flamethrower set the theatre alight, the pranks of the acrobats who walked on their hands and gave the chars a fright. Her companion finds this extremely amusing. When he laughs there are creases at the sides of his eyes which begin in the shallows and then deepen. This is how she knows he is genuine. One cannot fake those lines. So on she goes to the knife thrower with two fingers missing who had wooden replicas made. The strongman who was frightened of mice. She likes making Jack laugh.

His comebacks and comments are funny too. His mind is keen, able to whizz like a busy bee from subject to subject, bud to bloom, cross-pollinating her comments, marvelling at her thoughts.

They recharge their glasses. The sun comes out from behind the clouds and shines down on them.

Jack sees how the light plays upon her hair. Her eyes sparkle. He thinks she is beautiful but says only, 'I bet you look marvellous onstage.'

She takes the compliment and another port with ease and asks him about his life.

Born in Canada. His mother was a society girl and met his English father when he was posted at Halifax. He was in the navy and soon after Jack's birth was sent overseas. The family moved around a lot. His mother, he tells her, had some kind of nervous condition which made caring for a baby exhausting for her. A few years after his younger sister was born, it was decided he was old enough to be packed off to an English boarding school. A cloud passes over his face as he speaks of holidays spent in the deserted grounds – one of two boys who couldn't go home. The other had been an orphan and sometimes went to visit his uncle. Jack was often unsure what country his family were living in.

One of the teachers, who lived in married quarters in the grounds, had an older son who fancied himself as something of an inventor. Jack was fascinated by him and would spend days in a small rickety shed at the edge of the school grounds with the young man, Freddie, making anything from powered carts to rockets and other projectiles. It was the beginning of a vocation.

Daphne finds the conversation easy and fluid, like the several ports. Talk of an ill-fated rocket launch prompts Jack to muse on the Cone that they are building and the abruptly reduced timescale. 'I think it's doable,' he says. 'But I worry we might not run enough tests. Unfortunately I know what happens when you don't do that. Though Jonty, of course, seems to be professional. I can see why you work with him. There's genius there, I'd say.'

'Oh yes.' Daphne is pleased to be able to contribute again. 'His family have been in the business for decades. They are well known in magical circles.' She is going to drop in a prestigious award that Jonty's father had won but notices Jack has stopped listening and tilted his head towards a bench, where a couple of older men are hunched over their drinks.

'Did you hear that?' Jack asks, abruptly changing the subject. He frowns hard and looks at his watch.

'Hear what?' She is a little put out that he has not been attending to her.

'That fellow just said he was off for his tea.'

'Oh,' she says, nonplussed. The villager's daily routine is of no interest to her.

'It's a bit early, isn't it?' Jack is watching them now.

'Oh, I don't know. What time do they have it round here? My dining times are irregular because of the shows. It depends on matinees and evening performances.'

The creases in his forehead blacken. 'I make it quarter to four. What do you have?'

Daphne does not have a watch.

Jack rises to his feet. 'Must check.'

He swings his legs over the bench and jogs over to the table, where one of the men is collecting his things together in a leather bag.

Jack speaks. An older man holds out his wrist. Jack takes it and twists it. He sucks in his lips and bobs his head tightly. Now he is running back. 'Look, I'm sorry,' he says. He shakes his wrist, puts the timepiece to his ear and curses. 'Damn. I think it's stopped.' Undoing the strap, he hands it to Daphne, presumably seeking confirmation.

Yes, it has definitely stopped. She turns the crown. 'What time is it then?'

'Five to six,' says Jack, most vexed. 'I'm late. Got to go. The cog. I'll miss them.'

She does not know why he is so bothered. Surely he could go tomorrow. Although, yes, she thinks, time is of the essence. Ironically.

Jack backs away from the table, hands up, palms facing her. 'I'll have to run. You can . . .' he says scratchily, as if his breath is catching in his throat. 'You can talk to the girls, can't you?'

'Well . . .' begins Daphne. But he has broken into a gallop, weaving through the tables and disappearing out of view.

Daphne sits there on her own. She has not expected to be abandoned like this. Part of her thinks it is slightly rude. The other part thinks he is doing his job. She remembers he mentioned it this morning. It leaves her in a bit of a quandary.

What is she to do? Wait here and hope he returns? What if he doesn't? Perhaps she ought to make her way back to Burleigh Hall. Not that she has a clue where it is. But she is a resourceful woman. Of course, the lumberjills know the forest well. They might help point her in the right direction. She gazes over.

Their numbers have diminished significantly. She has been so caught up in conversation with Jack that she has not noticed any movement outside of their little bubble. Now the dark trees over the hedgerow have lengthened their shadows. There is just the one bike parked against the oak. The garden has emptied to a handful of drinkers.

Fortunately, Penny is still there, conversing with another girl with her hair in plaits.

'Did you say something to make him run?' Penny asks as Daphne reaches the table.

'I don't think so,' says Daphne, though she is not entirely sure.

'You never know with men,' says Penny. 'Different species.'

'Oh no, it's not that,' Daphne says, more to reassure herself. 'His watch stopped. We lost track of time. He had to run for an appointment.'

Penny nods at Daphne's hand. 'What is the time actually? I'll have to get back soon,' she asks, and Daphne realises that she is still holding Jack's watch.

'Oh, blast it,' she says. 'Though I've wound it. It's working now.' She holds the watch to her ear and hears the regular tick.

'Oh gosh,' says Penny. 'Jack might need it. You should try to catch him.'

Daphne scowls. He's got a good ten-minute start on her. Could she catch up? She doesn't even know where he is heading.

But Penny says, 'I saw him take off in that direction,' and points south, to the lane outside.

Daphne glances out. She remembers the road had been long and twisty.

'He didn't take the truck,' says Penny. 'Went on foot. Here, use my bike.' She motions to the solitary cycle leaning against the oak tree.

'That would be helpful.' Daphne thanks her.

'Of course. Just make sure you bring it back. I have to cycle eight miles to camp and I really don't fancy a long walk.'

Daphne latches the watch around her wrist.

Penny asks her if she knows how to ride.

'I'm used to unicycles,' says Daphne. 'So I think I might be able to cope with two wheels.'

She ignores Penny's open mouth and grabs the pushbike, rolls it out of the beer garden.

After a few wobbly revolutions she masters the vehicle. Then she is off, cycling up the hill as quickly as she can manage.

The lane cuts into the forest. The air dampens, becomes thicker, full of smells: pine, dry leaves, hot earth. She pedals furiously, moving into the shadows, the feral centre of the land. A shiver goes through the trees, their leaves thresh at each other. A wind is coming up.

At ground level the forest is almost library-quiet, hushing. Her bike rattles and clangs, the only man- or woman-made sound in the vicinity.

She crests the hill. The road opens up before her. A good hundred yards of it unfurl in a straight line before it curves into darkness. There is no sign of Jack. Where could he have gone?

Something snaps in the bracken to her left. The noise makes her react reflexively, her head swivelling in its direction. There is a gap in the undergrowth. Barely visible, camouflaged by two large holly bushes and overhanging branches, a track meanders off the lane. She would have missed it if it weren't for the noisy creature in the bushes there.

She squeezes the brakes and slows down, circling round to the entrance, calling out, 'Jack! Jack!'

For a split second she registers a flash of royal blue against the trunks, so turns up the path. Or was it royal blue? Perhaps the colour was darker – navy.

The wood is dense here, the shadows deeper.

She coasts the bike down the lane. After a few yards it drops and judders. She steadies the handlebars and looks at the ground.

'Damn it!' she says. Potholes and dips are everywhere. Tractors must come this way when it is boggy and leave their impressions to become hard-baked grooves. No, she wouldn't be able to ride over them. But that is all right – she has almost caught up with him.

She dismounts. Up ahead, the blue shirt has disappeared from view.

He must have taken another path into the forest.

No matter.

Tensing her biceps, she gives the bike a good shove. It lurches, clattering and bumping over the dried mud. She makes sure to avoid the large stones and roots that straggle across the track.

As she progresses, she peers into the woods on either side. It is so much thicker here. Quieter too. The density of trunks absorbs the sound, though every now and then she can hear a distant bird call, the rustle of unseen creatures trampling over the sticks and twigs strewn across the forest floor.

Rubber tyres crunch over leaf litter. Her legs brush against weeds and long grass on the verge. The pungent smell of animal droppings, maybe the manure of the ponies, pricks her nostrils and makes her sneeze.

A jackdaw shrills out in fear. The call echoes eerily through the trees. Or perhaps it is another bird responding. Either way, she finds she is unnerved. A rash of goosebumps creeps up her forearms.

The temperature has dropped.

Now she is becoming aware of the dimness in here. Should she really have come out alone? She might get lost. Has she been foolish? Perhaps. It is only a wristwatch after all.

She is on the verge of giving up and returning when she sees a squat figure in amongst the trees. 'Jack!' she calls again.

This time he hears her. Or at least he responds by unfolding himself into a standing position.

'Your watch,' she yells. 'I've got it!' and begins to jog/wheel towards him.

The figure remains still.

She can't see his clothing in this light – he is just an outline.

A fleeting thought passes over her that this might not be Jack at all.

She breathes in and smells an odd fragrance – something chemical, sweet but very very strong. And as her mind begins to process it, there is a gruff cough behind her.

Ah, perhaps this is him. She clamps on the brakes, jerking up the front wheel to turn round.

Something, a cloth, comes over her mouth. A weight connects with the back of her head.

Hard, heavy, targeted.

Hot, white light, a searing pain, the roaring of a voice – 'No!'

She is unconscious before the tyres hit the ground.

Black. Torches illuminate meagrely, held aloft in the hands of ten, eleven, twelve solitary figures, each clad in dark robes. Faces obscured by hoods and shadows. Cold marble beneath bare feet. A mosaicked spiral. At its centre, flames warping into a twisted pillar of light – blue, orange, red – and clawing high into vaulted darkness.

Cold altar. Metal.

With a channel.

To collect . . .?

Murmurs.

No, not murmurs.

Words, voices, together.

In unison.

Quiet whispers.

Slowly building:

IN NOMINE DE LUCIFERI

REGO MEI SPIRITIS

Echo, echoing off cold walls.

Hellish words pricked with filth.

Infection.

Corruption oozing.

IN NOMINEE DE LUCIFERI

DARE ME TUI SCIENTIA

The air flexes

and buckles under the weight of

stifled breath and

expectation.
AUDI NOS NUNC FRATER BALDUR
LARGIRE SUPER POPULUM TUUM BENEDICTIONEM TUAM
Dripping poison
Into the world.
Birthing something new
Something old
Something ancient.
And the circle of acolytes opens
to give way to . . .
DAMUS TIBI SOLI TERRAE NOSTRAE
Enters the sandman, red-robed, spear in hand.
Spear.
Sacred.
Who intones:
WIR SCHENKEN DIR DAS BLUT DIESES LANDES
TAKE OUR GIFT
Under the hood, spectacles reflect the glassy eyes of others.
The time is right. He can feel the thing preparing to cross over.
He nods to the darkness.
Another man, only skin and bones, is hurled into the circle.
Shaven-headed, bruised, bearded.
As bare as a newborn lamb
he sprawls quaking on the floor.
Lips tremble
but in his eyes there is no fear.
No panic.
Only the blindness of the overwearied
pushed beyond endurance into another state.
His soul has already vacated its shell.
Waiting for the end.
Waiting for it to end.
So that

even when he is pulled up by his arms
and fastened onto the black strap of the altar
he is mute, wordless.
Even when the sandman raises the spear,
its head glinting in the light of the twisting flame.
Even when it is brought down hard into his thigh
and again rips through into his stomach
and again higher, slashing his throat.
Even when his arterial blood sprays high in an arc.
RISE FROM THE DEPTHS AND INTO THE LIGHT
Still he makes no sound.

CHAPTER TWENTY-SEVEN

A wail rises up from the pit of her soul. Not this again. The terror of the nightmare knows no limits. Out, she has to get out of it and sends her mind up, up, up into consciousness. It rises like a diver clawing for the top of a well.

She bursts and breaks the surface to gulp down air.

'Quiet!' A man's voice. Gravelly, hoarse.

Jonty? No. Too rough.

A thump on wood.

She blinks, confused by her surroundings. Why is there straw on the ground? This is not Farnham Castle. There was no hay there.

No, she is not in Surrey now, is she? She has moved. Been transferred. Gone somewhere else. Now, where is it? Here? No, she does not think so. Her lodgings are better than this.

It is . . . She reaches into her bruised memory and tries to untangle the aching mess there.

Burleigh Hall – that is it! She has been sent on a mission.

Operation . . . Operation . . .

Like a fox.

Operation Reynard.

But this is not Burleigh Hall. She squints into the darkness. This is . . . this is . . .

No, she gives up. It is not familiar. Perhaps from a better angle . . .

She tries to sit up but finds she cannot move her hands. Well, maybe a little. Something restricts them.

It is too dark to see much. She looks down. Why is it dark? And why does her head feel like it is bulging, swelling against her hairline? There is going to be a lump there, she knows, though she can't remember how she knows. She puts a hand to the back of it. As she lifts one arm, the other goes with it.

Fingers grope around each other and work down to the wrists. Someone has tied her. At first she wonders if this is a new trick.

Still no recollection.

She decides to give up trying to work all of this out. She is very tired.

And thirsty, her mouth is dry. Acrid. There is an aftertaste of rust on her tongue as if she has bitten it. Her lips are rough. She spits out fibres that have come from a cloth. The odour of a solvent lingers. She closes her eyes and then opens them. Better. She is adjusting to the dark.

Now she sees she is in some kind of room. Rustic. No, not rustic. An outhouse of some sort. Tall walls, uneven, pitched. A door, wooden, illuminated by a low, silvery wash.

Where is the light coming from?

She rolls over and tries to chivvy up her mind. Focus, Daphne, she tells herself. Do what you're good at. Assess your surroundings, dimensions, space.

Yes.

Her eyes sweep the room.

Somewhere nearby she hears a hum and sees a phantom dragonfly hover before her. Beautiful, almost translucent in the thin light, it darts up away and settles on . . . what is that?

A window, or opening, is letting in moonlight.

A good eight feet up the wall, though. And small.

The dragonfly disappears through it.

Moonlight.

What time is it, then?

Not a clue.

What has happened?

She pauses again and tries to clear the fog from her mind.

Yesterday, or was it today, yes, out at the camp. The pub, Jack, the watch. The forest.

Someone hit her.

Who?

Why?

For the watch? She peers down and sees that it has gone from her wrist. She wonders if it was expensive or sentimental and hopes Jack will understand. She wasn't able to prevent its loss. She had the best intentions.

Didn't she?

Yes, it is coming back now – someone coshed her over the head and made off with the timepiece. That must be it. People are desperate these days, it is true. But if that is the case, why have they taken her with them? There is no sense in it.

Still, relief is to be found in the fragments of memory that are congealing into an explanation. Even if there persists a fuzzy sense of dissatisfaction.

Anyway, does it matter why she is here? The reasons are irrelevant to the unequivocal fact that she must get out. She is not meant to be here, of this she is sure.

Pushing herself back, she stretches out her legs and discovers her feet are tied too.

Why bind her like this?

Such restraints are a poor choice, for she has been tied up many times before. Usually onstage. So this goes in her favour. If she can bring a clarity to her brain then she might strategise and think.

There are various positions and poses that might be put to

good use to in order to free oneself from such a situation. Bound feet are one. They have double the strength when applied as a singular unit. She needs leverage, though.

Wriggling over the ground, she feels the surface of the floor and locates a nook. There are lots of dips in the uneven gravel and dust. Without further thought she puts her feet into it and pushes hard. Her derrière is propelled swiftly across the ground. Repeating the action several times, she squirms across the floor like a caterpillar until her head comes up against something hard, a bumpy wall. Using it as resistance, she inches her way up and manoeuvres into a seating position. The exertion has her gasping. Inside her ribcage her heartbeat is accelerating quickly, so she takes a couple of deep breaths and smells the fetid perfume of animal dung.

Strong. It makes her gag.

She recovers and regulates her breathing.

Oxygenised more fully now, her brain processes the surroundings: this has to be some kind of sty or barn or storehouse, though it is presently uninhabited, empty but for some logs against the other side of the room.

Voices. She sits up, alert.

There are people in the next room. Or outside.

Men.

Two.

A jolt of fear crosses her stomach. Who are they? The kidnappers? Or could they be her liberators?

Perhaps she should shout out for help?

Or might they hurt her?

This thought, as it is processed, shocks out a foamy ripple of emotions. The tide of unease tugs at her. No, she will not give in, be swept out into a churning sea of terror. It will only paralyse her. Pointless. The important thing is to stay calm and measured.

She draws in more air. The haze in her head clears, though a dizziness remains at the edges, born of physical injury. Her shoulder hurts. Perhaps she has fallen on it. Though this is not the time nor the place to inventory the damage she has sustained. Right now there are more pressing problems.

Daphne flexes her wrists, enabling her fingers to slip over the skin of the back of her hands. Stretching them out, she reaches the material that binds. Rough, bumpy, fraying. She twists her hands and hears the creak of the fabric: rope. Not very strong rope at that. The kidnappers have been opportunist and grabbed something close to hand.

Good. Not only does this mean it has not been planned, it is likely that the rope has been used before. Its fibres will be weakened.

Any box jumper worth their salt should be able to get out of this.

Now to see if her unconscious body has reacted to the touch of chains and ropes, after Houdini. Have the muscles in her arms, legs and shoulders filled out the space around her? She is tense now, so there is little give. If she can only relax . . .

Relax.

Difficult, but not impossible.

Think.

Yes! Only last year a troupe of levitating Tibetan monks, or at least a group of men who had told her they were such, had tipped her with some techniques on clearing the mind and relaxing the physique. What were they?

She rolls her shoulders, which are not restricted, and lets her head tilt gently from side to side. *Shake your elbows*, she remembers. *Tense your hands. Push them out to the extreme limits of what curtails your strength. Breathe in deep, pure, bright aether, hold. Exhaaaaaallllle . . .*

The exercise draws in more oxygen which permeates her body.

A calmness begins to fill her. A kind of lethargy too, as if her body is absorbing the shock of her present trauma ahead of her mind.

She thinks too of Miss Sabine: '*Empty your mind of thoughts . . .*'
Magnificent white . . .
Inhale . . .

And so she finds her muscles *are* softening. There is less friction at the points of connection from ankle to ankle, wrist to wrist.

Repeating the exercise slowly, focusing on all parts of her body, she begins – yes – to feel, at last, a tiny gap opening up. Not much, true, but sufficient to create enough space to move her finger down between the palms. Gently she inserts, so it becomes another lever pushing her hands out, creating more slack.

One of the men has raised his voice: '*Was sollen wir mit ihr machen?*'

Sweat breaks out over her body. She tenses again. Her heart quickens, for she has spent enough time with Grandfather Günter to understand German when she hears it. *What are we going to do with her?*

She lays still, barely breathing. What is the other man saying?

He is further away, maybe outside; his voice is not as deep so does not carry. She cannot make out what he says.

'*Morgen*', though, she recognises. *Tomorrow.*

Now a scuffling at the door. In the lock a key turns. Just as she manages to throw herself prostrate on the straw, it opens.

Tobacco smoke wafts towards her, and the stale stench of days-old perspiration soaked into clothes that have not been changed. Definitely men.

A syrupy sour smell of alcohol on breath. Strong stuff. Spirits.

Worrying. If they are drunk it could go either of two ways.

Her eyes, though shut tight, detect a change in the light. Behind the lids the blackness transforms to a bloody brown.

One of them coughs, a shrill, unpleasant, clattering sound. His chest is heavily congested. He spits on the floor. *'Sie ist noch bewusstlos. Wir werden eine Weile keine Probleme mit ihr haben.'* She remains unconscious. *We'll have no trouble with her for a while.*

The other grumbles. Something untranslatable. The door closes. Keys jangle in the lock again and the voices become muffled once more.

Whatever they plan to do tomorrow, she does not want to be around for it.

She *will not* be around for it.

Because Daphne Devine is *used* to escaping: a locked room is surely no more challenge than a locked cabinet. There will be a way out, she just has to find it.

Indeed. For she is not just any box jumper, but a most excellent assistant to the fabled Grand Mystique.

Quite so.

She resumes her efforts on the rope. Locating the knot, she is able to slide it closer for inspection. It isn't one she knows. In fact it is irregular and untidy. Amateurs. She gets her fingernails into it. This is just a matter of time.

There is some give there now. A bit more manipulation and she guides the ties up to the widest part of her hand, the palms. She pulls them together, draws her thumb and her little finger right in, then squeezes.

The pain is intense. She grits her teeth, suppressing the urge to cry out – but then one more push and the rope is off. Her hands slip free. She caresses them for a moment and then reaches for her feet. With nimble fingers on the clumsy knot there, it is mere seconds before that rope comes off too.

But what if the men come back in to check her?

Mmm. That won't do.

Everything, all the tricks she and Jonty have ever pulled off, are all about timing.

She will need to bide hers. Find the right moment.

Though it galls her, she fastens the ropes back on, but ensures they are sufficiently loose to rip them off when the hour comes.

Then she will make her move.

It is like a chess game.

But for now she waits.

ACTIVITY IN THE AREA – *The Post*

More than twenty parachutes have been found in the south-west after several hours of enemy fire. A parachute made of silk was discovered by a police sergeant who was patrolling the outskirts of a village situated in the New Forest. It is understood that this caused some alarm, as German markings were all across the canopy. Experts are currently investigating to discover for what purpose the device may have been used. The silk cords are thought to be able to hold a load of approximately 400 lbs, and we can only speculate what the parachute may have delivered. Further parachutes have been recovered. These were scattered over the outlying area, in trees and ponds and across fields. However, despite search parties, no parachutists have been found.

The police sergeant has stated that he had heard a 'swishing' sound. When he went to investigate the source, he found the parachute knotted in a large tree. The harness, though somewhat destroyed, was still attached. A neighbouring farmer has also come forward. He has testified that he found two parachutes in his chicken run and was relieved to find that both were empty.

Church Bells

When the first parachute was found, the vicar of the village was immediately informed and made the decision to ring the church bells. Although it was still in the early hours of the morning, it was felt that local people should be warned of the possibility of airborne troops. Police in the area went door to door to advise the public to be on the lookout for invaders and suspicious strangers, specifically those in civilian clothes, who might be armed with guns and dangerous.

Farmer Thomas Acrington said, 'The parachutes were located very close to my land. Though myself and my workers looked, we could not find any trace of men landing. Which is strange and perplexing . . . There's a few of us now who are wondering if this is all a German hoax.'

One parachute was found in the middle of a village's cricket pitch, another was caught on a rambler rose growing up the side of the nearby inn. Police stopped and searched passing vehicles and checked drivers' and passengers' identification cards. One man said that he had been questioned over twenty times within five miles. Otherwise, there was minimal disruption to the inhabitants. One witness said, 'The noise of the planes woke us but it didn't occur to us that there would be parachutists. Though, at the time, it seemed that they were circling overhead for hours.'

A police spokesman has said that so far there have been no reports of any planes crashing in the New Forest.

CHAPTER TWENTY-EIGHT

When Daphne wakes, the sky outside the wall opening is no longer black. Navy cracks into a dark russet splinter. Dawn cannot be far away.

Her head hurts violently.

Even her teeth ache.

In the pit of her stomach she hears a grumble. It has been a long while since she has eaten.

Action. Daphne sits up straight, supporting herself on her hands, still insecurely tied, and bends her ears to the door. They keen like a radar for any signs of habitation.

All is quiet.

She waits, still, and presently is rewarded with a loud snore.

Good.

They are clearly untrained: the alcohol reveals a lack of discipline on active duty, as do the knots in the rope, both so ineffectively tied. And although she has been taken hostage, they have not interrogated her.

Now is the time.

Come on, Daphne, you can do it.

Yes.

She can.

A deep breath.

Slowly out.

Slowly in.

Then she casts off the ropes and awkwardly gets to her feet. Her limbs have seized up, the fleshier parts of her body throb where she has slept on hard ground. The fog in her head still lingers, not as thick as before. Her shoulder burns.

She ignores the thirst. The adrenalin that has begun hurtling through her veins chases away further symptoms of hunger.

On her feet, she surveys the wall with the glassless window up high. Her hands run over bumps and nooks. It has been constructed when outbuildings for non-humans were thrown together from rubble and materials that had long outlived their function. About nine feet high, with the opening right at the top there. Dips and hollows might be used again for footholds. They are small, but she has small feet. And tiny toes, which are flexible enough to curl up in cabinets.

The lowest potential cavity she finds at about five feet up – far too high even for a dancer to reach.

She steps back and lets her eyes wander.

A log, one of those stacked against the wall, might give her sufficient height.

The pile is also high. Again, too tall for her to be able to sufficiently scale.

This will not defeat her.

Pressing hands against it, she fingers the surface: the uppermost log is knobbly, rough and not yet stripped of bark and nodules.

Yes.

Retrieving the rope that tied her hands, she secures it to the far end of the log. Then she takes the ends and moves to the other side of the pile.

In the same style with which she snaked against the wall earlier, she pushes her feet hard but steadily, in a precise and restrained thrust, against the largest trunk at the bottom, and transfers her weight back so she can pull hard and add to the gravitational effect.

She takes another breath and drags it towards her.

The log scrapes along the floor but then hits a bump on the wood beneath it. She stops, gathers her breath, and inspects the blockage. No, she won't be able to nudge it over using sheer force – it is too big and will probably make too much noise. She needs something to help slide it.

But what?

Straw? Too flimsy.

There is nothing else in the outhouse that she can put to any use. Not even a pail of water.

But there are her clothes.

Her beautiful satin-lined skirt.

Daphne hears herself exhale and notices the fiery determination in the noise. She takes heart from her own conviction. It is strange, as if there are two of her now: a former self occupied by the superficial trappings of the old life, and a new one emerging from the chrysalis of this prison – dedicated, intense, driven to survive. She likes and admires this new person, is astonished by her, as though she is a stranger she has just met. She finds herself propelled onwards.

Off comes the skirt. She turns it inside out and digs her fingernails into the seams. The garment is too well made.

No matter. She works at the fabric with resolved ferocity, elbows out, brow furrowed. Time, time. Why do things always have to be so difficult? No matter. They are what they are.

Eventually she tears off a length and holds it up into the lightening air like a warrior brandishing an enemy's trophy.

With fresh energy she sets about the task and drives the fabric into the space between the wood and the lump. Quickly returning to the other end, she grabs hold of the ropes and tugs.

After two attempts it begins to move.

Bit by bit, inch by inch, sweating with exertion, gritting her teeth, she guides the log to the end. Progress is slow, yes, infuriatingly so, but this way she keeps noise to a minimum. There is no other option.

Finally it reaches a point where another wrench will topple it off the pile.

This is going to be challenging. If she fails to catch it, there will likely be a loud noise as it hits the floor. Though it is only lime dust and stones, she thinks. But still it needs muffling.

She gathers up straw and throws it around the bottom of the log pile, pausing to put her ear to the door.

The alcohol still has the men in its sleepy snare. Two snores – one light and quick, the other deeper and irregular.

Right, she thinks, once everything is in place. If she is going to do this, it has to be now. If the log falls, if it knocks its neighbours off too or unbalances the woodpile, then she is done for. She will have to hide behind the door and take her chances to flee when it opens. Though she understands that realistically escape is improbable that way. Indeed, it might hasten the other plans they have made for her.

She hopes it will be a bullet in the head. She does not want a drawn-out death. Perhaps a run for it will force their hand.

No. No, this is not the way. This is her other self.

She compels her focus back to her primary plan. This log will be her liberty. She is not stupid, she has thought it out.

And she *forever* tries to do her best.

You have always had a courageous heart, of which no one can doubt.

A final deep, composed breath, then she starts to haul.

The log scratches and creaks as it begins its downward slide. She tenses herself and throws up her arms to slow its descent. One hand catches the end, and though it deflects its trajectory to the side, it is not enough to prevent the log crashing down.

It strikes the floor with a hollow bang and plunges sideways. Another loud *thunk* as it rolls along the floor, coming to a pause inches short of the adjoining wall.

Full of nervous dread, she runs and hides behind the door, pressing her frame into the corner as far as she can. Quaking, she holds her hands in front of her chest to stop it being crushed when the men burst in.

Good God – if they haven't heard that, then surely the drum of her heart will alert them?

But there is . . .

. . . only a grunt.

She struggles to hold her breath and keep the lid on a howl of horror building in her lungs. An urge to weep threatens to overwhelm her resistance.

The crackle of straw or hay as someone outside shifts their weight.

Oh God, this is it.

Carabella flashes across the screen of her mind, then her father too. Her death will destroy them. And what if, like Giuseppe, she is never found, her body disposed of somewhere dark, never to be seen again? She cannot let that happen.

It *will* not happen.

Clenching her hands, she exhales as shallowly as she can manage.

Breathe. She does, steadily, quietly, remembering Miss Sabine's instructions. *Relax.*

Silence.

Though is it silence? she wonders.

Nobody is rousing, nor hurrying to the door.

What now? Does she dare peek through a crack in the wood?

If she rallies her nerves and looks, it will prepare her for what is to come. The chink is only a sliver, but very carefully she bends her eye to it and squints. Through the tiny gap she can

see a lean-to of sorts, stacked with hay. Dust circles in the air
there – the sky has lightened significantly. Sunrise. It will make
her plan even more dangerous.

On the ground are a pair of boots and trousers. They are not
moving, yet the sight has her leaping back against the wall, the
notion of impeding assault punching into her mind.

A nasal snuffle follows a shrill congested cough – the younger
of the two.

Her heart stops for a full second.

She closes her eyes.

But still no one comes.

This is positive.

She holds on to it.

Although tremors continue to wrack her, she feels a change
in herself once more and becomes aware of her heart, recovering
from the pause – a small death – beating again with newness
and vigour and life. It feels as if the entire world is waiting for
her next move. Like she is being watched, tested.

There is something that has been blocking her, she thinks.
She finds it, then surrenders it. It is fear. And now it gusts from
her. Though far from at ease, the release makes her shoulders
drop a little.

She galvanises her resolve.

To survive, to win, to evade a fate at the hands of these
incompetents is the goal now set. Her determination doubles.

Invigorated, she creeps out from behind the door and fetches the
scraps of her skirt, slowly bending down over the log.

With care she rolls it towards the window. When she has got
as close as is required, she attaches the fabric to its top end,
though this will make it slippery. Despite the chill of early
morning she takes off her sweater and wraps that over too,
tying the sleeves tightly, so that the log now looks like a giant
green match. Gently she loops one of the ropes around the top

and fastens the other around her waist. She will need that later. Using her feet as a stop, and pulling hard at the rope on the log, she succeeds in lifting it quietly against the wall.

She pats it. Not the sturdiest of stage props, but it will do.

Taking one last sweeping look at her prison, she puts a foot on the lowest protrusion, where a branch has been lumpily sawn off. Her other hand reaches up for the wall.

Using the rope to help take her weight, she makes her ascent. Handholds in the walls provide grip, and she swings back and forth from the wall to the log like a showman's monkey. Delicately, without rushing, she arrives at the top. A silent prayer goes up to the god of logs. For once she is grateful to the rations for ensuring her body is light.

When she manages to get both feet on the stump, she is able to grip the window frame and, with a jump and a heave, shifts her bottom onto the ledge so that she is half sitting, half dangling out of the opening.

Before she swivels her legs over, she reaches back down and snatches the jumper and cream lining.

Outside, the sky is becoming a pale grey.

The barn must have been dug out of a hillside, because the ground beneath the window is higher than that inside. Her jump down is only three feet or so.

Hallelujah.

This has to be somewhere remote and barely used – there are no signs of life, just a small verge of grass and mud straggling around it which spreads to a clearing full of bracken and ferns that have not been cut down for at least a harvest or two. Insects hum above, waking for the day. Beyond, about twenty yards away, the forest stands up darkly against the cloudy sky.

Looking down, she studies the barn. Yes – good. It has not been maintained either. There are large ferny bushes, thistles, a small tree growing from the side.

On tiptoes, minimising the sound, she leaps to the ground and steals along the line of the building, turning down the side that is shadowed. The sky to her right is hazy, filled with smoky clouds. This must be the west. The shrubs here are bulkier, fuller, more verdant. She brushes leaves, twigs and branches away and sees a dip in the earth between the wall. From it sprouts a bushy wide-leafed plant like a green parasol.

This will be the place.

Onto her knees. She digs with her hands, scooping soil, carving out something that resembles an infant's shallow grave.

When it is deep enough she breaks off a couple of overhanging branches, collects handfuls of leaves and sets them to one side.

Back at the north window, she reviews the environment. Halfway to the treeline stands a solitary jagged tree. It is partially dead, maybe struck by lightning, a blot on the bucolic terrain. No one has yet chopped it down. It is conspicuous in its contrast to the lush vegetation. She makes her way over, ignoring the cuts and scratches from bracken and thorny weeds, and removes her jumper. Shaking it out, she drapes it across the lower branches, where it sways softly like a flag at half mast.

The forest is so close. Only yards away.

The thought crosses her mind that she should take the opportunity now and run.

But then she hears a buzzing in her ear. A dragonfly hovering near. Though it is absurd, she has the feeling it is watching her. Waiting to see which decision will be made.

It begins to fly to the trees, then stops abruptly and retreats, spins off back to the barn, pausing to hover over a large thistle about three feet high, dark and fleshy. Its vivid purple head nods back and forth in the breeze.

'Yes,' she whispers. 'Thank you, that will do.'

The creature floats a moment more then flies up over the outhouse.

With long strides Daphne makes her way back to the thistle and wraps the light-coloured satin tatters of her skirt across its spiky leaves. More pointers, flags.

Reaching the barn, she climbs up to the window one last time, unwraps the rope around her waist and throws it down so that it is half across the verge, half over the bracken.

There. The last thing done. Distraction, misdirection, deception – all in place. It is time to pull off the most important trick of her life.

With one foot at the top of the log she kicks it away.

Before it has tumbled to the ground she pivots round, catching her flesh on something as she does so. The stab of pain provokes her to let out an unplanned yelp.

Without waiting to inspect the damage, she springs to the ground as the log collides with the mud floor. This time there is no doubt: the noise and her scream are certain to rouse the Germans.

She races back to the ferny bush, crushes herself into the shallow grave, covers her body with soil, branches and leaves, and makes herself as tiny as possible.

Inside the barn the door flies open and clatters against the wall.

'Hey!'

Steps.

'*Verdammt!*'

More noises. Some sort of physical fracas. One of them cusses.

Pounding footsteps.

The internal door slams against the wall with such force that she hears it rattle open again.

A shout. Clearer, unmuffled by the walls.

They are outside now, searching the clearing for her.

She makes herself even littler.

Rivulets of sweat trickle down her body into the mud,

Her heart becomes hectic again. Like the staccato beat of a battalion's drummer boy, she thinks. It sets the pace for the men running wildly.

If they were dogs they would be sniffing the air now, salivating as they fastened on to her scent.

She breathes lightly and folds inwards, ignoring the fullness of her bladder pressing against the damp earth, the cramps beginning in her arms and legs. With the pain and the tension, it will not be long before she has to change position. Though even a minute movement might draw attention. Might give her away.

Tumbling, tangled thoughts cross her mind. She exhales and releases them.

A hard voice. The younger man is near. She understands his words: 'You take the forest!' An awful racking cough, bubbling with phlegm.

'*Ja*. And if I find her?' The other, switching from German to English. Just as harsh as the first, but louder. Closer.

'Then,' he says with cold distinction, 'just kill her.'

'*Ja*.'

The heavy tread of boots pauses. The weightier of the two men pants. Then, slower, he comes towards her.

Thud, thud, thud.

So near, perhaps only inches from where she lies.

Is this it?

But then, sharp: '*Schau!*' Look.

'*Dort! Da hängt was am Baum. Sie ist in den Wald gegangen.*' *She's gone into the forest.*

The man brushes past her ferny cover.

Then onwards.

They are taking the bait.

Bracken crunches and breaks underfoot.

Their footsteps grow faint.

The impulse to make a run for it is making her legs physically twitch. But she knows she must stick to her plan: if the men have a gun, it will be the end of her. And this is not the objective.

Minutes pass.

She remains motionless, perspiring in her shallow grave.

Then she hears them – at a pace, returning.

This time they do not pelt past her hiding place but to the other side of the barn.

The doors of a vehicle slam. An engine fires up. The driver hits the accelerator.

Then the car speeds away.

CHAPTER TWENTY-NINE

Ninety-nine. One hundred.

Time.

Her breathing is approaching something that almost resembles normal. Gradually she extends her body and rights herself, stretching out her legs. Leaves, earth and branches fall off her.

They have gone.

Well done.

She pulls herself out of the hole, using the branches of her saviour, and clambers out of the side.

Standing up, shaking out the cramps in her limbs, massaging her shoulders, she allows a sigh of extreme relief to fill the air. She raises her head to stretch her neck and as she does she feels her new self step up and out, no longer a latent image camouflaged by skin and hair, blurred by lack of focus, but a real flesh-made being that springs from her heart and reaches into the ends of her fingertips, the bottoms of her toes.

This new Daphne takes charge.

It is not over yet, she says. There is still much to do.

A dirt track leads west, away from the barn, down into another part of the forest.

If they have gone that way, then she should choose the opposite and aim for the east.

Ensuring there is no sound of a car or engine, she emerges from the shadows and heads for the trees.

CHAPTER THIRTY

The noises come before she sees them.

Voices.

They are singing a song.

Something about little fishies swimming. Jaunty and cheerful. Oh, how wonderful to feel like that. She hopes, one day, she might also sing with such verve.

And they swam, swimmy, swam, bam, over the dam . . .

One foot in front of the other, she follows the noise.

Though she does not know it, all that is propelling her forwards is the sheer force of her new-found will. Extreme exhaustion, dehydration and a ballooning, immense lightheadedness have been nagging at the edges of resolution, whispering that she should wind down. Her limbs are certainly getting heavier and heavier, urging her to sit and rest.

If she was to do that, she knows she would sit on the forest floor forever and nobody would ever see her again. That's what happens with fairies, isn't it? Something about mushrooms in a circle. If you sit down in them you'll end up in Fairyland. And never be seen again.

That wouldn't be too bad. She could trade war for fairies.

Her parents always did say she was off with them anyway.

But she can't do that to her parents.

Not when she's come so far.

Not when she's come *this* far.

Not when . . . she does not remember what she is thinking.
The end of the sentence – what is it?

Something about Carabella.

She needs to move.

Walk.

On.

Yes, just a little more.

One foot in front of the other.

That's all it takes. All it takes.

Left, right, left, right.

Marching drill has sunk into her brain at a subconscious level.
Internalised, the rhythm beats out silently in her mind and
coordinates her body. Or at least she thinks it does.

She ploughs on.

Up, over the logs, slipping on moss, avoiding bogs and mires,
lashed by long grasses and yellow gorse.

The forest had sometimes seemed to surge against her, grow
stronger and thicker in its vegetative lustre, shimmering greenly.
Creatures had come out and regarded her progress unafraid, as
if they realised she was becoming one of them, part of the
woods.

It was only the dragonfly that popped back now and again,
gliding on, a luminescent guide that kept her on track. Not that
she knew where it was taking her.

She just kept on. Trusting in the insect, so sage.

Keeping as straight as she could.

Must not mind those scratches about the legs, she thinks,
and the aches and bumps and the lightness – oh, there it is again.
Lightness. Just a little rest.

Not now, fatigue! I will NOT give in!

Out over the grass. Not scratchy. Good. *Step, step, whoopsie,
straight, Daphne, steady! Step, yes, that's it, step.*

She can see them at last. They are loading freshly felled logs onto a truck, their uniforms glowing amongst the trunks. Sun shining down on them. Singing about the swimming fishies.

Back to the pond in the field they swam . . .

And there is Penny from the pub. She is probably worrying about her bicycle. Will she be angry?

It doesn't matter.

Penny becomes a target.

Daphne stumbles across the clearing and tries to raise her hand. Exhaustion will not allow it. Instead she attempts to call, 'Penny!' but there just comes a hoarse, rusty noise, as if her vocal cords have dried up.

No matter – she treads on and on towards them. *Left foot in front of the right. That's it.*

One of the girls sights her and, taken off guard by the peculiar sight, recoils and drops her end of the log.

The lumberjill up the other end begins a rebuke then, reading her partner's expression, turns to see what has dismayed her so.

The weird being coming towards her like a staggering fawn, dirty, brown, ruddy and in tattered rags, confuses her and she too dumps the log. Instead of standing there dumbstruck and useless, she cries out, 'Oh God. What's happened to you?' and flies over to Daphne.

A strong arm under her shoulders and the weight of her body decreases, enabling her to move-stumble-hop-falter that little bit further on.

Other girls are appearing out of the trees, drawn by the spectacle. Crowding round. Concerned faces. Hands clamped over mouths.

Here is Penny. 'What's happened? Did he . . .? Was it that man who did this to you?'

Another pair of arms, and she is lifted onto the back of the truck.

Someone says, 'Where's it all coming from? Can we stem it?'
A different voice: 'Burleigh Hall. There's a medic there.'
'No, the blood. Look, her leg.'
'Poor dear.'
Jumpers are pushed under her head. Hands grab her feet and swivel them up and into the truck. Clothes are whipped off and laid across her.
'There's a gash here too.'
'Quick. Start it.'
Penny's face lowers to hers. She dabs a handkerchief on her tongue and rubs at Daphne's face. 'What happened to you, old bean? What has he done?'
It is important to counter that idea, Daphne thinks. It is not Jack's fault. 'Kidnapped. Germans,' she tries, unsure if the words have made it out of her brain into the air.
Two bodies slide into place either side of her. Females. Stabilising her as the truck takes off, jogging her weary body from side to side. How grateful she is to these wondrous beings, these strong Amazonians.
Finally safe, in the presence of angels, she closes her eyes and sleeps.
Nine lives.
Eight lives.
Seven lives left.

CHAPTER THIRTY-ONE

'And then when Jack arrived without you, we assumed you'd be walking back,' Jonty is saying. 'I thought it strange when you didn't appear at the workshop.' He is explaining the process of how the alarm was raised. Or rather not raised. 'Well, I went over to your hut and . . .'

She lets him talk. It appears to calm him. He is the more upset.

Daphne, perversely, has come through the experience of the past days relatively unhurt. Relatively.

At least the medics have given her a clean bill of health – that is, as clean as is necessary for someone whom the country urgently needs to get back in the saddle right away.

The wound in her leg has been stitched. At the back of her head the contusion does not need further attention. It will heal naturally if she takes care of it and washes it with salt water once a day. She promises she will.

There has been some talk of brain injury. However, it is the opinion of the medical staff that none has been sustained. The patient is as coherent as is necessary to perform Operation Reynard and does not need convalescence.

Nurses were sent to administer a good meal, and then she became dozy. One of them stayed. And she dreamed that a doctor came in and checked her *down there*. It occasioned some discomfort but then he said, 'Intact.' After that she slept.

She was awoken in the middle of the night, or was it the day, by Septimus. Furtive and saturnine in the shadows cast by the bedside lamp, he recorded as many details about the barn and its location as she could remember. And he waited quietly as she recounted the events that had led to her miraculous escape, though concern lurked in the furrows of his forehead. He interrupted when she spoke of the totemic dragonfly who had 'guided' her getaway. 'There was no divine intervention here, Daphne,' he said with gravity. 'No "Miracle of the New Forest". It was all you. Remember that.'

And she would.

There was nothing extraordinary she could bring to her descriptions of the assailants, more's the pity. One she thought had been older, though could not peg an age. He had worn boots and brown trousers and was of a heavy build, or so she had gathered from his exertions. Of the other she had seen nothing, only heard his voice, which she guessed had been used for fewer years than his partner's. Certainly it was higher. This younger man's tread had been lighter as he had torn around searching for her. He had more agility, though his chest was heavily congested.

Of her outhouse prison, she could only say it faced south. That it was formed of an external lean-to and a larger chamber. She gave a good description of the walls, however, recalling the bumps and glitches, but of the colour she found she had no idea. It could have been white but was probably grey. Perhaps parts had been built with brick. It was a building much like those found on other rural farms. She had headed north to the treeline but had no idea if she had continued in that direction once she had lost sight of the sun behind the foliage. Crossing several streams and rocks had altered her trajectory. And she had no idea how long she had walked for.

The agent nodded her on. 'Any detail is helpful.' It relieved her of a portion of guilt.

There was something about him, she thought, that was similar to Miss Sabine's presence, though Septimus soothed the air through which he moved. There was a certain composure in his features when his mind was occupied elsewhere, an attitude of quiet absorption, as if he were carefully routing out explanations, clues, plans. There was no judgement in his words, only gratitude and interest.

She was glad that they had someone like this on their side. Power lay within. Which type of power, she didn't know. He had the attitude of a sceptic but the knowledge of a believer. She wasn't sure what made him tick, where he stood on the spectrum of possibilities that started in magic and ended in science. Or what his persuasion was. But then again, she reminded herself, it didn't really matter, did it? Lots of things that had seemed so important mere months ago had been reduced in significance. There was nothing like a close shave with death to focus the mind.

And that is exactly what Septimus told her before he left. 'The ordeal has been unpleasant and frightening. But if you can take something constructive from it, remember how your senses heightened and your resolve did not fail.'

And, as he shut the door, she ruminated on the notion until marvellously she fell back into a restorative sleep.

Then, this morning, Jonty has been allowed in to see her. And he has spent the past twenty minutes apologising for not acting sooner. He has not asked for details of what had happened, so she assumes he has been briefed by Septimus. As the words and justifications tumble from his lips, he sits by her bed and occasionally strokes her hair.

She lets him. He needs the reassurance that she is truly here.

And curiously, when she replays the events in her head, it is as if they did not happen to her but to someone else who was infinitely more capable.

At other times she remembers the strange feeling of a new self emerging. A butterfly self. What a thought.

But she *has* survived. That is worth spending time on. And when she does linger over that, as her body strengthens and her health returns, she feels an unusual build of energy bubble up. Sort of . . . zesty. She is very aware that she is alive. In fact, right now, if Jonty weren't here she would have a mind to rip off the blankets and go and find Jack and do something unspeakably carnal to him. The thought makes her cackle with wicked delight.

'Are you laughing at me?' Jonty's eyes are still watery and full. He must have drowned his anxiety and sorrows last night.

'No, of course not.' She lays a hand on his arm. 'I just . . . it's contrary, I know, but I am thrilled to be alive. Really I am. I feel full of life, ready to go out and do all sorts of wild things.'

Jonty's face compresses. 'Are you sure? You're not just saying that?'

'Sincerely,' she says. 'I mean it. I have a slight pain in my leg where I cut myself, but I've slept, eaten and woken refreshed. I've not felt as fit for a good long while.'

'Well, that's just as well,' her friend replies. 'I'm glad you said that.'

'Really?' she says, alert and keen.

'Yes, because they've brought Operation Reynard forward.'

'To when?'

'Agents in Bavaria have reported that Hitler has ordered a conference at Berghof to discuss the invasion. Plans have been accelerated.'

Somehow she has wondered if that might be the case. The noises in the manor have indicated a distinct increase in activity. 'Again?'

'Indeed. So, we have been in consultation with the mystics and such. The new date is one that Gerard Potter and Miss

Sabine tell us is on the Celtic calendar – Lammas, Lughnasadh. A pagan festival. The section heads believe this will amplify everything. Powerfully. Which of course is our purpose.'

She is listening to him but not processing his words.

'We shall start the ritual at ten o'clock at night and continue into Lammas morn. Captain de Wohl has specified that the thirty-first is auspicious astrologically, which will worry Hitler. So we are hastening to complete in time.'

She registers the date with shock. 'But the thirty-first is tomorrow, Jonty. That cannot be achieved, surely?'

He picks up her hand. 'Dear old bean. You've lost a day, I'm afraid,' he explains. 'The thirty-first is tonight.'

31 JULY 1940

CHAPTER THIRTY-TWO

One last inspection of the device has been permitted.

Ernie has greeted her as if she is a returning goddess, come to breathe life back into the land. And Jack, well. His eyes are red and thick-lidded. She does not want him to feel bad, but she is pleased he does. It is confirmation.

Only the English can understand how many layers of advancement, stages, points of courtly behaviour are cut through, flouted, ignored, when Jack flings his watch-less arms around her and holds Daphne tight.

The other men avert their eyes.

She gives into it. Feels the flush of peachy pleasure spread through her. The thrill of his closeness, of his touch.

'So sorry,' he says, pulling apart. 'Damn that blasted cog.'

'It was an accident of happenstance. Not your fault.' Daphne steps back, aware that Jonty and Ernie are waiting to resume.

The physical distance between the young people has been reinstated to a level of clean propriety, so Jonty feels he can take charge again. 'There it is,' he says with pride. He wants his Daphne to see his work, to marvel at it. He needs this, and suddenly appreciates how much more she has become than an assistant – now friend and surrogate daughter. Though immediately his brain rationalises that it is important that she is happy with the mechanics of the contraption. She will have to play her role.

He does not like the fledgling romance, blaming Jack's negligence for the pitch-black hours he spent in the grips of palpitations once her absence was finally noticed. He will never go through that again. Never.

'Much better,' says Daphne. The team have clearly worked fiercely on the 'cone'. Much of the grass around it has been worn away by tracks of feet and wheelbarrows, the heavy lugging of machinery.

Now it is impressive. Decorated with curious ciphers, the five-sided lantern is what they would call at the theatre a 'showstopper'. Pentacles, cursive script, runic symbols, the alpha and omega and more occult imagery from Gerard's grimoire, the *Key of Solomon*, cover the surface, giving it an aura of the sacred and occult. The hinges that were to allow the top to slide open and the sides to fall back are now hidden discreetly, no longer visible even as she walks close to it. Only the very cynical mind could remain unmoved by such an object, especially when it was to be encountered in a circle of 'all the witches of England'.

They have done well.

Across the ground, the cabling that runs to the rotator has been dug out of its trench, ready to be transported.

Watching her, Jonty says, 'There are men digging a new path for the cabling up in Boulderwood Forest. That's where we'll perform.'

She has a notion that she had passed the place with Jack that day: a sloping wood away from the road. Private, secluded.

Prowling around the cone, Jonty kicks dust at the base. 'We need you to light the tinder at the bottom of the box. There's a grate there. Shouldn't need much. But it will be moving.'

'No, we can't,' she says. 'The bombing in Christchurch—'

He cuts her off. 'The instruction has come from above, I'm afraid. Though I've been in touch with, er, a source. He tells me it was likely to have been a Heinkel. They deliver their entire load of bombs. We think the ghastliness in Christchurch was due to an accidental drop from a returning bomber. Or one that was offloading leftover munitions. If you were the target it would have rained down bombs.'

Daphne remembers the hellfire and shudders. It is strange to think that they have been lucky.

Jonty sees her reaction and does his best to reassure. 'We've scaled down what we were working on. There will be an effect. It will be momentary, sudden – perhaps the equivalent to four or five fireworks going off at once. The lantern will flare briefly and then go out. Not much.'

'The risk will be minimal,' says Jack. His mouth is fixed, shoulders tense, eyes pleading.

She nods to please everyone.

And Jonty is satisfied. 'As the cone rotates,' continues the magician, 'it should burgeon to give the necessary impression – of a dazzling cone of energy. Although fleetingly.'

Daphne bends down and examines the tinder. It is accessible through a saucepan-like section with openings in its sides. If this cone/lantern is to be in motion, it will be harder to light unobtrusively. She will have to time the rotations.

Jonty's face is at her shoulder. 'You must remain close to it. I know you will be dancing, performing some sequence of steps. Don't let it out of your sight. Keep your *eyes* on it, though – hands up, all the twirls, direct the audience upwards.' His instructions are exactly as if he is teaching a new trick. 'When the ritual nears its climax, use this taper.' He hands one from his pocket. 'You may also borrow my cigarette lighter.' It is well-loved and reliable, a present from Mrs Trevelyan, so she bows her head in respect as she takes it. 'I hope they are both small enough for you to conceal in your . . . on your person,' he whispers in her ear. 'Sleight of hand, my dear.'

'I can do that,' she says and puts them in her pocket.

'I believe Miss Sabine, Gerard and the man who is to perform the role of the priest are to meet you at Bolderwood Farmhouse. You can work out a trigger word with them.'

'A trigger word?'

'A cue to light the lantern.'

'Do I need one?'

'Yes, because there will be a distraction at that very moment.'

'And can you tell me what that will be?'

He does not answer her question. 'The priest, is it Alex?'

'Yes, though I have not been formally introduced.'

'Then I will brief Alex on the distraction.'

'Which is?'

Jonty casts his eyes around. 'Need-to-know basis, you understand how it is.' He pats her shoulder. She flinches. It still throbs.

'Oh, come on, Jonty. It's not as if you have to hide anything from me.'

'Yes, but you know what they said.'

'I should be prepared.'

'All right. I will tell you this. Think "Bobo". "Coco" too.'

Ernest pipes up from the side. 'Oh, I could do with a cup of that.'

But Daphne smiles. It is all she needs. 'Got it, Jonty. Thank you.' She files it in her mind.

'I will be hidden by bushes,' the magician continues. 'At the rotator with Jack,' he adds. 'Ernest will be on the perimeter with fire buckets and ash. Not that they'll be necessary. Need I remind you – no long sleeves or anything that might catch light.'

'No, you don't need to. I'm a professional.' She snakes an arm round his waist, the way she used to with her father, and gives him a squeeze. Her sense of being alive is giving way to a feeling of invulnerability. She thinks he probably needs more reassurance than she does.

'Good.' Jonty presses her hand against his waist too.

'Then you're ready?' asks another voice. Septimus appears in their circle. He is carrying a cloak in his arms that looks like a toga. Something an ancient emperor might wear. He sees her run her eyes over his costume. 'When in Rome,' he says with a shrug.

She laughs.

'Costume is part of the theatre. It will help with conviction. Ready for Bolderwood?'

'As I'll ever be. It all seems feasible.'

'It is,' Jonty says, then in his terrified/offhand way, he says with irony, 'What could possibly go wrong?'

What indeed?

CHAPTER THIRTY-THREE

The farmhouse is vast, with wings on each side. Daubed in whitewash and structured with heavy black beams, it looks more like an Elizabethan manor than an agricultural building.

It has been opened to the military. Or possibly requisitioned. It is hard to tell what is voluntary and what is not these days.

In the spacious grounds, huge lawns. Long tents have been erected over them. Across the gravel drive under tarpaulin, a workshop. Here servicemen, not just British but Canadians too, are bent over trestle tables, tugging at sewing machines. It does not look right to her. In amongst them she spots Vivian, hands on his face, fingernails digging into his cheeks, trying to contain hysteria.

'We had to make do,' Septimus says as they pass. 'There's not been enough time for Mr Steiner to complete production of all the robes. It's become necessary to order the airmen to embroider their own dressing gowns.'

'I bet they're delighted about that,' Daphne says grimly, thinking about the terrible mess they are likely to produce.

'Might have been worse,' says Septimus. 'They could also have been required to perform a silly dance.'

'Pah ha ha. As if.' She glances at the agent to see if there is eye-rolling going on and braces herself for a reprimand: she has spoken back and out of turn. But nothing. She feels herself warm to him.

They cross the lawn, pausing to let a frantic woman with a tray full of threads skitter over their path.

Instead of entering through the front door, Septimus heads for the side of the east wing, to the tradesmen's entrance. A long narrow window leads up to it and Daphne, looking through, catches sight of her reflection.

It is not what she is expecting. Her face is swollen, with dark patches above her nose, and her hair has been let down as instructed by the doctor. It is wild and loose about her shoulders. The general impression is of unkempt abandonment or a desertion of duty – if all females must indeed aim for beauty. However, even in the dirty window she can see that her eyes blaze with a new light. She tries to smooth down her locks.

Without looking directly at her Septimus says, 'You've been through a lot, I'm aware. We still haven't managed to track down the men you described, or the outhouse.'

She takes his words for a slight. 'Well, I'm not making it up. It happened. They are in the forest somewhere.'

'I'm aware of that,' he says, quietly. 'I don't think you have fabricated your story. It may be that they have camouflaged the place and left the area.'

She calms down. 'Yes.'

Then, before they cross the threshold, he turns and halts. The action forces her to come up short, almost crashing into his chest. This time she thinks there certainly will be a reprimand on its way. But he asks, 'Are you sure you are quite well? Gerard has said that tonight's ritual will take effort and may well use up what he calls "bodily resources". I don't know if that is true, but I am aware that the working will continue for a few hours. It may exhaust you, this, what shall we call it – magic?'

Daphne nods. 'Magic I can do with my eyes closed. But usually I prefer a blindfold.'

This time Septimus lets go a chortle. 'It is rare to find such spirit in one so young. Initially I had doubts: compliance is fundamental to efficiency. However, you are no secretary, are you?'

She is too shocked by his honesty to reply.

'There are other qualities that can be more useful. You've got spunk, girl.'

No one has said that to her before. Daphne thinks about his words then responds with a candour that matches his. 'While I was captive, I think I learned that I'm braver and more courageous than I imagined.'

Septimus touches her arm lightly. It is another gesture that seems out of character, and a surprise of sorts, but welcome. 'We all are. I know it might not seem it right now, but you've been fortunate to . . .' He pauses. A contraction of the brows, then, 'It is a gift to discover this early on in one's life. Often people learn it too late. Some don't learn it at all.' They pass over the threshold and meet a kitchen door. 'You'll do well now, Daphne. You may have already exceeded your potential. Imagine what more is in store.'

'Thank you, Septimus,' she says, using his name for the first time. 'I'll take that on board. I feel odd calling you by your code name. Should I call you by your proper name now?'

As he pushed the door open, she glimpses amusement playing on his lips. 'That's quite all right. Septimus will do just fine.'

Inside, the kitchen is a hive of activity. Maids, civilians and servicemen rush at different angles, all purposed with a task of ultimate importance, jostling against each other, cursing under their breath. The air is steamy. Great vats of water are boiling on the range. A man in a suit is shaking a quantity of salt into a bucket.

They dodge the bodies charging back and forth and come out into a hall of grandiose proportions.

If the kitchen had been frenetic, it is nothing like the scene that grips them here, which resembles a haberdasher's January sale. Men are hoisting black cloaks on hangers onto the picture rail, puffing at them with water sprays. Others rummage through trunks, pulling out different brightly coloured garments. Several soldiers are carrying farming equipment out through the main door. There is a feeling of desperate urgency in the air.

'We're upstairs,' Septimus calls over his shoulder and they pick their way over to the large mahogany staircase. It is decorated with portraits of the previous owners. They stop at a minstrels' gallery.

Daphne is still looking at the old paintings on the wall, mostly men, although there is an old woman with a lace ruffle who looks disapproving. Septimus's voice draws her.

'The Order is inside, preparing.' His words are precise and solemn.

Of course they are. She remembers the night of the bomb. The ritual and strangeness that had come with it.

'One moment,' he says, indicating that she should wait outside. 'I'll let them know you're here.'

She is not sure why but finds herself pressing her ear against the door.

There is Septimus's voice and others. The words 'ordeal' and 'personality' are flung around on the other side of the wood.

Then, after a minute, the door opens and she jumps back. If he has noticed what she has been up to, Septimus does not comment, only bids her to enter.

Inside are various members of the group. There are cushions on the floor where some sit cross-legged, or on pieces of furniture dragged against the walls. She is sure that she has not seen all of them before. There are some very old women with untamed grey hair, and middle-aged men with accents from different reaches of the country which speak of a journey to these parts. Certainly, in numbers, there are many more than had taken part that night in Christchurch.

A woman steps out in front of her. 'Hello, Dee, I hear you've been through the wars. So to speak.'

Daphne takes a moment to place her, then realises it is Brigit. The two embrace briefly before pulling apart. 'What are you doing here?' asks Daphne. 'I thought you were in Farnham?'

'A few of us have been sent up to pad out your numbers tonight. The more the merrier,' she says.

Daphne grins. 'I'm not sure it will be very merry. It's good to see you though.'

'I'm to be taught some kind of dance. Is it you who'll instruct us?'

'Not sure there's time now, but it's all quite straightforward.' Daphne hears herself and adds, 'Not that there's really anything straightforward about conducting a ritual at night in the middle of a forest. Yet the steps are easy and the incantation simple. You'll pick it up as we go along.'

'Ah,' says a familiar voice. 'Our protégée.'

With a glance of recognition, she waves to Miss Sabine, who has been conversing quietly in the corner with two men – Gerard and Alex, he who had played the part of the priest.

'I'd best go,' she tells Brigit and hurries to the little group.

The priest steps forward to greet her and says, 'I have been informed that we need to confer.'

'That's right.' Daphne is aware once more of his shining robe, symbols and jewels. At his midriff is the thick golden belt. Dangling from it – the sharp knife. It has not been used before, though she is aware it will be tonight.

'Yes,' he says. 'The athame – knife – for the ritual, you know.' Eyes intense, he hooks into her as if he is trying to project words into her mind.

'I saw it before,' she says.

He motions to a chair by the window. 'Shall we withdraw?'

Miss Sabine, however, steps between them and asks with customary frankness, 'I trust your honour remains preserved? Septimus has let us know about your "ordeal".'

There is no sympathy there, only enquiry. It is typical of the woman.

Unafraid to make eye contact with Miss Sabine, Daphne holds up her chin haughtily. 'Of course.'

This seems to satisfy the older woman, who leans forward and says, 'Then the time has come. The country is grateful for your gift, your sacrifice. Everything is in place, the portents are favourable. Let the magic hereby commence.'

The words produce a shiver. Again the notion of someone walking over her grave.

CHAPTER THIRTY-FOUR

Night cloaks the land with rich darkness.

Under blue moonlight the robed figures gather. It is impossible to distinguish the Order from the servicemen.

There is not a glimmer of frivolity. A sense of solemn intent pervades. The esoteric gowns provoke feelings that not all can identify.

Some feel wonder and reverence, others expectation and excitement. A few feel that it is profane. All these emotions infiltrate their perception, despite the doubts of even the most cynical.

At the head of the procession the Order assemble, their bright ceremonial wear swapped for black.

Flanked by Miss Sabine and Gerard, Daphne advances.

She has become aware of a difference in the way she is treated tonight. Both women and men of the Order have been respectful, parting as she moves to allow her unblocked passage. Some drop their eyes when her gaze touches them. Others look with curiosity, like she is a foreign princess come to visit. One woman, older and matronly, shoots her a look that can only be described as compassionate, full of pity.

If she was more vigilant, she might wonder why. But her recent experience has made her audacious, invincible. She is also occupied by the new part to play, upon which the high priest has instructed her only an hour before.

He holds aloft a hefty wand. It is a strange object, not used before. She knows what it is, though, has seen it in photos.

Albeit a replica, the Spear of Destiny is a powerful symbol which provokes veneration and awe. The uninitiated soldiers have been allowed to overhear talk of it and now a ripple of enervated excitement and fear blenches through their ranks. So much of the magical working is about drama. These emotions will be a powering factor.

Movement ahead. Alex hits the floor with the spear.

Though the noise it makes, wood upon earth, is not loud, the line of supplicants – those real *and* those acting – detect a change, a call. They still.

Dipping his hands into the sky, he clears his throat, stiffens, and then with command in his low voice offers up a prayer, magical words she has not heard before in a language she does not understand. They prick the air and tense it to attention.

Everything, everyone becomes alert.

It is happening again.

A pregnant silence falls.

After a moment, which seems to last an extraordinarily long time, the priest takes a step forward. He hoists the spear into the air and points to the woods. The action rouses the assembly. Moving like a herd, they make off across the paddock in deliberately slow steps.

Daphne is conscious of a stirring in the atmosphere, a sense of being scrutinised, as if the gods have parted the aether to look down upon their work.

Even the soldiers at the rear have stopped their jostling and become subdued, privately amazed that about them the tension and drama have transformed each other's drab dressing gowns into remarkable ritual robes. Some of them grow scared.

None of this is ordinary or usual.

It is fantastical, unorthodox, worrying.

A swarm of moving torches and candles in the windless July night, they enter the forest, above them sounds like rain pattering on the leaves, beneath their bare feet the bone-dry ground.

Pitter patter pitter patter into the occult enigma, the line of disciples snakes its way along a twisting path. Into the dark, deeper, deeper, past the trunks of trees and the creatures that skit across them, through a gap to the theatre of their Orphic endeavour, onto the stage, under the eyes of an unseen throng.

Bracken, leaves, grasses cleared from the glade have created a perfect circle.

Daphne is pleased that tonight the props within it have been staged to tremendous effect: the altar shines, its lethal tools glittering. Feet away, the lantern is at the centre, dominating the scene. The spluttering torchlights cast dark shadows over the symbols and animate them. She blinks but the illusion persists: some of the characters painted in gold appear liquid and alive, moving, running like streams. It is a stunning illusion, unsettling, arcane, and creates an impression of intense, vibrant, barely contained power.

Around the edge ash, cedars and birches tower like giants above the gorse, bowed down to listen. A fleeting thought passes over Daphne as she searches them for her team: They will be there for me, won't they, if anything goes wrong?

But she cannot see any humans in the bush – they have hidden themselves well. So expertly, in fact, she wonders if they might not be there at all.

For an instant her ebullience dips. Cold reality grips her. Her nerve endings begin to jangle.

She checks herself. She should not feel like this, she remembers: fear has been banished. It is simple to think that but less easy to slow her own worried pulse.

Silently, obediently she slides into the circle.

They wait, heads down.

A tall, robed man at the end of the procession, features obscured by his black hood, closes the line of salt and seals everyone in. 'Do not step outside the circle. Creatures, forms, elementals will draw to our energy. Inquisitive, hungry. We are protected only in here.'

Torchbearers root their flaming branches in the ground so they form another ring of light. Shadows and darkness dance with each other, like ghosts rising from this now consecrated ground.

And so it begins.

'I offer to the spirits of the air,' the priest sings out.

He drinks of the chalice then passes it along the circle. Returning, he claps his hands. The sound magnifies and hits everyone, seeming to change the particles in the air, recalibrating the frequency.

All lingering notions of absurdity, hilarity, ridicule, are swept up in a volcano of psychic dust, spewed out over the forest to fade away.

'I call upon thee, Gabriel: bestow protection now.'

To her right the chalice is passed.

The taste of well water, wet, rusty, thick, organic, combining elemental forces – fire, earth, air.

They have begun to move, hand in hand, skin upon skin.

'Demeter, Hecate, Diana, Selene, Ishtar,' all intone.

Though she has been through this before and knows what to expect, she is not prepared for the extraordinary sight of it. The sheer numbers here, focused and committed or giving the appearance of being so, paint a tremendous picture of unison, determination and shared goal, if not dark vision. No witness would doubt the conviction of these scores of black-robed occultists staring with grim intensity into the lantern.

And something *is* happening.

The night, the darkness, the light and smoke swirl about them.

Aromas: spicy, warm, amber. The sap in the nearby trees rises – she can almost hear the sizzle as it moves.

Above the torches peculiar creatures like fireflies have begun to flutter and twirl. Is it her or is the leafage jewel-bright?

A crack! Wood splintering in the forest around them, like an immense hoofed beast is prowling near.

A prickle of unbidden anxiety crawls up her neck. She swallows.

No, focus.

It is important to ground oneself.

Deep breath in, deep breath out.

The priest is looking at her.

Ah, yes. It is now.

She breaks free of the circle and goes to him. Her left leg is shaking. A strange compulsion makes her drop her head in submission. He touches her chin and lifts her face. Then, taking her hand, he leads her to the altar.

Be brave, Daphne. Hold your courage. It is theatre. Theatre is all. Isn't it?

The high priest seizes the chalice as she mounts the altar and then, with a sombre bow, passes it.

Her palms are greasy with perspiration. She takes the chalice, drinks again, sets it down once more.

Untying the knife from his belt, the holy man raises it high above her. The athame's blade glints in the flickering light.

She can sense some of the circle bristling, fidgeting, understanding, intuiting that something horrible is about to occur. Just like her old audiences.

Just like her dreams.

'We give up this offering to thee.' Alex brandishes the knife for all to see, then without warning he plunges it down.

A red spray arcs in a semicircle.

Someone screams and tries to break the circle. Others hold them back.

She feels the liquid on her cheeks but cannot move.

The force with which the knife has sliced through the air and hit the chalice has caused her to lose her balance on the altar. She falls and hits her head. The pain is sharp enough to momentarily stun, but does not prevent her continuing.

Alex does not speak or ask if she is all right, but helps to raise her up.

It is vital there are no interruptions – he must progress through the steps of the rite.

He takes the chalice.

'The offering, the offering.'

Through a confusing light-headedness she knows that has been a close call. An inch either side and he would have carved through her flesh into her femoral artery. She would have bled out in minutes.

The priest returns to his position in front of the cone.

She follows too.

Seeing she is unhurt, the circle settles down. The chanting develops consistency; the members breathe as one again.

Down at the base of the lantern, kneeling, she removes the taper and lighter from her brassiere.

And now for my next trick . . .

Again the priest needs her attention. A minute signal passes between them.

He throws his hands wide and high and shouts out the invocation in a firm, determined voice: 'Arise now from the earth, oh spirits of Albion. Arise, arise.'

Close to him, only Daphne hears the click and the spring of a coil, before a hundred white things fly out of the bowels of the earth, up past Alex, chirping and squawking into the sky.

A collective gasp from the gathered.

'No, look!'

'Be ghosts.'

'Spirits.'

'They fly east!'

But still the circle holds.

With all eyes focused on the doves in the heavens she lights the tinder and sees the spark. An orange glow.

'Jupiter, Isis, Amunet.'

'Project your minds, your spirit, your being. Build the cone with power.'

Crackle, spit. The rest catches fire.

She steps away so it appears the lantern has self-ignited, become a vivid manifestation of the power of all those filling it. It begins to rotate, flames billowing out.

The witches' voices strengthen.

Streams of fire twist, spiral, up, up into the sky.

And then something incredible – a charge, a hiss, sparks.

A great whooshing sound. From the base of the lantern a brilliant, blinding light explodes, rising, solidifying into a pillar of intense luminosity, building up, growing higher, higher than the trees, projecting into the heavens for all the gods to see.

'We take this power and we turn it against you.' The priest's words ring out across the glade. 'Turn east, turn east.'

Open-mouthed, she takes in the sight. Phenomenal, unbelievable. How have they made that happen? It is truly extraordinary. Preternaturally beautiful.

She can see it clearly, in focus, as if a new lens has been inserted over her eyes: a tightly woven fabric of dense angelic gossamer. It is as if the beam is fashioned of the same spectral fibres as Jacob's ladder.

Of course.

Magic!

It has worked.

Oh, it has!

The air fills with vapours, spices, woody bark, fungus, pollen, and something golden.

A tremor passes through the forest, warping the glade for a second.

She starts to move round the enormous radiating column, hands up to the gods, then down to the ground, chanting, chanting, possessed by an impulse to praise this, worship this great power. And as her body works, a separate sensation boils up from within, like a wave, changing perception as it washes over her.

Beneath the collection of voices, she feels a hum vibrating her body, breathes in deeply, but as she does the wave crests again. More strongly this time, as if she has inhaled a gas, and she – *no, could it be?* – she is incredibly light: all the weight in her bones and her flesh has disappeared.

A dizziness seizes her and she puts down a foot again to steady herself.

But it does not touch the grass.

Instead, she is lifted up.

Up.

Up.

Raising her hands to her eyes, she sees that her fingers are golden and transparent and wonders at them silently as she ascends.

Could it really be so?

Floating now, she is like an angel.

There comes again the smell of sap, pulsing in the veins of the trees. She can see it now, moving through the bark, little gilded bubbles taking flight into the air.

Another fragrance. Something holy, like myrrh or frankincense.

Something holy.

Something sacred.

Something . . .

She has reached the top of the luminous pillar of light and laughs. Swimming, dancing, twirling in the air, feeling the heat of the fire on the soles of her feet.

This is madness.

There she is, like a bird or an airborne phantom, looking down, omniscient, seeing the entire glade. Everything that is there and everything that is not there. Yes: here is the altar, the priest, and there is herself, Daphne Devine, a small girl, still dancing around the lantern – the implausible pillar of light – the black witches, the sacred soldiers, dark trees, blanket of night, and then her eye, roaming out, out of the circle, latches upon a movement. A rustle in the trees. She sends her mind to it, flying over the tree-tops, a witch without a broomstick, and peers down.

Bushes retract before her eyes and she perceives there, hiding in the brush, a man she does not recognise, but . . .

There is something about him that evokes familiarity, though she does not like it.

He coughs, a high rattling sound, and immediately she understands that this is one of her captors. The younger. She flies closer. Pale, concentrating intensely, his hands fumble with . . . a small device, black and hard. He brings it up to his eyes and clicks.

A camera. He is taking pictures of the rite.

More clearly now, closer: there on his back is strapped a rifle. Beside him, a machine gun.

The sight of the metal jolts her. Breaks the spell. A judder goes through the air and she feels herself pitch, then she is sucked down, down – snap! – into her body.

Something pulses across her forehead and she clicks back into place, inside her physical form.

There is no luxury of time to question this. Not when the enemy may be about to spray bullets across the circle. She must warn them right now.

She finds her voice, which is hoarse and weak, and calls out, 'There!'

But no response.

The circle swirls, the members as if in a trance, all eyes transfixed, mesmerised by the tremendous column pulsating and growing with every word uttered.

'German!' she shouts again, or thinks that she has shouted.

Still nothing.

He will kill us all if . . .

Before she has completed the thought a decision has been made by some higher or lower self and already her muscles are twitching, tendons contracting . . . and she leaps across the circle, pushing through the ring of dancers, out, off into the darkness, off into the forest.

She knows where to go, she has seen him in her mind's eye, no, her bird's eye, no, not that. Not real. But onwards she goes.

Outside of the glade the ground has not been cleared. Thistles and roots bite into her bare feet, stones bruise the tender underside of her soles, weeds bring her down, bushes thrash, reluctant now to grant passage. Nevertheless, she persists. And it is paying off: she is closing in on him. Daphne knows instinctively where he is and intends to circle round so she may come up from behind. She has been taught that the element of surprise can sometimes counter inequalities of physical strength.

As she separates the branches to reach him in his hollow, she realises that she has made a noise. Emerging from the shadows, there is a sudden flash of light and a click.

He has taken a photo of her. Dammit.

She stops, blinks, holds up a hand to shield her eyes.

Another flash.

No time to hesitate.

Immediately she opens her eyes and launches herself in the direction of the enemy agent, hands first. One connects with the camera and knocks it from his grip. Another step forwards and she throws her fist up, aiming for where she thinks his chin might be. It strikes soft flesh. His cheek, maybe. Still, it is successful in disorientating him. He staggers back.

She takes her chances and throws herself at his feet and wraps her arms around his legs, clutching onto him as if she might crush his bones.

But she is no match for a man. He fights out of her hold and kicks hard. His foot comes down on her sternum between her breasts and lays her flat.

Winded, she rolls onto her side.

He has fallen over too, into a bush of prickly gorse.

She draws air into her lungs; the exertion creates a noise like a dying man's death rattle. Chanting from the circle is loud, drowning out the wheeze. Her lungs hurt, her skin burns, but she must keep on or else become terribly undone. She presses up from her palms, ignoring the pain spreading across her chest, the terrible ailing hiss coming from it.

Her opponent, too, is trying to stand.

But she is on her feet, resting her weight with her hands on her thighs, hunched over and panting.

He wipes his mouth with his sleeve, then looks up.

She is astonished to see that his eyes are not wide with violence but with the horror of discovery. They are unfocused to such an extent that he looks confused, unsure of why he is here at all. Nor is his build that of a Wehrmacht agent – he is weedy, concave-chested, sickly. Dressed in cheap, shoddy trousers, covered in mud.

Though her own energy is diminished and she is aware her

build is slighter, she senses an easy kill and hurls herself again, this time higher, throwing her arms around his waist. Grappling to gain a fingerhold somewhere, she latches on to his braces.

They overbalance and hit the ground in a huddle.

His shirt rips in her fingers – cheap, threadbare fabric. She lets go of it and claws at his face, scratching his skin with sharp fingernails.

Now fear has made the man wildly violent. He grabs at her hair and pulls it back hard.

Daphne yelps in pain. Perhaps, at last, the noise may wake up the circle.

But the cry is caught up in the flap of disturbed night birds taking fright.

'*Scheisse. Verschwinde!*'

Her head follows the hand pulling it until she is yanked over and drawn off. He kicks out again, hits her shin. Her legs are bare and his boot heavy. The sting of it drives her to wince and recoil. A gap opens up between their bodies and the man is able to throw a punch.

This time he hits her forehead. She feels the thud inside her skull. It judders her neck and vibrates through her skeleton so that she gasps out and reflexively clutches her head.

He paddles back on all fours.

But she is not done for yet. As the initial pain subsides she opens her eyes and sees him on his knees, trying to get up. Panic has whacked him like a hammer and knocked awry his normal cerebral processes. She sees he is a stricken beast, and a sudden energy returns to her limbs. It is imbued with impassioned understanding that she must abandon all self-interest and commit now to the greater good.

With a scream of reckless fury she springs up, raises her arm and would strike, but something stops her. Resistance. An unknown force pins her robe. She is jerked backwards, off her feet, straight down, hitting the forest floor with a crack, breaking twigs and shrubs, bruising her coccyx painfully.

Still, she must get on with it. There is too much at stake here.

She flips over onto her hands and knees and closes in on . . . feet. Two. Black boots. Her eyes slide up regulation khaki trousers, body, to hare-like eyes, dark locks slicked back and . . . oh so surly expression.

Captain Tuckett.

'What are you doing?' she cries out breathlessly. 'Don't stop me!' The enemy agent is scrabbling around, grabbing his photographic equipment.

She scrambles into a kneeling position and grabs Tuckett's trousers, points. 'He's escaping!' It's true – he is vanishing into the shadows.

But Tuckett does not go after him. He hooks his hands under her armpits and hoicks her up. 'Too precipitate. I knew you would be.'

A rising sense of injustice fills her. Tuckett might be a traitor, but she is certainly not.

He grabs again at her arm.

She tries to struggle out of his grip. 'But *he's* the one who kidnapped *me*.'

Hesitation tightens the Captain's vocal cords. 'Oh.'

'And he's taken a photograph. Of me.'

A new course of action may have been developing in the officer's brain, but Daphne's last plea changes his mind and he returns to his regular impassive expression. 'There are some sacrifices we will all have to make. This will be yours,' he says.

The shock of this causes her to slacken. She stops resisting, although her heart is still pumping at speed and she has not yet recovered from the fight.

Tuckett loosens his grasp and frees her.

She bends over, puts her hands on her knees and catches her breath. Finally standing, she shakes her head. 'What? You're letting him go?'

Tuckett tuts infuriatingly. 'I understand your anger, but this is what we want, *remember*? This rite, the photographs, it will get back to Germany. And quickly too. They've a Morse lamp out there.'

'But—' she says between pants, ready to protest.

The captain does not heed her. 'That Jerry will have been parachuted in or landed on the coast, to prepare for the invasion. We know they've been in the area. *You* know that more than any. He'll have access to a radio.'

She cannot understand his meaning.

'Do not lose concentration,' he continues. 'The pomp and ceremony is all well and good, but impotent if it fails to reach the eyes and ears of the Third Reich's High Command. That's where our true power lies. Not in "magic", for goodness' sake!'

And his words finally make sense.

She wipes the sweat off her brow. 'You could have warned me . . . us . . . there were agents in the area. I might not have . . .' She does not finish.

Nor does he speak. Her accusation is valid but will elicit no new response. He will merely refer her once again to sacrifices and duty and none of this will provide a satisfactory response.

Officer and assistant stare at each other. An impasse.

She is audacious, he'll give her that. Though it is unattractive in a woman to be so, he reminds himself.

Daphne is not sure whether she is right to be angry, or is being immature, or what she should do. In the end she breaks the deadlock. 'I'll get back to the ritual.'

'No you won't,' says the captain. 'You've left the circle. They will be going on for hours and don't need any more interruptions from you.'

'But,' she says, incredulous at such abrupt dismissal, 'I'm needed!'

'You'd do well to remember that no one is indispensable,' he says, his voice grave and quiet. 'Daphne Devine, your work here is done.'

AND ON . . .

CHAPTER THIRTY-FIVE

It had been an unexpected ending to a night stranger than any she thought possible.

She was full of thoughts, some clear, others opaque. And she was furious too.

How could she be discharged? Especially like that? Brutal, considering all she had done. Was nothing valued?

And that man, the German, someone surely should have followed him? To see where he went? He might have had help in the area. There was certainly another spy out there. The other, older man.

She had staggered back to the black and white farm and found a housemaid there who had supplied her with cocoa and a blanket then returned to other chores.

The house was still busy with preparations to welcome the practitioners and servicemen home. Tea was brewing, cocoa already on the stove, brandy laid out for warming those who were chilly, bedspreads, coverings, rugs and quilts piled up in the hall. Servants and support staff, although thinner on the ground, continued to speed across the floors.

With the mug and blanket she returned to the gallery where there was a cosy armchair. She was so exhausted and spent, it did not take longer than three minutes for her to fall into a long sleep.

When she did awake a while later, it was to a full room. But there was a difference in those who lay on the floor and those who tended to them. Lifeless husks, their eyes were glazed, sucked dry with the effort of what they had done. Whatever that was. She was confused about it.

Half an hour later, when Jack showed up to collect her, he too had the look of a man who was a shell of his former self and lacked the lustre she had seen in him before. Though there had been warmth in the exchange, both were physically depleted. They fell into an easy embrace, which immediately became awkward as soon as they realised others were looking, and they pulled apart. And now the adrenalin had faded her bruises and cuts were aching. The wound on her leg stung.

Jack's eyes were dull. 'Are you all right? One minute you were there, the next time I looked up, I could not see you. Though it was dark. I thought you might have donned a hooded robe?' It seemed an effort to ask these questions.

She found that she did not want to tell him what had happened. It would necessitate a lengthy explanation of her 'flying', and she had not the energy nor the mental rigour to align her thoughts before they tumbled out of her mouth and might disgrace her. 'I felt . . . strange,' she said.

He did not ask her why. It was simply left like that.

They reached the car.

In the army vehicle she found Septimus, grey-faced, and Jonty, also fatigued. The lines under his eyes, shadows on his neck, sagging jowls and limp posture suggested that he had been working for a very long time, and now the feat had been accomplished, his stamina had run out.

Ernest had, apparently, left not long after they had begun, finding the effort of patrolling the flaming circle unaccountably draining.

'But it worked,' said Daphne, trying to inject a little life into the morose atmosphere.

No one replied.

Silence filled the car. And remained like that until they reached the manor, when she could not keep in her question any more.

'How did you create the pillar of light, Jonty?' she asked before he got out.

The magician frowned. 'The pillar? The fire was tinder and gunpowder. I told you, the rotating motion allowed the flames to spiral.'

'No,' she said, now irritated by the vague reply. 'After Alex released the doves from the trap, there was a great explosion, and a beam went up right into the sky. I've never seen anything like it before. It was astonishing. And I felt like I could fly. I saw the man, the spy . . .'

Jonty shrugged. 'Not sure what you're talking about, old girl.'

She looked at Jack for an explanation and support, but he could not meet her eyes.

As Septimus descended from the vehicle he muttered, 'I'm sure they put something in that bloody water.'

But Daphne picked it up. 'They would never dose us. The military, they would never . . .' And then she saw he might be referring to the dramatic arc of liquid that had sprayed out as she sat on the altar. 'Oh yes. I slipped in the dye and turned the water red.'

Jonty briefly raised his eyebrows to the stars and mumbled, 'So sensational . . . too modern.'

Daphne persisted: 'But the column of light?'

The agent, however, did not reply but headed off wearily to his quarters, stopping only to yell over his shoulder before entering the manor, 'In the meeting. We'll discuss it all in the debriefing tomorrow.'

* * *

But the debriefing never happened.

The next day a car arrived, and she and Jonty were packed off back to London with an instruction to 'continue as normal'. Which she thought completely mad. Whatever was normal now?

Such an extraordinary time.

Full of peculiar incidents and feelings, she has still not turned all of it over in her mind. So many aspects remain unanswered, and Jonty is ignoring them. His silence is uncharacteristic, though she is aware magicians hold their secrets close to their chests.

Jack did not see the pillar of light, apparently, nor Tuckett. But she certainly did. She *had*.

If only she might speak with Miss Sabine and Gerard or Alex. She is convinced that they would have something to say on the matter, even if she might not believe their explanation.

There is no way of contacting them. Miss Sabine's address was never revealed – she was dropped off there by a driver and collected after the night of the bomb. Although Daphne can remember where it is, she is unable to locate the bungalow on any map, and can't buy a new one: they have all been removed from the book-shops, should the Germans use them to their own ends.

It is anticlimactic, and there are problems in not being able to talk about anything. Jonty refuses, even in private. 'The walls have ears,' he says. Which is true – the papers are full of a fifth column in the country, and she has had her own experience of the enemy on home ground. But surely, in their dressing rooms, when they are alone?

It is not purely the need for secrecy that she fathoms in his reticence. Whenever she tries to speak about that night he takes on a frayed look and asks about the knock to her head. She thinks, after a few days off under the maternal watch of Mrs Thomas, that she has recovered well.

The whole thing is a conundrum. She worries that her friend thinks she is going mad. It makes her feel like bursting. Especially as there was the weightlessness and the bird's eye perspective that had led her to the German. Had there been something in the water? Or had she glimpsed the Unknowable beyond? But then why was the chalice so important? The liquid they all had to share? Had it affected her perception? Why would they want to manipulate her? All of them? But is that not what the Nazis are doing, have done? Is that the point – has she fought fire with fire? Or has she, the trickster, finally been tricked by a grand illusion? So many questions and no answer to any.

At one point she tries to get into HQ at Wormwood Scrubs and seek answers from those there. But her services being no longer required means no access is forthcoming. She is removed from the premises and told not to return until bidden.

With Brigit back at Farnham there is only herself to talk to or think through the issues presenting themselves.

Some are understandable, of course. Like why Captain Tuckett had failed to apprehend the spy. Though it is troubling that there might be a photograph of her somewhere out there. Jonty doesn't mind talking about this, her apprehension of the spy *outside* of the circle. It is only her recollections of what happened inside that perturb him. He has calmed her with the suggestion that the German, in his startled state, would have been unlikely to frame a good and regular snap. It was more likely that only a pair of feet and a tattered robe were captured on the film.

That helps, though she still lingers over why she was taken by the Germans at all. Just unlucky? Wrong time, wrong place? Perhaps she interrupted something. A meeting. If so, who was the man in blue? If he had even *been* in blue. Her recall was perhaps untrustworthy, though she had thought it sharp at the time. Some details were hard to remember at all. And maybe she shouldn't try.

'Best not to dwell on these things.' That is what everyone tells her, and maybe they are right.

The advice is well applied to the dreams that still snap at her heels when she experiences bodily or mental stress. Vicious, satanic apparitions chase her through nights: monks moaning, castles leering, purple skies burning with effulgent dread. It is easy to explain these away by referencing her recent experiences and upset – they might be a caution manifesting from some inner part of her. Yet at night, when she lies under the rafters failing to find sleep, she cannot help but worry they are more than that, some sort of warning or a premonition of sorts. Though the thought chills the very marrow of her bones.

Of course, she will find these answers presently.

Three lives.

Two lives.

One life in.

Of this she is ignorant, only meditating as positively as she can that her time with Section W has, if anything, been an adventure. One full of different emotions, diverse turns, myriad aspects. But full.

And an adventure that has come to an end.

One day, she thinks, when this is all over, I will tell my grandchildren, and they will listen open-mouthed and admire my courage.

If I ever have any.

Daphne might never say it aloud, but life presently seems rather . . . flaccid, despite the new illusions that The Grand Mystique is keen to build into their act.

Like her, Jonty has returned changed. A fresh purpose has

filtered into him. He is drinking less and as he plays upon the boards he displays a spring in his step which she thinks is not entirely performative. The audiences are increasing, infected, thrilled by this new enthusiasm that a recent review has declared 'brings a certain panache to the show that had been lacking before'.

But she misses the life, the urgency, and finds her mind spinning over some of the opportunities she has lost.

Namely those with Jack. And when she is wrestling with her unanswered questions, returning to the nightmare barn, her mind reaches for him – their fumbling clinch, the afternoon in the beer garden, the joy of reunion, the dance in the pub – and she remembers how she thought she would never see him again, and is reassured by a conviction deep inside her soul that this story has not yet concluded.

In fact, a letter turned up at the theatre two weeks since. Jack's tone was friendly, with a recurring undertone of apology. He had been posted up north to be inducted further on wireless operating and other techniques he referred to obliquely, and said he would look her up when leave came his way and he could visit London. Though there are no dates yet, she gives much of her thinking to what they might do: tea at the Ritz, the construction of the new Waterloo Bridge, Westminster Abbey, the British Museum. They could even go for jazz at the Café de Paris, which is safe and underground and has the most handsome of men and—

'. . . as my brave assistant is tied to the firing board.' The Grand Mystique coughs and glares, then repeats himself again. 'Watch as with superhuman precision I fire a bullet which will miss her skull by only an eighth of an inch!'

Daphne has missed the cue. She blinks into the spotlights and works out where she is in the unfolding act. She needs to bow, so makes up for lack of concentration by twizzling over to the large wooden board, painted with a red, blue and black bullseye.

All the twirls, he likes that.

Two stagehands tie her hands and feet while Jonty marches over with great strides and wraps a silk blindfold around her fully healed head.

His brief firearms training has inspired all sorts of unusual ideas. She does not mind too much, as it has increased the takings. And despite her attempts and those of others to assure her that she is not invulnerable, her fear has lessened. Fear of physical harm.

Her work with Section W has unleashed something else in her, and she has from time to time experienced an abnormal resentment that The Grand Mystique is able to reap all the glory when it is her hard work that makes the illusions successful. But for the moment she will acquiesce.

Jonty uses blanks, rather than the real ones she believes might liven the act up a bit. He is as reluctant to use live ammunition as he is to talk about *that* night.

Bound to the board, Daphne need only pull a wire, and the paper which is painted to match the bullseye falls away. It is concealed behind her mane of hair and hides a real bullet hole made weeks ago.

The band in the pit hits the drums.

Tension mounts.

Then a shot, a gasp.

When she steps away from the board unharmed, no one notices the discrepancy in her height and the hole.

And it is all over.

Again.

To roars of applause, together they take a bow.

She is starting to find it dull.

* * *

Assuming it is Charlie, the usher, she covers herself with a loose silk robe when she hears a knock on her dressing room door. Though the days are shorter, there is no need yet for her to light the fire in the grate.

But it is not the usher who stands outside in the dimly lit corridor.

Flowers are thrust forward, held by a tall man in a trilby hat.

Beneath the shadows on his face, his lips broaden.

It takes a fraction of a second to place him.

'Hugh! Mr Devereaux!' she says, with genuine delight. 'Come, come in. Is Jonty not in his room?'

'No,' he says, and takes off his hat, revealing the strong features she had once found attractive. 'It's you I'm looking for.' The irises in his eyes dilate, one darker than the other. She had forgotten about that.

He is certainly fetching, but not in the same way as Jack. He lacks youthful vigour.

She finds a jug and fills it with the flowers.

'Oh,' she says, returning, and sits down on her rickety dressing table stool, beckoning him to take the remaining 'good' chair. It is threadbare but still cushioned. Aware of her state of undress, she pulls her gown together.

He conceals a smile of appreciation and settles. 'I wanted you to know first. We have located your uncle.'

A thrill, then a pause. 'Is he alive?'

'Very much so. Currently he is on a ship bound for Australia.'

'Really? Can I tell Mother? Do they know yet?'

'You can. Of course. I expect Carabella will be most relieved. But before you do, I have an important question that needs to be asked.'

She glances at the bouquet, curious. 'Yes?'

He crosses his legs. 'We are still at war.'

'Yes?'

'And a man must make decisions, with speed, that might otherwise require deep thought and care. Women too. But we have not that luxury. You and me. Things change at a lightning pace.'

'Yes?' She swallows.

He leans forward. 'Daphne.'

'Yes, Hugh? Mr Devereaux.'

'Have you ever been to Iceland?'

'Oh,' she says. 'No. Why?'

'Apparently it's very pleasant in autumn.'

'It is?'

'We invaded earlier this year. Strategic, of course. And, you see, there's something odd happening on the island.'

For a moment she is speechless. This is not the proposal she has been expecting, though she is glad of it.

'You did so well in the New Forest,' he continues. 'And are spoken of highly.'

'I am?' Her voice croaks, and she silently curses her weakness.

'Yes.' He glances around the room, and she realises he is aware of being overheard. 'Clearly you are busy here, but I have come to see if . . . well, if you would like to take a trip?'

A quickening in her heart. It is not unpleasant.

'I think,' she says, her voice low, confidential, 'it would be rude to refuse such an offer.'

The world rights itself and brightens.

Outside, the globe hurls through time and space and
shifts on its
axis.
In the darkness of Europe's soul, embers spit.
The black eagle spreads burning wings.
Growing,
heart enlarged with vanity,
manifesting inwardly
ambitions
for eternity.
Above, beyond the present purgatorium
in flux, Past and Yet to Come
Consider the maelstrom.
What may portend.
And wonder how
the human
story
will
ever
end?

Extract from the documentary *Hitler's Failed Invasion*

What we do know now is that despite his conviction that Operation Sea Lion should absolutely be executed, late on the night of 31 July 1940, Hitler withdrew to his private rooms with his inner circle. By the morning of 1 August, he had impulsively changed his mind. Instead of focusing on Great Britain, his sole remaining enemy, he emerged from that night intent on turning his gaze to Russia in the east, which had long been central to his master plan. It was one of the most catastrophic decisions of his career, and in fact would cost him the war.

ACKNOWLEDGEMENTS

This story, the first of three novels, has been inspired by events alleged to have taken place in England over the summer of 1940.

Many books have helped me in my research and are too numerous to mention here, but some that may be of interest to those wishing to find out more are Eric Kurlander's *Hitler's Monsters*, Philip Heselton's *New Forest Coven* and *Lumberjills* by Joanna Fort.

My heartfelt thanks goes out to the Combined Military Services Museum for sharing with me their original documentation.

Roy Waight has produced the most comprehensive history of Farnham Castle, *A Convenient Place*, and has been so helpful in answering some of my queries about the remarkable building and its surrounding land. I must also thank Francesca Cribb, who took time out of her busy schedule to guide me around the castle when we were emerging from the pandemic and not entirely opened up yet.

Of course, as always, I have taken liberties with the truth, however, the Farnham Castle section of this story fictionalises the antics of the Camouflage Training and Development Centre that trained there from 1940 to 1944. Hugh Cott was an eminent zoologist, and it is he who gave lectures about camouflage. Much of the information gleaned came from his book on the subject, *Adaptive Coloration in Animals*. As bizarre as it seems, I have not had to do much with the men at the castle, who did come from a range of extraordinary backgrounds and occupations. They included the artists Blair Hughes-Stanton, Edward Seago, Frederick Gore and Julian Trevelyan, a West End theatre designer, an electrician, Oxford dons, a circus manager, an art critic, a magazine editor, designers, sculptors, cartoonists, artisans and, indeed, a surrealist poet. Victor Stiebel, a well-known fashion designer, was also stationed there, as was the magician Jasper Maskelyne. The eagle-eyed amongst you may notice a resemblance to The Grande Mystique. Unlike Jonty, however, Maskelyne departed Farnham for the Middle East. Jonty is pure fiction.

More authors and more books will be referenced in my next novel in this series, due to be published in 2025. So thanks also go to Emily Sullivan at Leigh Library, who has helped me procure various obscure texts from strange places, and who I hope will continue to let me draw on her phenomenal librarianship.

Continuing my appreciation, I must acknowledge Gareth Owen ACIfA, archaeologist at the New Forest National Park Authority, and Hayden Bridgeman, an obliging ranger who directed me to the memorial to the Canadian Airmen. If you are in the area, it is modest but extremely moving. Many thanks also to Phil Stride of the New Forest for the helpful advice and the anecdote about his dad seeing the witches, which sparked some very interesting ideas. 'The Lumberjills' was inspired by lots of poems I read about them, and those penned by the Women's Timber Corp members. Some can be found in Joanna Fort's fascinating book, others at www.womenslandarmy. co.uk. Incidentally, it's worth pointing out that the WTC were not treated very well after the war. They were not even allowed to take part in the annual Remembrance Sunday parade in London until 2000. Obviously by then many had died.

I must also thank the Imperial War Museum London and Churchill War Rooms, whose staff have been fantastic and able to immediately answer questions that would have taken me weeks, if not months, to research. Julie Ann Miller at the Combined Military Services Museum in Maldon has also been a great help to me in fact-checking various military and counter-espionage details, and as a beta reader too. I have to add here that the museum is also an absolute must for anyone with an interest in this area.

I am grateful to Professor Alison Rowlands, who I worked with on a fantastic project reclaiming the voices of the women lost to the 1645 Manningtree witch hunt, and who helped me with the German in this novel.

Other thanks extend to Ian Simmons at the *Fortean Times*, Gary Hardiman and also Phil Baker, author of *City of the Beast*, an excellent biography of Aleister Crowley's time in London.

It was the economist Tyler Cowen who was once asked about dying. 'The worst thing about death,' he said, 'is not knowing how the human story turns out.' It's something I have thought about too. The atrocities of the past don't end there. Despite the fact that we can learn lessons from history, we often don't. Many comments about the nature of humanity and its bent for destruction discussed here could easily be set in our contemporary landscape.

Parts of this book were written when I was writer-in-residence at the White Rabbit in Brighton as part of the Writers in Hubs initiative. Big thanks to the staff there for making me feel so comfortable, especially Sam and Jake.

Thank you to Steph and Julian. Sorry that you emerged from the New Forest with so many bites and scratches. You were a tremendous help to me and I am grateful for your friendship.

My league of extraordinary school chums, Sherry Bexfield, Midge Jackson, Lizzy Rant, Jo Oats, Tammy Peters, Hobbit, Rachel Simnett, Caroline Evans are all appreciated for their cleverness and insights. And to Riley, who never reads my books.

But most of all thanks to all the staff at Oneworld for their continued support, particularly Juliet and Novin, Julian Ball, Lucy Cooper, Beth Marshall-Brown, Mark Rusher, Margot Weale, and my sterling agent, Sandra Sawicka. My gratitude extends to Sarah Terry, my very thorough copy-editor, who also helped with German translation.

Wonderful supportive chums from the crime and folkloric community include Caroline Maston, Olivia Isaac-Henry (who convinced me my idea was a good one), Kate Bradley, Paddy Magrane, Erin Kelly, Colin Scott and Hugh Foster – always in my thoughts and no doubt sipping absinthe with Sartre somewhere in the blue beyond. Friends and famalam of course, as ever.

My final vote of sincere gratitude goes to my editor, Jenny Parrott, who in her own inimitable style has transcended all regular requirements of the role to become sage, guru and adviser, truly a diamond in the dark night.